Photographs
from the
Cove

Jennifer Bardsley

BOOKS BY JENNIFER BARDSLEY

Photographs

from the

Cove

JENNIFER BARDSLEY

bookouture

Published by Bookouture in 2024

An imprint of Storyfire Ltd.
Carmelite House
50 Victoria Embankment
London EC4Y 0DZ

www.bookouture.com

ISBN: 978-1-83790-538-6
eBook ISBN: 978-1-83790-537-9

To my sister-in-law, Monica Prescott, and our joint belief in the motto "if it's free, take it."

ONE

Mary was too heartbroken to speak. Words were there, on the tip of her tongue, but she was crying so hard there was no way she could talk. How could Aidan do this to her? Come back from Kansas with a pregnant wife? She'd known that maintaining their long-distance relationship for four months had been difficult, but she had thought they were on solid ground. Hell, she'd been expecting Aidan to propose. They'd dated for three years straight, ever since she was nineteen years old. She'd loved him right from the start, which was perhaps foolish of her, but that's how Mary had always been—an open-hearted romantic. Well, that was going to change now. Starting today, she wouldn't trust anyone who wasn't part of her inner circle. Mary would guard her heart.

And that ring... Her heart fractured just thinking about it. Thank goodness for Hannah, who stood by her side, like always.

"I had no idea you were such a jerk." Hannah pointed at Aidan right between the eyes. "How dare you treat my sister like this? Lying to her. Cheating on her. Manipulating me into telling you what type of engagement ring she'd like and then buying it for someone else."

Pear-shaped white sapphire. Aidan had selected the perfect ring and then given it to another woman. *Not just any woman, the mother-to-be of his child.* Mary felt like he'd punched her in the stomach.

"I can explain," Aidan said as the two sisters stared him down in Hannah's office at Seaside Resort, the vacation property she managed. "It was an accident," he said, his voice scratchy, like his spring hay fever might be bugging him. His light brown hair was parted down the middle in a style Mary had always found unattractive on him but had never mentioned. She was supportive that way. Just like how she'd encouraged him to become a traveling nurse since it paid more than local jobs in Sand Dollar Cove. What a fool she'd been! What an outrageously trusting fool!

"Here, Mary, take one of these." Hannah offered her a tissue. "And sit here next to me, in the comfy chairs." She maneuvered Mary into one of the two desk chairs. "Behind my desk and away from the lying, cheating asshole."

"That's a bit harsh, don't you think?" Aidan asked, sounding affronted. "I'm a medical professional who saves lives."

"Oh, so you got that woman pregnant with your blood pressure cuff, did you?" Hannah snapped. "Or maybe it was your thermometer." She held out her index fingers two inches apart. "Seems about the right size."

"Crude jokes, really?" Aidan sat in a scratched wooden chair. "I'm surprised at you, Hannah."

Mary was shocked, too—not shocked that Hannah was defending her. Her big sister always protected her. Mary was twenty-two years old, and the one constant in her life was Hannah trying to keep her safe. But Hannah's face was so red she looked like she was about to drop the F-bomb, and her sister never swore. Hannah had even kept her composure that time Mary had talked her into letting her cut her hair and it came out three inches shorter on one side because Mary didn't know what the hell she was doing.

"It's all going to be for the best." Aidan fidgeted with his brand-new wedding ring. "You'll see. You haven't gotten the chance to meet Lara yet, but I think you'll really like her."

"I... I... I..." Mary stuttered, unable to get words out. She looked at her sister for help.

Hannah, taking Mary's cue, slammed her palm on the table. "Are you mad? We're not the Sand Dollar Cove welcome committee. Mary's not going to become besties with your wife. She's the longtime girlfriend you screwed over." Hannah flipped on her desk lamp and angled it straight at his face. "Now start from the beginning, and tell us how this happened."

Aidan held up his hands to block the light. "Is that really necessary?" He squinted and scooted his chair away from her light-assisted interrogation.

"Yes. I think so." Hannah adjusted the lamp, so it hit him again. "Light always helps identify cockroaches."

"Why are you even here, Hannah?" Aidan asked. "This is between me and Mary."

Hannah looked at Mary. "Do you want me to leave?"

Mary blew her nose and shook her head. The lump in her throat was so big that she could barely breathe right now, let alone stick up for herself.

"Mary deserves answers," said Hannah. She clicked off the light but rapped her knuckles on the desktop. "Start explaining."

"It was like this." Aidan squirmed in his chair. "It was a four-month position in the Midwest, and I was lonely. Winter was brutal. I'm not used to snow like that and—"

"Snow made you cheat on Mary and knock a woman up?" Hannah asked.

"Let him finish," Mary said, finally finding her voice.

Hannah nodded and patted Mary's hand. "Whatever you want."

"Like I said," Aidan huffed in the slightly superior way that was so like him. "It was snowing and there weren't many things to do in Hutchinson once you'd visited the salt mine and Cosmosphere. My Airbnb happened to be next door to Lara's place, and..." He looked at Mary. "It was an accident, I swear."

"Wait a second." Hannah folded her arms across her chest. "Lara looked pretty darn pregnant to me. How far along is she?"

Sweat trickled down Aidan's forehead. "She's due on November twenty-first."

Mary quickly did the math. "She got pregnant in February. But you only left town five days before Valentine's Day."

"This wasn't about you being lonely," said Hannah. "This is you going on a business trip and immediately having a fling."

"I told her I didn't want it, but she wouldn't listen," Aidan protested.

"I'm assuming we're talking about the baby here," said Hannah, "in which case, you absolute turd."

"Stop." Mary held up her hand. Her heart was bleeding right now, but Aidan still held a piece of it. She raised her brown eyes to look at him. "Is this the first time you cheated on me?"

"Let's not put a number on it," Aidan said cagily.

Mary's tears stopped as her grief turned to anger. "What?"

Hannah looked at Mary. "Maybe you should be tested for STDs."

Aidan scoffed. "That won't be necessary. I'm always careful."

"Obviously not." Hannah scowled.

"I mean about the testing," Aidan protested. "I'm a nurse, after all."

"I'm such a fool," Mary whispered. The shred of love for

Aidan she'd clung to went up in smoke. She never should have trusted him. "You're a habitual cheater."

"I wouldn't say habitual." Aidan shook his head. "Once in New Jersey and a couple times in Florida. But only when I was stressed to the max. Working in the healthcare industry is brutal. I've told you that."

"That's no excuse for cheating." Hannah's eyes flashed with rage. "And Mary was faithful to you that whole time. Weren't you, Mary?"

Mary nodded.

"Yeah, but... I deal with trauma daily," said Aidan. "I endure stress that you can't imagine." He tilted his head to the side and looked at Mary. "No offense, but I'm an ER nurse, and you're just a barista."

The accusation stung. He'd never said it so plainly before. Mary had always felt like Aidan's parents thought that she was beneath them, but she had no idea Aidan felt that way too.

"She's not just a barista, she's also going to school full time to become an interior designer," said Hannah.

"I was faithful to you," Mary uttered her words softly. "Every second for three years, whether we were in the same room or across the continent." Had she been foolish to expect that he'd done the same? "I've loved you since the moment you drove up to my coffee stand and ordered a vanilla latte with extra whipped cream."

She'd taken a chance and written her phone number on the cup along with a smiley face. Aidan had asked her out the next day via a curt text: *hey coffee girl wanna hang out*

No question mark. No introductions. Straight to the point. That's one of the things she'd liked about Aidan. His directness. Now she realized he was probably using those same skills on women all over the country.

"I loved you, too," said Aidan. "You know that. But Lara and I are a much better fit. We're on the same page about how we want our child to enter the world, and how we want to raise it. With a mom and a dad and responsible grandparents who can help."

That was a low blow, and Aidan knew it.

Mary and Hannah's father had died twenty-one years ago, when Mary was a baby. Their grandmother had gained custody after their mom nearly killed them while driving under the influence of alcohol.

Mary clutched her stomach, feeling physically ill. The back of her neck felt icy. Her skin was clammy. Was this what going into shock felt like?

"Mary will be an outstanding mother someday," said Hannah.

"Hopefully so." Aidan said in a sickly-sweet tone. "But it'll be a steep learning curve, don't you think? Since you had such a messed-up childhood. All I'm saying is—"

"Gran gave us a lovely childhood," Hannah interrupted. "As a parent, she's worth both of yours."

"You don't know my parents," said Aidan.

"I've heard stories," said Hannah.

"You've never met them." Aidan narrowed his eyes.

"But I have," said Mary, refusing to let Aidan belittle her grandma. "Hannah's right. Gran's better." Cheryl was the best parent any child could ask for. The shock was passing. It was still there, ever present, but her nervous system was coming back to life. Instead of cold and clammy, her hands felt sweaty. Mary's fists clenched involuntarily, like she was ready to fight.

"It's not your fault you come from a broken home," said Aidan. "But part of you will always be broken, too. How could it not be?"

"That's a load of crap!" Hannah shouted.

Mary stared blankly ahead. Who was this man in front of her saying such horrible things? She felt Aidan's words like they were being etched on her soul. *Part of me will always be broken.*

Mary saw Aidan's familiar brown eyes, and the mole on his left temple that wasn't melanoma. She recognized the shirt she'd helped him pick out at a shop on Main Street, and the jeans she'd ordered for him online. Here was her boyfriend of three years, and although every inch of him was familiar, he already felt like a stranger.

"Cheryl did the best she could, but your grandmother was a housekeeper," Aidan continued. "Lara's father is a doctor, and her mother teaches at school. She comes from a white-collar background like mine."

"Our father graduated from the University of Washington School of Engineering." Hannah leaned forward, pressing her elbows against the desk. "There's nothing wrong with blue-collar jobs like our grandma had, but don't lie about our background just to make you feel better about your despicable behavior."

Aidan looked directly at Mary. "I'm not lying, and I'm sorry the truth hurts. If you'd had better guidance, you'd never have run off to LA to pursue that stupid fantasy of yours to become an actor."

"Dreaming big isn't stupid," Mary said, her voice growing stronger. "I learned a lot in Hollywood."

"I bet you did," said Aidan. "About brewing espresso and frothing milk."

"That's not true," said Mary. *He doesn't know and I'm not going to tell him.*

The truth was, Mary had landed a starring role in a film that had never been released. A film she didn't want to talk about. *Zombie Prom at the Disco* was supposed to be an avant-garde look at the way social media turned teenagers into the walking dead, but had been sleazier than Mary had expected. She had felt uneasy about the director from the very beginning but had been so excited about making her acting debut that she'd put her faith in him, only for him to exploit her naivety.

Instead, she spoke of a job she was proud of. "I learned set design while working in local community theater. Now I have an entire career in front of me as an interior designer."

"What career?" Aidan scrunched up his face. "Picking out fabric samples hardly qualifies."

"I'm going to be a certified interior designer, not a decorator." Mary gripped the edge of her chair. "There's an enormous difference." Why was he belittling her ambition? "What does Lara do for a living?" she asked, sensing competition.

"She's a medical billing specialist," he said. "It's the perfect job, really. She can work from home wherever she wants so long as there's a strong internet connection."

"How is that better?" Mary asked.

"It's not," Hannah scoffed.

Aidan stood. "I'm not sure there's much more to say beyond I'm sorry."

Hannah rose, too. "You bet you'll be sorry. This is a small town, and people have long memories. Nobody's going to forget what a rat you are for screwing Mary over. So take another one of your traveling nurse gigs, keep on going, and don't come back."

Aidan shook his head. "I don't take orders from you, Hannah." He looked at Mary, who was still seated. "Like I said, I'm sorry. I hope we can still be friends."

Friends? Aidan thought they could still be friends? Not only was he a backstabbing liar, but he was delusional as well.

"Hannah, could you please leave us alone for a minute?" Mary asked. Some things were better said in private.

"Sure." Hannah picked up her keys. "I'll be right outside if you need me."

As soon as the door shut, Mary wiped her eyes and rose from her chair. Emotions swirled inside her like a tempest, beginning to boil over. Blood pounded in her temples, and she felt that shaky sensation again, like she was becoming too upset to speak. It had been a mistake to send Hannah away. That had been a rash move. She realized she needed her sister's help after all. But then Mary found the perfect words, words she'd memorized as a hopeful teen when big dreams and true love still seemed possible. It was the speech she'd given during the final scenes of *Zombie Prom at the Disco*.

Mary squared her shoulders, lifted her chin, and looked Aidan straight in the eyes. "Friends? We can never be friends. You've murdered my love for you. Your cursed heart means nothing to me anymore." Tossing back her golden hair, she strode out of the room with a swish of her skirt. It was only after the door closed behind her that she whispered the last line to herself. "I don't dance with the dead," she murmured into her cupped hands, before bursting into tears.

TWO

Christmas Eve was cold that year. Mary knew she should be downstairs with her family and friends, but she was holed up in her room nursing her wounded heart and a lukewarm Coke Zero. It had been seven months since Aidan's deception had ripped Mary's life in two, and she still felt the tear like it had happened yesterday.

It's not your fault you come from a broken home, he had told her. *But part of you will always be broken, too. How could it not be?*

Was that true? Was she a fractured piece from a busted-up family that would never have the chance at a normal life? If she did find a partner who was worthy of her someday, would she be too damaged to have a healthy relationship? And what about motherhood...? The only thing Mary had learned from Kelly was how *not* to parent.

She knew she wasn't to blame for Aidan cheating on her, but it *was* her fault for choosing him in the first place. Mary had always been the wide-eyed and trusting sister, whereas Hannah was usually more guarded. Now Mary saw that Hannah had been right all along. Mary was too quick to believe in people.

She rushed into relationships and ignored red flags. That needed to stop immediately, or her life would be permanently ruined. If only she could build a huge wall that would protect her heart. But how? These thoughts and more had weighed on Mary's mind for months, dragging her down into a pit of depression she struggled to escape from.

To make matters worse, Aidan had not taken Hannah's advice and left town. Instead, he'd found a permanent position at Grays Harbor Community Hospital. Now, Aidan, Lara, and their newborn son Larry—seriously, who named a baby Larry? —lived with his parents, Stewart and Heather DeLack. And their house just happened to be next door to the house Mary, Hannah, and Cheryl shared with their landlady, Brittany, and her teenager, Jeremy.

Mary loved living in Brittany's house, which had a view of the golf course on one side, and a canal on the other. She usually left her window cracked open so she could smell the ocean breeze. But living so close to her ex complicated things. The bedroom she shared with Hannah on the second floor offered a clear view of the DeLacks' driveway. On nights like this one when the wind carried, she could hear whatever the DeLacks said while they parked their cars.

It's not that Mary approved of eavesdropping, or Facebook stalking, or listening to Aidan's Spotify playlist while stress-cleaning the bathroom. But she was curious about Larry. Was he cute? Did he have that mole on his temple like his father? Was he a good sleeper, or did he wake his parents in the middle of the night? Mary turned off the lights and crept closer to her window. Tonight, Aidan and Lara were arguing over whether the car seat was properly installed in the Beemer.

"I told you to take it to the fire station months ago to check the installation," Lara chided. "That's not how the seatbelt's supposed to go."

"It looks good to me," said Aidan.

"You don't use the latch system and the seatbelt at the same time."

Mary didn't know what a latch system was, but it sounded like something responsible fathers ought to know about.

"Putting a car seat in my X6 is a bad idea to begin with," Aidan complained. "It might scratch the leather."

"Which is more important," Lara asked. "Your son's life or your precious car?"

Good point, Mary thought. Although if they were concerned with the baby's well-being, maybe they shouldn't have named him Larry.

"I just don't understand why we can't take your Corolla," Aidan complained. "It can handle baby puke a lot better than mine."

"My car is out of gas," said Lara. "Remember?"

"So why didn't you fill it up?"

"Are you serious right now?" Lara's voice rose. "I had a level three perineal tear, you bastard, and then a clogged milk duct, and then thrush. I haven't slept since November."

Bingo. That answered *that* question. Lara and Aidan weren't getting any sleep at all.

"Unlike you, you selfish jerk, who never helps with Larry in the middle of the night," Lara continued.

Ooops. Mary realized she shouldn't have been so quick to make assumptions.

"I have to work!" Aidan shouted. "Twelve-hour shifts!"

A tiny wail raged through the night as Larry joined the conversation.

"Now you woke the baby, moron," Lara shrieked.

Mary peered through the blinds but couldn't see much besides the glow of Christmas lights that Hannah's boyfriend Guy had hung all over the house, including the vine maple next to her window. She scooted to the left, so the glow was less bright, and she could see the driveway better.

The baby had stopped crying, and Lara stood outside the car. "I don't want to take Larry out in freezing weather like this."

"Why not?" Aidan opened and closed the back door of his car. "This is nothing compared to what you're used to in Kansas."

"Yeah, but in Hutchinson they plow the roads and people have snow tires. Your driving makes me nervous. Let's stay home."

"We can't. You heard what my mom said. Everyone's expecting us at church tonight."

"That's another thing," said Lara. Even from this far away Mary could hear the panic in Lara's voice. "I don't want to take our five-week-old baby into a crowded space like that. He might catch the flu."

"That's always a risk, but—"

"Why aren't you in the car yet?" boomed a voice. Stewart DeLack shut the front door after his wife, Heather. "We need to hitch up and move out, or we'll be late."

"I want to stay home," Lara said in a clear voice. "It's safer for Larry to avoid germs."

"I would never put my grandson in danger," said Heather.

Mary leaned closer to the window to hear better.

"What are you doing?" called a voice behind her. Hannah flipped on the light. "Why are you hanging out in the dark?"

Mary spun around and brought her index finger to her lips. "Shh. I'm trying to hear," she whispered.

Hannah marched over to the window and slid it shut. "We've been over this before. Eavesdropping isn't healthy." Hannah adjusted the blinds so that only the tiniest hint of Christmas lights peeked through. "It's been seven months. Time to let Aidan go."

"I *have* let him go," Mary protested.

"Really?" Hannah raised her eyebrows.

"Yes, really. I can see how self-absorbed he is now. In fact, I almost feel bad for Lara having to put up with him." *Almost.* "It's good for me to see how awful my life might have been."

"You say that, and yet you're slinking around up here like a spy in one of Gran's detective shows."

"I wasn't spying. It was more like I was observing someone self-implode on Twitter, but it was happening in real life."

"But focusing on Aidan could be holding you back from moving forward." Hannah pointed to Mary's framed diploma on the wall. "When are you going to quit your job at the coffee stand and start that interior design business you've always wanted?"

"Soon..." Mary didn't want to talk about it.

"You did a great job redesigning the Seaside Resort lobby."

"That was a pity job, and you know it. The only reason I was hired was because you're the general manager and your gazillionaire boyfriend owns the place. I don't want to score clients because of your connections, I want to earn them by merit."

"So maybe you could create a website?" Hannah suggested. "I could help you formulate a business plan."

"Do you have to talk about this again? On Christmas Eve, no less!"

The truth was, Mary didn't feel stable enough to embark on a major life decision like starting a business. She clung to her barista job because it was all she could manage. Sure, the job was going nowhere, but it was relatively stress-free.

Too much stress, and she might crack into pieces like her mom had after her dad's death.

Mary shuddered, not wanting to think about Kelly and her history of substance abuse right now. She'd only spent the first three and a half years of her life with her mom, until her grandma had won custody of the sisters. But Mary's childhood trauma was always there, at the back of her mind, and no matter how hard she worked at acting like it didn't bother her, it did.

She didn't remember much about those early years because she'd been so little. But every now and then an image would float across her memory. An empty six-pack of beer... The stench of vomit... Needles on the kitchen counter... And then there had been the elementary school years to deal with, which Mary *did* remember. Friends questioning her about why she lived with her grandma. *Because she loves me.* "Where's your dad?" they would ask. *He died in a car crash when I was a baby.* "Where's your mom?" *That was harder to explain...* The rare visits with Kelly had only made matters worse. No wonder Mary had grown up to become such a poor judge of character. Kelly's influence on her childhood had been confusing.

"I'm sorry I pressured you." Hannah sat on the floor next to her. "Let's go downstairs. Everyone is gathered around the tree waiting for you to open presents. Come on." She gave Mary a side hug. "I can't wait for you to see what I bought you."

"Socks. You bought me socks, like you do every year."

"Yeah, but are they wool socks, athletic ones, or no-shows? The suspense must be killing you."

Mary laughed. "It's kept me awake at night, wondering, that's for sure. The real question is, what did Guy get us? Those three matching rectangular boxes are mysterious. I resisted the urge to shake them in case they might be jewelry."

Last spring they'd discovered that Guy Barret, the former personal trainer at Seaside Resort, was actually Guido Barret Blanchet IV, heir to the international Blanchet Maison hotel chain. That realization had been a shock to everyone, but especially to Hannah, who had just begun dating him. Mary was glad when Hannah forgave Guy for hiding his identity, not only because he made her sister happy but also because he brought them home-cooked meals on a regular basis. Unfortunately, they were vegetarian meals, but nobody's perfect.

"I hate to burst your bubble but there are actually six matching boxes," said Hannah. "Guy bought gifts for Brittany, Jeremy, and Keith, too."

"Bummer," Mary frowned. "There goes my jewelry fantasy."

"I'm not sure Guy's the jewelry type. We've dated for eight months, and he's never given me anything like that."

"Even though he could buy out Tiffany's? That seems unfair."

"I wish you weren't so easily swayed by bling," said Hannah.

"I am not," Mary protested. But then she thought back to the day when Aidan had first rolled up to her coffee stand in his freshly washed BMW. Would she have given him her number if he'd been driving a Kia? *Probably,* her heart murmured, the hurt as fresh as ever.

"You're like a Steller's jay who's distracted by shiny objects," said Hannah.

"There's nothing wrong with maintaining an appreciation for flair." Mary stood. "Speaking of which, how do I look?" Her sparkly gold eyeshadow matched her shirt, which was almost the same shade as her hair.

"Marvelous," said Hannah. "Let's go open presents."

The sisters had an upstairs bedroom at Brittany's house, and Cheryl had one of the ground-floor rooms, which was essential because her osteoporosis made it difficult to manage stairs. The shared housing arrangement worked well for everyone. Before the Turners had moved in, Brittany had found it difficult to afford her mortgage payment post-divorce. As for Mary, Hannah, and Cheryl, they'd been priced out of the rental market because of skyrocketing property values. Together, the two families had created a happy home that was easier on everyone's budgets. Hannah's boyfriend Guy, and Brittany's boyfriend Keith, were frequent guests.

Tonight, the downstairs smelled like coffee and ginger. The coffee was from a pot of decaf that was brewing in the kitchen. The ginger was from the plate of cookies on the coffee table. Already an excellent cook, Guy had taken up baking as well, to the point that Mary had to watch it, or she'd consume her entire daily allowance of calories in baked goods every time he came over. Luckily there was a teenage boy in the house, because Jeremy usually scarfed down every sweet morsel.

"Well, look who finally decided to come down from her room," said Cheryl, who sat in her recliner in front of the fire. Physical therapy had helped improve her mobility, but she still preferred the comfort of her La-Z-Boy.

"Hello, everyone." Mary waved.

"Do I have to be here for this?" Jeremy asked.

"For my grand entrance into the living room?" Mary winked. "Yes, you do."

Jeremy laughed. Only five years apart, the two of them enjoyed an easy rapport. "No, I mean hanging around for hours doing nothing but sitting here looking at the Christmas tree."

"It hasn't been that long," Brittany clarified.

"Do you want some more cookies?" Guy asked. His hair was chestnut brown now, his natural color, unlike the blond shade he used to wear. Mary thought he looked like Ryan Reynolds.

"Are there any more peanut butter balls?" Jeremy asked.

"We're all out," said Guy. "But there's plenty of peanut brittle."

Jeremy wrinkled his nose. "Gross. No thanks."

"Jeremy, don't be rude," said Keith. Brittany's boyfriend Keith was the director of the senior center where Cheryl hung out. Brittany was the center's nutritionist.

"You're not my dad." Jeremy pulled down the stocking cap he wore to keep his long hair out of his eyes.

"Please don't talk to Keith that way," said Brittany,

defending her boyfriend. Her sparkly nose ring matched her necklace.

"I'll talk to him however I—"

"Hey, Jeremy," Mary said, interrupting the teen before he could get himself into trouble. "Did you see what happened to the snowman somebody built by the T Bone Bluff steak house?"

"Yeah." Jeremy chuckled. "It wasn't me, I promise, but I might know someone who was involved."

"What happened to the snowman?" Cheryl asked.

"Ah, you probably don't want to know," said Hannah.

"What?" Cheryl asked. "Was a boner involved?"

"Gran!" Hannah squeaked.

"I'm eighty-three years old and successfully raised a teenage son back in the day," said Cheryl. "This isn't the first snowman with a boner that's popped up in this town. Chill out."

Mary and Jeremy exchanged conspiratorial glances. She liked the teenager, and had a lot of empathy for him. It must have been hard for him only seeing his father a few weeks a year on brief visits to Seattle. Living in a house full of women must be rough, too. Jeremy would go off to college next year, but in the meantime, she wanted him to know that she was his ally rather than yet another adult telling him what to do.

"Are we going to open presents, or what?" Mary asked. "Let's get this show on the road."

"Fantastic." Guy leaped to his feet and began rustling under the Christmas tree. "I'm so excited to give these to you all. I almost gave them to you early, but I used an incredible amount of self-restraint."

"Now you've got our attention." Cheryl held out her hand and Guy passed her a package.

"Uh... I didn't realize you and I were exchanging gifts, Guy," said Keith. "If I'd known..."

"Don't worry about it." Guy waved away his concern. "There was a deal if you purchased in bulk." He passed out a present to everyone. "Okay. Now that you all have one, go for it. Open them at the same time."

Mary ripped apart the wrapping paper as quickly as she could, but she wasn't fast enough to beat Jeremy.

"A DNA kit?" he asked.

"Yes," Guy said, a giant smile on his face. "Because knowing your roots is really important."

"That's right." Hannah patted him on the back. "Thank you for this. I know how much family ancestry means to you."

"Yeah, uh... thanks," said Mary. "If only a DNA kit could tell me what I really wanted to know."

"What's that?" Jeremy asked.

"How my family became so broken," said Mary. She didn't want to admit it, but Aidan's cutting words to her about her *messed-up childhood* haunted her.

"Our family isn't broken," Cheryl said indignantly. "What gave you that idea?"

"Gee," said Mary. "Maybe the fact that my mom is an addict who almost killed Hannah and me in a car crash, which made you have to fight—literally fight—the courts for custody to save us?" She wouldn't admit it to anyone, but Mary worried that Aidan had been right. That her traumatic upbringing had scarred her for life. That she couldn't handle stressful situations without cracking.

Perhaps if Mary had grown up with a mother and father in her life, she would have had the confidence she had needed to stand up to the sleazy writer/director of *Zombie Prom at the Disco* who had convinced her that of course her character Jenaly Macintyre needed to disrobe in the locker room. It didn't make sense that she'd seduce the quarterback while still wearing her bra and panties. Mary could only imagine how horrified Hannah would be if she'd known that Mary had stripped on film for money. Full-frontal nudity! It wasn't porn, but it was definitely R-rated. Hopefully the film stayed stuck in limbo forever and never reached theaters.

"Let's keep opening presents," Brittany suggested.

"No, wait," said Guy. "You still need to spit in the tubes."

"What?" Keith asked.

"To collect your DNA," Guy explained. "That way we can mail them off tomorrow and get the results as soon as possible."

"But tomorrow's Christmas," said Keith. "The mail won't be collected."

"Let's just get it over with to appease him," said Hannah. "He's like an excited puppy dog."

"Ruff!" Guy barked.

"Good boy." Hannah patted Guy's head and then squealed when Guy licked her.

"Gross!" Mary exclaimed. "Nobody wants to see that."

"Yeah," said Cheryl. "Save your spit for the tube. Can someone help me open this thing? The packaging isn't arthritis-friendly."

"Here, Cheryl, let me help," said Brittany.

"Gran, what do you think of doing DNA tests?" Mary asked. "These weren't invented when you were my age."

"No, they weren't," said Cheryl. "But I wish they were. Family ancestry has always fascinated me."

Ten minutes and a considerable amount of spitting later, they'd moved on to opening more presents.

"A graphing calculator?" Jeremy asked. "Um... Thanks, Mom."

"What?" Brittany asked. "Your teacher said this was a good one and you know you need to bring your math grade up."

"How nice of you to remind me of my mediocre math grade," said Jeremy.

Brittany's cheeks turned pink. "There are a few other things under the tree for you to open tomorrow morning. But that calculator was expensive."

"I thanked you, didn't I?"

"You did," Brittany admitted.

"Hopefully your dad gets you something cool," Mary whispered, trying to cheer him up. She knew Jeremy was sensitive about his report card.

Mary didn't remember Christmases with her dad. The Christmases she had spent with her mom, back when Kelly still had custody, were horrible. Mary didn't recall much except for eating Cheerios next to Hannah and watching *Elf* while their mom slept next to them. Passed out, maybe? Yeah, that must have been why Kelly slept so hard. At the time, Mary had just thought her mom was extra tired from waiting to see if Santa would come.

Mary's shoulders curled forward, and she looked down at her hands. It didn't matter how many lovely holidays she'd celebrated after those days; part of her would always be the little girl on the couch. The girl from the troubled family. The woman Aidan didn't think had the skills to be a mother because she'd never learned how.

It had turned out that Aidan was a lying jerk whose opinion didn't matter, except why had it taken her so long to understand that about him? Why did Mary have a hard time recognizing who was worthy of her love, and who wasn't? Her inability to judge people's true intentions threatened to ruin her life. She could see that, and it terrified her.

"Here you go." Hannah passed her a package. "Just what you always wanted."

Mary plastered a fake smile on her face and opened up the gift. "Socks. Thank you."

"Not just any socks," said Hannah. "They're Merino wool. Thin, so they aren't too bulky, but extra warm so your toes won't get cold."

"Wool socks can save your life," said Keith. "I learned that in the Boy Scouts."

"I got you something I think you'll love," said Cheryl. "My present is over there with the silver ribbon."

"Thanks, Gran." Mary retrieved the package right when Jeremy opened the one from her.

"Dune Buggy tickets. Cool! Thanks, Mary."

"I thought you could take a friend. But wear a helmet, and follow all the rules, okay?"

"Will do." Jeremy gave her a high five.

"So, did you get me a present?" Mary asked, intentionally putting the teenager on the spot.

"I did..." he said cagily. "But I didn't wrap it."

"What's the gift?" Mary asked.

"I'm going to stop swiping your Coke Zero."

"Jeremy!" Brittany exclaimed. "You know we're not supposed to take food from their side of the pantry."

Jeremy shrugged. "I know, but..."

"That's a great present," said Mary, with a chuckle. "I'll take it. Now I'll open this one from Gran."

"They're coasters," Cheryl said, before Mary had even undone the ribbon. "I found them in the antique shop on Third Ave."

When Mary finally opened the present, she found four purple glass circles. "They're gorgeous," she said as she held them up to the light. "Thank you."

"I knew you liked shiny things," said Cheryl. "As soon as I saw them, I thought of you."

"Thanks, Gran." Mary got up and gave Cheryl a hug.

"And now for the present we've all been waiting for," said Hannah.

"What would that be?" Mary asked, thinking her sister was joking. "More socks?" Too late, she realized everyone in the room was staring at her—everyone but Jeremy, that is, who must not have been in on whatever crazy scheme Hannah had hatched. "Why are you all looking at me like that?"

Much to her surprise, it was Guy who stood up. He walked across the living room and handed her a manila envelope. "Here you go," Guy said. "The senior center awaits your magic."

"What are you talking about?" Mary slit open the envelope and removed the papers that were inside.

"You're going to redecorate the senior center!" Cheryl exclaimed.

"With a generous grant from Blanchet Maison's foundation," said Hannah as she patted Guy on the back.

"Why?" Mary asked, feeling confused.

"Our foundation is investing in the local communities that surround our hotel properties," Guy explained. "Several of our former employees benefit from the senior center, so this seemed like a good organization to support."

"Oh. Interesting..." Mary looked at the contract. "But I was going to be a designer, not a decorator." Not that it made any difference. Before Aidan had broken her heart, Mary had created huge plans for her future. She had wanted to open her own design firm with a focus on refreshing Airbnbs and long-term rentals. Now, all she could manage was her barista job at the coffee stand.

"There will be design work too," said Brittany. "Some outlets in the kitchen don't work."

"There's enough in the budget to afford new kitchen counters," said Keith. "But it'll be tricky because we won't be able to do a complete remodel as the seniors will be there every weekday."

"I thought you could work on the weekends when the center was closed," said Hannah. "And then use the weekdays to get your business off the ground."

Damn Hannah and her meddling. Mary didn't want this job, even if it had been dropped in her lap. She wasn't ready for it. She didn't have the energy. Maybe if she had been at full force. But not now, not when Mary felt so low that the only thing she wanted to do was go back to her room, turn off the light, and crack the window so she could hear Aidan and Lara argue when they returned from church. What was wrong with her that she continued to wallow like this? Mary, who had once been so happy and full of life.

She was damaged, that's what. And she was too fragile to handle stress, just like her mother. What if she developed a liquor habit? What if she was doomed to a life of substance use disorder, like Kelly? What if the sins of the past repeated themselves, and someday it was Mary's daughter enduring a crummy Christmas? What if it was Mary passed out on the couch next to her little girl? Sleeping Christmas Day away with nothing to eat but a box of Cheerios didn't seem that bad to Mary right now. It was certainly better than pretending that she was happy, and feigning excitement over this design job. But if there was one thing Mary was good at, it was pretending.

She had been an actor, after all. Mary had been acting all her life.

Pretending she was happy when her mother neglected her. Pretending she didn't miss her mom when Kelly was sent away.

"Thank you so much!" Mary said, with a huge smile on her face. "This is an amazing opportunity, and I appreciate all of you." Stress was already cracking her foundation, but Mary maintained her cheerful facade.

"We knew you'd love it!" Hannah squealed.

Darkness washed over her, but Mary kept smiling. If her life couldn't be perfect, at least she could make her surroundings look beautiful. Interior design was like acting at a material level.

"Now, who's ready for cheesecake?" Cheryl asked. "Jeremy, we bought three so make sure you save two for the rest of us."

"What's the matter?" Jeremy whispered when the rest of them had wandered to the kitchen. "I thought you wanted to be a designer."

"I do, but..." Mary sighed. "I'm kind of in a rut that I can't get out of."

"Maybe you're depressed. There's medicine for that, and it can really help." He pulled down his hat. "I was on it for a while when my parents went through the divorce, but now I don't need it."

Touched that the teenager would share something so personal with her, Mary spoke from the heart. "I'll ask my doctor about that if I can't get myself unstuck, but right now I don't think medicine would help me."

"Here you go," said Brittany, entering the room and handing Jeremy a plate. "Three slices of cheesecake just for you."

"Thanks," he grunted.

"Here's a piece for you too, Mary."

"I appreciate it." Mary ate the cheesecake slowly, letting every rich bite melt on her tongue. She stared at the snow falling outside. Jeremy could be right. Perhaps she was depressed. But where did that sadness come from? When her father had died, her mother had gone to pieces, turning to alcohol and shopping sprees to take the edge off her grief. Kelly had never recovered, and had spilled her pain over onto her young daughters. Now here Mary was, in the darkest place she'd ever been, all because of Aidan. No, that wasn't right. She was here because of her stupid, over-trusting heart. She needed to figure out how to protect herself better, pull herself out of this funk, and reclaim her power. She needed to rebuild her life one piece at a time, starting with her career and then hopefully finding new love in the future. But most important of all, Mary needed to find out how to stop herself from becoming her mother. Whatever happened next, she couldn't let history repeat itself.

THREE

"Thanks for letting me know," Mary said. "I understand getting trapped by Hood Canal Bridge traffic. I'll see you when you get here." It was Saturday morning, February 1st, and Mary was parked in front of the senior center speaking to the subcontractor who was bringing the brand-new dishwashers to install that morning. Mary had a whole team of professionals coming out that day. A crew would arrive any minute to paint the walls a creamy shade of yellow that would really perk up the place. The stonemasons were delivering the new quartz countertops for the kitchen, and her UPS notification said the cabinet hardware would arrive by noon. It was going to be a big day, and Mary would be lucky to be home by midnight.

A little over a month ago, when Hannah had orchestrated this job for her, Mary had been irked by her sister's interference. Embarrassed, really, because it was a clear indication that Hannah thought Mary needed help. That she was incapable of launching her business without her sister meddling. And okay, maybe she was. But now that she was in the thick of it, her creative juices had begun to flow again, and it was easier to move forward—at least where design work was concerned. The rest of her life was still stuck in neutral.

Mary climbed out of her car and stepped into the wind. Her blonde hair whipped out of its loose ponytail and hit her in the face. She tied it back again before opening the trunk of her car. The weather was a balmy fifty degrees out, and the sky was overcast. Mary reached into the trunk and brought out three big bags of cleaning supplies. She needed to stay out of the painters' way today, so had decided to use the time degreasing the kitchen cabinets.

Her phone buzzed right when she closed the trunk. It was a text from Jose, who owned the painting company.

Hi, my favorite client, he wrote. *Just letting you know that we're headed your way.*

See you soon, she answered.

Mary didn't know if Jose was this friendly with all his clients, or if he was flirting with her, and she didn't have the energy to find out. Dating was the last thing on her radar. But it did make her see positive qualities in Jose that Aidan had lacked from the very beginning. Unlike Aidan, Jose showed up when he said he would and cleaned up after himself. And he wasn't too lazy to use punctuation. How had she missed those warning signs about Aidan? Okay, so maybe punctuation wasn't a deal-breaker, but a total disregard for her time was unacceptable. Thinking about Aidan now made her angry, so she pushed him out of her mind and focused on work.

Mary entered the building and clicked on the lights. She wore a comfortable pair of sneakers since she'd be on her feet all day, but had also chosen tight jeans and a form-fitting, long-sleeved T-shirt. After setting her bags down by the door, Mary toured the main room to make sure that Jose's crew had prepped last night to her approval. There was only one tiny spot by the front window that had come undone.

Walking carefully, so as not to disturb the prep work, Mary

carried her bags to the kitchen. She removed the cleaning supplies she'd brought and placed them on the old countertops. The spray bottles and scrub brushes were here. But where were the microfiber rags? She must have forgotten a bag. Probably they were in the car. Grabbing her keys, Mary walked out the back door this time so she wouldn't interfere with the drop cloths.

The senior center used to be a roller rink, and the back exit still had a giant mural of roller skates on the outside wall. Keith had asked her if repainting it would be part of the makeover and she'd told him no, it was too iconic. Today, she came outside to find a tall man in baggy pants and a torn leather jacket staring at the skates. His long hair snarled and blew in the wind. He had the scruffy appearance of someone who might be living on the beach, which occasionally happened in Sand Dollar Cove, since it was a popular vacation destination and also because there was an affordable housing shortage all across Grays Harbor County and not enough shelters.

"Why do the skates have faces?" the man asked. "Who would want to put their feet into sentient beings?"

"I don't know," Mary said. "I've never thought about it."

"It's the first thing I noticed." The man turned around and Mary yelped.

"Snake!" she cried, pointing at the yellow reptile coiled around his wrist.

"Who? Elvis?" The man stroked the snake's skin. "Yeah, he's my ball python."

"Sorry," Mary said, feeling foolish. "That was an involuntary response."

"No need to apologize." His eyes sparkled like he was laughing at her but was too polite to say so. "Not everyone has been lucky enough to have a personal relationship with reptiles." He held up his wrist and flicked his tongue back at the snake. "Isn't that right, Elvis?"

Mary chuckled. *Who pretended to kiss a snake?* She had a schedule to keep, but curiosity got the better of her. "Where's the rest of Elvis? I only see his head."

The stranger undulated his arms like he was doing the Wave. "He's in my sleeves, absorbing my body heat. This is the first day we've been here when it was warm enough to go for a walk. Is it always this cold in winter?"

"I'd say so. We don't normally get snow very often but it's usually pretty chilly." *This guy must be a drifter,* she figured. Mary had met ones with dogs before but never pet snakes. "Well, uh... you and Elvis have a nice day. Try to stay warm." She thought about telling him about the cold weather shelter that sometimes operated in the Catholic church on Second Street, but it only opened when the temperature dropped below freezing. He would be long gone before it got that cold again.

Mary headed to her car, unlocked the trunk, and took out the rag bag. She walked up to the front entrance of the center. From the corner of her eye, she saw Jose's van drive down the street. Right on time, like usual. Mary opened the front door and was just about to walk into the center when the man with the snake surprised her from behind.

"Say, you wouldn't know where I could find Mary Turner, would you?" he asked.

Mary yelped for the second time that day and dropped her bag. "Gah!" she cried. "Did you have to sneak up on me like that?"

"Sorry." He immediately stepped back three feet. "I didn't mean to jump scare you. I thought you heard me come up the ramp."

"No," Mary said in a stern tone that reminded her of Hannah's. "I didn't." She took a closer look at him. The man appeared to be just a couple of years older than her and his skin was tanned like he'd spent serious time outdoors. "Why are you looking for Mary?" she asked cautiously. The stranger was over six feet tall.

"I got her name from Nick."

The former maintenance man at Seaside Resort? Mary knew that Hannah had been about to fire Nick last spring, but he had quit instead and started his own construction firm. "Why is Nick talking to you about Mary?" she asked, feeling awkward that she was talking about herself in the third person.

"He referred her to me as an interior designer." The man gently poked Elvis's body back into his sleeve and held out his free hand to shake. "I should have introduced myself earlier, but I was too mesmerized by anthropomorphic roller skates to think. My name's Steven Clarke and I'm the new owner of Sand Dollar Cove Cinema."

What the actual...? Mary's mouth gaped open. She'd heard that the historic movie theater had sold last fall, but she'd assumed a corporation had bought it. "Mary Turner," she said, shaking his hand briefly. "Nice to meet you."

"So *you're* Mary. Well, this is a lucky coincidence. Nick told me to look for you in the senior center, but I thought I'd stumbled upon the roller rink."

"Good morning, sunshine," Jose hollered from the bottom of the ramp. Three men stood behind him, dressed in white, holding paint cans, rollers, and brushes. "I've been looking forward to this job all week."

"Great." Mary flashed him a thumbs up.

"There's nothing like paint to make a dramatic transformation," Jose said, as he marched up the ramp.

"Excuse us," said one of his crew. "We're coming through."

Mary opened the door wide for them and stepped over to the corner of the porch. Steven followed her.

"You did a great job prepping last night," Mary told Jose. "I did notice one little section of the front window that might have come undone, though."

"Thanks for the heads-up." Jose brushed back his thick, dark hair. "I'll be sure to take care of it myself." He looked Steven up and down and wrinkled his forehead. When his gaze drifted down to Elvis, he frowned. "Is this bum bothering you, Mary?"

"Bruh." Steven snapped his head back like Jose had wounded him. "Why would you say that?"

"It's okay." Mary shot Jose a reassuring smile. "This is Steven Clarke, the new owner of the movie theater."

"*Cinema*," Steven corrected her. "The Sand Dollar Cove Cinema."

"Seriously?" Jose raised his eyebrows. "Good luck with that. I heard the HVAC system broke, and it developed a major damp problem."

"That's been taken care of." Steven put his free hand in his pocket. "Now it's a toasty seventy-three degrees."

"Sounds too hot if you ask me," said Jose.

Steven narrowed his eyes. "I didn't, but you can add your comment to the suggestion box once the cinema reopens. I can also direct you to some literature on how to respectfully refer to people struggling with housing insecurity."

Jose scoffed. "Is this guy for real?" He caught Mary's attention and pointed with this thumb. "I'll be in here if you need protection from the word police. Just holler."

"Thanks." She nodded and looked back at Steven, her first impression of him rearranging itself like modular furniture. *Tall, tan, scruffy... and sensitive.* "So why did Nick send you my way?" she asked. "I barely know the man."

"He said that you were the best interior designer he knew."

She was probably the *only* interior designer Nick knew, but Mary kept that information to herself. "That was nice of him. Are you in need of interior design services?"

"Yes, actually. I am."

"For your home or business?" As soon as she said it, she felt a buzz of excitement. Was Steven hiring an interior designer to renovate the movie theater? That would be a dream job.

"The cinema." Steven pinched his sleeve and lifted up the leather to make more room for Elvis. "Insurance is paying for almost everything. Luckily, we caught the damp issue in time. That's been taken care of by professional mitigators. Now it's time to put the pieces back together, and there are so many choices I'm overwhelmed. Nick's my contractor, but he's no help when it comes to picking out tile and carpet. He suggested you'd be the right person for the job." Steven nodded toward the senior center. "I take it you're in charge of this renovation?"

"It's more like a facelift, but yes. I'm a certified interior designer and I've recently opened my own business. I can show you a portfolio of my work. My most recent projects are the lobby renovation of Seaside Resort as well as the temporary restoration of one of its buildings, Strawberry Cottage. What are your goals for your renovation?"

"Being able to sell tickets again, as soon as possible, but also keeping the character of the place, if you know what I mean."

"I'm not sure I do. It has good bones, but hasn't had any character at all since they remodeled it in the early 2000s."

"The turn of the century, huh? I wasn't sure how old that brown granite was in the restrooms."

"It's been there for ages. I remember because my mom took me there one day and we watched a musical. It was so boring we both fell asleep."

Was that what had happened? Or had Kelly passed out? Mary was only realizing certain things now. Sometimes memories were like that. You held onto them your entire childhood, thinking they were innocent, and then they hit you in the face as an adult when you realized their true significance. The day they'd watched *Chitty Chitty Bang Bang* together, a burning plastic smell had clung to Kelly like it so often did before she took long naps. Mary looked down at her feet for a minute, lost in thought. It had been a rare unsupervised visit with Kelly, when she had been in fifth grade.

"Musicals bore the hell out of me, too, except for *The Rocky Horror Picture Show*. I'm a horror buff, myself. The more gore, the better."

"Cool." Mary lifted her gaze and inspected him closely, realizing that the target audience of *Zombie Prom at the Disco* was standing before her. How devastatingly awful it would be to know that strangers would see her naked if the film ever did make it to theaters. Her body might be perfect, but her reputation would be in shambles. But renovating Sand Dollar Cove's movie house... That would be amazing. "I have some time on Monday. Could I stop by the th—" she caught herself from saying "theater." "Cinema, to show you my portfolio and discuss an estimate?"

"That would be great." Steven hooked a finger in the belt loop of his baggy jeans and tugged upward to keep them from falling. "You know where to find me. Does nine a.m. work, or is that too early?"

"Nine works perfect. See you then." Mary spoke with confidence, but as she watched him go, she wondered what she had gotten herself into. The possibility of managing two large-scale projects at the same time excited her, but working for Steven? She didn't know anything about the man, except that he had a snake up his sleeve.

FOUR

The Sand Dollar Cove Cinema was a dilapidated wreck; that was Mary's professional opinion. She stood in front of the building Monday morning and took in the peeling exterior paint, the ugly landscaping, the missing letters from the marquee. "Sand Dollar Cove Cin," she read out loud. "Charming."

Despite the missing letters, the marquee was the one thing she liked about the exterior—or the marquee's background, that is. It had clean, futuristic lines and neon lights that spoke of its original 1960s style. This was a sign built for a generation that had gone into space, put a man on the moon, brought TV dinners to family rooms across America, and still found time to go to the movies—dressed up in miniskirts, Gogo boots, and mohair sweaters. But the 1980s font on top of the marquee background was ugly. Mary loved experimenting with mixtures of old and new in her design work, but this was an example of experimentation gone wrong.

She tucked her portfolio under her arm and walked up to the front door of the theater, with a clear vision of how she wanted to renovate the place. The question was, could she win

Steven over with her concept and land the job? She hoped so. The more she'd thought about the opportunity this presented, the more excited she'd become. Not only would it be fun, but this was her chance to leave her mark on Sand Dollar Cove. People would see her design aesthetic on display for years to come. That would lead to future jobs.

This morning, she'd chosen her outfit with care, wanting to look both creative and professional at the same time. Mary wore light blue corduroy pants over soft leather boots, and a green angora sweater with embroidered hummingbirds on the sleeve. Underneath, she'd added a silk undershirt, since the yarn was itchy. Topping it all off was her bright turquoise raincoat and knit scarf. There was nothing Mary could do about her young age—twenty-three now; or her relative lack of experience—she'd only graduated last summer. But at least she looked artistic. Knowing that added a spring to her step as she opened the double doors and walked into the movie house, six minutes ahead of schedule.

The lobby hummed like a thousand beehives, which wasn't what she was expecting. But it was no wonder the noise level was intense. Mary counted seven industrial dehumidifiers, all of them running at full force, sucking moisture out of the air. Where the concessions area had once been was now a zippered wall of plastic. She couldn't see inside, but it sounded like there might be additional fans behind the plastic screen. Wow. The mildew damage must have been worse than Steven had indicated. She needed more details about that.

"Hello?" Mary called out, trying to be heard over the hum of small engine noise. "Steven? Are you here?" She checked her watch and confirmed she was early. "Hello?" she called again. Mary walked over to the doors that led into the screening room, but they were locked. Five minutes later, she was still waiting, only now she was uncomfortably warm. Steven hadn't been joking about the thermostat being cranked up to seventy-three degrees. Jose had been right: that was too warm by Pacific Northwest standards, especially considering how Mary had dressed for the cold. She needed to remove her raincoat and scarf, pronto.

Just strip off a layer or two, Zeke had said, in front of the cast that day. *The locker room's hot and steamy. You're a zombie with a lust for blood.* Mary pushed the memory away. She hated thinking about that horrible event. She refused to think about it now.

Not finding any place to safely rest her portfolio besides the floor, Mary wedged the binder between her knees and clenched her calves tightly to hold it in place. Then she used both arms to escape from her raincoat and scarf. Right when she had one sleeve on and one sleeve off, a zipping noise cut across the roar of the dehumidifiers. The plastic wall in front of the concessions stand split into two and Steven poked his head through.

"You didn't tell me you were a contortionist," he said as he came into the lobby. "Add a boa constrictor and people would pay good money to see that act where I come from."

"And where's that?" Mary asked.

"Las Vegas."

"Nice." Mary, who was sweating, wrestled out of her coat, but accidentally dropped her scarf on the ground. When she swooped down to pick it up, the binder fell, and the clips sprang open, scattering pages everywhere. "Oh, no!" she threw out her hands trying to collect them, but it was too late.

"Whoops. Let me help with that." Steven trotted over to where she knelt on the carpet and crouched down. "Were these in any particular order?" he asked as he collected the papers.

"Yes, and now they're all messed up." Mary put her scarf and jacket in one hand and picked up the shell of the portfolio binder with the other. The three rings poked open, with only a few pages still hanging on by one hole. This was a disastrous way to start out a pitch presentation. Embarrassed, Mary tried to recover. "I promise that I'm better at designing inspiring interiors than I am at balancing acts and raincoat removal."

"I don't know. I was entertained."

"Glad I could amuse you." Mary flashed him a wry smile. For the first time since he'd entered the room, she got a good look at his outfit. What the hell was he wearing? Steven swam in a silk shirt so voluminous it looked like a poncho. Hula dancers and palm trees decorated the fabric along with what appeared to be pineapples strumming ukuleles. Mary couldn't stop staring.

"I see you've noticed my shirt." Steven continued to gather pages. "It was so gray outside I figured we could use some Hawaiian sunshine."

"Good thinking." Mary looked away, embarrassed to have been caught staring. "I've never been to Hawaii, but always wanted to go."

"It's one of my favorite places on the planet. I've even thought of buying a timeshare, except they're either a hassle or a rip-off." He handed her the last page. "Looks like we got them all now."

"Thanks. Sorry to be such a klutz." Mary stood, and as her body moved upward, she felt a creep-crawly sensation that she couldn't identify. Her hair, which she'd spent ten minutes flat-ironing into submission that morning, floated diagonally across her chin and stuck to the bustline of her sweater. She'd never seen static electricity so bad. Desperately wishing for the hairbrush in her purse, Mary attempted to finger-comb her locks back into place. Only that didn't work.

"I see that the dehumidifiers have attacked you," said Steven. "I'll be glad when the moisture mitigators are done."

"Is there someplace we can go that's quieter?" Mary asked. "These machines are loud."

"That's the understatement of the year." Steven waved his hand. "Let's go into the auditorium."

Steven led her through the lobby, past the concessions stand, and into the movie theater's auditorium. The place had been gutted and didn't look how Mary remembered it at all. "Whoa!" she exclaimed. "You've been busy."

"Yeah, that whole left-side wall had to go, because that's where the mildew was the worst. We've torn down the acoustic cushioning, replaced the insulation and drywall, and covered everything with mold-resistant paint."

"But the seats are still here?" Mary went over to the first chair she saw and pressed her hand into the scratched velvet cushion. "I'm surprised these aren't mildewy."

"They probably are, but the insurance adjustor said someone could reupholster them. I wasn't sure if that was worth fighting or not. That's what I mean about needing help."

"Hmmm…" Mary set her belongings on one of the seats and then turned on the flashlight of her phone so she could get a better look at the cushions. The houselights were on, but the flashlight helped her see more detail. "Could be," she said. "These chairs have good bones. I can't tell for sure, but they look like they're made of cast iron. I'm surprised I'm not seeing rust, but the powdered coating must have held up."

"They have intricate feet." Steven pointed at the ground. "That's what I noticed."

Mary looked at the base of the chair where the metal splayed out in an ornate design. "That filigree reminds me of the late 1940s, not the 1960s when this place was built, but maybe they got a deal on the seats. They could have already been used when they bought them." She leaned down and sniffed the cushion. "Yup, damp. These cushions need to be replaced."

"Did you just smell my chair?"

Mary quickly stood. "Uh, yeah. Sorry."

"Don't apologize. I admire your nosy approach."

"Thanks." Was Steven being serious, or was he cracking a

not-very-funny joke? Mary couldn't tell. "I need to reassemble my portfolio before I show it to you since the pages are all messed up, but maybe you can explain what's happened to the building while I do that."

"Sure. Sounds like a plan."

"So, the HVAC broke, and the building developed a mildew problem that the insurance company is fixing?" Mary asked as she sat down.

"That's right." Steven sat a few seats to her left. "I purchased the building at a foreclosure auction in September but didn't arrive to take possession until early December. By then the building had been cold for over two months. Combine that with a roof leak, and it's no wonder mildew took hold. Once Nick started tearing up walls, we learned that the damage was worse than we'd thought. There must have been many leaks over the years that were patched instead of being dealt with properly."

"I'm not surprised." Mary added another section of papers to the binder. "The owners lived in Port Angeles. They bought the business for their son to run, but he was a total dipsh—" Mary caught herself, just in time, remembering that she was trying to present herself as a competent business owner, not someone who flung around the word "dipshit." "Disappointment," she said instead. "Anyway, I'm assuming they thought he was a disappointment. For most of the time he was in charge he only showed movies on the weekends. The rest of the time he surfed."

"Surfed? Isn't it way too cold to surf here?"

"Not if you're wearing the right type of wetsuit."

"No, thank you." Steven shivered. "So... the cinema was empty the rest of the week?"

"I think so. At least, I remember it being closed a lot when I was a kid."

"What about summer in tourist season?"

"I think it might have been closed then, too. But when I was in middle school, things improved a lot because the owner married, and his wife became involved. There was a good stretch there when they opened every night of the week. Thursday nights at eight p.m. were teen nights, where anyone thirteen to nineteen years old could get in half-price." Mary grew wistful. "This theater and the roller rink were *the* places to be. But then, in my senior year, the roller rink closed and became the senior center. And sometime after that the couple running the theater separated."

"What happened then?"

"I'm not sure exactly. I moved to California after high school for a couple of years. By the time I'd returned to Sand Dollar Cove the business had gone back to only showing movies on the weekends again."

"How did he make any money only working two or three days a week?"

Mary pulled a lock of blonde hair behind her ear. "I have no idea."

"Your explanation lines up with what Nick told me, too," said Steven. "And also explains why the place is a mess. You won't believe some of the junk we've found. Wait until I show you the storage room."

"I'd be curious to see it." Mary clasped the three-ring binder shut, narrowly missing pinching her finger in the process. "Would you like to see my portfolio? Or would you rather show me around first and explain what needs to be done?"

"How about I show you around first? But leave that binder of yours in a safe place so it doesn't fall apart again."

"Will do." Mary stood. "I'm ready for the grand tour."

"Follow me, madam."

Steven spent the next ten minutes showing Mary parts of the theater she was already familiar with as a previous guest, like the balcony, concessions area, and women's restroom, as well as places she'd never visited before like the projection room and the men's restroom.

"Gross," she said when she saw the stained urinals. "Those look like they've never been replaced—or properly cleaned."

"That's nothing. You should have seen my office. It was so rotten that Nick had to rip out the ceiling tiles and subfloor. I'd show it to you now but the moisture mitigators are in there. But I can show you the basement."

"This place has a basement?" Mary's eyes grew wide. "I had no idea."

"It's pretty creepy, but it has some fun memorabilia in the storage area." Steven took her through a back hallway and opened a door to a flight of stairs that descended into darkness. He flicked on the lights before taking the first step. "I'll go first so you can follow me, but please hold onto the handrail. These stairs are narrow. Watch your head, too, because the ceiling is low."

"This sounds like the beginning of a horror movie." Mary eyed the stairs nervously.

"It does, doesn't it?" Steven smiled. "I knew I liked you." He ducked his head and walked downstairs, leading her into a cold, but surprisingly dry, basement. "The leak didn't reach down here, thankfully."

"This place is huge." Mary surveyed the space. Mainly it was empty, but there were some cardboard boxes that looked like the original packaging that the popcorn machines came in. "Does that furnace still work?" Mary asked, pointing to the corner.

"No, it's hooked up to an oil tank that was decommissioned in the 1980s. The previous owners must have left it here because it would be too expensive to remove. I'm not sure how they got it down here in the first place."

"I wonder if you could put a roller rink down here? You've got the room for it."

Steven raised his arm and touched the ceiling. "If I were wearing skates, I'd hit my head."

"Oh." Mary felt stupid. "Right. Sorry." She was five feet five inches and Steven towered over her.

"The best part of the basement, or should I say the only good part of it, is the storage room. So far, I've found over two dozen vintage movie posters." He brought her to the far side of the room and opened a door. An earthy smell greeted them. Steven pulled a string attached to the ceiling before stepping aside so Mary could enter.

"I'm getting horror movie vibes again." Mary stepped inside the tiny space. "I'm trusting that you're not a serial killer." She tried to make light of it, but safety concerns were no joke. Her professors had warned her about that. Interior designers often met with clients in private homes, away from prying eyes, and that brought an element of danger with it. Mary was glad she had told Hannah and Cheryl where she was going before she left.

"Wait until you see Godzilla." Steven pointed at a rubber statue of a lizard that nearly matched him in height, propped next to a stack of cardboard boxes.

"Whoa! That's actually kind of cool." Mary went closer to investigate.

"Ten bucks says you're thinking about smelling it."

"We can't use it if it stinks." Mary took a whiff. "Thankfully, all I smell is rubber."

"You think we could use that thing?"

"Maybe. It would make a fun selfie station, and that would give you free advertising on social media."

"If it's free, take it."

"Exactly." Mary looked at the boxes next to Godzilla. "Anything else interesting in here?"

"Probably lots of stuff. I've barely scratched the surface." Steven walked over to the opposite side of Godzilla. "Over in this corner is where I found the posters, but I already brought those to my apartment, so they'd be safer." He lifted the lid to a wooden crate. "I don't know what these are. I can't figure them out."

Mary peeked into the box. "They're glass coasters," she said, picking up a circle of purple glass. "My grandma gave me some for Christmas that she found in an antique shop in town."

"Sweet. Maybe I could sell them online." Steven put the lid back on. "I haven't been able to look through the rest of this crap yet. It's overwhelming. Then, on top of that, I have to figure out what to tell Nick about which carpet, and paint, and light fixtures to choose. I'm in over my head."

"That's where I can help. Let's go back upstairs and I'll show you my portfolio and explain how my services can make things easier for you."

"I like the sound of that."

After they returned to the screen room, Mary paged through her portfolio and walked Steven through her past projects, most of which she'd done in her design school course-work. "Hiring a designer costs money up front, but often ends up saving funds in the long run. I can save you time. I can help you prevent mistakes. I help communicate with the contractor to make sure the job is done right. I can follow up with the city permits office. A job like this requires a million details, and I'm here to help."

"That's exactly what I need." Steven leaned forward and rested his elbow on the seat back in front of him. "The insurance company has given me a budget, but no direction. How much do you charge?"

"One hundred and eighty dollars an hour, and I require a ten-hour retainer to get started. After that I would invoice you weekly." She was lowballing herself, but wasn't sure if he knew it. Experienced designers charged $200 an hour, or more. But Mary didn't feel comfortable charging that much until she had more experience. Plus, she really wanted this job. If Steven got other bids, at least hers would be the cheapest.

"One hundred and eighty sounds more than reasonable." Steven flipped through the pages of her binder. "I'm enjoying looking at your work, but everything is a lot simpler than what I'm used to."

"Simpler?" Mary asked, her voice rising. What a horrible way to describe her creative vision!

"In a classy way. None of this looks like what I grew up with in Vegas."

"Oh. You mean my designs aren't..." *Gaudy; ostentatious; hideous; tacky*—Mary struggled to find an adjective that wouldn't insult him. "Flamboyant? I can do flamboyant. I always listen to my clients and incorporate their wishes." Maybe Steven wanted something as wild as the ugly shirt he was wearing.

"I don't know what I want," said Steven. "Like I said before, that's why I need you. Or someone like you," he added quickly. "I'm twenty-eight years old and have never owned a house before, let alone a movie theater. I don't know how to sort through carpet samples. So you tell me, what do you think needs to be done around here to turn it into a place that runs seven nights a week to a packed crowd?"

This was what Mary had been waiting for. She loved telling people how to re-envision their spaces. "Well, the way I see it, you have three options." She held up her fingers. "Option number one would be to bring the theater up to modern design standards in every way. Make it look like an AMC or Regal like you'd find in Seattle. That would mean investing in leatherette reclining seats with dual cupholders, putting in a high-traffic carpet, and redoing the restrooms with touchless faucets and soap dispensers. The benefits would be you'd give tourists the moviegoing experience they were familiar with. The drawback would be a loss of charm, and the reclining seats would reduce seating capacity. However, with that type of theater you could charge twenty bucks for a bucket of popcorn, and nobody would blink an eye."

"You're right," said Steven. "Except it wouldn't be like theaters people were used to back home because I only have one screen."

"True." Mary held up a second finger. "Option two would be to go vintage. Sand Dollar Cove Cinema was built in the 1960s. You could take it back to the past, with all the sleek, futuristic, mid-century modern details that are so popular right now. Keep the original seats, but reupholster them. Bring the marquee back to its former glory. Do vintage tile work in the bathroom. Hire a muralist to paint popcorn and soda bottles dancing around with smiley faces. Like the roller skate mural on the senior center, only movie theater-themed."

"Play up the whole anthropomorphic thing. You've got my attention."

Mary didn't know what that word meant, but she pretended like she did and kept going. "A benefit of this plan would be you'd keep your current seat capacity. You'd also give tourists a unique experience that they couldn't find elsewhere. Maybe you could lower the price of popcorn, or show double features like the old days." Cheryl had told her about that when Mary had asked her grandmother what the movie theater used to be like. "My gran said that when this place used to show double features, people would load up on food during intermission."

"What's option number three?" Steven asked.

"That would be a mixture of both plans. Go vintage in the lobby and screen room but put modern amenities like touchless faucets in the restrooms. Those are more hygienic."

"In that option I might want to change up the seats." Steven put his hands on the armrests of his chair. "These are really narrow. A lot of people wouldn't be able to comfortably sit in them, especially since the armrests don't go up."

Mary hadn't noticed that. "You're right," Mary said, feeling ashamed. She believed in creating spaces that made everyone feel welcome. "And the rows are so close together that it makes it difficult for people with mobility challenges." *Like Gran.* "If you hired me, my goal would be to create a place that was inclusive and exciting. I believe you could use the fact that this is a historic property to your advantage. This could be a normal movie theater—or it could be a movie theater and tourist attraction."

"Wow," said Steven, his mouth gaping open.

"What? Is static making my hair stick up again?"

"No. Wow to you being so impressive."

"Really?"

"Yes, really. I'm on board. Option three all the way. Do you think we could have Martians meeting children wearing space helmets?"

"Huh?"

"For the murals. Or maybe robots. Like Tomorrowland at Disney World, only here in my cinema. That's the type of vintage 1960s vibe you mean, right?"

Mary nodded quickly. "Yes. Exactly." Steven might have horrible fashion taste, but she was excited that he understood her vision.

"The concessions packages could have space themes too," said Steven. "The Jupiter pack. The Neptune bundle."

Awesome. He'd really taken the space theme and run with it. Mary brainstormed quickly on the fly. "We could have a selfie wall that says 'Sand Dollar Cove Cinema is out of this world'."

"And one of those painted boards with cutouts for people to poke their heads through that turned the whole family into astronauts."

"Or aliens."

"Or robots." Steven leaned forward slightly, his eyes flashing.

"Or Godzilla." Mary felt energy rush through her. Steven's enthusiasm for her ideas was the ultimate elixir. She'd walked into this building hoping to get the job. Now she desperately wanted it with every fiber of her being. "I realize you're probably considering other candidates," she said, trying not to get her hopes up. "I understand if you need some time to get back to me with your final decision."

"There are no other candidates," Steven said, not taking his eyes off her. "I mean, there were, but not anymore. Not now that I've heard your presentation. You've got the job."

Hallelujah! Mary needed this win. Her broken, wounded spirit craved this. The senior center project had been given to her. But this job she'd earned all by herself.

"Thank you," Mary said, feeling a flush of pride. "You won't regret it."

FIVE

Unfortunately, the funk Mary found herself in was still there. Her excitement over landing the job at the cinema while also redesigning the senior center had pushed some of her gloom away, especially since that had allowed her to quit her job at the coffee stand. But on gray days like this one, when nobody else was home, Mary cracked her window, angled the blinds, and kept her ear out for Aidan's BMW. It was like poking a festering wound.

Looking back, there had been a multitude of signals Mary had ignored about Aidan's true character. She had acted like things were okay, even though at some level she knew they weren't. If she didn't figure out why she'd done that, she might fall into the same trap again, and become bound to someone who was unworthy of her. There must be something inherently wrong with her that she would pretend like things were great when, deep down, she knew them to be awful. That was the reason she was obsessed with studying Aidan and Lara's relationship. Mary was desperate to avoid repeating her past mistakes.

Aidan usually arrived home at ten thirty a.m. on the dot,

especially Fridays through Tuesdays, his workweek, and today was Tuesday, February 11th. What were he and Lara doing in a few days for Valentine's Day? Would Heather and Stewart watch Larry so they could go for a fancy night out? Mary scoffed at the notion. Aidan hated expensive restaurants. As for Valentine's Day, the nicest thing he'd ever bought her was a car wash coupon.

Mary frowned, remembering coming out to her car and seeing a giant heart written in the dirty window with 'wash me' in bold letters. She had been seconds away from unleashing her fury at the jerk behind the message when Aidan smiled and presented her with the coupon with *for my valentine* written on the top. He'd used red ink, which looked like blood, and his usual atrocious punctuation, but Mary had thought it was romantic. She'd baked Aidan brownies, tracked down a boot-legged concert recording of his favorite band, and hand-drawn a Valentine's card with a beautiful note expressing her devotion. And had accepted a discount coupon in return. The broken part of her psyche had told her that a car wash coupon was all she was worth.

Why? Why had she done that? Why had Mary been so confused about love that she'd been eager to build her life around Aidan? Why had she been so needy for stability that she'd ignored clear warning signs about him? One thing was for certain: going forward, Mary would be vigilant about defending her heart.

Thinking about Aidan had gotten her sidetracked, and she knew she needed to get back to work, so Mary took one last peek through the blinds to make sure the BMW wasn't there. Nope, all she saw was Lara's Toyota parked in the driveway.

Refocusing her attention back on her computer screen, Mary continued researching which movie theater seats to buy. Already she had learned that in the 1940s, when she suspected the current seats had been made, the average American male weighed 166 pounds. Now that had increased to 198 pounds. Steven was right; keeping the original seats—which were incredibly narrow—excluded many moviegoers.

Mary felt strongly that the space should be inclusive. Everyone who came to Sand Dollar Cove should feel comfortable no matter their ability level or size. That meant adding additional seats that were accessible to wheelchairs as well, and redesigning the entrance so that the wheelchair ramp wasn't an ugly bandage on a previous design, but part of the thought process from the very beginning.

Her eyes drifted over to the sketch she'd made for the new entrance and she felt a zip of excitement, momentarily pulling her out of her gloomy mood. She couldn't wait to show the drawing to Steven. She'd already imagined rolling Cheryl up the new ramp and down the red carpet like she was a glamorous movie star, instead of a retired housekeeper with a bad back.

When her phone rang, she looked at caller ID and her excitement curdled like sour milk. It was Zeke, the writer/director of *Zombie Prom at the Disco*.

"Hi, Zeke," she said after picking up on the third ring. "What's up? I haven't heard from you in ages."

"It's been at least a year," he said, "but that doesn't mean I haven't been working behind the scenes making things happen. Mary, I have fabulous news!"

"You do?"

"We've finally found a distributor!" Zeke exclaimed. "As well as additional financial backing."

"Oh... ah... wow." Mary's hands gripped the phone gently, like she was palming a live grenade. "What does that mean exactly?"

"It means that *Zombie Prom at the Disco* is coming to theaters across America!"

"Holy crap." Dread pooled in her stomach.

"It'll be a limited distribution, unfortunately. Not every city will show it, of course, and not every theater either. But yes, there will finally be showings, and after that, who knows? I have a meeting with Netflix next week."

Panic washed over her. "But the locker room scene," she protested. "That can't be on Netflix."

"Sure it could, with the right editing."

"Like editing it out?" Mary asked hopefully.

Zeke laughed. "You're hilarious. Why would we edit it out? You're gorgeous in that scene, and it's a pivotal role."

"But—"

"Besides," Zeke continued, not letting her finish her thought. "If Netflix doesn't want it, MAX will. The more tits and ass the better, as far as they're concerned."

This was her fault. All of it was her fault for being so stupid. She hadn't been beautiful or talented enough to land an agent, and when it had come time to finalize contract negotiations, Mary had signed her life away, without understanding what the contract meant. Then, when the locker room scene was lined up, she'd gone through with it because she had no other choice.

Take off your shirt, too, Zeke had said, with the entire cast and crew watching. *Don't be such a prude.*

If it had only been her shirt, maybe Mary wouldn't have minded so much. If the camera was angled at her back, maybe she could have gotten over it. But letting Zeke persuade her into the rest of it, when she had been so incredibly uncomfortable... Should she fight for herself now? Could she? Mary wanted to. The thought of total strangers seeing her naked made her feel sick. What would happen if future design clients googled her and the first thing they saw was a YouTube clip of her naked body covered in blood? That was disturbing. And what if she had kids someday, and they saw it? How would she explain that to them?

Mary had seen her own mom's naked body lying on the apartment floor, and never gotten over it. That was one of her first clear memories of Kelly. One moment Mary had been watching cartoons and the next, she had looked across the room and seen Kelly stumble against the coffee table, pitch forward, and fall to the ground, holding a bottle of alcohol.

"Mom," Hannah had yelled. "Put some clothes on!"

Kelly hadn't responded, so Mary had helped Hannah pull a blanket off their bed and cover their mother. Together they had picked up the bottle, which was made of such thick glass that it hadn't broken, and sopped up the pungent liquid from the carpet as best they could.

"Mom's sleeping," Hannah had said. Mary, who had been preschool age at the time, had believed her.

Now she knew that her sister had lied to protect them both. Kelly had been so drunk that she hadn't bothered getting dressed before passing out.

"I don't like the nude scene," Mary told Zeke. "The movie would be better without it."

"Don't be ridiculous. That scene is brilliant."

"But I don't want—"

"It doesn't matter what you want," Zeke said, in a harsh tone. "Why do you have to be such a buzzkill? I call with amazing news, and you bitch about that scene again."

"I'm not—"

"Real actors do nude scenes all the time. It's not a big deal."

"Then why was I the only one with the frontal nude shot?" Mary asked. "Why didn't the football players have to strip off their clothes, too?"

"Because nobody would know they were athletes without their jerseys on. Any idiot knows that."

Mary fumed. She wished she knew what to say to make Zeke listen, but she'd been down that road before and he always ignored her.

"Now about your contract," Zeke continued. "You agreed to

promote *Zombie Prom at the Disco* for three months prior to and post release. That starts now."

"How?" Mary glanced quickly at her design plans. "I can't leave town now, I have work to do."

"I'm not asking you to fly anywhere. Our budget has increased but we certainly don't have the funds for plane tickets. No, most of the promotion you'll do is online. I've had our marketing person create a document for you that I'm sending you. Does your old email address work?"

"It should."

"Great. I'm sending it right now." A few seconds later an email from Zeke with an attachment popped up in Mary's inbox.

She clicked to open the PDF. "Online interviews, Zoom presentations, and a few print interviews as well," she read. "Okay. I can do that." She felt relief at first, because it seemed like it was manageable. But then she read the next section. "You want me to create a TikTok account? But I don't do TikTok. I'm on Instagram and Twitter."

"Which would be fine if our prospective audience didn't skew younger," said Zeke. "But TikTok is where it's at for our target demographics. We'd like you to post every day and hopefully build your account up to the thousands by the premier. Be sure to use the list of included hashtags."

"Hashtag Zombie Movie. Hashtag Horror Movie. Hashtag Sexy Zombies." Mary felt sleazy just reading the descriptors. What would she tell Hannah? Or Cheryl? She heard the sound of a car driving down Ocean Court Place and looked through the blinds in time to see Aidan park next to Lara's Corolla. A horrible thought occurred to her. What would Aidan think when he found out about the movie? He could watch her naked self for the rest of his life and there was nothing she could do about it. Even worse, his parents would see it, too!

Mary saw Aidan climb out of his Beemer, walk over to

Lara's Toyota and draw a heart on the road-stained window. *He wouldn't give the same Valentine's Day gift to Lara, would he?* she asked herself. But then he did! Aidan wrote 'wash me' in messy letters. *What a jerk!*

She pulled away from the blinds. "Does the TikTok account have to be under my own name?" she asked. Maybe if she was clever there was still a way out of this. "What if I build up the account under my character's name, Jenaly Macintyre? I could do the whole thing from her point of view."

"Brilliant! Character confessions are hot right now. This is why I've always loved working with you, Mary. You've got imagination oozing from every pore."

Every naked pore that was now immortalized on the big screen, for ever and ever.

"When will the movie come out?" Mary asked.

"May fourteenth. We have from now until then to build as much buzz as possible."

"Okay. I'll do my best." Mary said goodbye and hung up. She *would* do her best, despite her humiliation. Except for the locker room scene, Mary was proud of the film. Over three hundred women had auditioned for the role of Jenaly, most of them agented and with a long list of credentials behind them. It was an honor to have been chosen—at least, at first. If it weren't for the sleazy locker room scene, the job would have been a dream come true.

Mary headed downstairs for a cup of coffee. As she walked, she mulled things over. She could shield her identity on the TikTok account by wearing zombie makeup and using a fake name, but hiding behind theatrics would only work for so long. Once the film hit theaters, she was done for. How would she tell Hannah and Cheryl?

Walking into the kitchen, Mary was shocked to see Jeremy and a teenage girl sitting at the table eating instant noodles. Shocked on a multitude of levels, because one, school was still in session; two, who was this girl with waist-length hair and a navel ring? And three, instant noodles? Brittany never let those in the house—she called them "sodium bombs."

Best to play it cool, Mary figured. Especially since teenagers were concerned. "Hi, Jeremy." Mary walked over to the coffeepot like nothing was amiss. "Who's your friend?"

"This is Kenzie." He put his arm on the table, like he was shielding the noodles from view.

Mary took a mug from the cabinet. "Nice to meet you, Kenzie. I didn't realize today was a half-day at school."

"It's not," said Kenzie. "But we had AT so we left early."

"What's AT?" Mary poured the last drips of coffee and drank it black.

"Achievement Time," said Jeremy. "It's the best part of the day because you get to hang out."

"Or study." Kenzie poked him in the arm with her chopsticks and then tickled him, making him laugh.

"Yeah," Jeremy said with a chuckle. "Study."

"I take it there's a lot of studying happening in this kitchen." Mary rinsed out the coffeepot and immediately began loading up the machine to brew another pot.

"Absolutely," said Kenzie.

"That's why we're here," said Jeremy, blushing.

"Uh-huh." Mary counted out beans into the automatic grinder. "Cover your ears," she said, as she put on the lid. "This is going to be loud." Seconds later, she hit the brew button and the coffee machine whirred to life. She'd made decaf, since it was officially the afternoon. When she turned around, she caught Jeremy and Kenzie whispering behind her back. "If I were you, I'd finish those noodles before your mom gets home," said Mary. "You know how she feels about MSG."

"MSG?" Kenzie asked. "Is your mom a chemist or something?"

"She's a nutritionist," said Jeremy. He looked at Mary. "I'm going to take the trash out before she gets home and destroy the evidence."

Mary leaned against the counter. "That seems suspicious, don't you think?"

"How?" Jeremy raised his eyebrows.

"*You* taking the trash out without Brittany reminding you first?"

"Ha, ha." Jeremy rolled his eyes. "You're a comedian."

Mary added her mug to the dishwasher. "I happen to love instant noodles. Hannah and I practically grew up on them. Your secret is safe with me."

As she walked out of the kitchen and into the living room, she heard Kenzie ask Jeremy a question. "Was that the younger sister or the older one? I couldn't tell."

Burn! The nerve of that girl! Mary marched up the stairs, her ego smarting. When she reached the landing, a yucky thought occurred to her. Here she'd been so worried about telling Hannah and Cheryl about the zombie picture. But Jeremy would see it, too. *Probably he and Kenzie will have a good laugh at me,* she figured. It shouldn't have mattered so much, but the idea stung.

SIX

Valentine's Day was a bust—for Mary, at least. For her, it had been an ordinary day so far except for her dentist sending her a postcard that said: "At Sand Dollar Cove Dental, we love to see you smile." Hannah, on the other hand, had learned that yes, Guy believed in gifting jewelry. She'd texted a picture of herself that morning wearing diamond earrings the size of Skittles.

As for Mary, she was once again holed up in her room, burying herself in design projects. She'd cracked the window, but it didn't appear as if any of the DeLacks were home, so the twenty-four-hour soap opera happening next door was quiet at the moment. Mary held pins in her mouth as she put up posters. She'd already covered the walls with vision boards for the senior center renovation, and now she was overlapping them with designs for the theater as well. She didn't worry about destroying Hannah's side of the room, since Hannah was rarely there. Usually her sister was at work, or Guy's apartment, but she'd promised to swing by tonight and bring takeout from The Summer Wind, Seaside Resort's signature restaurant. *Hannah probably feels sorry for me being alone on Valentine's Day,* Mary realized, and the thought stung.

Her phone buzzed with a text. When Mary saw who it was from, she spit the pins into a cup so she wouldn't injure herself. A text from Kelly was dangerous enough without adding puncture wounds to the equation.

Can I talk to you?

Her mom was texting her? Mary hadn't communicated with Kelly in several months, not since the last time Kelly had asked to borrow money. Mary had said no but had sent her a gift card for the grocery store instead. She hadn't told Hannah because she knew her sister would flip out. Hannah still hadn't forgiven Kelly for stealing her credit cards at Christmas a few years back.

What did Kelly want this time? More money? Maybe Mary hadn't been clear enough with her mom that she was the wrong person to ask. Steeling herself, Mary kept her reply terse.

I have a few minutes she texted.

The phone rang seconds later.

"Hi, my darling girl, how are you doing?" Kelly asked, her voice raspy from years of abuse: drugs, tobacco, alcohol—you name it. Time had wreaked havoc on Kelly's vocal cords.

"I'm pretty busy right now, actually." Mary shuffled through fabric samples. "I have two design projects on at the moment. What's up?"

"A lot, actually." Kelly cleared her throat. "That's why I'm calling."

Uh-oh. Mary's stomach clenched. Here came the big ask.

"I'm staying at a new place in Aberdeen. A... uh... friend put me up here. Anyhow, I've been doing a lot of thinking and I wanted to call and tell you how sorry I am for the things I've done in the past, and also that I love you and hope you'll be able to forgive me someday."

A blanket apology? That's what this call was about? Mary didn't believe that for a second. In her experience Kelly usually apologized before she asked for money. Plus, what was Mary supposed to say to a fill-in-the-blanks apology like that? I forgive you? Mary could say the words, but they'd be a lie.

"Taking some time to sit with the past is a good idea," she said, choosing her words carefully. "I appreciate you apologizing." That was as much as Mary felt capable of offering her mother.

"This place has been really good for me," said Kelly.

"Is it a new apartment?" Mary asked. *Or rehab, hopefully?* she wanted to ask but didn't.

"It's like a group house with a counselor who comes in each day to talk to us."

"Oh. Wow." So maybe rehab, or maybe a court-ordered type of thing. Mary didn't feel close enough to Kelly to ask for specifics.

"I'm realizing that I never should have been a mother because I was born to be awful at it."

"What?" Mary exclaimed, startled by the confession.

"And that was unfair to you and Hannah," Kelly continued. "You deserved better than what I had available to give."

Mary didn't know what to say, so she repeated something that Cheryl had told her when she was a little girl and would ask about her mother. "Addiction is a disease."

"It *is* a disease," said Kelly. "Thank you for recognizing that. It's a disease that's caused me to make a lot of bad choices over the years, and I want you to know that I love you and I'm sorry."

"Mom, I—"

"I need to go now," Kelly said, her voice breaking. "Bye." She hung up the phone before Mary could stop her.

What the hell? Mary slumped over her desk and rested her face in her hands. Of all the things that could happen on Valentine's Day, her mother calling to apologize wasn't something she'd expected. But it wasn't only an apology... Kelly had all but admitted that she shouldn't have had children. How was Mary supposed to process information like that? She needed Hannah. She needed to know if Kelly had called Hannah, too. Mary called her sister, but the number went straight to voice mail. Hannah was either still at work, or with Guy.

For a few seconds Mary was annoyed with her sister for not being available. But that feeling was immediately followed by guilt for being so needy. Seriously, when had she become so pathetic?

Aidan... her heart whispered. She'd become needy after he abandoned her. But she was damaged before that, too, and been so good at hiding it that nobody knew.

It was easier to act like she was hopeful than admit she was afraid. It was simpler to put a fake smile on her face than reveal that she was sad. A lot of that had to do with Kelly. It was her mom who had first given her acting lessons, after all.

During a rare visit with her mom when Mary was nine years old, Kelly had coached her to stumble at the grocery store, cry on cue, and provide a distraction while her mom shoplifted from the liquor aisle. Hannah had refused to do it, but Mary had complied. They'd pulled the same stunt three more times until they were caught in the middle of a Sand Dollar Cove gift shop on First Street. Mary's tears over her supposedly bruised knees became real when the shop owner had plucked her up by her collar and accused her of stealing. The unsupervised visits had ended after that. All the visits had. Kelly hadn't bothered to contact either of her daughters until years later when she first called to ask them for money.

A car drove down the street, the road noise sneaking into the room via the cracked window. Mary walked across the room and slammed the window shut. That's what Hannah would tell her to do if she were here. Focus on work. Focus on her future! Feeling slightly more in control of her turbulent emotions, Mary went back to work. But her mind continued to wander.

This weekend Jose's crew was coming to paint the kitchen

cabinets in the senior center. She was a teensy bit curious to know if he was dating someone or not, considering how much he flirted. Mary took her phone out and scrolled through Instagram, trying to ferret out Jose's romantic status. His painting company had a social media presence, but she couldn't find any personal accounts tied to him. His sister, who lived in Port Angeles, had tagged his business account with a shout-out to her brother and the great job he'd done repainting her house, but that was the only personal detail about Jose that she could find.

What about Steven? Mary wondered, not that she was attracted to him at all. When she'd stopped by the theater yesterday to share tile samples for the bathroom, he'd been wearing a baggy purple sweatshirt and yellow sweatpants. Mary tried not to judge people based on their appearances, but it was hard not to notice Steven's eccentric outfits. Was he color-blind?

She was also curious about what type of background Steven had that would give him the funds—at twenty-eight years old—to purchase a movie theater. Where did he get the gumption to pack up and move to the West Coast?

"Steven Clarke," Mary said, as she typed his name into Google. "Who are you and why did you come here?"

Whoa! The first five articles were not what she expected. They were about someone named Vick Clarke, who was apparently Nevada's attorney general. Mary clicked on the first link to find more information and saw a picture of Vick, a handsome man with silvery hair, dressed in a tailored suit and speaking in front of a crowd.

"Vick Clarke announces his campaign for governor," she read aloud. Her eyes skimmed the article until she found Steven's name. "Vick Clarke, who, early in his career, made his name by prosecuting major kingpins of organized crime, has announced his bid to become the next governor of Nevada. He announced his candidacy in front of a packed audience that included his wife, Pamela, and his son, Steven Clarke, who works as a public defender."

Steven was a lawyer? That seemed odd. He didn't strike her as the lawyerly type. She checked the date of the article and saw that it was from two years ago.

Scrolling back to the original search page, Mary clicked on the next link, wanting to see if Vick had won his campaign or not. She recognized that she should have a vague notion of who the governor of Nevada was. It was only a few states over from Washington, after all. But Nevada politics wasn't on her radar.

Nope. It looked like Vick had lost his bid for the governorship but was still the attorney general. Interesting... She scrolled down and found a photo of him giving his concession speech, only this picture included his wife and son. Mary read the caption. "Vick, accompanied by his wife, Pamela, and his son, Steven, addresses supporters and concedes the election."

But wait a second... That man standing next to Vick... that couldn't be Steven, could it? Mary rubbed her eyes and peered forward. Instead of the colorfully dressed man with unruly hair that she was used to, she saw a much larger man with short hair, wearing a three-piece suit. He didn't look like Steven at all. Except maybe... Mary blew up the picture. There, underneath the neatly trimmed beard, she thought she saw a glimpse of the quirky man with a passion for horror films. But the suit-and-tie version of Steven had a haunted look in his eyes, like the crowd was attacking him. There wasn't one ounce of the good humor that Mary associated with him.

Mary looked up the other articles that included Steven's name but found little beyond him being mentioned as Vick's son.

It was closing in on dinnertime and Mary was getting hungry. Hopefully Hannah would be home soon with the seafood chop-chop salad Mary had requested. In the meantime, she'd tide herself over with a Coke Zero.

Turning off her computer, she left her room and headed to the laundry room downstairs to check on the prom dress she'd tossed in the wash. She'd purchased it at a thrift store and intended to slash it up, add some fake blood, and use it for her Jenaly Macintyre TikTok videos. She'd also scored elbow-length gloves and a satin coat. The washing cycle was done now, and when she removed the garments from the drum, she was grateful to find them still intact. Now the question was how to hang them up to air-dry without anyone discovering them and asking awkward questions. Mary tapped her chin as she thought the problem over. Maybe she should take a risk and throw them in the dryer on low. If the heat ruined them, it would add to the zombie aesthetic.

"Here goes nothing," Mary mumbled as she set the dryer going. She was so focused on the perplexities of laundry that she didn't pay close enough attention to the elevated voices coming from the kitchen. Mary accidentally walked straight into the middle of an argument between Brittany and Keith.

"If Jeremy were my son," Keith was saying, "I'd take away his car keys until he brought up his trigonometry grade."

"Well, he's not your son, is he?" Brittany folded her arms across her chest. "And as Jeremy's mother I know that if I revoke his driving privileges, he won't be able to get to work, and his after-school job means everything to him right now."

Mary opened the fridge, found her soda, and kept her opinion to herself. She didn't think Jeremy would describe his job at McDonald's as "meaning everything to him right now," but she agreed with Brittany that taking away the car keys wouldn't help improve his math grade. The two things had nothing to do with each other.

"How is Jeremy going to learn to be responsible if you let him get away with everything?" Keith demanded.

"I don't let him get away with things!" Brittany pulled her curly hair away from her face. "How can you say that? I hold

Jeremy accountable. He pays for his own gas and car insurance. He does his own laundry."

Mary slunk out of the room, pretending she hadn't heard anything. As she crossed the hall, she heard a knock at the front door. Opening it, she found Kenzie standing on the porch wearing flared jeans, Doc Martens, and a crop top sweater that revealed her glittery navel ring. How her abs weren't freezing was a mystery, but Mary admired the teen's self-confidence for showing off her midsection like that.

"Hi, Mary," said Kenzie, as she readjusted the straps of her giant purse. "I'm here to see Jeremy."

"Not me?" Mary pressed her palm to her chest. "I'm crushed."

Kenzie laughed—or pretended to laugh—Mary couldn't tell.

"I believe he's upstairs," said Mary. "I'll go get him for—"

"No need." Kenzie brushed past her and raced up the steps to Jeremy's bedroom.

Well, then. Mary thought about letting Brittany know that there was a hot teenage girl in her son's bedroom on Valentine's Day, but didn't want to get caught up in her argument with Keith. Hanging out with Cheryl in the living room seemed like a better plan.

Mary entered the living room and curled up on the couch next to Ferdinand, their cat. "Hi, Gran."

"Hey, kiddo." Cheryl pointed at the TV with her remote control. "I turned up the volume because..." She nodded toward the kitchen. "You know."

Mary cringed and nodded. She'd never seen Brittany and Keith fight like this. As far as she had known, they had a happy relationship. Apparently not, given the noise level coming from the kitchen.

"How can our relationship progress if you refuse to acknowledge how Jeremy's coming between us?" Keith asked.

He wasn't yelling—exactly—but he wasn't speaking in a normal tone, either.

"Jeremy has nothing to do with you and me, so why are you giving advice about something you know nothing about?" Brittany shot back.

"Nothing?" Keith asked. "My dad's a math teacher. Of course I have an opinion about trigonometry."

"Oh boy." Cheryl pointed the remote at the evening news and turned the volume up two more notches.

Mary set her soda on the glass coaster. At least Jeremy was upstairs, not having to listen to this. If Kenzie overheard, that would be even worse. That's probably what the two teenagers were doing in Jeremy's room right now. Avoiding embarrassment.

Or not...

"I'll be right back." Mary popped up from the couch and raced upstairs. Probably Jeremy and Kenzie weren't doing anything worth telling Brittany about, but Mary's guilty conscience would feel better once she'd confirmed that. *Trust, but verify.* She knocked on Jeremy's door a few times and then opened it without being invited inside.

"Hey!" Jeremy exclaimed. "I didn't say you could come in."

He and Kenzie sat on the carpet in front of his bed surrounded by books and papers. Mary spotted his new calculator among the school materials.

"Sorry about that," said Mary. "It's so loud downstairs I thought you couldn't hear me."

"What do you want?" Jeremy asked, more rudely than he normally was with Mary.

She thought quickly, improvising a reason to be there. "I wondered if you would like some snacks and drinks?"

Kenzie smiled, her lips shiny with ruby-red lip gloss. "That would be great. Thanks."

"Diet soda okay?" Mary asked. "Or would you rather have water, or coffee?"

"Soda would be great," said Kenzie. She looked at Jeremy. "The caffeine boost will be just what we need to keep going all night."

Keep going all night?

Jeremy must have read the look on Mary's face because he quickly explained. "Kenzie is helping me study for my trig test. She's the smartest person in school."

Kenzie blushed and leaned ever so slightly closer to Jeremy.

"Good for you," said Mary, uncertain which teenager she was addressing. "That's great." Leaving the door cracked open, Mary hurried downstairs to get soda, crackers, and a bag of baby carrots. After delivering the load, she once again left the door ajar, and returned to the living room. She arrived just in time to witness Keith stomp through the downstairs and out the front door.

"Whoa," said Mary as she sat on the couch. She picked up her own soda and took a drink, setting it back on the purple coaster.

"Whoa is right." Cheryl cringed. "That's a side of Keith I've never seen before. But I guess I always suspected it was there."

"I thought you said he was a catch because he owned his own condo and had a pension plan?"

"That doesn't mean he's not a controlling jerk," said Cheryl. "You heard him just now. What a pompous toad."

"Sorry about that," said Brittany, as she slunk into the living room like a wet cat. "You probably heard, but Keith and I had an argument."

"How could we not hear?" Cheryl asked. "You can't let him talk to you like that. There was no need for him to raise his voice at you."

"You're right." Brittany sat next to Mary. "But to be fair, I was yelling, too. I learned a lot of bad habits from Ian, my ex-husband. And my parents. They fought like cat and dog before they got divorced."

Bad habits that Jeremy might have learned too, Mary thought. It was none of her business. But there was something about the teenager that made her want to protect him. *How dumb can I be?* Mary asked herself. Jeremy was her friend, not her family member. But she felt the urge to protect him nonetheless, which was weird because, like her mother, there probably wasn't a maternal bone in her body.

"Maybe you should see a family therapist to help you deal with uncomfortable conversations," said Cheryl.

Brittany leaned back into the couch cushions. "We saw one, back when the divorce was happening, but it's been a while." She squeezed her eyes shut. "I guess I need to go back for some unfinished business."

"That might be wise," said Cheryl. "It's not good for Jeremy to witness a man yelling at his mom like that."

"It's not good for any of us to witness it," said Mary.

Shoot, she had thought this shared housing situation was a great setup for all of them, but not if it meant being mixed up with relationship drama. At least now, unlike last year, Mary and Hannah had the financial means to find a different living situation if needed. Still, she didn't want to have to move again. *Or leave Jeremy in an uncomfortable situation on his own.*

The awkwardness was broken by the sound of the front door closing. "I'm home," sang a friendly voice. Hannah walked into the living room carrying takeout bags. She took one look at them and frowned. "What did I miss?"

SEVEN

The following week Mary met up with Steven at the movie theater to discuss details about the renovation. The plan was to finalize the carpet selection and discuss what do to with his private office. Mary hadn't seen that space yet, because Nick's crew had been working around the clock to replace the subflooring and drywall.

"Hi, Mary." Steven opened the front door for her, which was helpful since her arms were full of carpet samples. "Can I help you with some of that?"

"That would be great. I can barely see where I'm going." Mary stood still as Steven unburdened her. "I brought a wide selection for you to choose from."

"I can see that. Let's head to my office where it's warmer."

"Warmer?" Mary had barely stepped foot into the theater, and she was already glad she'd chosen to wear a tank top underneath her sweater. She'd need to remove that layer as soon as she could so she wouldn't turn into a sweaty mess. "Have you gotten your first heating bill yet?" she asked, curious.

"Yeah, and it wasn't too bad, thanks to hydroelectric power.

I was expecting it to be a lot worse than Vegas, but it's comparable, I guess because I haven't needed the air conditioning yet."

"And you might not need it for years. Usually our summers are mild here unless there's a horrible weather event like a heat dome."

"Still, I'm glad I have the AC. Maybe the cinema could be an emergency cooling shelter. I'd love to give back to the community." He repositioned the carpet samples over to his left arm and opened the door to his office with his right. "Watch your step," he cautioned. "There are boxes everywhere."

"Thanks for the warning." Mary entered the small space and felt like she was walking into a furnace. "Is the heater broken? It's cooking in here."

"Not broken." Steven set the carpet squares on top of a white rectangular box—a chest freezer, Mary realized. "I Just cranked the thermostat up to eighty-eight degrees like Celine and Dion like it." Steven took the carpet remnants from her and added them to the pile.

"Celine and Dion?" Were those the snakes he had mentioned previously? Mary didn't know what they had to do with the theater until she turned around. "Holy cow!" she exclaimed, just barely stopping herself from using a stronger word. Two giant snakes in individual glass enclosures took up half of the room.

"Meet my babies." Steven walked up to the glass with a goofy smile on his face. "This here is Celine. She's my reticulated python who's native to Southeast Asia. One hundred and seventy pounds of pure love." Steven crouched low and stared into the coil of brown and black snake. "Isn't that right, sweetie pie?" He shifted his attention to the right-hand enclosure where a white snake was draped over a rock underneath a heat lamp. "And here we have the handsome Dion. He's an albino Burmese python who's a much more compact one hundred forty pounds." Steven made kissy faces at the snake. "But it's not a competition, is it, slugger?"

"Um... My... They're a lot bigger than Elvis, huh?" Mary's feet were rooted to the ground. When she'd accepted this job, she didn't know that snakes were involved. Sure, she knew about Elvis, but Celine and Dion were on a whole different level.

"It's too bad you weren't able to come yesterday," said Steven.

"Oh? Why's that?"

"It was feeding day. That's what the chest freezer is for."

Mary's gaze drifted over to where her carpet samples rested on the freezer. "What do they eat?" she asked, even though she didn't want to know.

"White feeder rabbits and the occasional guinea pig."

"Frozen?"

"I defrost them first. When they were little, I fed them live rats but now they prefer prey with more girth." Steven stood and patted his stomach. "Which I understand. I'd rather have steak than salad."

"I'm actually... ah... terrified of rats, so I guess that makes Celine and Dion my heroes," Mary stammered, trying not to look at them.

Steven's eyes widened. "You're okay with reptiles though, right? I'm sorry. I should have asked first before I sprang them on you like this."

"I don't have any reptile experience," Mary admitted. "Unless you count Elvis."

"Next time I bring Elvis to work with me I'll let you hold him," Steven promised. "That'll make you more comfortable."

"Right," Mary chirped. "Good plan." *Horrible plan.* How would she get out of it? "Let's get to work, shall we?"

"Absolutely." Steven offered her a folding chair and sat down in the one next to it. Mary was grateful that the chairs were positioned on the opposite side of the room from the snake enclosures. A tiny window above the chairs provided a smattering of daylight.

"One second," she said, as she took off her sweater. "I need to adjust for python weather."

"I have the opposite problem." Steven pulled his shaggy hair behind his ears. "I don't own warm enough clothes for Sand Dollar Cove."

"Is it always hot in Las Vegas? Even in winter?"

"Yes, and no. The temperature drops at night since it's the desert, but we don't have anything like this. I'm used to dry heat, not this damp, moody, chilly stuff. Yesterday the fog was so bad I thought I was in a Stephen King novel."

"It's only February. Wait until March comes. That's when the gloom becomes even worse." Mary bit her lip and studied him. The short-sleeve T-shirt he wore was many sizes too big. Fabric billowed around him like a cape. Maybe he didn't know what clothes to buy to deal with the Pacific Northwest weather. Or perhaps he hadn't bought new clothes for himself in quite some time, after losing weight. He was thinner now than the picture she'd seen of him on the internet, standing next to his father. Mary didn't want to be awkward about it, or interfere where her input wasn't wanted, but she didn't want him to be cold, either. "Do you own a fleece jacket?" she asked.

"No." He shook his head. "Should I?"

"I would never tell someone what they *should* wear, but speaking personally, I'd freeze to death if I didn't have the three bedrocks of Pacific Northwest fashion: fleece, wool, and Gore-Tex. Right now I have on a cotton tank top because I knew you kept the theater nice and cozy, but this sweater?" She pointed at the pink fluff poking out of her bag. "It's wool, which means it stays warm even in the damp. Wool can be itchy, so a lot of people like synthetic fleece better. I have a lot of that too."

"And Gore-Tex?" Steven asked.

"For coats. You need a warm raincoat and a lightweight raincoat. If you can afford it, it's good to have a puffer coat, too, for days when it's cold but not raining. That one doesn't need to be waterproof."

"Why not just wear the warm raincoat all the time in cold weather?"

"You could," Mary admitted. "But they don't breathe very well. So, let's say you were on a walk on the beach, and it was forty degrees but not raining. If you had your warm raincoat on, you'd sweat, and since the coat didn't breathe well, your sweat would make you cold. But if you were wearing something more porous, like a down jacket, you'd be fine." Now that she was thinking about it, maybe she should have added down to her list of must-have Pacific Northwest fabrics.

"I think I need some help shopping because I don't know any of this," Steven admitted. "Where do I buy clothes like that? The only clothing stores downtown are for tourists."

"The Walmart in Port Angeles would have things at a good price," she said. "Or, if you had a bit more money to spend and wanted something that would last longer, you could order clothes from REI, or one of the big brands around here like North Face or Columbia." She pulled a notebook out of her bag and uncapped a pen. "I should have mentioned the thrift shop, too. Sustainable is always best."

"I'll keep that in mind." Steven took a deep breath. "Thanks for the advice. I know I'm paying you for your interior design skills and not fashion expertise, but I appreciate it. I hate buying clothes. I really, really hate it."

The emotion in Steven's voice made Mary feel honored that he'd confided in her. "Where did you buy clothes in Las Vegas?" she asked, genuinely curious.

"I didn't. Usually, I'd wear whatever my mom or aunt gave me for Christmas. That was fine by me since it meant I didn't have to go shopping. Only they never got the sizes right. My aunt bought things that were too big, and my mom gave me things that were too small."

"I *love* shopping," said Mary. "And nobody ever buys me clothes except for my sister Hannah, who gives me socks." She pulled her foot out of her slip-on sneaker and wiggled her toes. "Once again, wool saves the day."

"I need to get me some of those, too." Steven held out his foot. "To go with my Crocs."

"Or maybe buy shoes that keep your feet dry," Mary suggested. *And weren't hideously ugly.* "Are you ready to talk carpet?"

"Sure am." Steven hopped up from his chair. "Should I get the samples?"

"That would be great."

They spent the next twenty minutes evaluating the pros and cons of each option, including back-order specifics and shipping dates. After Steven had selected choices for the theater and lobby, the conversation turned to his office.

"Right now, it looks like a cave," Mary said. "With snakes." She looked at the bare walls. "But at least that gives us a blank slate to work with. What are your goals for this space? What's it's functionality?"

"You mean beyond making it comfortable for Celine and Dion?"

Mary's gaze darted over to the pythons before looking back at Steven. "You're intending to keep them here and not at your house, then?"

Steven nodded. "I'm renting an apartment right now and my landlord doesn't allow pets." He leaned in and whispered. "He doesn't know about Elvis though, so shh."

"My lips are sealed." Mary zipped her mouth shut and threw away an imaginary key. "Okay, so snakes and what else?"

"I need the usual office stuff—filing cabinets, a desk, a place for the printer—that sort of thing."

"Office suite furniture," Mary said as she jotted down her notes.

"As for style, I'm thinking horror."

Mary looked up from her papers. "Horror?"

"I want this room to scream 'slasher flick.'"

Mary's mouth gaped open for a few seconds before she closed it. "We're sitting in the horror room." She glanced at her notes and wrote that down. "Got it."

"You think it's weird."

"No, I don't." Mary scratched the back of her head. "It was just an unexpected request, that's all."

Steven scooted his chair closer. "The whole theater has to be genre-neutral. It needs to be a space where I show G-rated Disney films all the way up to the latest PG 13 Marvel movie, am I right?"

Mary nodded. "I agree."

"Okay, so then the only place I can express my personal taste in movies is right here in my office where the public won't normally see."

"And you love gore."

"Not just gore," Steven clarified. "Horror. Scary movies don't have to have blood in them to be effective. *The Blair Witch Project*, for example, or *The Ring*, or *Invasion of the Body Snatchers*. Have you seen any of them?"

"Yes, but I'm more of a romcom person myself."

"Romcoms are a level of horror I can't usually tolerate."

"Rude!" Mary squeaked.

Steven laughed, and his eyes twinkled. "I'm just teasing you."

"Oh."

"But your passionate defense of romcoms is noted."

"Thanks."

"Back to horror though, I've collected some vintage posters that I thought could work." Steven crossed the room and opened one of the cardboard tubes in the corner. "Only this movie appears to have blood in it." He pulled out a poster of *Psycho* and showed it to her. "Hitchcock used chocolate syrup for the blood, but you probably already knew that."

"I did," said Mary. Would that work for her zombie costume? If she shot her TikTok videos in black and white?

"So what do you think?" Steven asked. "I know I just sprang this theme on you, but you're a creative person, what have you got?"

With no time to overthink it, Mary threw out the first ideas that came to her mind. "Paint the walls black," she said. "But with a satin finish so that they catch the light." She pointed to the back wall. "Install floor-to-ceiling red velvet curtains with an ornate brass rod, to give the effect of a second window. Then over there, by the actual window, let's add security bars, so it looks like a dungeon. Maybe with some manacles hanging off the wall."

What was she doing? Why did she just say all of that? It was like her old set design background had come out to haunt her. She looked at Steven, afraid to see his reaction.

"Love it!" He pulled his fingertips away from his face like his head was exploding. "I can't believe how in sync we are on this."

Amazed that he appreciated her campy creativity, she kept going. "Your posters deserve ornate frames and places of honor next to the red velvet drapes. But over on the dungeon side of the room, let's secure the file cabinet to the wall with fake chains."

"Sick." Steven closed his eyes and smiled. "So sick." His eyelids opened, and he gazed at her. How had she never realized his eyes were hazel before? They were the same color as his shirt: greenish brown. "What about an extraterrestrial element, or maybe zombies?" Steven asked.

Zombies... Mary squeezed her pen so tight that her wrist

hurt. What would Steven say when he found out about *Zombie Prom at the Disco*? He'd probably love it, but Mary couldn't stand the thought of him watching the locker room scene and seeing her humiliated. She glanced down at her notes to steady herself before looking back up at him. "We could stencil 'Zombie Emergency Kit' above the chest freezer with arrows pointing down. Then, to add an alien element, we could put up a sign showing how many miles it was from Sand Dollar Cove to Roswell, New Mexico. That's where all the supposed alien abductions have been, right?"

"Brilliant. And this is just what you came up with spur-of-the-moment, too. Mary, you're impressive. I hope you know that."

The praise felt good. Mary drank it up like a deer lapping water. "Thanks." It was one thing having Hannah and Cheryl tell her she was good at her job, but quite another to have a client tell her that too. "How did you discover your love of horror films?" she asked.

"From my Aunt Helena. She was my great-aunt, actually. I used to hang out at her house on weekends and watch movies with her. That's where the snakes come from, too. Celine and Dion were like her children. They're both almost twenty years old and won't live much longer." His attention shifted to the glass enclosures, and his hazel eyes grew misty. "I try not to think about them no longer being with me."

"It's sad, losing pets."

"I feel guilty about moving them, too," said Steven. "But Celine and Dion seem to have adapted well. I think this has been less stressful on them than it has on me, in fact."

For the first time since she'd met him, Mary realized how daring Steven had been. It took courage to move to a new state and open a business, especially one in an entirely different field. She thought about asking him about his life as a lawyer but didn't want him to know she'd been stalking him on the internet.

"This room is nice and warm," she said. "I bet they're happy here."

"I think so." Steven let out a deep breath. "I just hope I can be happy here, too."

Something about the way he said it pinged her heart, like the melancholy in his tone was contagious. She searched for a way to relieve it. "Don't worry," she said. "By the time I'm done with your new office, it'll be so horrific that you'll have to be happy."

Steven grinned. "I'm glad you're my scream queen."

Mary chuckled. "Me, too."

EIGHT

"Am I smelling peanuts?" Cheryl asked. "What exactly is that delicious aroma?"

"I'm curious too," said Mary. The foghorn sang in the distance. "It smells amazing."

They stood on the porch of the newly rebuilt Strawberry Cottage, one of the delightfully charming vacation properties at Seaside Resort owned by the international hotel conglomerate, Blanchet Maison. Strawberry Cottage was where they had temporarily lived last year before they'd rented rooms from Brittany. Now, the cottage was the command center for Guy's remote work as CEO of Blanchet Maison. Guy had inherited the company in its entirety after his father passed away from a stroke. Hannah managed the other forty-nine cottages at Seaside Resort, renting them out to guests from all over, but Strawberry Cottage was Guy's domain. He was hosting dinner here, and not at his second-floor apartment, because it was more accessible for Cheryl. The cottage had a synthetic wood deck, a wheelchair ramp, and a remodeled bathroom that met requirements for the Americans with Disabilities Act.

Mary lifted her fist to knock on the front door and Guy

opened it before she had the chance. He wore an apron that said: *Vegetables Change Lives.*

"Welcome to Strawberry Cottage." Guy held out his arms for a hug. "Are you excited to open your ancestry DNA kit results?"

"Not as excited as you appear to be, but sure." Mary pushed Cheryl's wheelchair inside and set the brake before hugging him. "Thanks for inviting us to dinner."

"I love it when a man cooks for me," said Cheryl, as Guy leaned down to give her a gentle embrace.

"You might not say that after you discover that we're eating collard greens," said Hannah, while she set the small table in the corner.

"What's wrong with collard greens?" Mary asked. "I've never had them before."

"They're bitter." Hannah folded a napkin. "He served them to me in a salad last week and I thought I was eating spinach gone bad."

"That sounds like the name of a paint color." Mary took off her coat. "'Spinach Gone Bad.'" She looked around the room, admiring the renovation. The original footprint of the cottage was the same, but it had been rebuilt from the ground up. Triple-paned windows blocked out the foghorn that crooned every three minutes, and the thick, insulated walls kept the space cozy, even on a blustery evening in late February such as this one.

"I learned my lesson about your sensitive palate for greens." Guy kissed Hannah's cheek. "But tonight you'll discover that collard greens can taste differently once they are cooked. I think you'll really like this recipe. At least I hope so... I really want tonight to be a success."

"What are you making?" Cheryl asked.

"It's a creamy peanut butter and black-eyed pea stew." Guy opened the small refrigerator. "Can I get you a drink? We have iced tea, lemonade, or I could mix them together for an Arnold Palmer."

"Oooh." Mary sat down on the couch. "That sounds good. I'll take an Arnold Palmer."

"Me, too," said Cheryl. "That's as close as I get to golfing these days. The table looks beautiful. I love the new dishes."

Hannah held up a plate. "They're actually old dishes that Blanchet Maison doesn't use anymore, so Seaside Resort was able to acquire them for free. Cost-effective and environmentally wise."

"A win-win." Mary nodded her approval. "The rest of the place is great, too. It looks so different from when we lived here." She thought back to when she had decorated the apartment with a second-hand sofa bed, a thrifted dresser, and her grandmother's recliner. Now the cottage boasted a sleek desk with multiple computer screens, as well as a standing desk in the corner that perched over a treadmill. But there was also a sitting area, with a couch, coffee table, and easy chair.

Guy looked at Mary. "I should have you work your magic once you're between projects. I'm sure you have strong opinions about the bare walls."

"I like them," Mary replied. "It reminds me of a museum gallery when you're supposed to focus on the paintings and not the decor. Only in this case, the artwork is the view."

"Which we can't see now because it's dark," said Hannah.

"True. But we know it's there." Mary glanced over at Guy's treadmill desk. "Why did you angle your desk that way? If you slid it over two feet to the right the flow would be better."

"You don't think that would be weird, having it farther from the window?" Guy asked.

Mary shook her head. "No. And you'd likely have less glare on your computer screen."

"I'm going to try that." Guy crossed the room and shoved the treadmill over. "Luckily this thing is lightweight."

"It doesn't look lightweight to me," Cheryl commented. "Careful with your back."

Mary was so focused on furniture arrangement that she barely heard the knock on the door.

"Oh, jeez. She's ten minutes early." Guy let go of the treadmill and swept a lock of hair off his forehead. "Well, okay... I guess being early is better than arriving late."

"Why are you acting so weird?" Mary asked.

"Yeah," said Hannah. "Who's here? Housekeeping isn't supposed to come until morning."

"It's not housekeeping." Guy smiled sheepishly. "I have a surprise. A good surprise, I hope." He spread his arms out wide like he was blocking the entryway. "Before I open the door, I'd like to remind you that I love you all and only have good intentions for you."

"What's that supposed to mean?" Mary asked, feeling nervous.

"Yeah," said Hannah. "What are you up to?"

"Never trust a man who offers to make you dinner," said Cheryl. "It usually means he has ulterior motives."

"Ulterior motives?" Hannah frowned. "Guy, explain yourself."

"I can't handle any more stress!" Mary proclaimed, her palms already sweating.

Guy took off his apron, hung it on the coat rack. "It'll be fine, I promise. Remember what I said about me wanting the best for you." He opened the door.

There, standing on the porch, stood Kelly, wearing jeans and a black raincoat. Her bleached hair was pulled into a ponytail and her leathery skin made her appear ten years older than her actual age, but her eyes were the same color brown as Hannah and Mary's. "Hi, girls," she said, waving slightly. "Long time, no see."

"Mom?" Hannah gasped.

"Oh boy," Cheryl muttered. "Here we go."

Mary's sweaty palms felt even more disgusting. Her whole body tensed. Every time she saw Kelly something bad happened. At least, it felt like that. The only thing she knew for certain about her mom was that Kelly brought trouble with her wherever she went.

"Come on in." Guy held the door open wider. "Let me take your coat."

"Thanks." Kelly removed her raincoat and passed it to Guy. Underneath she was wearing a black shirt and matching fleece vest. "Nice to meet you."

"You haven't met?" Mary asked.

"Not officially," said Kelly. "But we've spoken over the phone."

"Guy, you should have told me," said Hannah. "What's going on?"

"Why don't we sit down to a nice family dinner and talk about it?" Guy hung up Kelly's coat and closed the front door. "Mary, could you please roll your grandma to the table?"

"Hello, former mother-in-law," Kelly said, in her raspy voice.

"Hello, former daughter-in-law." Cheryl narrowed her eyes and glared.

"Let's get you rolling in that wheelchair," said Mary, keeping one eye on her grandma and the other on her mom.

"I can walk," Cheryl said indignantly. She pushed onto the armrests of the wheelchair and gingerly rose to her feet. Then she shuffle-walked toward the dinette.

"I'll pull out your chair for you," said Mary. Cheryl was ambulatory, but usually relied on her walker for support.

"I guess I need to set an extra place," said Hannah.

"Which I have ready to go, right here." Guy handed her a place setting that he'd stacked on the counter.

Hannah pressed her lips together in a thin line. "You were really planning ahead there, weren't you?"

"I try..." Guy cringed.

"I'll just go and, uh, wash my hands," said Kelly. "Is the bathroom over here?"

"It is." Guy nodded.

As soon as Kelly shut the door the Turner women laid into him.

"How could you do this!" Hannah whispered hoarsely.

"Yeah," said Mary. "This is a low blow."

"I'm trying to help," he explained. "She just got out of rehab, and I thought—"

"Wait," Mary interrupted. "Rehab? How do you know?" She thought back to that awkward phone call last week when Kelly had called her out of the blue.

Guy's cheeks turned pink. "Because I arranged it myself. I found a nice place and made her the offer of going if she wanted to." He looked at Hannah and then at Mary, and then back to Hannah again. "And she *leaped* at the opportunity. She really wants to change."

"That was kind of you," said Cheryl.

"Or stupid," said Mary. "Did she ask to borrow money afterward?"

"Please don't call my boyfriend stupid," Hannah said in a pert tone. But then she glared at Guy so intently it was like laser beams shot from her eyes. "Well, did she?"

Guy held up his hands, palms up. "She needed to get back on her feet. She told me that the place she was living was a bad environment, so I gave—"

"She already got a quarter of Dad's life insurance policy last year!" Hannah exclaimed.

"Yeah," said Mary. "Where did that money go?"

Guy shrugged. "I don't know exactly."

"Why'd you get involved in the first place?" Hannah asked. "Did you look her up in the phone book or something?"

"Something like that. I had my lawyer track her down." Guy's cheeks turned even redder as he turned to face Hannah. "You're the most important person in the world to me, and you deserve a mother who is sober." He looked over toward Mary. "You deserve that, too. I thought maybe with my financial resources, I could help."

"That's sweet of you to care so much," said Hannah. "But Mom could be clean for the rest of her life, and she'd still not have her issues under control."

Mom's broken, Mary thought. *Like me.*

The bathroom door opened, and Kelly came out. "What did I miss?" she asked.

Everyone took a deep breath and for a moment nobody said anything. Then Cheryl piped up.

"Guy was telling us how you graduated from rehab," said Cheryl. "Congratulations."

"Thanks." Kelly scratched the back of her neck. "It was a really nice place. Classy. Wallpaper and borders, and embroidered guest towels and everything." She waved her hands around like she was drawing a picture.

Mary studied her mom's hands. She hadn't seen them close up like this in years. Kelly wore a French tip manicure with black and white edges, like tuxedos. It looked like a professional job that must have been expensive.

"How about everyone take a seat while I serve dinner?" Guy suggested. He pulled out a chair. "Here, Kelly, you can sit here."

"Thanks." She sat down and scooted closer to the table.

Mary took the seat closest to Cheryl, which meant that Hannah had to sit on one side of Kelly, with Guy on the other. *The only thing that could make this dinner more awkward would be Elvis slithering across the table,* Mary thought to herself. Imagining the tiny python made her smile, which caused Hannah to shoot her a look of betrayal.

"I promised to feed you, and I always deliver." Guy circled the table dishing out big scoops of fluffy white rice. "Wait until you taste this stew. It's been slow-cooking all day."

"What are the chopped peanuts for?" Cheryl asked, pointing to a bowl on the table.

"Garnish." Guy came back with a second pot and began adding a nutty mixture of beans and greens to each pile of rice. "It's such an easy recipe that anyone can do it. Sauté some onions and ginger, add creamy peanut butter, mix in some black-eyed peas and collard greens, and then let it slow-cook all afternoon. Cheap, vegan, and full of calcium-rich nutrients to fortify the bones."

"Guy's been force-feeding us vegetables to ward off osteoporosis," Hannah explained to Kelly.

"Smart man," said Cheryl. "I wouldn't wish my condition on anyone, let alone my beloved granddaughters."

"I'm hoping that the DNA test results will provide some medical history answers about that," said Guy.

"DNA kits?" Kelly asked.

"Guy gave them to us for Christmas," Mary explained.

"And we're opening the results tonight," Hannah added.

"Oh." Kelly looked down at her stew and stirred it with her spoon.

"Which reminds me." Guy hopped up from his chair, opened a nearby cabinet, and pulled out a small box. "I have a kit for you, too, Kelly. It'll just take a while to receive your results."

Kelly shrank back into her chair. "No, thanks. I never give my DNA unless there's a court order."

"Oh." Guy's forehead wrinkled and he pulled the kit away. "Sorry. Never mind about that."

"Besides," said Kelly. "I don't need a scientist to tell me I'm Swedish. I can look in the mirror."

"We're Swedish?" Mary asked.

Kelly nodded. "I think so."

"That explains your love of pancakes," said Hannah, as she poked Mary in the arm.

"Was your mom Swedish, or your dad, or both of them?" Guy asked.

"My dad." Kelly scratched her arm. "Well, that's what my mom told me when she was alive."

"Your mom who owned the video rental shop in Aberdeen?" Cheryl asked. "Amy?"

Kelly nodded. "That's right. Her name was Amy. It's closed now. Netflix put it out of business."

Mary didn't know anything about her maternal grandparents besides the fact that they were both dead. "What was your mother like?" she asked.

Kelly took a sharp breath, like Mary had punched her. "She had a big heart and was a hard worker. I gave her hell as a teenager, but she never kicked me out. In fact, she opened her home up to lots of kids in trouble. And then..." Kelly looked across the room like she was staring at Guy's desk, only her pupils didn't focus. "Then she had a heart attack a couple of months past my eighteenth birthday."

"That's so sad," said Hannah.

"It is," said Guy. "I'm sorry for your loss."

"What happened after that?" Mary asked.

"I kept the store running as long as I could. Then I met your dad and got married."

"What about your father?" Guy asked.

"Never really knew him." Kelly took a bite of stew and chewed slowly.

Everyone ate in silence for a minute or so until Mary tried to revive the conversation.

"So... uh... Mom... What are you up to these days?" she asked.

"I just got settled into a new apartment, but I'm not sure I like it because the neighbors are so loud." Kelly ate a bite of stew and swallowed it.

"Are you working?" Hannah asked.

"I always work," said Kelly. "Right now, I'm bartending." Her eyes squinted, and she inspected Hannah closely. "Those are gorgeous earrings. Are they real?"

Hannah's hands shot up to her earlobes, covering the diamonds from view. "Yes. Guy gave them to me for Valentine's Day."

"How many carats are they?" Kelly asked.

Mary was curious too but hadn't pried, since she suspected Hannah felt slightly uncomfortable wearing something so expensive.

"I don't know," said Hannah.

"Well?" Kelly asked, looking at Guy. "Let's hear it."

Guy's face paled underneath Kelly's interrogation. "Each stone is a little over a carat."

Kelly whistled. "That must have cost a pretty penny."

"Hannah's worth it," said Mary. "They look beautiful on you and they go with everything." She squeezed Hannah's hand. "A practical accessory. Or, as practical as diamonds can be, that is."

Kelly raised her eyebrows. "It must be nice to have a rich boyfriend."

"Mom!" Hannah exclaimed.

"Of course, I wouldn't know." Kelly clicked her fingernails on the table. "The most expensive thing my last boyfriend bought me was a tank of gas."

"Gas is really expensive," said Mary. She looked at Guy. "Should we open the DNA results now?" The peanut stew was yummy, but she wanted to get this meal over with as quickly as possible.

"Sure," said Guy. "We could—"

"It took me a quarter of a tank to drive here," said Kelly. "My car's practically on fumes." She looked pointedly at Guy.

"Do you need gas money?" Hannah asked. "If so, I'll give it to you. Don't ask Guy."

"Hannah," Mary whispered, even though everyone could hear. "What are you doing?" That's what Mary said, but what she was thinking was: *We agreed never to give Mom money!*

Hannah was already opening her wallet and pulling out two twenty-dollar bills. "This should get you back home," she said as she handed the cash to Kelly. "Now let's enjoy this wonderful meal Guy made for us."

Mary evaluated Hannah's frozen smile and stiff shoulders and knew that her sister was mustering all her self-discipline to make it through the evening in peace, and not all-out conflict, with their mother. But why? It was Guy's fault Kelly was here. Why not let things go off the rails and allow Guy to see what Kelly was really like?

Looking over at Guy though, Mary guessed he could already tell. "Shoot," he said, crumpling his napkin. "I forgot the lime wedges." He got up and opened the refrigerator, bringing a container of citrus back to the table.

Guy was working so hard to make things perfect for Hannah that Mary felt sorry for him. He was a good person, who made her sister happy. Hell, he might be Mary's brother-in-law someday. As much as she wanted Guy to share her burning mistrust of Kelly, she didn't want to scare him away from her family. Guy made Hannah happy and that was the most important thing. So instead of triggering Kelly, Mary followed Hannah's lead and tried to maintain a semblance of calm.

"I'm helping to renovate the senior center and the movie

theater right now," she said. That led to a solid twenty minutes of animated conversation as they finished up dinner. Then Guy brought out a tray of chocolate brownies, which made everyone happy.

When Kelly left the cottage an hour later, Mary had to admit that the visit had been fairly pleasant. But the first thing she did was check her purse to make sure her credit cards were still there.

"What are you doing?" Hannah asked.

Caught red-handed, Mary opened her wallet. "Oh, you know..." She pulled out her Visa. "Protecting my credit rating, that's all."

"Good idea." Hannah went over to Guy's desk. "I'll check my cards, too."

"Gran?" Mary asked. "Would you like me to get your purse?"

"The only thing in there worth stealing is a bottle of chocolate Ensure," said Cheryl. "Brittany was passing it out at the senior center this morning."

"Why'd you give Mom money?" Mary asked, looking at Hannah.

"What was I supposed to do? Let her cry poor in front of Guy?"

"I would have been happy to give her gas money," said Guy. "I wouldn't have minded."

"She won't necessarily spend it on gas." Mary frowned. "That's the problem."

"Oh..." Guy brushed hair off his forehead. "I didn't think about that."

"And you didn't think about how we'd feel having you spring her on us like that," said Hannah. "Or getting involved in something that was none of your business."

"But we're in love!" said Guy. "We're planning a future together. How can your mom not be my business?"

"Because I don't want her to be my business, either," said Hannah. "I keep her at arm's length for a reason."

"I was trying to help." Guy cleared dishes from the table. "Sometimes an outside party can come in and really make a difference."

"You're not an outside party at this point." Hannah put her hands on her hips. "You're my boyfriend and should have been on *my* side on this one."

"I *am* on your side," said Guy. "I'm on all of your sides."

"That's our cue to leave." Cheryl rose unsteadily to her feet. "Mary, could you please bring me my chariot?"

"Wait," said Guy. "You haven't opened the DNA results yet."

"Maybe we should do that another time." Mary pushed the wheelchair toward Cheryl and set the brakes so she could safely climb in.

"It'll only take ten minutes." Guy folded his hands. "Please? I'm sorry I messed up by inviting Kelly, but tonight was supposed to be special. I wanted you to have a family bonding moment where you got to discover more about your past and really dive into it."

Mary rolled her eyes before looking at Hannah. "How do you put up with this type of earnest enthusiasm? Don't you find it annoying?"

"I love it," said Hannah, her voice softening. "You really went to all this trouble for us?" she asked Guy. "So we could have some sort of weird family reunion?"

He nodded. "You know I want you to be happy. I thought if your mom was more stable then that would be less stress for you, and maybe you could have a better relationship in the future."

"That's so sweet." Hannah threw her arms around him and kissed his cheek.

"Misguided," Mary said loudly. "But sweet." She sat down

on the couch next to Cheryl's wheelchair. "Okay. Let's open the ancestry results and get this over with."

Everyone except for Guy pulled out their phones to check their email.

"I still remember when I opened my results last year," said Guy. "I told you how my paternal ancestor was part Irish, and that I can trace my family tree all the way—"

"Yes, you told us," Cheryl said, seconds before Mary had been about to cut him off as well. She didn't want to hear *that* boring description again.

"On the count of three," said Hannah. "One. Two. Three."

Mary clicked on the link. "Huh," she said. "Mom's right. We're part Swedish."

"I think my official definition is 'European mutt'," said Cheryl.

"And mine is 'granddaughter of European mutt'," said Hannah.

Mary looked at the results with a growing sense of disappointment. Part of her had been hoping that they could have provided proper answers. Solutions to problems she really wanted to know. Why was her family a cesspool of drama? How did she end up with such a mess of a mom? What could she do to keep herself from turning into Kelly? But no. If anything, the results were a huge letdown.

"These are interesting," Mary said, feeling deflated. "But they don't explain anything."

"What do you mean?" Guy asked. "Your family tree? That's a separate program, but you can sync your results up."

"No, I mean..." Mary sighed. Part of her felt too tired to get into it. Another part of her could never rest until she'd said her piece. "It doesn't tell us why we're not like normal families. Why—"

"We're normal," Hannah protested.

Mary shot her a look. "You know what I mean. What drove

Dad to leave us and take jobs in other parts of the world, instead of here? Why did our mom make such crappy decisions? Is there something deep inside us that drives us away from quiet, happy lives and into trouble?"

Cheryl put down her phone, her face grim. "Your dad wasn't a drama seeker. But he was profoundly impacted by the September eleventh terrorist attacks. It stirred his sense of patriotism." She folded her hands in her lap. "Originally Max wanted to join the Army Corps of Engineers, but then he saw a private contractor job that offered more money and a little bit more flexibility." She looked at Hannah. "You were two years old at the time."

"I didn't know Dad thought about joining the army," said Hannah.

"Me neither," Mary added.

"He left for Afghanistan a month after you were born, Mary," Cheryl continued. "That was one of the benefits of choosing that particular job. He was able to be home for your birth, which was important to him."

"Okay, that explains why Dad left us," Mary began to say.

"Temporarily," Cheryl cut in. "It was only supposed to be temporary."

"But what about Mom?" Mary asked. "She left us, too." Mary thought about the DNA results they'd just read. "Fifty percent of me comes from Mom's genes, and they seem to be lousy."

"We don't have lousy DNA," said Hannah. "We come from pioneer stock. Our Swedish ancestors helped settle the Pacific Northwest. Some of them probably came on the Oregon Trail."

Guy cupped his hand around his mouth. "Wagons ho!" He took his hand away. "Sorry, not helpful."

"I think there's something more," said Mary. "But I don't know what it is." She looked through the window to the dark night sky. Her dad was a hero, but her mom certainly wasn't.

With Kelly being as damaged as she was, was it possible for Mary to have a stable future? Or was there a fracture running through her, that could crack at any moment? The last thing Mary wanted to become was the deadbeat mom asking her grown daughters for gas money. She needed to make sure she never became that person. But how?

NINE

"Friends? We can never be friends." Mary angled her face against the wind so that the ocean breeze made her blonde hair streak behind her. She ripped the corsage of dried roses off her breast and threw it on the sand. "You've murdered my love for you," she said, lifting her hands up like claws. "Your cursed heart means nothing to me anymore. I don't dance with the—"

Shoot! The tripod tipped over and her phone careened backward. Mary dove forward to rescue it, but it was too late, her phone was covered with wet sand.

Filming TikTok videos was harder than it looked.

Mary used her tattered prom dress to wipe off her phone. She set the tripod back up, clipped it to the pincers, and tried again. It was late Sunday afternoon and she only had about forty minutes of sunlight left to film. She'd rushed here directly from the senior center, where Jose's crew had finished the final coat of paint on the kitchen cabinets. Now she had these damn TikTok videos to make. After brushing sand off the decrepit corsage and pinning it back on her dress, Mary hit record and tried again.

"Friends? We can never be friends. You've murdered my

love for you. Your cursed heart means nothing to me anymore. I don't dance with the dead!" After delivering the cutting line, Mary jerked her wrists up and flailed, whipping her limbs at awkward angles, in a funny dance routine she'd invented herself. She spent ten minutes filming three more takes, each one with a different view behind her. The ocean, the dunes, the endless white sand. When the sun began to set Mary filmed a few more, this time pretending like her character, Jenaly Macintyre, was speaking directly to viewers.

"Did I want to murder the entire football team? No, not at first. But after they secretly recorded me in the locker room? Hell, yeah, I did. They weren't so tough after all—once I added a bit of meat tenderizer and some ketchup." She licked her lips and cackled wickedly.

Mary threw on a raggedy satin cape and elbow-length gloves. The light was perfect now. Everything around her glowed like gold. She pressed record once again.

"The only thing anyone at my high school cared about was that video. It was like YouTube controlled their minds. But you say *I'm* the zombie?" She pressed her hand to her heart. "At least I'm honest about who I am. I'm me, Jenaly Macintyre. I'm not your prom queen—I'm your nightmare."

There, that ought to do it. Now she had a new video to post each day, all of them saved in her drafts folder. Shivering, Mary took off the gloves and cape and put on her warmest raincoat, the one with the fleece lining. She used makeup wipes to remove the pasty foundation she'd smeared on her face and the blood-red lipstick. Now it was impossible to tell what she had been up to. Not that it would have mattered; the beach was abandoned.

That was one of the beautiful things about life in Sand Dollar Cove. During the summer months, tourists came in droves, but the beaches were so vast that the sand swallowed them up. Instead of a checkerboard of beach towels and sunbathers, you'd find cars parked here and there. Each visitor had their own patch of windy paradise. Horses galloped beside the waves.

But now, at the tail end of February, it was even easier to commune with nature. The tourists who did visit hung out around the fireplaces of the Airbnbs, or the day spa at Seaside Resort. It was too cold to sunbathe, and too frigid to swim unless you brought a wetsuit.

That's why, on her trek back to the parking lot, Mary was surprised to see a lone figure running parallel to her. They must have been a hardy soul, she figured, because the wind was picking up so much that she felt grit in her mouth. Luckily, they were so far off that there was no way they could have seen her in her zombie attire. Just in case, Mary zipped her coat up all the way. As the figure changed angles, and began to come closer, Mary saw it was a male runner. As he grew closer still, she saw that it was Steven!

Mary almost didn't recognize him. His hair was pulled back under a cap and he wore black athletic pants, as well as a neon green shirt that clashed with his orange reflective vest. For once, his clothes fit him properly and she could see the shape of him, which appeared sturdy and strong. Sweat poured down his face, drenching his neck and soaking into his clothes. His face was fire engine red, and he had a glazed look in his eyes that spoke of exhaustion. But when he saw her, he grinned, slowed his pace to a walk, and wiped the sweat from his brow. He came to a halt ten feet away.

"Don't worry," he said. "I won't get too close. I stink so much I can smell myself."

Mary chuckled and mustered a bit of small talk. "It's a cold night for a run, isn't it?"

"That's why I bought running gloves yesterday when I went to Port Angeles." He held up his hands. "So much better. Are you headed to the parking lot?"

"I am. The sun's setting fast now, so I'd better hurry."

"Same. I'll walk with you."

"Great." She didn't fancy the idea of walking with sweaty Steven, but it would have been rude to do otherwise. "How long have you been a runner?" she asked.

"Just ten months or so. I can barely run five miles."

"I think that's a lot. I've never been able to get into running. What made you pick it up?"

"It's complicated." Steven gazed at the water for a moment. "Everything got away from me these past couple of years. My job, my social life, my health..."

"That *does* sound complicated." Mary was surprised by how much he was sharing. It made her feel special, that he was confiding in her.

"A friend suggested I start running to clear my head." Steven looked back at her. "And she was right—it really did help."

Ah... ex-girlfriend drama. Now things were starting to make sense. "Friend?" Mary asked, still curious about what had prompted Steven to move here.

"Lady Whisper from the Cobra Ballroom."

"What?" Mary stopped in her tracks, not sure if she'd heard him right.

"One of the best drag queens in Vegas." Steven waved his hands in an hourglass shape. "Lady Whisper was a regular performer at my aunt's nightclub, the Cobra Ballroom. It wasn't really a ballroom, it was more of a dinner theater space with live snakes."

"I see..." Mary said, even though she didn't.

"And then on the other side of the building was a reptile zoo."

"Oh?"

"Which is still going strong. Both of the businesses, in fact. Lady Whisper bought the ballroom after my aunt passed, and the head reptile keeper took over the zoo. All the snakes are as happy as ever. I made sure of that."

"That's..." Mary struggled to find words. "Sweet." It was, too. Mary might not have understood Steven's love of reptiles, but she appreciated that he cared so much about animal well-being.

"But I never have warmed up to running." Steven wiped sweat off his forehead with his gloved hand. "Lady Whisper was right about it clearing my head, but only because I can't think about anything besides putting one foot in front of the other and trying not to keel over."

That was something Mary could relate to. "I hate running," she admitted. "I'd much rather go for a walk, or kayak, or bike."

"I've always wanted to try kayaking."

"It's a blast. The house where I live is on one of the canals and we can kayak from our private dock. It's weird, though, because my landlady never steps foot on it. She's scared of the water."

"That's too bad. We had a backyard pool growing up, and it was wonderful."

"That sounds fun. Most pools are indoors around here."

"I can see why." Steven rubbed his arms to keep warm. "I'm thinking about buying a treadmill so I can run indoors. This wind is brutal."

"Especially on a cold afternoon like this one." The sinking sun kissed Steven's face with an orange glow that accented his tan. Until now, Mary had never noticed how his chin ended in a square shape with a little cleft in it, almost like a dimple. It was a strong jawline, except for that divot, which gave his face some character. "If you'd like to run out of the wind without buying a treadmill, you could get a community day pass to the wellness studio at Seaside Resort."

"I thought that was a hotel?"

"It is a hotel. My sister's the general manager there and she started a new program last fall. Sand Dollar Cove residents can buy memberships to the wellness studio, which is like a tiny gym, and even sign up for private sessions with the personal trainer."

"That sounds intimidating."

"How so?"

"I don't mix well with gyms. I don't like people staring at me, and I never know how to use the machines."

"I'm not sure you'd have to worry about that at Seaside Resort. It's a hotel, not a gym. Like I said, the wellness studio is minuscule. But it has all the basic equipment. I love going there. Hannah sneaks me in for free."

"It *would* be nice to run indoors and away from this wind," Steven admitted. "But I don't know... The risk of humiliation seems high."

"You'd be fine, I promise," Mary said, mainly because she was defending Hannah's new program. Seaside Resort was her sister's baby, and Mary felt like a protective aunt.

"I guess I'm just shy around gyms."

"You're the least shy person I've ever met," said Mary, thinking of his Hawaiian shirts. "Did you or did you not strike up a two-hour conversation with the carpenter last Friday?"

"Power tools get credit for that one. I've always been fascinated by them. But like I said, I have a bad history with gyms, so I guess it's hypothermia for me. I love everything about Sand Dollar Cove but the weather."

Mary didn't know what it was, but something inside her couldn't bear to see him look miserable. Maybe it was his unhappiness with the weather... Maybe it was his confession about gym-phobia... Maybe it was that even though she barely knew him, he was willing to be so vulnerable with her. Her heart compelled her to make the offer before her brain could think it through. "I'll go to the wellness studio with you."

"What?"

"I can show you around your first time so you can see there's nothing to worry about."

"Thanks, but... I don't want to waste your time."

"It's no big deal." How could she make him see that? "There's a lovely restaurant there, too. The Summer Wind. It's my favorite place to eat in all of Sand Dollar Cove, except it's so expensive."

"I'd be happy to buy you lunch if you'd show me around the gym."

"Sure," Mary said, glad that he agreed with her. A few seconds too late she realized what she'd done. *Did I just agree to a lunch date with Steven?* She needed to protect herself from bad relationships, not rush into new ones. "Just to be clear, I'm pretty sure they don't allow snakes."

Steven tossed his head back and laughed. "Elvis doesn't like elevated heart rates, so he'll be happier at home, anyway."

Was *her* heart rate elevated? *It was...* Just a little bit... Shoot! How did she get herself into this, and how would she get herself out? Lunch with Steven didn't necessarily mean the beginning of anything. They were business colleagues, after all. But still... she should be on her guard. "Unfortunately, I'm really busy this week," she said. Maybe she could put him off indefinitely—or maybe it was better to get it over with quickly? Like ripping off a bandage? "I'm free tomorrow, though. I promised my sister that I'd help her pick out new desk furniture for her office."

"Great." Steven smiled broadly. They were at the parking lot now, and there were only a few cars in sight. "Does ten a.m. work for you?"

"Uh... okay." Mary took out her car keys. "I'll meet you in the lobby."

"I'll look forward to it. Promise you'll be gentle."

"Ahh..."

"With the gym tour, I mean. Don't make fun of me if I fall off the treadmill."

"You won't fall off the treadmill."

"But those elliptical machines. You need serious coordination skills for those things."

"I'm sure you can handle it."

Steven shook his head. "Your confidence in me is completely undeserved."

"I'm not so sure about that."

"At least there will be lunch afterward. I'll look forward to that."

"The chef at The Summer Wind never disappoints," Mary promised.

"Good food and good company." Steven laced his fingers behind his head and took a steadying breath. "That's the carrot at the end of the stick."

"I'm not going to beat you with it. We don't have to go if you don't want to." Was Steven as wary about this plan as she was? For some reason, that annoyed her.

Steven dropped his hands. "No, I want to go, I just—don't want to go. Does that make sense?"

"Not in the slightest," Mary said, feeling miffed.

"I was always the last to be picked in gym class. Always the slowest, or the least coordinated. Until high school when the coaches practically forced me to play football, because of my size, and then I spent four years being knocked around because I was horrible at it. I got a concussion senior year, and my mom begged my dad to let me quit. So, I *want* to go, and have it not be awful, and I especially would like to go with you. But the whole idea of it makes running on the beach like a frozen popsicle seem easier." Steven stared out at the horizon for a second before looking at her with eyes full of hurt.

"Oh." Her heart softened. This was something she could understand—feeling less than, like you weren't good enough, or that you would never be good enough no matter how hard you tried. "I promise I'll be with you the whole time, and if I see any mean teenagers or football players come near you, I'll charge them like a zombie."

"Like a zombie, eh?" His hazel eyes lost their haunted look.

"With a bloodstained prom dress and everything." She crossed her heart. "But I'm ordering the sockeye salmon for lunch, and it's expensive."

"Deal." He held out his hand to shake.

Mary put her palm in his gloved one, shook hard, and wondered what she had gotten herself into.

TEN

How was she going to get out of this? Mary parked her car in the lot at Seaside Resort and grabbed her gym bag. Her impulsive offer to show Steven around the wellness studio had been a mistake. Not only did it risk giving him the wrong idea about their relationship, which would only ever be professional, but now she had to deal with Hannah, too. As soon as Mary had told Hannah about the plans and asked to score two free guest passes, Hannah's eyes had lit up like fireworks. There she was now, walking down the path to the parking lot, and Mary wasn't even out of her car yet. Her sister's enthusiasm cranked Mary's anxiety from medium to high.

"There's my little gym rat." Hannah opened Mary's door for her. "Are you all ready for your big date?"

"It's not a date." Mary frowned and stepped out of the car. "This is a business meeting, or whatever." She slammed her door shut.

"Ambiguity is fine. I'm just glad you're doing something productive that doesn't involve you being cooped up in your room eavesdropping on the DeLacks."

"It's *your* room, too, only you're never there anymore

because you're always with Guy. And in case you haven't noticed, I'm managing two major design projects. Either I'm on the job site or making plans for the next project."

"I'm so excited for your business meeting then." Hannah hugged her.

Feeling Hannah's arms around her made Mary realize how much she'd missed her sister's presence. Hannah was her rock. Her solace. The person she had counted on for protection. When Mary had turned four years old, and they'd moved in with Cheryl, she had enjoyed her grandmother's support as well. But even then, Mary had clung to Hannah like she was her savior. Could she ever be as strong as her big sister? As responsible and fierce? Mary was great at pretending to be okay. She could act like everything was perfect. But true happiness was always out of reach because she was too fragile to claim it.

The sisters pulled apart and Hannah waved the two tickets. "Here are your guest passes. All you need to do is show them to Alicia and she'll hook you up."

"Who's Alicia?" Mary asked, as they began walking up the path to the resort.

"The new personal trainer who replaced Guy."

"Oh yeah." Mary tightened her grip on her gym bag. "I forgot."

"She's not nearly as good as Guy, of course, but she's making an impression."

"How so?"

"You should see the TripAdvisor comments about her."

"What do they say?" Mary asked.

"A bunch of complimentary things, but only from men."

"Oh."

"Creepy old men," said Hannah. "And young men. And middle-aged men. And in one case, a reviewer I'm pretty sure was a fourteen-year-old boy who somehow opened a review account just to share how hot she was. His exact words were:

'The GOAT who rules the gym is extra lit.' I'm not exactly sure what that means but I assume it's favorable."

"It shouldn't matter what she looks like so long as she does her job well, right?"

"Right," said Hannah. "And she is. Just not as good as Guy, but who could be?"

They were at the entrance to the lobby now. A winter garden of purple cabbage, bright pink camellias, and creamy-white hellebores bloomed along each side of the path. Hummingbirds zoomed up to bird feeders hanging from the roof eaves. Out in the distance, the silvery-blue edges of the Pacific Ocean beckoned, as the foghorn sang. Mary looked around but didn't see any sign of Steven yet, which made sense, since she'd arrived early. "Is it okay if I grab a coffee in the lobby?" she asked, referring to the complimentary beverage station.

"Be my guest," said Hannah. "I have to go follow up with something at housekeeping, but text me if you need anything."

"Thanks. I'll meet you after lunch to pick out that office furniture. And Hannah?" Mary paused, feeling needy.

"What?"

"Could we maybe spend some more time together? I miss you."

Hannah's expression softened. "I miss you too, sis." She gave her one more hug before taking off.

Mary entered the lobby and enjoyed a boost of confidence when she encountered her own work. Unlike the dreary and dated interior of a year ago, the lobby now reflected Pacific Northwest artistry mixed with mid-century modern panache. Low-back leather couches with Pendleton Woolen Mills cushions circled the hearth. Sepia-toned photos of old-growth cedars graced the original wood-paneled walls, which glowed from the orange oil and elbow grease Mary had worked into their grain after painstakingly removing the 1980s-era wallpaper. It was like entering a cabin perched above the Pacific Ocean and feeling instantly at home.

The coffee in the beverage station was piping hot, and Mary was putting a double sleeve on her cup when two women burst into the lobby, in animated conversation.

"It just makes no sense, Brenda," said the first woman, who appeared to be in her early seventies. She wore velour sweatpants and a matching hoodie along with giant hoop earrings and bright pink lipstick. "I've never known Carlos to pass up the chance to fish. He's been talking about that charter cruise for months."

"So has Vicente." Brenda folded her arms across her chest. She, too, appeared to be the same age as her friend, but had the toned physique of someone half her age. "And since when has he wanted to go to the gym? I've begged him to go to Silver-Sneakers with me for years, and he's always had some excuse not to."

Mary stepped to the side since the women were headed to the beverage station. She found a seat in one of the leather chairs and engaged in her favorite pastime—eavesdropping.

"I think we know what changed Vicente's mind about exercise." The first woman stopped by the beverage station and refilled her water bottle. "Ooh! Mint infusion! I love how they spice up the water."

Mary loved the spa water, too.

"The water's the same, Elena, but this whole place feels different now that Guy's no longer running the wellness studio." Brenda waited her turn to refill her water bottle.

Ooh. Hannah's not going to like that negative review, Mary thought as she sipped her coffee.

"Guy did meet us for lunch yesterday," said Elena. "And he asked about your grandkids, too."

"But it's not the same, is it?" Brenda asked. "The whole reason we came back here was the 'Two Weeks to Fitness' program with Guy. You and me, getting fit and having spa treatments each day."

"We're still doing that," Elena pointed out. "But now our husbands are doing it, too."

Brenda threw her hands up in the air. "Instead of fishing."

"If I had wanted to see Carlos sweat, I would have stayed home in Seattle and sneaked peeks at him watching football."

"Maybe we should go fishing tomorrow," Brenda suggested. "Just to get away from them."

"I don't think so." Elena shook her head. "It will be freezing, and I might get seasick."

The two women were leaving the lobby now, and Mary had to lean over the arm of her chair and crane her neck to catch the last bit of their conversation.

"Dramamine," Brenda suggested. "That'll fix you up."

The door closed behind them, and Steven entered. Mary was already so off-balance on the chair that she stopped herself just short of keeling over.

"Are you okay?" Steven rushed over to help her.

"Never better." She pushed herself up to sitting. "I was stretching," she said, not wanting to admit that she'd been eavesdropping. "Are you ready for the gym?"

"Sure." He pulled out his wallet. "Where do we pay for the day passes?"

"That's already been taken care of." Mary picked up her bag and stood. "Compliments of Hannah."

"Hannah?"

"My sister."

"Oh. That's right. You mentioned her."

"Are you ready?"

"As ready as I'll ever be." He pulled back a lock of hair that had flopped over his forehead. Steven wore black shorts and a blue athletic jacket.

"You look the part," Mary said, as she opened the front

door. "By the way you're dressed I'd never know you weren't a regular gymgoer."

"Thanks." Steven paused at the threshold, his cheeks turning pink. "That means a lot." He took a deep breath before walking outside. "Those who are about to die salute you."

"Huh?"

"Gladiator reference. My best friend Corey worked at Caesar's Palace to pay for college."

"As a gladiator?"

"Yeah. Corey would wander around, pose for pictures, and fend off handsy drunk people."

"Did he make a lot of money?"

"Loads. Here, I'll show you a picture." Steven pulled out his phone, scrolled through his gallery, and handed her the screen. "This is the two of us sophomore year of college."

Mary looked down and saw a greased-up man wearing a short skirt and holding a shield. Corey's plumed helmet added an additional six inches to his frame. The gladiator's arm muscles were like tree trunks. Meanwhile, standing behind him was Steven, wearing the same Hawaiian shirt with the dancing pineapples she'd seen him in before, only this time, instead of swimming in the shirt, he stretched it out. He had on baggy cargo pants, Crocs, and a huge smile. "You look happy," she said.

"Free beer and nachos will do that for you." He took his phone back. "That was right before Corey dropped out of college and entered massage school."

"Is he a masseur now?"

"He developed carpal tunnel syndrome the first month of training and dropped out. But he eventually went back to school, got his degree, and now he practices law in California." They were at the entrance to the wellness studio, and he looked at the sign warily. "Maybe we should skip this and just go to lunch. I'm not sure—"

"It'll be fine." Mary gave him a short, quick pat on the back. "I'll be with you the whole time—except in the shower." *Dang it.* That had come out flirtier than she had intended.

"You promise?"

"To not shower with you?" Mary nodded. "Yes, I promise." *Shoot.* That sounded mean. Luckily, Steven took it like a joke, which was what Mary had intended.

"Okay," he said, laughing. "It's a deal. But you're going in first." He held open the door for her.

Mary walked inside and saw two sweaty old men on benches lifting free weights. Standing next to them was a pint-sized woman with silky black hair flicking around in a high ponytail, demonstrating the correct form for using weights that were twice as large as the ones the men carried.

"I think that must be Alicia," Mary explained. "The new personal trainer."

"It looks like she's busy with clients already. Maybe we should find a locker first."

"Sure." Mary waved her guest passes in Alicia's direction and put them on her desk. Then she showed Steven where the locker rooms were so they could stow their gear. "I'll meet you by the cardio machines in a couple minutes," she said.

Five minutes later, Steven still hadn't emerged from the men's restroom. Mary began to worry. Maybe she shouldn't have encouraged him to come after all. Sure, Steven was super outgoing in other ways, but something about all of this was rattling him. He seemed to have a hang-up about gyms that she didn't understand.

"You must be Mary," said Alicia as she trotted over to say hello. Her thick eyelash extensions gave her a doe-eyed look, and her teeny-tiny sports bra showed off her abs. "I'm Alicia Wong."

"Nice to meet you." Mary shook hands. "My guest should be joining us soon." Should she mention Steven being nervous?

She didn't want to talk about him behind his back, but it might be helpful for Alicia to have a heads-up about what she was dealing with. Mary glanced over Alicia's shoulder to make sure Steven was still in the locker room. Then she looked back at Alicia. "His name is Steven and he's really skittish about gyms, so please be gentle with him."

"I can be gentle." Alicia tightened her ponytail.

"Take it slow."

"I will."

"He barely exercises at all," Mary continued. "Except for running. He told me he's only worked out for the past ten months."

"Running's a tough form of cardio. Good for him."

"Yeah. Good for him." From the corner of her eye, Mary saw Steven exit the locker room and walk across the gym floor. Only instead of wearing the warm-up jacket he had on earlier, now he wore a tank top over his barreled chest. His hair was pulled up into a knot at the top of his head. *A man bun,* Mary realized. *Wow.* And his arm muscles showed such intense defin-ition that she stared.

"He must do something besides cardio." Alicia looked back at Mary. "Are you two together?"

"Like dating together?" Mary shook her head. "No. We're more like acquaintances."

"Glad to hear it." Alicia arched her back a bit so that her chest stood out, lifted her hand up, and waved. "Yoo-hoo! Over here, Steven. I've been waiting for you."

That wasn't taking it slow! Alicia was going to scare him off before Steven had turned on the treadmill. But much to her surprise, Steven didn't flinch. He walked toward them with a firm gait, holding a gigantic water bottle. "Hi," he said, with a nod.

"Steven, this is Alicia," said Mary. "Alicia, this is Steven."

Alicia hopped forward and batted her eyelashes. "I am so glad to meet you. I hear you're a runner, just like me."

"I wouldn't say I'm a runner yet." Steven rubbed his jawline. "More like a person who runs a few times a week."

"What's the difference?" Mary asked.

"There's a huge difference." Alicia pointed at Steven's calf muscles. "You look like a runner to me."

"If so, I've been a freezing cold runner. That's why Mary suggested finding out about your gym, so I could use the treadmill on rainy days."

"Sounds like a great plan to me." Alicia peered at him while pursing her lips. "Do I know you?"

"I don't think so," said Steven.

Mary rolled her eyes. *What a cheesy pickup line.* Did Alicia treat all her male clients like this? No wonder the Yelp reviews were off the charts.

"Are you sure?" Alicia put her hand on her hip. "You look *so* familiar. I could swear we've met before."

Steven shrugged. "I must have one of those faces."

Alicia waved her hand in the air excitedly. "I know! You look like Austin Butler only with longer hair. That's it!"

"The *Elvis* actor?" Steven shrugged. "I don't think so."

"Why don't you give us a tour of the gym so we can get going?" Mary said, trying to keep the trainer on track.

"Oh. Right." Alicia went to work showing them the intricacies of the treadmill. "You can push this button here, pull up the app screen, click the Netflix button and watch whatever you want so long as you use closed captions or bring your own earbuds," she said. "Do you like Netflix?"

"I love Netflix," said Steven. "And MAX, and Amazon Prime, and basically anything that involves watching high-quality TV."

"I just knew we had that in common," said Alicia.

"Cool." Steven put his water bottle in the holder.

Big deal, Mary thought. Almost everyone loves watching TV. That wasn't a special connection Alicia had with Steven that nobody else had.

Alicia rose on the balls of her feet, so she was a few inches taller, and a little bit closer to eye level with Steven. "I love hanging out and watching TV after a hot shower and a good run. What about you?"

"Um... It depends." Steven bent over and tightened his shoelace.

What did Netflix and cozy evenings have to do with treadmill operation? Mary gave Alicia a hard look. Was she flirting with Steven? No, she wasn't. Was she? *She doesn't know about the snakes, and the weird clothes, and the horror-office-dungeon,* Mary told herself. All she sees is... what? Mary looked at Steven as if for the first time. A burly man with a rugged jawline and a man bun? A dead ringer for Austin Butler? Her eyes drifted across his broad shoulders and up into his hazel eyes. A hunk of a man who wasn't afraid to be vulnerable and try something new?

Shut the front door.

Had Mary just thought of Steven as being *hunky*?

She had, in fact. And that was ridiculous because he wasn't hunky, he was Steven. The quirky stranger in the ridiculous Hawaiian shirt who'd showed up to her workplace holding a pet snake. What the hell!

Mary gathered herself, realizing too late that while her thoughts had been traipsing all over the place, Alicia had made Steven laugh, positioned herself closer to him, and was now leaning on the treadmill's handlebars in a saucy way.

"Why don't you tell us about some of the other treadmill features," Mary suggested pointedly. "Like, how to turn it on."

"Oh, silly me. I got so carried away talking about Vegas that I forgot the basics."

Vegas? Jeez Louise. Mary needed to pay closer attention.

"This is how you start the treadmill. This is how you stop it, and this is how you increase the speed and incline." Alicia pointed to each button with French-tipped fingernails. The edges were black, instead of the typical white, with sparkly crystals at the centers. *Like Mom's...* That made Mary even more annoyed.

"Back to the special features," Alicia said, clicking her fingernails on the dashboard. "If you'd rather save TV-watching for a cozy evening with a special someone, you can choose one of the preset programs instead, like running through the virtual woods or on the virtual beach."

"Instead of running through the real woods or on the actual beach?" Steven peered down at the screen.

"That's right." Alicia nodded. "It's not nearly as fun as running with a friend on the beach, but it's still a good time. Climb aboard and give it a go." She looked at Mary. "You, too. Need any help?"

"I've used a treadmill before," said Mary, as she picked a machine and pressed the start button.

"I have too, years ago," said Steven. "But never one this fancy."

"Fancy is my specialty." Alicia grinned at him. "I bet you'll be a natural at this machine."

"Alicia?" called one of the men near the weight rack. "Can you show my friend Vicente over here how to do a proper triceps dip?"

Alicia's smile froze into place. "Sure," she called over her shoulder. "Be right there." She looked back at Steven. "If you need anything, and I mean *anything*, let me know. Promise?"

"Thanks, but I think we'll be fine." Steven pushed a button to up the speed on his machine. He kept his eyes focused on his feet as Alicia walked away. Once she was out of earshot, he looked at Mary. "Well, that was humiliating."

"What do you mean?"

"The trainer, offering me so much help, like I was a toddler. What's the opposite of mansplaining? I don't know, but that's what she was doing to me."

"Huh? That's not what was happening."

"She practically offered to babysit me."

"I think you misinterpreted."

"How?" Steven gripped the handlebars of his treadmill. "She took one look at me and realized I didn't belong here."

"What? No!" His interpretation shocked her. "She was flirting with you, Steven. I'm surprised she didn't come straight out and ask you if you were on Tinder."

"Tinder? Why would I be on Tinder?"

Mary looked sideways at him. "For the same reason anyone would be on Tinder."

Steven shook his head. "There's no way that a woman like that would—" He stopped mid-sentence because Alicia was scampering their way.

"How's it going, you two?" she asked, looking directly at Steven. "Are you all warmed up?"

"Seems like it," Steven grunted.

"Great." Alicia beamed. "After you've had a nice sweaty run, we can do the weight machines." She reached out and squeezed Steven's biceps. "And you can tell me all about how you acquired these."

"Snakes," said Steven. "Nothing but lifting snakes."

"Ooh!" Alicia's eyes lit up. "I'd love to hear about your snake."

"Plural!" Mary blurted. "There's more than one of them." She looked at her treadmill dashboard, wishing she had brought headphones. She needed some sort of ear protection to block this conversation out.

ELEVEN

Normally when Mary had the opportunity to use the wellness studio's women's locker room, she spent over an hour relaxing. The eucalyptus-scented steam sauna detoxed pores, and the dry sauna was the perfect temperature to lie down and relax. But today Mary hurried. She changed out of her stinky gym clothes and showered quickly. After toweling off, she slathered on the complimentary Blanchet Maison body lotion, and swished her mouth out with mouthwash. Then she blow-dried her hair and helped herself to one of the hair ties in a basket on the sink. While she was at it, she added one of the travel-sized containers of deodorant to her gym bag. *If it's free, take it,* she figured. Wasn't that what Steven had said about the six-foot Godzilla?

Shoot. Now she was quoting Steven.

And thinking about him.

And rushing through her shower for him.

Seriously! What the hell was wrong with her? This was Steven. Steven, the fashion criminal.

But even though she hurried, by the time she left the locker room it appeared that Steven had already been waiting for her for a while. He stood by Alicia in animated conversation. The trainer perched on the edge of her desk and leaned forward slightly, like she was intentionally offering Steven the perfect view of her cleavage. So unprofessional of her! Mary frowned. She was all for women supporting women, but did Alicia really need to wiggle like that?

At least now that Steven was changed out of his gym wear into street clothes, he looked closer to how Mary expected him to look. *Less hot.* No, on second thoughts, that wasn't exactly true. Steven wore well-fitting jeans and a black Henley. His wet hair was slicked back behind his ears, like he hadn't bothered to dry it. But it was his belt that really caught her attention. Was it made from snakeskin?

As if he could sense her eyes lingering on him, Steven turned around at the exact moment Mary was staring at his waistline. He waved. Mary blushed and looked up to see him grin. Busted!

She tried to shake off the fact that he'd caught her ogling him, and walked forward as if nothing had happened, all the while arguing with herself. *I wasn't ogling.* She was headed to a working lunch. That's all this was. But then she saw Alicia pluck a business card out from a little box on her desk, write something on the back of it, and hand it to Steven with a flirty wink. Her phone number, perhaps? Unbelievable! Did Alicia not see that it was Mary going to lunch with Steven and not her? She had told Alicia that she and Steven weren't an item, but still... it was irksome.

"There she is," said Steven. "I thought you'd drowned in there."

"I rushed as fast as I could." Mary pointed to her blonde tresses. "This is a lot of hair to blow-dry."

"You did better than me." Steven picked up his gym bag off the floor. "I didn't bother."

"I can see that," said Mary. "My gran would say: 'you'll catch pneumonia.'"

"I like it wet like that," said Alicia. "You look like you're in a motorcycle gang."

"The only motorcycle I've ever ridden was a kiddie toy in front of the grocery store." Steven turned toward Mary. "Ready for lunch?"

"Looking forward to it," Mary blurted. She was, too. And not just because Alicia looked like she was about to lick her client like an ice cream cone. Mary wanted to escape this Bermuda Triangle of a gym space where Steven had suddenly become hot, and get back to the real world where he was the possibly color-blind guy who talked about feeding dead guinea pigs to pythons.

Once they stepped outside into fresh air, things immediately felt better. Steven must have felt the return to normalcy too because he let out a huge sigh of relief. "I'm so glad that's over with," he admitted. "Thanks for taking me, but I don't think a gym membership is right for me."

"But you did great in there." Mary led him up the path to the restaurant. "You used almost all the machines."

"Yeah, I just don't enjoy exercising in front of strangers. It's too awkward."

"I can see that. Especially with the way Alicia was leering at you the whole time like you were a sirloin steak."

"She wasn't leering."

"She was one step away from squirting ketchup on you."

"Who puts ketchup on steak?"

"Lots of people."

"Sounds like a way to ruin a perfectly good steak if you ask me."

"Did she give you her phone number?" Mary asked, honestly curious.

"Yeah, but only because she wanted to find out when the cinema reopened."

"Sure, that's why."

"No, really. That's it."

Mary stopped in her tracks and looked at him sharply. Was Steven really this clueless? "She could have found out that information online."

"I suppose so, but does it matter?"

"Of course not." Mary zipped up her coat. The wind whipping off the Pacific was chilly. "Let's go eat lunch."

"Wait a second." Steven touched her sleeve. "Are you angry with me about something?"

"I'm not angry," Mary said indignantly.

"Then why are your cheeks so pink?"

"Because I took a hot shower. Maybe I have circulation issues. I don't know. Let's go eat. I'm hungry."

"I'm always hungry. Especially after a run." The foghorn sounded and Steven looked out at the horizon. "I'm still not used to that noise."

"I barely hear it, unless I'm specifically listening for it."

"Sometimes I find it soothing, other times it's annoying, but mainly it's a reminder of how far I am from Nevada."

"It must feel like worlds away."

Steven nodded. They were approaching a viewing platform that looked out above the cliffs and directly at the waterline. "Is it okay if we stop here for just a moment?"

"Sure. I never say no to admiring the view." Mary had meant the ocean, but as Steven climbed up the steps ahead of her, she found herself ogling again, only this time she was ready to admit it. *Nice view,* she thought. How had she not noticed that before? She'd been distracted by baggy clothes and wild prints, that's why. Mary was pattern-sensitive. How could she not be? She was an interior designer, after all. Aesthetics were her life's work. But was she really so shallow that she hadn't realized how handsome Steven was until today?

Mary stepped up to the deck and leaned against the railing as she took stock of herself. Her eyes were on the horizon, but her focus directed inward. It wasn't so long ago that she'd been working at the coffee stand, scribbling her name and number on Aidan's order cup, all because she thought he had a cute smile and drove a flashy car.

Her mom had been into sports cars, too. Kelly had once owned a Corvette. Maybe Mary was shallow, like her mom. That thought horrified her. She remembered what Hannah said about her too. That she was attracted to flashy objects, like a Steller's jay.

But that couldn't be entirely true. When Steven had been wearing his outrageously hideous Vegas clothes, she hadn't been attracted to him at all. But that snakeskin belt he had on now... What would it be like to hook her fingers behind it and pull him toward her for a kiss? Mary shivered. That's not what she should be thinking about at the start of a quasi-business lunch.

"Are you cold?" Steven asked. "I have a jacket in my car you could borrow."

"Thanks, but I'm fine. The wind got me, that's all."

"Here." Steven angled his body toward her. "I'll block it for you." He licked his finger and held it up to the breeze. "I think it's coming from that direction. Better?"

"Better," she said in a weak voice.

Not better.

Not better one bit.

They were close enough that she could feel heat radiate from his body. He was still a foot away from her, but it was near enough that she could smell his clean scent, the same fragrance as the Blanchet Maison shampoo, Sandalwood and Ivy.

"Views like this make the move from Vegas worth it," Steven said, looking at her and then off at the ocean. "The Strip can't compare with Mother Nature. Every time I see the ocean, I know I made the right choice to come live here."

"It feeds the soul."

"I bet it does, especially for someone with an artistic personality, like you. With a view like this, it's no wonder you're so creative." He said "artistic personality" like a compliment instead of a slur. Which made Mary think about how Aidan had used to complain about her career choices, and how *art would never pay the bills.*

"Thanks." Mary smiled.

"But this is enough of standing at the edge of a cliff for me. You might get the wrong idea and throw me off."

"What?" Mary's eyebrows shot up. "Where did that come from?"

"Horror movies. Look, it's the perfect setup. Man standing quietly looking out at the jaw-dropping scenery. Everything is calm until—bam! The gorgeous woman standing next to him turns out to be the serial killer the town sheriff has been looking for the whole time."

Mary held out her hands and fake pushed him. "Bump."

Steven jumped back. "You're a real comedian."

"I wouldn't be a serial killer, though. I'd be a zombie." She didn't know why she had said it, but she had. It was as close to confessing her secret as she had come, and to Steven of all people. How had that slipped out? "Let's go to lunch before someone dies," Mary said. She walked down the steps and back to the sidewalk, not waiting to see if Steven would follow.

But he did. She could feel his presence a few steps behind her. *And wait a minute,* she thought. Did Steven say she was gorgeous a minute ago? That felt good. Almost as good as when he'd said she had an artistic personality.

"How are Celine and Dion doing?" she asked, trying to veer the conversation away from this fluttery feeling in her stomach. There was no way in hell a lunch date with Steven was giving her butterflies. Besides, it wasn't a date. But when he caught up with her and flashed a friendly smile, she felt the butterfly wings beat again.

"They seem to be cozy in the office space, but I don't know how they'll do next week when we move them into the concessions area while Jose's crew paints."

"Could you sneak the snake enclosures back into your apartment without your landlord knowing?"

Steven tilted his head. "I might have to. I don't care so much about breaking the rules, but keeping a consistent heat level there is difficult. There are these old wall heaters that you have to turn on one by one, and they are either so hot that they'll burn you or they won't turn on at all."

"Sounds like cadet heaters. We used to have them in the house we rented growing up."

"Celine and Dion like it hot but I don't want to accidentally scorch them when I'm not home."

"We'll figure out a way to keep them happy in the cinema while the work happens," Mary promised. "Maybe we can reuse those plastic walls that the moisture mitigators left behind. Worst-case scenario, maybe they could hang out in the senior center for a while. There's a storage closet we could heat for them, so they'd stay warm. I'm not sure Keith would say yes, but we could ask him."

"Keith?" Steven stopped walking, right before they reached the path to The Summer Wind. "Who's Keith?"

"The senior center director," Mary explained. "He's dating my landlady, Brittany."

"Oh. Cool. Good idea."

Mary and Steven walked up onto the porch of The Summer Wind just as two older women exited. Brenda and Elena, the ladies Mary had seen in the lobby that morning, walked out. Only instead of wearing workout gear, both women wore slacks and sweaters.

"Hubba hubba," said Brenda as Steven held the door for them.

"Brenda, don't be rude," her friend barked. She lifted her

chin and looked at Steven. "Please excuse my friend for her aplorable behavior.'

"Aplorable's not a word," Brenda interjected. "I might have had three mimosas but even I know that."

"Two mimosas. We only had two mimosas."

"It was three mimosas, and you know it, Elena. You lost count."

"I never lose count!" Elena exclaimed.

"It was two pitchers of mimosas, but three drinks each." Brenda hiccupped. "Remember now?"

"Oh..." Elena palmed her forehead. "Well, three mimosas at brunch would explain your explorable behavior."

"I think you meant deplorable." Brenda linked her arm with Elena's. "This is why I always beat you at Wordle."

"Do not."

"Do too," said Brenda.

The two women wandered away down the path to the lodge.

"Hubba hubba," Mary said to Steven, who was still holding open the door.

They both burst out laughing.

"Mimosas with lunch?" Steven suggested. "I hear they're popular."

"Sure," Mary said, even though she knew that adding alcohol to the mix pushed this meal further away from business lunch territory and more into quasi-date territory than she had originally wanted. Only now, she realized, as her heart thumped in her chest, she was beginning to change her mind.

When the hostess directed them to a table by the floor-to-ceiling window, she took a seat next to the glass and tried to steady herself. She didn't look at the view. She kept her gaze away from Steven. Instead, she focused on the menu even though she already knew what she wanted to order: the Copper River salmon from Alaska.

"You mentioned yesterday that the salmon was good?" Steven asked.

"Yup," Mary mumbled, not taking her eyes off the menu. She had to decide what to do about her sudden attraction to Steven. Maybe she was imagining it. Better double-check.

Raising her chin, she looked straight into his hazel eyes and felt nothing. There! She felt nothing. He was just Steven after all, not a hunky shapeshifter. Still... there was something about him... "Your hair looks different today," she said. "Slicked back like this, and before, when it was tied up in the knot."

"Like a *samurai*." Steven sliced through the air with an imaginary sword.

Still geeky, Mary thought. That hadn't changed.

"Not that cultural appropriation is in any way acceptable," Steven added.

And sensitive. Her heart melted.

Mary tried to remember how awful his hair had looked the last time she'd seen him, when he was running down the beach toward her at sunset. *When he was hot, and sweaty, and manly-looking.*

No! The time before that, when they'd met up at the hardware store to pick out paint samples. It had tangled around his ears. Mary hadn't found that attractive at all. Score!

"I haven't found a new barber yet," Steven explained. "It's been a couple of months now, and at least another two months since my last haircut in Vegas." He scratched the back of his neck. "But actually, I always wanted to have long hair but never could before, so this is a bit of a messy experiment."

"It doesn't look messy now," Mary said. "It looks good."

"Thanks. Water tamed it down, I guess."

"If you wanted a trim though, the hair design place on Fourth Avenue will hook you up. But don't cut all of it off unless you want to, I like it this way."

"You do?"

Mary nodded. "Why couldn't you have long hair in Vegas?"

"Because of my job. I used to be a lawyer."

"A lawyer?" Mary feigned surprise even though she'd already googled him.

"Yeah, a public defender. My heart was never in it though. So when I saw the— Oh wait. The waiter is coming."

It wasn't just the waiter; it was Jasmine, the head chef. Had Hannah put her up to this? Hannah and Jasmine had been best friends since middle school. Jasmine was practically Mary's older sister.

"Well, look at this cozy scene," Jasmine said as she pulled out a notepad. "How are you doing, Mary? Who's your friend?"

"Why are you here waiting tables instead of ruling the kitchen?" Mary asked, without answering Jasmine's question.

"Because a little bird told me that her sister was coming to lunch, that's why." Jasmine pinched Mary's cheek. "Look at how cute you are." She turned toward Steven. "I'm Jasmine, culinary genius, nice to meet you."

"Steven Clarke, movie buff and herper. Nice to meet you, too."

"Herper?" Jasmine asked.

Mary wondered what that word meant too.

"Amateur herpetophile," Steven explained. "Reptile lover."

Nerdy. Nerdy. Nerdy, Mary thought.

And cute... Damn!

"I'm sure you're super busy, so we'll give you our order so you can get out of here," Mary said. "I'll have the cedar-planked Copper River salmon with a side of mashed Yukon Gold potatoes and salad."

"In a hurry to get rid of me, are you?" Jasmine winked. "Got it." She looked at Steven. "And what will you have?"

"I guess I'll have the salmon too, although I don't really like fish. Mary raves about it though, so—"

"You'll love it." Jasmine picked up the menus. "Potatoes and salad okay with you, or would you rather have rice and roasted veggies?"

"Could I have potatoes and roasted veggies?" Steven asked.

"Sure."

"And mimosas," Mary added. "For both of us." One tiny mimosa wouldn't weaken the barrier she'd built to defend her heart. No matter what happened, she wouldn't rush into things. She promised herself that.

"Coming right up." Jasmine spun on her toe and walked away.

"That was Hannah's best friend," Mary explained.

"Oh. She seemed nice."

"I was going to say annoying." Mary straightened her hair. "She interrupted us right when you were telling me about not wanting to be a lawyer."

"Right." Steven leaned back in his chair. "I know it's a worthwhile career, and I admired my work friends for their devotion to the job, but my heart was never in it. I wanted to be a director. I double-majored in film studies and pre-law."

"That seems like a combo that could have helped you become a Hollywood lawyer." Mary poured two glasses of water from the carafe on the table.

"Yeah, except my passion was for directing. Or lighting. Or casting. Or something exciting like that."

"Never acting?"

"No, no, no." Steven shook his head. "The camera doesn't like me."

"That's not true. Show me that picture of you and Spartacus again."

"What?"

"You and your friend who worked at Caesar's Palace."

"Oh, you mean Corey." Steven took out his phone, tapped the screen a few times, and passed it over.

This time, Mary looked at it more closely. Sure, Steven's

friend was oiled-up muscles on a stick, but Steven looked darn good too, wild shirt, Crocs, and all. "Look at how winning your smile is in this picture," she said. "The first time I saw this picture I said you looked happy, but what I didn't say is that your happiness was contagious. It made me smile too, just looking at it." She passed the phone back to him.

"I *was* happy." Steven's face fell. "But I was also annoyed because tourists kept asking me to move out of the way so they could have their picture taken with Corey." He put his phone away. "That was before my dad convinced me that I'd never make it in the movie industry, in any capacity, and that I was stupid to focus on anything but law."

"That's not fair."

"It's not, but my dad can be very persuasive."

"Still, everyone should have the chance to pursue their dreams." She took a sip of water. Should she tell him about her experience in Hollywood? Sure, she figured. Why not? Somehow she sensed that Steven wouldn't make fun of her, or ruthlessly mock her for failing like Aidan had done. If he did, that would be a red flag, and Mary was looking out for warning signals like that. "I moved to Hollywood, hoping to become an actor," she confessed. "For a year and a half after high school."

"You did? That's amazing! What happened?"

"I spent most of my time working at Starbucks, and the rest of it going to open casting calls and never being picked. I had zero luck signing with an agent, probably because I couldn't afford decent headshots, and the first room I rented was so disgusting it came with bedbugs."

"Yikes to the bedbugs."

"Yeah, they were nasty. But I learned a lot by volunteering as a set designer at a local community theater. That's how I found out I loved interior design even more than acting. I came back home, trained for two years to become a designer, and the rest is history."

"You're amazing."

"I'm not."

"Yes, you are." Steven leaned forward and looked at her intently. "Do you know how courageous that was? To take off for Hollywood on your own, on a limited budget?"

Mary twisted her napkin. "Starving actors are a dime a dozen. Besides, you're being brave too. Moving to a new state and buying the cinema. All before you turn thirty!"

"I never would have done it without money, though. My Aunt Helena died, and that's what gave me the funds—and the courage—to do this."

"Your Aunt Helena who owned the Cobra Ballroom?"

"That's right. You remembered." Steven smiled softly. "She gave me my first paying job. I washed dishes in the Cobra Ballroom kitchen every summer in high school."

"Sounds like hard work."

"It was..." Steven looked thoughtful. "But it was also educational. I learned more in that kitchen about what real life in Las Vegas was like than I ever learned from my parents."

"What do you mean?"

"About how hard people struggled to get by. About how difficult things were for most people. I practiced my Spanish, learned a bit of Samoan, and a lot about how much Aunt Helena's employees loved her because she paid living wages—unlike at their previous jobs."

"She sounds like a good person."

"She was."

Mary noted the tone of sadness in Steven's voice when he spoke of his great-aunt. He must have felt her loss in a deep way. "Your parents didn't teach you about real life?"

Steven shook his head. "My dad is only focused on one thing: success. To him that meant me being a football star or following him into law."

"And your mom?"

"I love my mom."

"That doesn't answer my question," said Mary.

Steven leaned forward. "Well, let me put it this way. My junior year of high school I founded a film club where we sponsored outdoor movie nights at a local park. It was a great community-building event and completely free because we used the concessions stand revenue to pay for it. When I asked my mom to share a post about it on her Facebook feed, since I wasn't on Facebook and we needed the word-of-mouth advertising help, she refused."

"Why?" Mary asked. "It sounds really cool."

"My mom didn't like the fact that the park was in, as she put it, 'the wrong part of town.'"

"Oh."

"If it had been in *our* neighborhood park, or at the country club, she would have told *all* her friends."

"I see..."

Mary did, too. A clearer picture of Steven was forming in her mind. He might have come from a two-parent household, and an upper-middle-class life, but he didn't have the love and support that Mary enjoyed from Cheryl and Hannah. Yet somehow, he'd managed to follow his dreams to Washington State, and not give up on his ambition despite outside pressure. He was smart, creative, caring, and—how had she never noticed until today?—hot, in a nerdy film buff sort of way. Or, a sweaty runner on the beach way. Or, a "let's put on an amazing movie night for an underprivileged neighborhood" sort of way. Steven was dreamy. That was the truth of it. She didn't detect any danger signs at all.

Just then a waiter came over with two giant mimosas. "These are on the house, compliments of Jasmine," he said as he set them in front of her.

Mary lifted her glass and clinked it against Steven's. "To Jasmine," she said.

"To Jasmine," he echoed.

Their eyes locked together until Mary ripped her gaze away and sipped her mimosa. When the tangy taste of champagne and orange juice hit her palate, she felt the rush of knowing that yes, this meal might count as a date after all. And that thought excited her.

TWELVE

Today felt unlucky—really unlucky. Mary was up to her eyeballs in unfinished projects. She hadn't been able to check in at the movie theater at all; her laundry hamper was completely full; and she had run out of Jenaly Macintyre videos to post on her TikTok account. How did she get herself into this mess? The grand reopening party for the senior center was two days away, and she still had a million things to do. But instead of being able to work on them, she was stuck in traffic on the way home from IKEA. Normally the trek took two and a half hours, but work traffic in Olympia had doubled the journey time. Then, when she'd gotten to Elma, a logging truck with a flat tire had clogged the state highway. It was dark now, and Mary still had forty-five minutes to go before she reached Sand Dollar Cove.

She checked the clock. Shoot, she wouldn't be able to pick Cheryl up from the senior center in time before closing. Mary used Bluetooth to call Hannah.

"Hey sis, what's up?"

"Traffic nightmares, that's what." Mary flicked on the windshield wipers to swish away raindrops. "Can you pick up Gran?"

"Sure. But I thought the plan was for her to stay there and keep you company while you built the new bookcases."

"That was the plan, but now I won't be able to get there by pickup time to meet her. You know how persnickety Keith gets when members don't leave on time."

"Did you say 'persnickety?' Where did that come from?"

"I don't know," Mary said. But then she realized she did know. Steven had used that word yesterday when they were picking out tile for the bathroom and he said touchless faucets were fine, but motion-sensor soap dispensers were too persnickety, and he'd rather have manual ones. He frequently used colorful words like that.

Colorful, like the purple shirt he'd worn. It fit him well, too. Especially the way it hugged his shoulder line. Mary had wanted to hug his shoulder line. She'd thought about it when their arms brushed against each other standing at the sink display. For a moment there, they'd stood so close together, at first by accident, and then as the moments stretched from one to another like pearls on a string, it hadn't been an accident after all. It had been on purpose. Just like Mary wanted to hug Steven on purpose, and perhaps slide her hands along that broad shoulder line of his and...

"So what do you think?" Hannah asked. "About dinner?"

"What?" Mary jerked her attention from her wandering imagination back to the car in front of her, and then to her sister's voice coming out of the stereo system. "Could you repeat the question? The windshield wipers are noisy."

"Guy wants to take us out to dinner at the T Bone Bluff next week," said Hannah. "Gran, too."

"I'd never say no to a free steak dinner."

"Don't say yes until you hear the rest of it."

"What don't I want to know?" Mary asked, confused by the edge she heard in Hannah's voice.

"I want to invite Mom."

"What?"

"Guy's learned his lesson about not interfering, but I'm wondering if he was right after all. Maybe our lives would be easier if we could iron things out with Mom."

"There is no 'ironing things out,'" said Mary. "We're not talking about a misunderstanding, we're talking about abandonment. You know that."

"Abandonment, and all the years of her being a horrible caregiver. Squandering money. Losing the house. So much garbage."

"We were stuck with her, with nobody to see how much we suffered," Mary added. "I'm glad that I was too little to remember most of it."

"I'll never forget the car crash."

"I can barely picture it."

"Be glad for that," said Hannah. "I live with the memory every day and I want to tell Mom, to her face, how much that's scarred me."

"I don't feel any need for a confrontation like that. But I *do* want to know why she made such awful choices." *So I don't repeat history and make them too,* she thought to herself.

"I don't know why Mom did what she did," Hannah said. "But she was a grieving young widow. That must have been part of it."

"That's still no excuse."

"You're right."

Mary tightened her grip on the steering wheel. "Do you really want to have dinner with Mom?"

"I think so. I know that Guy had no business butting in, but his heart was in the right place, helping steer Mom through rehab. And maybe he was right. Our life will be easier in the future if Mom is stable."

"Maybe," Mary said doubtfully. "When do I have to let you know by?"

"Why don't you think about it, and we'll decide later? I want you to concentrate on the road. It's really starting to rain hard now."

"You're right. Love you," Mary said. The sisters hung up.

Mary drove for ten more minutes before she pulled into a gas station to stretch her legs and fill up the tank. While she was waiting by the pump, a text came in from Brittany.

Amazon delivered three giant boxes to the house this evening with your name on them from the blinds store. Were these meant for the senior center?

Yes, Mary replied. *Sorry. I was going to put them up tonight with the new curtains I bought.*

She had been hoping to install them right after she'd assembled the bookcases. But now it didn't seem like she'd have enough time to get everything done unless she worked all night.

I'll get the boxes out of the way by tomorrow, Mary promised.

No problem, Brittany replied. *I just wanted you to know they were here. I'll leave them in the entryway.*

Mary finished pumping gas and climbed in the car. There was barely room to sit down because the bookshelves took up space all the way from the trunk, across the folded-down back seat, and into the passenger side. Wedged into whatever crevice she could find were other purchases like the curtains, throw pillows, flowerpots, and baskets.

After clicking her seatbelt and turning up the radio, Mary drove away.

She reached the senior center after it had closed. Thankfully, Keith had given her a spare key to use for the renovation. Mary backed her car up to the door to the kitchen and went inside to find the dolly. Would she be strong enough to move the bookcases from her car, up the ramp, and into the building? She certainly hoped so.

Being careful to move one flat pack at a time, lifting with her legs and not her back, Mary loaded the dolly and began her slow ascent up the ramp. Rain drenched the cardboard boxes and poured down Mary's raincoat in rivulets. It took her two trips to move the furniture, and another three to carry in the bags of decor.

By the time all her IKEA purchases were safely in the senior center, Mary was exhausted—and famished. She was so hungry that she thought about scrounging some food from the refrigerator, but she didn't because she knew that Brittany carefully planned nutritious meals on a limited budget for all of the members. For the bargain price of $200 a month, seniors like Gran ate three square meals a day, five days a week. More affluent seniors paid four times as much to supplement the ones who needed extra help. Mary and Hannah had actually been talking about transitioning Cheryl off the food assistance program, but Cheryl didn't want to. Her social security payment was meager enough that she qualified for it, and after working fifty years on her feet, she felt like she had earned the benefit. That made sense to Mary.

So instead of stealing a chicken salad sandwich, she ate the chocolate bars she'd bought at IKEA that she had meant to save for later.

She was about to put her phone away when it chimed with a TikTok notification. She tapped the app and pulled up her Jenaly Macintyre account. Over the course of one week, she'd grown it to 642 followers. The first couple of videos had gotten over a thousand views. But now she was stuck in the two hundreds and didn't know how to fix it. She had also run out of content to post and didn't have time to film anything new. When she did have time, she wanted to film the dance to a trending sound instead of the ones she'd been using.

Mary clicked on the TikTok notification and saw that it was Zeke commenting on her post. She hearted the comment because she felt like she had to, but her stomach turned doing it. Just like it had three years ago, when he'd coerced her into taking her clothes off.

Try the scene again, Zeke had said. *Only this time take your panties off, too.* Mary had looked around at the cast and crew, her eyes silently begging for someone to protest. If just one person had stood up for her and told Zeke that was a bad idea, maybe he would have changed his mind. But the extras playing football players had salivated. The lighting director had cued the spotlight directly on her. The prop guy stood by with his spray bottle of blood.

Nobody had stood up for Mary, not even herself.

Mary shivered and focused her attention on the present. She couldn't go back and change the past, but she was trying to change her life for the better. And right now, a giant mound of IKEA furniture waited for her to torture herself with, using just a teeny-tiny Allen wrench.

She worked all night. By two a.m. she was so bleary-eyed that she could barely read the instructions. Luckily, she didn't need to. By then she was a bookshelf-building pro. Even the support shelf couldn't flummox her. Once the shelves were built, she shoved them carefully against the freshly painted walls, and used her toolbox to anchor the support straps to studs, so the shelves wouldn't fall over.

She didn't have the energy to unload boxes of books and board games from the storage room that were destined for the shelves. The bag of decor items she'd bought at IKEA sat abandoned too. All Mary could do was drag herself to her car when she finally reached a stopping point. She rolled into the driveway at four forty-five a.m., right when Aidan was leaving for his shift at the hospital. He looked at her curiously over the steering wheel of his Beemer. Mary waved like nothing was amiss. As far as he knew, she was coming home from a date.

Mary parked in her spot in the driveway and unlocked the front door. The porchlight beamed, but it wasn't enough illumination to prevent her from tripping over a gigantic stack of boxes in the entryway. Keeling over, she landed hard on the ground, but thankfully didn't break anything. In the faint glow of the darkened room, she could barely make out the shape of the boxes: her blinds.

"Is somebody there?" called a voice from the living room.

Shoot. Now she'd roused Cheryl. Mary picked herself up and went to greet her grandma.

"It's me, Gran," Mary said, entering the cozy living room. "Sorry to wake you."

"You didn't wake me. I woke up a while ago to go to the bathroom for the third time, and then couldn't get back to sleep so I came out here."

Mary tucked the blanket around her grandma. "Are you warm enough? The thermostat doesn't kick in until five."

"I'm fine. But what are you doing coming home in the wee hours like this? Hot date? Maybe I don't want to know."

"I was building bookshelves at the senior center," Mary explained. "I haven't been on a hot date in ages." *Not true,* her conscience whispered. Lunch with Steven on Monday was pretty spectacular. She pushed the thought aside.

"How's it coming?" Cheryl asked. "It looked like there's still a bunch of work to do."

"There is." Mary sank into the sofa. "And the party is tomorrow night. I don't know how I'll get it all done before then."

"What's there still to do?"

"Cosmetic stuff, mainly. I need to install the curtains, load the bookshelves, rearrange the furniture in the lounge area, and frame the hand-painted mural that everyone will sign."

"Plus sleep." Cheryl wagged her finger. "You may be twenty-three, but that doesn't mean pulling an all-nighter is good for you."

An all-nighter? The thermostat cranked on, signaling that it was five a.m. Apparently that was exactly what she'd done.

Mary yawned. "At least the party planning's taken care of. Keith is in charge of games, Brittany's arranging the food, and Jose volunteered to be DJ."

"Who's Jose?" Cheryl asked.

"The painter. You met him that day he touched up on the edge work." Mary had never managed to find out if he was single or not, but her curiosity on that topic had faded. "Steven said he'd bring his pet ball python to let people hold," Mary added. "That'll be a party activity too."

"Petting his snake?" Cheryl snickered.

"His name is Elvis."

"You've named it, I see."

"Gran!" Mary tossed a throw pillow at her. "Get your mind out of the gutter." Then she got off the couch and picked the pillow up so her grandmother, who was unsteady on her feet, wouldn't trip.

"I'd never say no to petting Elvis," Cheryl said, with a laugh.

"I'm heading to bed."

"You've earned it."

"Thanks."

Mary climbed the stairs, brushed her teeth, and crashed into bed. Hannah's side of the room was empty.

She woke up four hours later. A hot shower helped rouse her, and by the time she headed downstairs for a late breakfast, she was half human. When she brewed fresh coffee, it dawned on her that it was well past nine. Cheryl liked to arrive at the senior center by eight a.m. so she'd be there in time for chair aerobics. Could Mary do nothing right? She squeezed her eyes shut and pressed her face into her hands, wanting to cry. She didn't have the chops for this, running her own business and taking care of someone at the same time. Hell, she couldn't even take care of herself. No wonder she was so screwed up.

Just like her mother.

Kelly hadn't been able to work and take care of people either. Even to this day, Kelly was barely able to provide for her own needs, weaseling gas money out of her daughters, and still battling demons.

Was Mary like that too? Would she be like that in the future?

Taking a deep breath, Mary decided to give herself some grace. She was *not* like her mother. Not yet, anyway. She might not be as responsible or accomplished as Hannah, but she had her vision boards, and her portfolio of design projects. She had fresh coffee waiting to turbocharge her with energy. Mary wasn't the same person as she was a month ago when she camped out in her room, wallowing in grief. She was an in-demand interior designer who was cruising toward the finish line of her latest project. *Right?* she asked herself. *Maybe...*

Mary poured her coffee into a travel mug and headed out of the kitchen. "Gran," she called. "I'm sorry I overslept."

The living room was empty and so was Cheryl's room. In fact, the whole house was empty. Mary rushed to get her phone to see if there was a message. Sure enough, Cheryl had texted her.

Caught a ride with Brittany. Don't work too hard,
Sleeping Beauty.

I'm awake now, Mary texted back. *I'll be at the senior center soon.*

First, she needed to post another TikTok video. She found a trending sound, filmed herself hacking into an apple with a butcher knife, added a picture of her from her gallery in full Zombie regalia, and overlaid the images with text: *I'm not your prom queen—I'm your nightmare.*

She had just clicked post when her phone rang.

"Hello?" Mary said as she dragged herself up the stairs to her bathroom so she could finish getting ready.

"Hello, my favorite client, this is Jose."

"Hi, Jose."

"I'm sorry to do this to you, but I won't able to help with the party tomorrow night after all."

"What?"

"The music."

"Oh." This wasn't good. "Did something come up?"

"It did. My girlfriend works at the Squamish Clearwater Resort and Casino and she scored tickets to a concert there tomorrow night. We leave in a few hours."

"That's great," Mary said. *That's awful.* How could he flake on his DJ duties? But still, Jose was a professional contact she needed to maintain for future jobs. "Well, thanks for all your hard work on the senior center. Your team did an amazing job. I'll see you in around at the movie theater."

"Thanks for helping me get that job."

"You're welcome. Bye."

After Mary had hung up, she shouted down the empty hallway, "Can't I get a break around here? Everything's going lousy!" Yelling at the universe didn't help matters, but it felt good. She was about to enter her bathroom to fix her hair when Jeremy's door burst open, and he stood in his pajamas holding a baseball bat. "What's the matter?" he shouted.

"What?" she screamed.

"You screamed!"

"I didn't scream!" Or had she? Whoops, maybe she had. "Sorry," Mary said, lowering her voice. "I was just frustrated that the DJ canceled on my party."

"Oh." Jeremy lowered the bat. "I thought you were in danger."

"What are you doing home from school?"

"I overslept."

"You're welcome for waking you, then."

"I could DJ your party."

"What?"

"It's for the senior center, right?"

Mary nodded. "That's right."

"I could find a Spotify list that old people love."

"Really?" Mary felt instantly lighter. "That would be great. Thanks."

"I'd need a favor in return, though."

"Oh you would, would you?" Mary laughed. "What's up?"

"Would you talk to my mom about college?"

"What about it? I thought the plan was for you to live at home and attend Grays Harbor State?"

"That's still the plan, kind of... but I want to start out in Seattle and live with my dad for a year."

"What?" As far as Mary knew Jeremy didn't get along with his dad at all. According to Brittany, Ian was an egotistical jerk who only cared about himself.

"I mean, I *don't* want to live with my dad, but I want to live in the city."

Mary could understand that. She'd felt the siren's call of city living herself in the past. "Sure," she said. "I'll talk to your mom about it."

"Thanks."

Mary thought the conversation was over until a thought

flashed in her mind that she couldn't shut out. "What's Kenzie doing next year?" she asked.

The tips of Jeremy's ears turned red. "She's, uh... going to the University of Washington. Kenzie's super smart. Way smarter than me. She hasn't heard if she's gotten in yet, but I'm sure she will. The Paul Allen School of Computer Science is really competitive, but I bet they'll accept her. It's been really hard for her to wait and find out, though."

"I see." She did see, too. This explained Jeremy's sudden quest for Seattle. But there was something about the way he said glowing things about Kenzie's accomplishments and dismissed his own that bothered her. It both bothered her and felt familiar. "You're smart too," she said. "There are lots of different ways to be smart."

"That's what adults say to stupid people."

"No, I mean it. Sometimes it takes people longer to figure out what they want to do with their lives, and that's okay."

"Oh, I know what I want to do with my life."

"You do?"

"I want to be a firefighter. But it's really competitive too, so first I'll take classes to be an emergency medical technician at the community college near my dad's house. After I work as an EMT for a while, if I get accepted to the fire training program, great. If not, I'll come finish my degree at Grays Harbor State and then apply again. That's my plan."

"That's a great plan." Mary nodded. "Well done."

"I looked it all up online and then also spoke to my school counselor about it."

"You've done your homework."

"I have, except I haven't told my mom yet. So will you do it?"

"Wait a second, I though you only wanted me to tell Brittany about you moving to Seattle."

"That, and everything else. She's going to flip out and say it's dangerous. I know her."

"Give your mom some credit," said Mary "She might surprise you."

"Maybe." Jeremy yawned. "But I doubt it." He went back into his room.

Mary yawned too but didn't have the luxury of going back to sleep.

THIRTEEN

If sunshine and rainbows could be bottled into an emotion, that's what Mary felt as she looked out across the room. The senior center glowed like a pot of gold. Fresh paint had replaced peeling wallpaper. Cheery curtains framed the windows. Matching bookshelves stocked with books and board games lined the wall where a haphazard collection of shelving units had once stood. The old piano had been tuned. Now, when you walked into the senior center, it felt like entering a cool living room designed for important people instead of a grim emergency weather shelter.

"Well done, sis." Hannah threw her arm around Mary. "I can't believe how fabulous this place looks."

"Thanks," said Mary. Hearing her sister's praise felt good. "It's been a mad dash at the end here, and I'm not quite all the way done even though the party starts in an hour." She jammed the bottom of the balloon arch into its stand. "Thanks for coming early so you could help."

"My pleasure. I can't believe you're doing this in high heels and that dress. I brought clothes to change into later."

Mary tied on another balloon to the arch. "I was afraid I

wouldn't have time to change, and since the party is semiformal, I didn't want to show up in leggings and a sweatshirt at the last minute."

"Makes sense." Hannah picked up a balloon, puffed out her cheeks, and started blowing.

"Step aside," said Brittany, wearing a satin skirt and ballet-neck top. "Coming through." She held an enormous platter of sandwiches. Keith was right behind her with a tray of deviled eggs.

"I guess semiformal to Keith means chinos and a polo shirt," Mary whispered. Did people not understand the dress code? This was supposed to be a flashy gala, not bingo night.

"Need help?" Guy asked, looking especially dapper in a suit. He held Hannah's dry-cleaning bag over his arm.

"Yes," said Mary. "The sign still needs to be hung out front."

"And my car's loaded with food," Brittany called as she came back from the kitchen.

"Thanks so much for catering," Mary told Brittany. "And Jeremy's handling the music. Where is he?"

"He's driving separately," said Brittany. "I had to put the seats down in my car to hold all the food."

"I don't know how you blew up all these balloons on your own." Hannah gasped. "I've only done five and I'm out of breath."

"We can't stop now, though." Mary secured another balloon. "This is for the picture station. I have a trunk full of funny hats, boas, and glasses people can wear, too."

"Nothing like waiting until the last minute," Keith muttered as he walked past them with another tray of food. "Why didn't it occur to you to buy a balloon pump?"

"I was watching the budget," said Mary, feeling indignant. "And I didn't wait until the last minute. The balloons need to be done last or they'll deflate. I learned that in my test run."

"Yeah," said Hannah. "Everyone knows that." As soon as

Keith was out of earshot she whispered: "He and Brittany got in another fight right before we left. I think they're on the verge of a breakup."

"Oh no." Mary frowned. "That'll make their work situation difficult."

Hannah winced and nodded.

"Did you guys see Brittany made five different types of hummus?" Guy said, as he carried in another platter.

"I thought the blender sound would never stop," Keith muttered, as he followed with more food. "The roasted peppers almost blinded me."

Mary shot Hannah a look. "Hopefully the breakup happens soon," she said, once Keith was in the kitchen.

"Agreed." Hannah accidentally let go of a balloon and it squeaked out air as it fell to the ground.

"Where's Gran?" Mary asked, suddenly realizing that the most important person wasn't there. The senior center was Cheryl's special place, after all.

"Her friend Patti's bringing her." Hannah picked up the fallen balloon. After pinching the end, she finished explaining. "They wanted to get ready for the party together like it was prom."

"How cute." Mary clapped her hands together, getting excited. "That's exactly what I was hoping for with this party."

The next thirty minutes were a whir of activity. Mary and Hannah blew up so many balloons that they were both out of breath. Brittany set up the food display, Guy and Keith hung up the sign, and Jeremy and Kenzie arrived at the last minute to get the music going.

"What's the WiFi password?" Jeremy asked. "I need to sync my phone to the speakers."

"ForeverSexy," said Keith. "No space."

"I didn't want to know that." Jeremy fake-barfed.

"You literally asked me for the password," said Keith.

"Yeah, but..." Jeremy shook his head. "Who chooses a password like that?"

"It used to be ForeverYoung," said a voice at the front door, "but we voted to spice things up a bit."

Everyone turned and saw Cheryl carefully pushing her walker, wearing a sequined dress that sparkled. Behind her stood Patti, wearing a glittery pantsuit.

"You look amazing, Gran," Mary exclaimed. She'd never seen her grandmother look so fancy. "So do you, Patti, and Kenzie."

"Thanks." Kenzie twirled around and her pink skirt flared out. "This is what I would have worn to winter formal if someone had asked me." She looked sideways at Jeremy, but he was too busy staring at his phone to notice.

"You look gorgeous," said Mary. "Maybe you could wear it to prom." She made a mental note to give Jeremy a kick later, so he and Kenzie weren't stuck in the friend zone forever.

"I think I got it." Jeremy tapped his phone and looked up at a speaker in the corner. The opening bars of Chubby Checker's version of "The Twist" came on.

"Let's get this party started!" Cheryl wiggled her walker a bit, and shuffle-stepped forward.

"Nice choice with the music," said Brittany.

"You don't have to act so surprised," said Jeremy, sounding insulted.

"I'm not surprised," said Brittany. "I was—"

"It was your tone," said Jeremy.

"I was complimenting you!" his mother protested.

"Forget it." Jeremy turned away.

Brittany flashed a pained look at Mary. "What did I do wrong?"

Mary shrugged. "I don't know, but great job with the food. I really appreciate it."

A steady stream of guests arrived after that, and everyone

oohed and aahed over the results of Mary's handiwork. As the comments washed over her one by one, Mary felt proud of all she'd accomplished.

"This looks beautiful!"

"I feel like I'm in the lobby of a cozy hotel."

"I didn't think you'd ever get the scent of roller skates out of here, but all I smell now is paint."

Most of the comments were from strangers, or acquaintances. But the ones from Cheryl's personal friends meant the most to Mary.

"Thank you for doing this for us," said Patti, who was more like an honorary aunt than friend. She squeezed Mary's arm. "I've been feeling down ever since my husband entered a care facility after his memory deteriorated, but this is a huge pick-me-up. I've always loved coming to the senior center, and now it's even better. I feel we belong to an exclusive club."

"You *do* belong to an exclusive club." Mary swept a lock of hair off her forehead. "This place is so picky about members that Keith won't let me join."

Patti laughed. "Wait forty years and then I'll sponsor you."

"She'd only be sixty-three," said Cheryl as she joined their conversation. "Still too young by five years."

"Hey, dollface," said a deep voice. Everyone turned to look. A tall man wearing a tweed suit and bow tie grinned at Patti.

"Hi, Don." Patti blushed.

"Did you save me a dance?" he asked.

"Are people dancing?" Patti glanced around.

Don winked. "They will be once I spin a woman as beautiful as you around the floor."

"I haven't in years," Patti protested. "I don't know if I—"

"Absolutely you should," said Cheryl. "Show 'em how it's done."

It was just the encouragement Patti needed.

Mary smiled as she watched Patti take Don's arm and glide

across the room. Mary had hoped that people would dance. She'd arranged the tables so there would be room. Still, she knew that it might have been difficult for her grandma to watch, especially since dancing was something she could no longer do. Mary pulled out a chair. "Here, Gran. Let's sit down. I've been on my feet all day."

"Well, then, you should definitely take a load off." Gran held onto her walker as she carefully sank into the chair. "Oof! That's better," she said. "Sitting was a wise idea."

Mary sat down next to her and was relieved to take the pressure off her feet. Her little black dress and shiny black heels might have looked elegant, but they weren't comfortable.

"Don calls everyone dollface," Cheryl said bitterly. "He's such a player. I want Patti to have some fun, but I hope she doesn't get her heart broken."

"At least they got the dance party started." It had only been a couple of minutes, but a dozen or more seniors had joined Patti and Don on the floor.

"Don't give Don credit for that." Cheryl snorted. "Jeremy's doing such a good job with the music that it's impossible to keep your feet still."

Mary looked down and saw Cheryl's toes tapping.

"Snake!" someone cried. Or that's what Mary thought she heard. It had become so crowded that it was hard to hear distinctly. But when she turned in the direction of the voice, she saw Kenzie and three seniors crowding around Steven, who wore an oversized black silk shirt with tuxedo pants and sneakers. Steven was showing off Elvis, who was coiled around his arm.

Not hot at all, Mary thought, feeling confused. Why had she been thinking about him all week? This man didn't even wear clothes that fit. And since when did sneakers count as semiformal? But then Steven turned slightly, and she saw his smile, and her heart went pitter-patter like she was thirteen years old again and drooling over a boy band poster.

She wanted to trot over and stand by his side. What would it be like to scrape her thumb along the hard edge of his jawline, tangle her fingers in his hair, and kiss him?

Mary sighed, but then snapped out of dreamland when she saw her mother enter the room. *Kelly was here?* What the hell? Who had invited *her?* Kelly stood in the corner wearing skinny jeans and a jean jacket, looking like a much older—and wizened —version of Mary. Kelly's straw-colored hair was flat-ironed straight, and she held tight to her purse like she was worried someone would steal it.

"Oh, boy," Cheryl muttered. "This party's becoming more complicated than I'd expected."

"Where's Hannah?" Mary asked as she scanned the room. "Did Hannah do this?" She spotted her sister holding Guy's hand as they walked over to Kelly.

"Let's sit here and let them come to us," Cheryl suggested. "Less walking that way."

"Works for me." Mary felt every muscle in her body tense with irritation. This was supposed to be her big night, not a family dramafest. "I bet Hannah's behind this," she groaned. "Guy put ideas into her head about reconciliation, and now Hannah's acting delusional and thinks it's actually possible."

"She invited you to the T Bone Bluff, too?"

Mary nodded. "Like a steak dinner could fix anything."

"It couldn't, but I don't begrudge your sister for hoping for second chances. Or third chances."

"Or fourth chances." Mary folded her arms. She was unsure of how many times her mother had screwed her over.

"As it turns out, I learned that Guy didn't actually pay for your mom to go to rehab. I asked him point-blank, and he said no. He said that he had made the arrangements for her admittance, but that she used her portion of your father's life insurance settlement to pay for it. Guy had wanted to pay, but he honored Hannah's wishes of never giving Kelly money. He did write a check for the first month's rent on her apartment, though. He paid the property management company directly."

"That's good," said Mary. "I hope that Mom doesn't view Guy as just deep pockets."

The previous year a long-delayed insurance settlement over Max's death had issued in a four-way split. Mary had used her share, which was $50,000, to pay off her car, and set up a retirement account. It was a significant amount of money, but not life-changing, unless the index funds did extraordinarily well.

Mary sighed. "However Mom afforded it, I'm glad she got help. I hope her sobriety sticks this time." She was beginning to feel guilty that Hannah was able to deal with Kelly while she was too chicken to say hello.

"It appears they still haven't seen us." Chery scooted her chair closer. "Which means I can tell you all about my friend Ann and her grandson who looks like Colin Firth."

"Is Colin your friend with the bad toupee?"

"What? No! How can you not know—"

"Wait." Mary stood, guilt overwhelming her. "Sorry. I didn't mean to interrupt. But I should go join Hannah and at least say hello to Mom."

"Good idea." Cheryl held up her thumb. "Get it over with quickly, like ripping off a Band-Aid."

Mary's eyes drifted over to the circle of women standing around Steven admiring his pet python. She wanted to be in that circle of Elvis groupies too, not sucking it up and having an awkward conversation with her mother. But she should probably follow Hannah's lead. "You can stay here," said Mary. "I'll come back when I can."

"Sitting is one of the things I do best," said Cheryl.

Mary straightened her shoulders and walked forward confidently, with nary a wobble in her high-heeled shoes. When she passed Steven she smiled at him, wishing again that she could join him, but she headed straight for her mom and sister. Mary was glad she'd chosen her tallest pair of heels because it put her eye level with Kelly. "Hi, Mom," she said. "I didn't know you were coming tonight."

"Hannah called and said I should be here." Kelly shifted her weight from one foot to the other. "I almost don't recognize this place. Nobody would know that it used to be a roller rink."

"And now it looks amazing, thanks to Mary's talent and hard work." Hannah patted Mary's back. "I'm glad you got the chance to see how gifted she is."

Mary glanced sideways at her sister, but didn't say anything.

"I like the colors you chose, Mary." Kelly looked at the sunny yellow walls. "You always loved yellow crayons. Coloring kept you busy for hours."

Crayons... Thinking of the waxy scent of Crayolas triggered a memory. *Mary sitting on a hard plastic chair, her feet dangling, filling the black lines of a coloring book while Kelly sat in the corner.* Mary tried to place where the memory came from, but she couldn't.

"Yeah, Mary sure loved crayons," said Hannah. "Gran would buy her a fresh box with a built-in sharpener every Christmas."

Those memories were easier for Mary to picture. "Nothing beats a freshly sharpened crayon," she said. "Oh look, Gran's coming over now."

"Well, look who's here." Cheryl leaned heavily on her walker. "Glad you could make it, Kelly."

"Thanks." Kelly stuffed her hands in her back pockets and then pulled them out again. "Maybe I shouldn't have come. I don't want to keep Mary from her guests."

"They're not Mary's guests," Cheryl protested. "Most of these people are members. All of Mary's hard work is done, and we couldn't be prouder. Didn't she do a bang-up job?"

"She did." Kelly nodded.

Cheryl looked at Mary. "But speaking of members, I was just about to tell Mary about my friend Ann."

"Ann who drives the Avalon that you said to never park next to because she's had so many fender benders?" Hannah asked.

"Or Ann who carries her teacup poodle in her purse?" Mary asked. Both women were legends as far as Mary was concerned.

"Avalon Ann," Cheryl clarified. "Her car is easy to spot right now because it's missing the front bumper. Anyhow, we were talking, and it turns out that she has a grandson your age. He's not here tonight but she can show you pictures on her phone."

"I don't know if that's—" Mary started to say.

"I told you he looks like Colin Firth, right?"

"Who's Colin Firth?" Mary asked. "Is he here tonight?"

Kelly laughed. "She means the movie star."

"*Bridget Jones's Diary*?" Cheryl asked. "*The King's Speech*?"

"Never heard of them." Mary shook her head.

"*Pride and Prejudice*?" Kelly asked. "Even I've seen that."

"Oh!" Hannah brightened. "Did he play the annoying cousin?"

Kelly sighed. "No, he was Mr. Darcy."

"Back to Ann's grandson," said Gran. "I already asked, and yes, he's single. Don't worry, Mary, I gave Ann your phone number to pass along."

"Gran!" Mary exclaimed in horror. "Why would you do that?"

Cheryl raised her eyebrows. "Did I or did I not just tell you he looks like a young Colin Firth?"

"I don't care who he looks like. Please don't give my number to random strangers."

"He's not random. He's Ann's grandson." Cheryl pointed across the room. "That Ann, over there. The one talking to Mr. Man Bun holding a snake."

"Holding a snake?" Hannah whipped her head around. "Is Steven here? I want to meet him."

"Who's Steven?" Kelly asked. "Should I know who that is?"

"He's the owner of the movie theater I'm redesigning," said Mary, not wanting Kelly to know about him at all. Nor was she too wild about the idea of Hannah, Cheryl, and Guy meeting Steven. They'd either love him or hate him, and Mary wasn't sure how she'd feel about them hating him. *What if they think he's eccentric, or geeky, or both?* Those were all thoughts she'd harbored when she'd first met him, but now... Mary looked at him longingly. Now she just wanted to put the senior center project behind her and explore—with extreme caution—all things Steven-related. Or movie theater-related. That's what she meant, of course. But she'd be careful about it. No way would she let her heart get hurt again.

"Steven must love beer a whole bunch." Kelly eyed Steven up and down like she was grading meat.

"Why would you say that?" Guy asked.

"Yeah, why?" Mary asked sharply.

Kelly looked at them like they were clueless. "Because his shirt has the Sierra Nevada label on it. I'm a bartender. I'd recognize it a mile away."

Mary turned so she could see Steven again and saw that sure enough, underneath his billowing black shirt was a tight-fitting T-shirt with the craft beer logo. *Not semiformal wear at all,* she thought with annoyance. But she also found it adorable how he stooped his shoulders and crouched down a bit so that the elderly lady standing next to him could pet Elvis.

"What type of drink do I look like I'd order?" Cheryl asked Kelly.

Mary was curious what her mom would say. She knew her

grandma had never kept hard alcohol in the house because it was too expensive.

"I don't need to guess, I remember," said Kelly. "A Lemon Drop with sugar on the rim." She looked at her daughters. "And we used to order a Shirley Temple with extra cherries for Hannah, and a sippy cup of apple juice for Mary, when your father would take us out to a fancy dinner at the T Bone Bluff."

Mary had no recollection of that, and it pained her to dwell on that fact. She'd only been two when her father had died. It irked her that Kelly could remember happy memories of that time, and she couldn't. But she did remember what happened after Max's death. She thought about Kelly every time she smelled rum. Mary was about to say something she probably would have regretted later, something about her mother's affinity for rum and Coke and how it had almost killed them, when Steven showed up.

"Here's a crowd who hasn't met Elvis yet," he said as he held up his arm. The tiny yellow python emerged from his sleeve and flicked his tongue.

Steven's presence standing beside her immediately calmed Mary down, like he'd defused a bomb that was ready to explode. "Hi, Steven," she said, stepping an inch closer to him. She turned and looked at her family. "This is Steven." Then she looked back at his arm and gently stroked the snake. "And Elvis."

"Hi," said Guy. "I've heard so much about Elvis I feel like I've already met him. Is it okay to feel his skin?"

"By all means." Steven extended his arm. "You can hold him if you want, if you promise you won't drop him."

"Guy won't drop him," Hannah said. "I've seen him carry live rats to safety."

"I usually carry rats to their doom," Steven said, as he carefully transferred Elvis over to Guy. "But snakes need to eat, too."

Hannah elbowed Mary in the ribs. "Aren't you going to introduce us?"

"Sorry," said Mary. "I didn't mean to be rude. "Steven, this is my sister, Hannah; my mom, Kelly; Hannah's boyfriend, Guy; and my grandma, Cheryl."

"Nice to meet all of you." Steven waved. "Hannah, you and Mary sure do look like your mom."

"I'll take that as a compliment since both my daughters are knockouts," said Kelly.

"I agree with you there," Steven said, with a smile for Mary that made her blush.

"Well, Guy, aren't you going to say something?" Cheryl asked after Guy didn't comment.

Guy flicked his head up. "What, did I miss something? Sorry, I was so focused on Elvis that I wasn't paying attention. His tongue tickles."

"He's a charmer, all right," said Steven.

"Don't look now," said Hannah. "But here comes Ann-who-drives-the-Avalon holding her phone."

"Let her take a selfie with you, Mary, so she can send it to her grandson." Cheryl held out her thumb. "Here, lick my thumb. I can wipe away that smudge of mascara that's under your eye."

"Gross! Put your thumb away." Mary dabbed at her face to clear the gunk. "Did I get it?"

"I don't know." Cheryl licked her thumb. "Bend down closer and I'll check."

"Gran!" Mary stepped away from Cheryl and closer to Steven. She turned her face toward him. "Well?" she asked.

"There's a little something right there." He pointed to her cheekbone, and she was able to wipe it away. "You got it. What's this about a grandson?"

"Nothing," Mary said, with a note of exasperation. "Gran thinks she's a matchmaker, that's all."

"Quick." Hannah gave Mary a little shove. "You and Steven go get some food while Guy takes care of Elvis and I stop Gran from setting you up with every eligible grandson in the building."

"Thanks." Mary flashed Hannah a look of gratitude. Then, without thinking, she grabbed Steven's hand and led him away. "We're going to have to snake through the crowd," she said, as they made their way across the dance floor. Van Morrison's "Brown Eyed Girl" was playing, and some seniors were busting out serious dance moves. "Of course, you know all about snakes, so snaking should be no problem."

"No problem at all," said Steven as he followed. "Wanna dance?"

"What?" Mary wasn't sure she'd heard him right. She really needed to ask Jeremy to turn down the music since so many of the guests wore hearing aids.

"I said, do you want to dance?" Steven asked, leaning closer so that his lips were inches from her ear.

Mary, who loved to dance, didn't wait a beat. "Sure," she said. Dancing wasn't rushing into things, was it? She hoped not.

Steven slid his arm behind her back and pulled her close, rocking back and forth from one foot to the other like the seniors were doing. Then he pushed her away from him and spun her around. Mary squealed with delight and was back in his arms seconds later. "You're a good dancer," he said, as he navigated them around the floor.

"No, it's all you. Where'd you learn to dance like this?"

"My Aunt Helena gave me lessons before prom. And then when I got to prom nobody was dancing like this and I had to improvise." Steven spun her around again three times in a row, making it difficult to talk.

"Well, you sure know what you're doing now," Mary said, when she was back in his arms. "You've got all the right moves."

"Even in my beer shirt and tuxedo pants?"

"I was wondering about that. I thought maybe you didn't understand what semiformal meant."

"I tried on my suits, and they didn't fit."

"Oh."

"And this was the best I could do. Black T-shirt. Black button-down."

"You look great to me," Mary said, meaning it. She was about to say more when the music stopped abruptly.

"What the hell?" Jeremy exclaimed. "The WiFi cut out."

"ForeverSexy!" Don yelled.

A bunch of partygoers joined in and soon the entire room was chanting, "ForeverSexy! ForeverSexy!"

Steven leaned down so Mary could hear him over the noise. "This is a lot closer to how I thought my senior prom would be than it actually was."

"I can't work under this pressure!" Jeremy grabbed his phone and stormed out, with Kenzie chasing behind him.

"Jeremy!" Brittany called. "Wait!"

"There goes the music," Mary said, sighing. She stepped forward to the front of the dance. "Well, folks," she said in her loudest voice. "The party can still go on, but it looks like the music and dance portion of the evening has—"

A rumbling sound on the piano interrupted her. The opening notes to a familiar song caught everyone's attention. Mary turned to see who had brought the old keyboard to life and saw Steven sprawled on the bench, pounding on the keys, singing words that Mary recognized but didn't know.

"Jerry Lee Lewis!" Patti cried.

"Great Balls of Fire!" Don shouted before pinching his fingers and letting out an ear-piercing whistle.

Steven came to life at the piano. He put his whole body into the performance, singing and running his fingers up and down the keyboard. Mary couldn't believe it. The crowd surged forward, forming a horseshoe around him, pressing

Mary into a mosh pit of people who smelled like Old Spice and Shalimar.

"He's fantastic," the gentleman standing next to her said.

"Is that the young man with the snake?" his wife asked.

Elvis! Where was Elvis? Mary looked across the room and saw Guy tending the ball python like it was a baby. Hannah sat next to Cheryl and Kelly and was speaking to a stranger Mary didn't recognize. She turned her attention back to Steven right as he transitioned into another song. He paused to take off his overshirt, revealing the tight T-shirt he had on underneath.

"Any requests?" Steven asked, a huge grin on his face.

"Elvis!" the lady next to Mary called. "Like your snake."

Steven lowered his voice an octave. "Yes, ma'am. The King it is."

When he launched into "Hound Dog" Mary knew she was a goner. Her plan to take things slowly with Steven was becoming more difficult. She had protected her heart in bubble wrap so that it could never be crushed again. Yet here she was, with her hands dancing in the air, and her eyes drinking in every inch of him.

Don't be stupid, she told herself. After everything she'd been through with Aidan and her mom, she couldn't afford to be wounded again. She shouldn't be taking chances, not with Steven and not with anyone.

But it didn't matter what crazy outfit Steven wore or how he did his hair, Mary wanted more of him. More of him listening to her. More of him sharing his story. More of his colorful words and creative ideas. It was like her bubble-wrapped heart had a mind of its own.

FOURTEEN

"Show us the concept pictures again," said Ann-who-drove-the-Avalon. She sat on one side of Mary, and Ann-with-the-poodle sat on the other, her fluffy pup sleeping in her lap. It was Tuesday, March 11th, and Mary had just arrived at the senior center with Cheryl. She meant it to be a quick drop-off, but the seniors had talked her into a cup of coffee.

"I want to see it again too," said Cheryl. "I love looking at your design work."

"Okay, but I really need to get going after this." Mary flipped through her binder. "I'm supposed to meet Steven in twenty minutes. We're driving to Seattle to preview the order for the neon movie theater sign we've designed."

"And that's a two-person job?" Ann-who-drove-the-Avalon looked skeptical. Mary suspected that she still hadn't forgiven her for turning down a date with her grandson.

"It's a major investment, and I didn't feel comfortable signing off on it without Steven looking at it in person first," said Mary. "I wanted to visually inspect it, too, just in case the color was off."

"Still," said Cheryl with a twinkle in her eye. "That's a long way to drive together. I hope Steven knows that you'll need to stop at the restroom a gazillion times."

Mary pushed her half-empty mug of coffee away. "That's why I've been very careful with my liquid intake this morning." Pointing to her drawings, she brought the conversation back to the theater renovation. "My goal is to highlight 1960s Americana, which I've spent a lot of time researching, but I could still use some help on some things."

"What would you like to know?" Ann-with-the-poodle asked.

"Well, for starters..." Mary began.

"Hold on a sec." Cheryl raised her palm. "Patti and Don," she hollered. "Come on over here. Your advice is needed."

Soon the table was crowded with seniors, and Mary had all their attention.

"Hi, friends," she said, undeterred by giving an instant presentation. Mary loved the spotlight. "I'm helping to bring Sand Dollar Cove Cinema back in all its mid-century modern glory. There will be double features, inexpensive popcorn, and music played during the intermission. What I want to know is, what was your favorite part about going to the movies in the 1960s and 1970s?"

"Making out in the balcony," said Don.

"Dressing up," said Poodle Ann.

"Talking with friends at intermission," Patti offered.

"The carpet." Avalon Ann closed her eyes. "It was like red velvet. I can still feel how thick it was."

"The fact that it wasn't so gosh darn expensive," said Cheryl. "Back when I was in high school, you could see two movies, eat a bucket of popcorn and drink a couple of pops, and still have babysitting money left over."

"These are great details," Mary said, as she wrote them down on a scrap of paper.

"Balconies are tricky, though." Don scratched his chin.

Mary thought he was going to brag about his conquests, so what he said next surprised her. "I grew up in Seattle and thought they were a fun place to hang out away from prying eyes, if you know what I mean. But my late wife grew up in the South during segregation. She wasn't allowed to sit anywhere except the balcony due to the color of her skin. As soon as she told me that, I never thought the same way about balconies again, even though I have fond memories of them."

"Wow." Mary put her pencil down as she absorbed what he'd just said. "Thank you for telling me. I didn't know that."

"That's a good reminder," said Patti. "Be careful not to glorify the past too much, because a lot of it was crappy."

"Crappy's not a strong enough word for racism," Cheryl said. She looked at Don. "You almost never mention your late wife."

His eyes grew misty. "Doesn't mean I don't think of her every day."

"I used to love going to the movies with my husband," said Ann-who-drove-the-Avalon. "Except that he always got on my case when I ordered popcorn."

"He made comments about what you ate?" Mary was affronted. "That's not cool."

Ann swatted Mary's words away like they were houseflies. "No, no. He was right. Popcorn's bad for my digestion. Clogs me up like a cork."

"I hear you," said the other Ann.

This seems like a good time to leave. Mary looked at her watch. "Shoot, I gotta run or I'll be late. Thank you all for the help."

"Drive safe," Patti called after her.

Half an hour later, Mary sat in the passenger seat of Steven's minivan, relaying the conversation she'd had with the seniors.

"Maybe we should offer Pepto Bismol at the concessions stand," Steven joked.

Mary laughed. "Or prunes." She turned on the seat warmer since the March day was chilly. The drive from Sand Dollar Cove, through Olympia, Tacoma, and finally to Seattle, would take them two and a half hours. She was glad that Steven had offered to drive, although she had questions about his vehicle. "Why do you have a minivan?" she asked. "You're not a soccer mom in disguise, are you?"

"Don't soccer moms drive SUVs these days?" Steven looked at her and grinned. His hair was pulled back with an elastic and he wore jeans and an emerald fleece jacket that picked up the color in his hazel eyes.

"I wouldn't know. I never played soccer. I also learned the hard way never to get in the car with my mother. I have no idea what sort of car she drives now, not that she's the soccer mom type."

"Is she a bad driver?"

"I couldn't say."

"I get it. You don't want to judge."

"No, it's not that." Mary's heart twisted like a wrung-out rag. She hated telling people about Kelly and always avoided it if she could. Some people didn't care, which made her trauma feel unimportant. Other people—like Aidan's parents—viewed Kelly as a stain against Mary, like it was her fault her mother was such a mess. Usually when people asked, Mary said she'd been raised by her grandma and didn't know her mom very well, which was both true and untrue. But if she really liked someone, she told them the facts. Did she like Steven enough to tell him? *Yes,* her heart whispered. She did. Plus, this might be a way to ferret out red flags about him, depending on how he reacted. "My mom had trouble with drugs and alcohol," Mary said quietly. "When I was three years old, she almost killed my sister and me in a drunk driving crash."

"Oh Mary. That's awful. I didn't know."

Mary nodded. "I wasn't in a car seat. Hannah and I were buckled together in the passenger seat of Mom's Corvette. It was a miracle the airbag didn't kill us. That's what I've been told, anyway. I don't remember."

"What happened next?"

Mary shuddered. "We were in the hospital for a while. But I was so little I can't recall any of that."

Crayons... Mary remembered crayons. The waxy smell of Crayolas and the satisfaction of peeling the paper off to reveal the point. Bright lights and strangers with clipboards asking questions. Giving her one paper after another. Textured paper. Construction paper, maybe? And coloring books with clowns holding balloons and dancers riding elephants.

"Mary?" Steven asked tenderly. "Are you okay?"

"What?"

"There are napkins in the glove compartment. I'm sorry I don't have tissues."

Mary blinked her eyes into focus and tears splashed down. "Oh," she said, unaware that she'd been crying. "Sorry." She opened the glove box, grabbed a napkin, and wiped her eyes.

"You don't need to apologize. That's sounds traumatizing. Was your dad there to help?"

Mary blew her nose and shook her head. "He died the year before." Mary lifted her chin. "It was a car crash that killed him, here in Sand Dollar Cove. But before that he worked as a private contractor in Afghanistan building schools for girls."

"I'm sorry for your loss."

They were token words, but people rarely offered them because she never talked about her past. Mary didn't know what to say. "My mom lost custody, and Hannah and I moved in with our grandma. Gran did a great job raising us."

"Do you see your mom much now? That was her at the party last week, right?"

Mary nodded. "She showed up, but I didn't invite her. We don't have much of a relationship at all." Mary needed to change the subject fast, or her mascara would run. "But enough sidestepping the question."

"What question?"

"Why are you driving a minivan? I thought you were twenty-eight, not forty-five."

"I happen to like minivans." Steven tapped the steering wheel. "This baby is great for car trips, has room to move my snakes, and was a good car to have when I was a public defender."

"How so?" Mary asked. "The public defender part, I mean."

"A minivan doesn't freak people out. I could drive to any part of Vegas, rich or poor, to meet with my clients out on bail, their family members, or witnesses. No matter where I went, my van would fit in."

"It made you look trustworthy."

Steven nodded. "Exactly."

Mary stretched out her legs. "Well, it is pretty roomy, and I like the heated seats."

"If I had sprung for the upgrades, you could have sat in the back and watched cartoons."

Mary laughed. "I'd rather chat with you."

"Good, because I have lots of questions about Seattle."

"I'm probably the wrong person to ask because I don't go there very often."

"Because of the distance?"

Mary nodded. "Yeah, and the cost. Everything is so expensive there, even parking. I'm not used to having to pay to park. But there are lots of fun things to do. When I was in eighth grade, we took a school trip to the Space Needle and rode all the way to the top. Gran took us to the Woodland Park Zoo a few times, and once we went to the Pacific Science Center."

"It sounds like you could spend an entire week in Seattle doing tourist things."

"Definitely. Last summer, after I went through a nasty breakup, Hannah took me for a weekend getaway and we went to the MOHAI—the Museum of History and Industry, and the Seattle Art Museum."

"I didn't know you were so into museums."

"I'm not, but the MOHAI has some cool displays on fashion through the ages, and what interiors used to look like in different decades. I love things like that."

"I bet."

"We were going to go to the Seattle Underground Tour too, but we ran out of time."

"Hold on." Steven looked at her for a moment before turning his eyes back to the road. "The *what*?"

"The underground tour, in Pioneer Square."

"I still don't understand. You mean, like, sewer tunnels?"

"Eeew." Mary wrinkled her nose. "No. I mean... Well, I'm not sure I understand it exactly, since I've never gone on the tour, but parts of what we think of as ground-level Seattle are actually on the second story."

"Like Disneyland?"

"I've never been to Disneyland."

"You've never been to Disneyland?" Steven gasped dramatically. "That's tragic."

Mary chuckled at his over-the-top reaction. "It's really expensive, and Gran would have needed to take time off of work."

"But you lived in LA for a couple of years, right?"

"A year and a half," Mary corrected. "And I was broke the entire time."

"Well, there's nothing I can do to rectify you never visiting the happiest place on earth—not today, that is—but what would you say to doing the underground thing after we preview the sign?"

"Really? You don't have to rush back afterward? It's going to be a long day as it is."

"If you'd rather go home right away, that's fine, too."

"No, I'd love to go on the tour." And spend more time with Steven. Aidan had never wanted to go on the underground tour, or to the MOHAI, or to a movie, or basically anything Mary had wanted to do. He'd always put his wants ahead of her own. "I'll look up the website right now to see when the tours run."

"Sounds like a plan."

"This will be so much fun!" Mary wriggled with excitement.

"See if you can find a good place to eat lunch, too," Steven suggested. "Something we can't find in Sand Dollar Cove, like Greek food."

"I've never had Greek food."

"What?" Steven jerked his head back. "Never been to Disneyland *and* never had Greek food?"

"Do the two go together?"

"Not necessarily, but Mary, we need to get you out more."

"I would love to get out more, but that requires—" Mary stopped, not wanting to sound desperate or repetitive.

"Time?" Steven suggested. "Availability, and a scintillating dinner companion?"

Mary laughed. "Yes. All of that."

"It's a good thing you've met me then. I haven't gotten to take you out to lunch yet this week, but that changes today."

The drive to Seattle took another hour and a half, but they passed the time in storytelling and laughter. Mary told Steven about what life was like growing up in Sand Dollar Cove, and what a shock it had been to move to Hollywood, albeit temporarily. She told him about adopting Ferdinand as a kitten and how he'd spent the first five years of his life trying to escape from the house, refusing to be an indoor cat until he'd found peace at Brittany's house. Steven shared about his childhood dog: a beagle named Skipper. He told her about his giant suburban high school with metal detectors at the door, and how sometimes it was so hot at football practice that the players would pass out.

Their easy conversation continued as they arrived in Seattle and searched for a place to park. Steven's urban parking skills impressed Mary, who had limited experience with parking garages and found them intimidating. Steven taught her tricks about how to remember where she'd parked her car, and how to check to see if she needed to take the ticket with her for validation or leave it on the dashboard.

After they'd confirmed their order for the sign, they walked to lunch. Mary ordered a falafel plate with three types of hummus, and Steven ordered a greasy kebab platter. Both selections were delicious, and they swapped bites in addition to sharing a basket of French fries. When it came time for the tour, they had to find the van, drive to a different part of Seattle and park again. "I've never been to Pioneer Square before," Mary admitted. "Gran thought it was too dangerous because of things she saw on the news."

"If it bleeds, it leads." Steven locked the car. "This area looks fine to me but I'm not a grandma with two pretty granddaughters to worry about."

"I think it's charming," Mary said, as she fell into step beside Steven. "The trees, and the brick buildings, and that pergola thing over there."

"I'm not sure pergola is the right word. Arbor, maybe?"

Mary shrugged. "I'm an interior designer, not a landscape architect."

"I'll keep that in mind if I ever have a backyard."

"Bill Speidel's Underground Tour," Mary read from the

sign. "This is the place." She unzipped her purse and took out her wallet, but Steven beat her to it.

"Put your money away."

"This isn't the olden days." Mary removed her credit card.

"It's not, but my Aunt Helena was full of life advice and one of her favorite sayings was 'Never let a skirt pay.'"

"I'm wearing jeans. And you paid for lunch." Mary slid her credit card forward to the attendant. "Two tickets, please."

"Thanks for taking me on the tour," said Steven, as they waited for it to start.

"Thanks for wanting to come." Mary put her wallet away. "What other words of wisdom did your Aunt Helena release from her time capsule?"

"Lots. 'Don't be a sponge,' 'Keep your pad clean,' 'Watch out for people taking the five-finger discount,' and 'It's always better to be decked out than a slob.'" Steven sighed. "She'd hate my hair right now. I really need to go to that place you suggested on Fourth and get a haircut."

"I like it long. Especially when it's brushed."

"Good thing I brushed it today then."

"What's a sponge?"

"The shower tool?"

"No," said Mary. "From your aunt's life advice. What did the 'sponge' one mean?"

"Oh. 'Don't be a sponge' means don't leech off people. Pull your weight. Do your part. Pitch in—that sort of thing."

"She sounds like a real character."

"She was. Want to see her picture?"

Mary nodded. "Absolutely."

Steven pulled out his phone and showed her the screen a few seconds later. "This is me and Aunt Helena at the Cobra Ballroom when I was in high school."

Looking at the picture, Mary saw a petite woman with big hair, a sequined dress, and huge fake eyelashes standing next to a teenage version of Steven. He wore a wildly patterned shirt, as well as a large snake. The python—Mary thought it was a python—was draped around both their shoulders, connecting them together. "Cool," said Mary. "What type of snake is that?"

"That's Celine. Couldn't you tell?"

"Oh... ah... yeah. I was guessing that it was a reticulated python."

Just then, the tour guide called them to attention. Steven put his phone away and he and Mary joined the other tourists for the opening presentation.

The bare-bones story of what Mary already knew about the underground was elaborated on by a witty tour guide. In the mid-nineteenth century, early settlers had built the city on tidelands that flooded. Soon it became clear that they needed to elevate the city for safety. By using concrete walls, sluices, and wide alleys, they raised the city up to between twelve to thirty feet higher than it originally was. But what she didn't know was that vault lights were installed to illuminate the first level. When the tour guide held up an example, Mary was shocked.

"Those look like the coasters my grandma gave me at Christmas," she whispered to Steven.

"Why is the glass purple?" the tour guide asked the group. "Does anyone know?"

"For decoration," someone shouted.

"Nope." The guide shook his head. "Although they sure are lovely." He waited for more people to wager guesses, before explaining. "Originally the glass was clear. American glass-makers in the 1800s used to add manganese to their formula to produce glass that was clearer and less greenish. Almost like the manganese was a soap. It turns out that UV exposure changes the glass into this amethyst purple over time."

Amethyst... The word triggered a memory for Mary. Amethyst purple, like the crayon that colored the dancing woman holding the parasol. Mary could see the picture in front of her but couldn't remember where the image came from.

"Good thing we don't have kids with us," Steven said.

"What?" Mary jerked to attention. "Sorry, I couldn't hear."

"That's okay. The guide made a funny joke about seamstresses in the 1800s, but he was using it as a euphemism because of little ears."

Sometimes Mary couldn't understand half of what Steven said. Usually she nodded along, pretending she knew what the two-dollar words meant, but now she felt comfortable enough with him to ask. "What does euphemism mean?"

"It's when you say the wrong word on purpose because it's a gentler way of saying what you really mean. Like saying someone passed away, instead of died."

"Oh." Mary got in line behind the others. "And the 'little ears' part?"

"Those kids at the front of the group. The tour guide was using seamstress and sewing circles as euphemisms for prostitutes and brothels, so the parents wouldn't have to explain what those words meant to their children."

"And now you're having to explain them to me like I'm eight. Sorry." Mary felt like an idiot.

"Don't be sorry. I grew up being exposed to colorful language both from my dad, who was a lawyer, and from my mom who read a lot, but also from my aunt who could swear like a sailor."

"My dad graduated from the University of Washington with a degree in civil engineering," Mary said proudly. "But of course..." She didn't finish her thought. Instead, she held onto the handrail and descended underground. When she reached the bottom, she found a spot to wait with the group. Steven joined her.

"I know you're smart," Steven whispered in her ear. He

squeezed her hand for the slightest of seconds. "I'll stop talking like I'm still studying for the LSAT."

"The test you took to get into law school," Mary said, relieved that she knew that one.

Steven nodded. "Yup."

He could have belittled her just now, but didn't. In fact, she hadn't spotted any warning signals about Steven at all, even though she'd been looking for them hard. That made her feel safe, and that she'd been right to take a risk on him.

"Don't change how you speak on my account." Mary picked up his hand again and laced their fingers together. "I like how you describe things." She turned her attention to the tour guide and felt enormously pleased when Steven didn't let go of her palm.

FIFTEEN

She wouldn't let TikTok ruin dinner. Mary had promised herself that when she'd posted her latest Jenaly Macintyre video earlier this evening. It was a silly sixty-second bit of her dancing in front of a green screen in the slashed-up prom dress. Mary had filmed it quickly, timed it to a trending audio, overlayed a high school gym over the green screen, and posted. Then she'd tossed her phone in her purse, wiped off the ghoulish makeup, and put on her favorite dress. She just barely had enough time to apply matching lipstick when Steven arrived to pick her up for dinner at the T Bone Bluff. Ten days after their trip to Seattle, they were having their first official date.

Steven had asked her out on the ride home from Seattle after the underground tour. Feeling extra cautious, because she was still trying to be careful with new relationships, Mary had agreed to a date but delayed it a bit, to give her a chance to think things through. She needed to be sure about Steven before she let him into her life. Perhaps Steven wasn't so wonderful after all? But then, tonight for their date, Steven showed up right on time with a huge bouquet of red roses. He'd even washed his van! So far, everything about the evening was going great, except that as they were entering the restaurant lobby, Mary's phone chirped like a songbird from the annoying TikTok notifications.

"I'm sorry," she said, double-checking her settings. "I have it on mute, but the TikTok notifications keep coming through somehow."

"I wouldn't put it past TikTok to have bypassed the control settings." Steven opened the door for her. "At the risk of sounding like my dad, I don't trust that app."

Mary's phone chimed again. "I'll turn it all the way off." She held down the side button. "That'll stop it." She stepped into the lobby, and back in time. The T Bone Bluff had been a respectable family establishment since the early 2000s—and it hadn't been redecorated since then either. Every time Mary came inside, she amused herself spotting outdated trends. There were the arched doorways, the elaborate crown molding, the darkly dramatic paint colors, and the sponge-painted accent wall. Then, to give it a steak house feel, the owners had added giant pictures of cows everywhere you looked.

"I've never been here before," said Steven as he waited in line for the hostess to greet them.

"You haven't?"

Steven shook his head. "No. I'd rather go through a drive-thru than eat at a restaurant alone."

"We didn't eat here a lot growing up because it was so expensive," said Mary. "Usually we'd go to The Summer Wind for special occasions. But this place is known for their big portions of steak. When we did come, we'd split the Cattleman's Platter and it would feed all three of us. Mary and I loved coloring on the butcher paper they put down over the tablecloth."

"Sounds fun." Steven took off his coat and helped Mary out of hers. "I'm a huge fan of steak."

The hostess greeted them a minute later and led them to a

cozy booth underneath a wall hung with branding irons and a
picture of a covered wagon. Mary slid into her seat and put her
napkin on her lap. She saw Steven whisper to the hostess but
didn't hear what he said. A couple of minutes later, while they
were perusing the menu, the woman came back with a mason
jar of crayons.

"Here you go." The hostess set the crayons in the center of
the table. "As requested. Have fun, you two! Your server will be
right with you."

"You asked her to bring us crayons?" Mary put down her
menu.

"Kids shouldn't have all the fun." Steven winked. "What
are you going to order?"

"The steak salad with a side of French fries." Mary picked
up a crayon. "What are you thinking?"

"The 12 oz steak and a baked potato, and I guess the side
salad too, because I ought to."

"Their salads here are pretty good. Not as good as Jasmine
makes them at The Summer Wind, but decent." Mary peeled
back the paper on a sienna-orange crayon to expose the tip.
Then she sketched an oval.

"What are you drawing?" Steven helped himself to a
crayon.

"I don't know. I'm just doodling." Mary filled in the oval,
enjoying the toasty shade of sienna. She plucked an inky-black
crayon from the jar and drew a line from the circle, turning it
into a balloon. "So when am I going to hear you sing and play
the piano again?"

"Oh, ah... Start asking questions like that and you'll never
get me to shut up." He looked around the room. "Does this
place have a keyboard?"

Mary wasn't sure if he was serious or not, and didn't care.
She'd love to hear him play again, even if it meant making a
scene. She didn't recognize any of the other patrons anyway,

probably because most of them were tourists. "When did you learn to play the piano?"

"Second grade." Steven leaned forward. "My mom signed me up after my spectacular failure at soccer."

"What happened?"

"I cried."

"Oh." Mary waited for Steven to elaborate and when he didn't, she asked for more detail. "What made you cry? Was the coach a meanie? Did you hate your uniform?"

"My coach was nice, and the uniform was okay. But I was terrified of being smacked by the ball. Every time it came near me, I'd run in the other direction."

"And you played football in high school?"

Steven nodded. "Not very well. Only at least in football, I wore a helmet. In soccer, there was nothing but the shin guards and jockstrap."

"Seven-year-olds wear jockstraps?"

"Of course they wear jockstraps. Why wouldn't they?"

"I don't know. I'm not very knowledgeable about second-grade boys, I guess."

"One day in the middle of the season, the ball came toward me, and it ricocheted off my foot by accident. That was the only time I made direct contact with the ball the entire season."

"Was it a good kick?"

Steven nodded. "It went right into the goal. Entirely by accident on my part."

"That must have been exciting."

"It was... for the other team. I kicked the ball into the wrong goal and scored the winning point for them instead of us."

"Oops." Mary winced.

"Oops is right. My coach was nice about it, but some of my teammates flipped out. Called me every name a seven-year-old knows. Then my dad yelled at me in front of everyone and told me I needed to pay better attention. That only a moron would make a mistake like that."

"That's horrible! It was an honest mistake."

Steven nodded. "It was, but it was too much for me to handle. That's when I started crying. The next week my mom pulled me out of soccer and signed me up for piano lessons, which, it turns out, I was incredibly awesome at."

"I believe it."

"So awesome, in fact, that— Wait. Our waitress is coming. I'll tell you later."

Mary turned her head and just about lost her mind. The woman walking toward them in black pants and a white shirt and bolo tie was none other than Kelly. "Mom!" Mary exclaimed. "What are you doing here?"

Kelly pulled out a notepad from her pocket. "Taking your order. Welcome to the T Bone Bluff." She took a pen from behind her ear and wrote her name on the butcher paper. "My name's Kelly and I'll be your server tonight."

"I know your name, Mom, you don't need to do that." Mary spoke more loudly than she had intended.

"Would you keep your voice down?" Kelly whispered. "My manager's watching. I've only had this job for a week, and I intend to keep it." She poised her pen above the pad, ready to jot down their requests. "Now, what can I get you?"

"After you, milady," Steven said.

"I'll have the steak house salad with the dressing on the side and a basket of French fries." Mary watched as Kelly wrote the order down, not quite trusting her to get it right.

"And you, handsome fellow?" Kelly asked, smiling at Steven. "What'll you be having?"

"The 12 oz steak, medium rare, and a baked potato with a side salad."

"Would you like the dressing on the side, too?"

"No, ma'am. Load it up."

"Anything to drink?" Kelly asked.

"I'd like the IPA on tap," said Mary.

Kelly scribbled on her pad. "Great. I'll just need to see some ID first."

"You gave birth to me, Mom, you know how old I am."

"And I already told you," Kelly said pertly. "My manager's watching."

"Fine," Mary huffed, as she pulled out her wallet and removed her driver's license. "Here you go."

"Aww..." Kelly smiled as she inspected the card. "You look just like I did at that age." She passed the license back to Mary. "And you, Steven? Anything to drink?"

"I'll take the blackberry cider," said Steven, who had already taken out his ID.

Kelly walked away a minute later, and Mary fumed. How could her mom ruin her date like this? Couldn't she have switched tables with a co-worker?

"You look upset," said Steven. "Want to talk about it?"

"No, thank you." Mary picked up a cherry-red crayon and colored the next balloon with such fierce intensity that the crayon broke in two.

"How long was your mom in prison for vehicular assault?"

"What?" Mary looked up from the butcher paper.

"I'm sorry. You just said you didn't want to talk about it. That was wrong of me."

"No, um... What was that word you used? Or phrase, I guess?"

"Vehicular assault?"

Mary nodded. "Hitting someone with a vehicle?"

"Assaulting them. It's a Class B felony."

No one had ever explained that to Mary before, or if they had, she'd been too little to understand. She knew Kelly had gone to jail for what she'd done. Cheryl had said so on rare occasions when Mary and Hannah were being hard on their mom.

"Your mother has served her time," Cheryl would say. But Hannah never talked about it.

Mary stared at the jar of crayons. "I don't know how long she was in jail."

"Jail, or prison? I assume she was convicted."

Mary felt stupid again. Moronic even. Steven must think she was an idiot. "What's the difference?" she asked, feeling her face turn red.

"Jails usually hold people awaiting trial, or who are sentenced for less than a year, and prisons hold people who've been convicted and are serving longer terms."

Mom was in prison? The thought shocked her. As awful as Kelly was, Mary couldn't picture her in an orange jumpsuit, locked away. It must not be true. Steven probably misinterpreted, based on how she'd explained it. That was it. If Kelly had been in prison, Mary would have known about that. She'd ask Hannah about it later because she was obviously sketchy on the details.

"I should have known the difference between jail and prison," Mary said. "But I didn't take AP Government because I was taking AP English that year and one AP class was enough because I was also in Drama and—"

"It's okay, Mary. I don't expect you to be an expert in the criminal justice system. In fact, I'm glad that you're not. It's a relief."

"That my vocabulary's weak?"

"I don't think that's true. Didn't you give me a ten-minute lecture the other day on the difference between knockdown, orange peel, slap brush, sandcastle, and crow and shovel texture?"

"Sand swirl and hawk and trowel," Mary corrected. "Huge difference."

"See? I can't keep that stuff straight. You leave felony definitions to me, and I'll let you handle the gazillion types of tile shapes. What did we end up going with in the restrooms? I've already forgotten the name."

"You liked the Moroccan fish scale, but I thought the 3D hexagon tile would make the space look bigger, so we went for that on the backsplash above the sink."

"And you were right. It looks bigger now. It's like walking into an optical illusion." Steven leaned back in his chair, then suddenly sat ramrod straight. Mary didn't know why until she saw her mother approach holding a tray.

"Here's your side salad and drinks," Kelly said as she set the items down. "And your basket of fries. Ketchup is on the table. Can I get you two anything else?"

"A new waitress would be nice," Mary mumbled.

"Ha! What a kidder." Kelly attempted to laugh it off. But then her expression turned serious. "I told you, this is my first week on the job. Please don't ruin this for me." She stalked away before Mary could respond.

"What would you say to finishing our starters and getting the rest of our dinner to go?" Steven asked. "Would that be better?"

It was a kind offer, and Mary was touched that Steven thought to make it. Aidan wouldn't have noticed how uncomfortable Kelly made her. Aidan never noticed things like that. "Are you sure you wouldn't mind?" she asked.

"Not in the least."

"Where would we go?" she asked.

"The cinema's an option, or, not to sound totally presumptuous, but we could go to my apartment—just to eat dinner, of course. I'm not trying to lure you into the Cobra Bedroom on our first date."

"The Cobra *Bedroom*?" Mary laughed. "Is that where Elvis sleeps?"

"My ball python?" Steven shook his head. "Certainly not.

He has his enclosure in the living room next to the window that gets the most sun."

Mary thought the offer over. Was it a wise idea to go to Steven's apartment? She felt torn, mainly because her feelings for Steven were becoming stronger than ever, and she wasn't sure she could trust herself around him. But then again, it was just dinner after all. Dinner was taking things slow, no matter where they ate. "Elvis is probably lonely," she said, making her mind up.

"I haven't seen him all day."

"Let's go to your apartment then, and keep him company." Mary picked up her fork. "As soon as we finish our drinks and salad."

"You got it." Steven smiled.

An hour later, they were sitting on Steven's couch finishing their meal. Elvis slept peacefully in his enclosure in the corner. Dinner was delicious, and relaxing with Steven was even better. Mary kicked off her shoes and folded her feet under her. Steven's arm was flung over the back of the couch, almost like he was hugging her, but not quite. Mary inched closer, wondering where the night might lead. So far, Steven hadn't made a move to kiss her. Should she take the initiative herself? Maybe...

Or perhaps definitely.

Or definitely maybe?

Mary's pulse raced every time she *thought* about kissing Steven. He was kind, sweet, and fun to be with—the total opposite of Aidan in every way. It wouldn't be a hasty decision to take a chance on him. Would it? This wouldn't be a repeat of Mary scribbling her number on a stranger's coffee cup. No, this would be a more mature and wiser version of herself making a well thought-out choice. A choice that involved Mary sliding her hands up those biceps of his, and—

"I'm dying of curiosity," Steven said, interrupting Mary's train of thought. "What do you think?"

"What?" Mary asked, trying to regain her focus.

"Of my apartment. Give me your professional opinion."

At first Mary couldn't see if he was being serious or not. There was nothing about the apartment that was remotely appealing, besides Steven, and perhaps Elvis—if Mary was feeling generous.

"Um..."

"That bad, huh? Give it to me straight."

"This place is depressing. Everything's the same color as concrete: the walls... the carpet..." Her eyes drifted toward the broken miniblinds. "The window treatments. How can you stand it?"

Steven laughed. "I knew you'd hate it. I have so much going on with getting my business off the ground that I've barely unpacked. The pictures I was going to put up are in boxes. I'm not here that often, so it doesn't bother me."

"How can it not bother you?" Mary asked. "Every time I see you, you're wearing a bright color and then this place is like a—"

Prison cell.

Where had that come from? From the earlier conversation about her mom?

Mom was in prison, Mary thought. *I'm the daughter of a criminal.* Not just a criminal—a convicted felon. It was too awful to contemplate, so Mary focused on controlling her environment instead. That was her comfort zone, after all.

Act like things were perfect.

Decorate like things were grand.

Fake it until you make it.

"This place is like a cinder block," she said. "Even your couch is gray. I'd at least throw an afghan over it."

"I don't own an afghan."

"Quilt then? Comforter? Old blanket? That would be an instant fix."

"I like the sound of instant." Steven pointed to a door in the hallway. "The linen cabinet's right there if you want to dig through it. I might have something that would work."

"That sounds like a challenge." Mary hopped up. "If there's one thing I love, it's a design challenge." Plus, rearranging the furniture would give her more time to make up her mind about kissing him or not. "We need to take a before and after photo."

"We do?"

Mary nodded. "It's part of my process."

"I'm an admirer of your process, so let's do it. I'll get my tripod."

"You have a tripod?"

Steven nodded. "Is that weird?"

"No." Mary took out her phone. "I have a tripod, too." *For making those damn TikTok videos.* But why did Steven have one? "What do you use yours for?"

"Lots of things. Sometimes I'd video myself rehearsing my opening and closing arguments for my court cases so I could find ways to up the drama."

"Drama upping is one of my favorite things ever." Mary polished her phone screen on her shirt and clipped it into the tripod Steven had set up. "How much free range are you giving me for this challenge? Maybe I could do a hyperlapse video."

"You can do whatever you want to my apartment so long as Elvis remains unscathed. Should I stand out of the way though? I feel like I'm in the way."

"I'm going to put you to work in just a second here." Mary snapped a few photos and switched it to video mode. "Okay, on the count of three, I want you to go find the pictures you intended to hang, as well as a hammer." She stared at him.

"You're sure it's okay if I root around in your blankets and cabinets, and start moving stuff around?"

"I have complete confidence in you. This is already the best Friday night I've had in forever."

Mary grinned. "Me, too." She felt happy. Happy enough to picture herself trotting across the room, throwing her arms around Steven, and kissing him until she was breathless. But not in a place this depressing. First, she had to fix it for him. Her creativity flowed, and she felt energy seep from every pore. "Here we go. One. Two. Three." Mary pressed record.

The next thirty minutes were a blur. Mary moved the couch to the center of the room, and the TV to the side. She flip-flopped how the toaster and coffeemaker were arranged in his kitchen and flicked on the light above the stove to add a soft glow. Deep in the linen closet, Mary found a jade-green blanket that she folded into thirds and threw on the back of the couch for a pop of color. There was nothing she could do about the broken miniblinds except dust them well, to make them less dingy. By that point Steven had found his framed pictures, which were old advertisements for the Cobra Ballroom and not as sleazy-looking as Mary would have imagined, and a hammer. Mary helped him find the perfect spot to hang them. While he did that, she displayed a sage-color bowl she'd found in the closet. She set it on the top level of the bookshelf in the living room where it could be admired. It picked up the color in the blanket perfectly.

"I see you've found Aunt Helena," Steven said, as he pointed with his hammer.

"What?"

"That bowl. It's made from her ashes."

Mary looked at the ceramic piece with horror. "You're kidding."

"I didn't know what to do with it, which is why it was in the linen closet, but it looks really nice there. My aunt would be pleased."

Mary took a step back and looked at the bookshelf. It did look pretty. "So, her ashes aren't *in* the bowl, they *are* the bowl?"

"She liked to be useful and beautiful at the same time."

"That makes sense." It was weird, but it did. Mary looked at Steven. So much about him was unique, but he just made sense, too. His enthusiasm, his drama, his passion for herpetology. Mary knew that word now, and it was because of Steven. Being around him made her feel smarter and filled her with confidence.

"Need the hammer for anything else, or should I put it away?" Steven asked.

"Nope." Mary shook her head. "I think we're ready." She walked up to the tripod and hit the stop button. Her phone was almost out of charge, but she snapped a few pictures before it died. "Well, we're not going to see the final video tonight because my phone is out of juice."

"I don't need a video to see the final results. This looks a hundred times better. Thank you, Mary. You're amazing."

Mary scanned the room with a critical eye, seeing all the things she would do if she had more time and a can of paint. But she also felt proud. Steven was right, the apartment did look better. "I'm glad you like it."

"I feel kind of bad. I invited you out to dinner and ended up putting you to work."

Mary laughed. "It was fun, though. And now you won't live in an apartment of blah."

"Is that the technical word for it?"

"I believe so."

Steven flopped back down on the couch and threw his arm across the back. "It does look less blah. I won't say cool, because this is still my parents' old furniture, but definitely better than it was before."

"Is that where the couch came from?" Mary sat next to him, close enough that she was tucked in the crook of his arm. "I was wondering where the gray came from."

"That would be my mother, who replaced this gray couch with another one that was the exact same shade."

"At least it's comfy." Mary pressed her hand into the cushion next to her. "Must be high-end memory foam."

She didn't want to talk about couches. She didn't want to talk at all, not now that she was sitting this close to him. Close enough that Mary could see the five o'clock shadow shading Steven's square jawline. Close enough that she noticed the elastic that tied back his hair was the same green color as his shirt.

Her mind was made up. She trusted her intuition. Steven was worth the risk.

Mary lifted her hand off the cushion. Her arm acted on its own accord. Her fingertips brushed against the sharp angles of his face and she felt the emerging stubble.

"Mary, I need to tell you something."

"What?" Mary rubbed her thumb across his jawline.

"I really like you."

"You do, do you?" Mary raised herself upward until their lips were inches apart. "How much?"

Steven stared at her parted lips. "A lot." He put a firm hand against her waist and pulled her closer.

Mary moved her lips away from his mouth and whispered in his ear. "How much is a lot?" She kissed the corner of his jawline. "This much?" She kissed the hollow of his cheek. "This much?" Then, with both arms around his neck, she murmured, "Or this much?" When she pressed her lips to his, she felt a warm energy wash over her. Steven's arms encircled her, and she felt wanted and special. His lips were full and his body was larger than Aidan's had been. Mary felt enveloped. And as their kisses deepened, she felt consumed.

"So much," Steven said, when they paused for air. "I like you *so* much." He lifted her onto his lap like she was as light as a bag of feathers.

Mary's fingers gripped the front of his shirt. "I like you so much too," she said, before kissing him with all her heart.

SIXTEEN

"Thanks for meeting me," Mary said. "I know weekends are busy for you." She and Hannah walked across the sand, the waves of the Pacific crashing beside them.

"I'm sorry I couldn't see you yesterday when you texted." Hannah zipped up the down coat Mary had given her a couple of years ago. "Port Angeles Rotary Club arrived for their annual retreat at Seaside Resort, and it was a real zoo."

"And now I'm pulling you away from your lunch break."

"Which is wonderful." Hannah linked arms with her sister. "A walk on the beach is exactly what I needed. Plus, I need to apologize again for springing Mom on you like that at the senior center party. I know it's almost a month later, and I know I already apologized, but I still feel badly about how I handled it."

"You didn't think she'd actually show up," said Mary. "You already explained that to me."

"Yeah, and I was so proud of what you had accomplished, that I wanted her to witness your big moment." Hannah patted her arm.

"I'm still shocked that she came."

"Me, too." Hannah nodded. "But maybe Guy is right.

Maybe our family can have less drama in the future if we are willing to take a chance and make amends."

"Maybe..."

"Enough with my blathering. What's up? Is this about a certain adorable snake charmer we both know?"

Mary blushed. "Steven's not a snake charmer. He's a snake enthusiast. That's totally different. But yeah, it's kind of about Steven. Or rather, something he said to me the other night."

"What? Now you've got me curious."

She might as well come out and say it. The confusing thought that had been haunting her for the past day and a half. The misunderstanding that loomed over her like a rain cloud. "Was Mom in prison?" Mary blurted.

"Prison?" Hannah asked, in a guarded tone.

"Yes, prison. Steven used to be a public defender. When I told him about the accident, that's one of the first things he mentioned. I tried to explain that no, Mom had been in jail, not prison, but then I just changed the subject because it was easier."

Hannah let out a deep sigh and stopped walking, pulling Mary to a standstill as well because their arms were hooked together. "Mom *was* in prison. I thought you knew that."

"Wow."

"Yeah."

"Prison?" Mary asked again.

Hannah nodded. "Yes."

"Why?"

"Because of the drunk driving accident." Hannah pulled up her sleeve and exposed the silvery scar on her arm. "She almost killed us. You know that."

"I *do* know that, but... I thought she went to jail for a bit and then lost her license and did a bunch of community service, or something. I never thought about it." *Because it was easier to not think about Kelly at all.* Push her mom away because she wasn't part of Mary's life. If Mary could, she'd cut the maternal part of her DNA out completely.

"I'm surprised you didn't know this," said Hannah. "I thought you knew Mom had served time. Gran mentions that every holiday when she thinks we owe Mom a call."

"'Your mom has served her debt to society. She deserves a phone call,'" Mary said, in her best imitation of Cheryl.

"Put on elastic pants and push a walker and I'd swear you were Gran." Hannah chuckled.

"This isn't a laughing matter," said Mary.

Hannah wiped her smile away. "No. Of course it isn't."

"I thought serving time meant picking up trash on the side of the road."

"Mom probably did that too, after she left Gig Harbor."

"Gig Harbor?"

"That's where the Washington Corrections Center for Women is."

"Oh."

"We visited her several times, but you were probably too little to remember." Hannah shuddered. "I, on the other hand, wish I could forget."

"That sounds rough."

"Mom was there for three years. But we stopped visiting her after a bit."

"Why do you know this, and I don't?" Mary asked.

"I thought you did. But there were lots of legal things that happened to us when we were little, so maybe you got confused. Social workers... family court... We moved in with Gran right after the accident, but she wasn't officially granted custody of us until I was seven and you were four. I swear I thought you knew about Mom being in Gig Harbor, but maybe you were too young for it to sink in."

Mom's in Gig Harbor. The memory tickled like the scent of wax crayons. The long, endless drive in the back of Cheryl's

Buick. Mary so short that she couldn't look out the window, even though she was safely strapped into a booster seat.

"That's what Mom being in Gig Harbor meant?" Mary asked, suddenly remembering. "She was at the corrections center?" A euphemism for prison.

Hannah nodded. "So you *do* remember going to Gig Harbor. We'd listen to books on CD that we'd checked out from the library and stop for hamburgers on the way home."

"I had a coloring book," Mary said, testing to see if the sentence was true. The lion wearing the bow tie. The dancing woman who rode an elephant. The clown holding a bunch of balloons. Mary could suddenly picture the pages one by one.

"That's right." Hannah nodded. "It was full of zoo animals, or something."

"Circus animals," Mary murmured. "It was a circus theme."

"You loved that coloring book. Gran gave it to you to keep you busy during the long car ride."

Mary walked forward again and pulled Hannah along. Her feet moved so fast that she kicked up sand, but she didn't slow her pace. She charged along at top speed trying to make sense of things.

Hannah didn't protest at the frantic pace, as if she sensed her sister's distress.

I'm the daughter of a felon, Mary thought. *That's what's wrong with me. I come from bad blood.*

It was a bitter pill to swallow. She knew she was broken. She'd known all along. Something about her was stained on the inside. This was the reason why.

"Aidan was right about me," Mary said, without meaning to utter her thoughts out loud.

"About what?" Hannah asked.

"That day he dumped me. He basically said I had too much baggage and that my children would never have grandparents they could count on. He was right."

"Don't let that fool worm his way into your head. If you have children someday, they'll have you and they'll have me. Guy too, by the looks of things, and you know how much family means to him."

"Aidan's parents never liked me, and I thought they were being overly critical. But..." Mary bit her lip. She didn't want to say it, but she had to. "I wouldn't want my son dating the daughter of a felon either."

"Felon?"

"For vehicular assault. It's a Class B felony with a maximum sentence of ten years."

"How do you know that?"

"Steven told me."

Hannah froze and caused Mary to stop walking too. "That can't be right. Mom was... is... a felon?" Hannah took out her phone. "I'm looking it up right now."

Mary waited as her sister stared at the tiny screen. Waves crashed behind them, and wind whipped their hair. The cool ocean breeze pinked their cheeks. Hearing that Hannah was surprised by the revelation, too, made Mary feel less naive.

"He's right," said Hannah, still staring at her phone.

"Of course he's right." Mary spoke matter-of-factly. "Steven knows what he's talking about."

"I know, it's just..." Hannah put her phone away. "I guess I never thought about Mom in that exact way. Using that word, I mean."

"Felon?"

Hannah nodded. "It's a loaded word."

"You're making me feel better that it shocked you, too. I'm not the only clueless one."

"Being a little girl when something happens doesn't make you clueless. It makes you too young to fully understand."

"To process," Mary added.

"Yes." Hannah nodded. "Seven-year-old me must not have

understood the word 'felon' or it wouldn't have taken me by surprise just now."

"It doesn't matter how old we get," said Mary. "It will always be a lot to process."

"You're right."

The gravity of the conversation weighed Mary down, her heels sinking into the sand, as if the beach could swallow her. "Does this change your mind about engineering a joyful family reunion?" she asked.

"I never said joyful. I was hoping for neutral." Hannah started walking again. "Let's push my proposed dinner at the T Bone Bluff off a bit, to give everyone the chance to catch their breath."

"Good idea." Mary nodded.

"At least Mom lives in Aberdeen, so we don't have to run into her all the time."

"She's not in Aberdeen."

"Huh?"

"She doesn't live there anymore," said Mary. "I didn't tell you that part."

"What?"

"She's moved here to Sand Dollar Cove, or at least a lot closer."

"No!" Hannah exclaimed.

"Yes. She got a job waitressing at the T Bone Bluff."

"How did that happen?"

Mary shrugged. "I didn't ask. When we realized Mom was our server, we ordered our dinner to-go and hightailed it out of there." Steven had been so quick about it too, so polite and matter-of-fact. He'd helped Mary into her coat and sent her away with the keys to his van while he'd collected the food and paid the bill.

"Why didn't Mom tell me?" Hannah asked. "Was this before or after the senior center party?"

"I don't know."

Hannah secured her hair with a clip. "What do you think made her leave Aberdeen?"

"I have no idea."

"I liked having Mom live in Aberdeen, not here," said Hannah. "Aberdeen was a good distance."

"I agree. I'm not sure there's much we can do about it now. Maybe you and Guy got her hopes up thinking we'd be one big happy family."

"I don't think that's it. Well, I guess it could be..."

"You meant well."

"I did. But Guy's big speeches about healing people and second chances made me temporarily forget what Mom's like."

"That's understandable. I'm having a hard time coming to grips with her true nature, too."

"I'll explain to Guy about the felony conviction. Some reunions aren't meant to be."

"Good idea," said Mary.

"I'm glad we talked about these things, even though it's been hard, because shedding light on the past is important."

Hearing her sister say that made Mary want to unburden her soul. "Hannah, there's something else I need to tell you." For a moment, Mary was prepared to explain about *Zombie Prom at the Disco*. They were talking about family secrets, after all. Maybe it was time for Mary to disclose her part in this broken equation.

"What?" Hannah asked. "I'm listening."

Seeing the warmth in Hannah's brown eyes caused Mary to bail. She couldn't tell Hannah, at least not yet. It was only March. She still had until May 14th before the picture released in theaters. This was news that Mary could save for another day. So instead of revealing the worst thing in her life that she could think of, she shared the best.

"I like Steven a lot," Mary admitted. "He treats me well and we have so much fun together."

"I'm glad." Hannah hugged her. "I'm happy for you. Steven seems like a great person. Just promise me you won't rush into things."

"I'm not. I mean, I didn't. I was super careful before I took a chance on him."

"That's good to hear," said Hannah. "And now that you have taken a chance on him, don't start planning your wedding after only a few dates."

"That's unfair!"

"Is it? You're a dreamer and I love that about you, but..."

"But what?" Mary asked, feeling annoyed. "Spit it out."

"Sometimes you become so enthusiastic that you make your moves without fully thinking them through."

"I do not. Well, maybe I did with Aidan, but I don't now. I've changed." It hurt to hear her sister speak the truth so plainly.

"I hope so. You were all set to marry Aidan without taking the time to consider that he was a royal jerk."

"I would have said 'asshole.'"

"Asshole, then." Hannah frowned.

"I *did* think things through, to some extent, with Aidan," Mary protested. "I had this whole plan for us. He would be a traveling nurse and I'd follow him all around the country, doing one design project after another."

"And you were so focused on that dream vision that you didn't stop and see all the ways Aidan was unworthy of you. You rushed headfirst into the relationship without pausing to wonder if a relationship with Aidan was worthwhile."

"That's..." *Not true,* she wanted to say, but didn't because she couldn't. Hannah was right. Mary knew that in her soul. "I didn't rush into starting my design business," she countered. "I took my time on that."

"And look how great it's turning out."

"Are you saying you don't approve of Steven?"

"No. I've barely met the man. All I'm saying is take it slow and make wise decisions. Don't profess your love and redecorate his apartment on the first date."

"How'd you know about that?" Mary asked.

"Please tell me you're joking." When Mary didn't answer, Hannah swatted her arm. "You've already fallen in love with him? You've only known Steven for a month and a half!"

"No... I mean... I *did* redecorate his apartment." *And make out with him on the couch,* but Hannah didn't need to know that part. Mary would kiss Steven again, too, in a heartbeat. In fact, Mary had plans to see Steven later that evening. She was bringing over a houseplant, because a little greenery was what his apartment was missing.

"I'm not sure redecorating the apartment of someone you've just started dating is a smart idea," said Hannah. "That's like marking your territory and getting ready to move in."

"You make me sound like a dog peeing on a fire hydrant."

"Promise me you won't pee on Steven's carpet."

That made Mary chuckle. Knowing that Hannah was trying to lighten the mood with a joke made things better, too. "I swear it."

"Good. And don't buy a snake, either, because I'm not sure that reptiles are allowed in our lease agreement."

Mary felt affronted on Elvis, Celine, and Dion's behalf. Apparently she was developing feelings for the snakes, too.

SEVENTEEN

Mary had seen Steven every day that week. Her heart glowed like fire. Everything was going her way. She burned through one task after another, her productivity scorching hot.

"Slow down," Cheryl had told her last Tuesday when she'd unloaded the dishwasher at warp speed. "You might break something."

"It's my turn to do the dishes and I have to be fast because Steven's picking me up in ten minutes," she had said.

On Wednesday, when Zeke had called to harass her about posting more TikTok videos, Mary had slathered her face with ghoulish makeup, shot a video in the harsh bathroom light, and deadpanned to the camera saying: "I don't care what you think, I only care about what you taste like." She'd licked her lips and held up a fork. Then, she'd hit post. Within an hour it had reached over three thousand views, finally getting Mary's account out of the two hundreds' purgatory. It was another indication that things were going her way.

The movie theater renovations were making progress, too. Despite frustrations working with Nick, the general contractor, the subcontractors had done good work. The tile company was brilliant. Jose's crew had come in to paint. Electricians were installing new light fixtures next week, and the muralist had shown Mary and Steven concept sketches for the lobby that pleased them both. The muralist said it would take her five days to paint, and that was on the docket for early April.

Everything was going Mary's way except for her anxiety over the nude scene in the movie. It hung over her head like an axe, waiting to fall. When Hannah and Cheryl found out, they would flip out. Even worse, would this ruin her relationship with Steven? How could she tell someone she'd only been dating a week that in six weeks, the whole world would see her naked?

Today was Saturday, March 29th, and Mary intended to solve this problem once and for all. She went out to her car for privacy and dialed Zeke's number.

"Hi, Mary," he said. "What's up?"

She started the conversation on a high note. "Did you see my last TikTok? It got over three thousand views and dozens of comments. People are really getting excited about the movie coming out."

"Word of mouth is everything. Our distributor is really happy. That interview you did with the paper in Tennessee helped, too. Did you see my email about the Zoom meeting with the film festival people in Texas next week?"

"Yes, and I have it on my calendar. But that's not why I'm calling." Mary took a deep breath. She had to make Zeke listen. Her reputation depended on it. "Look, I'm excited about the release, but I want you to edit out the naked shots of me. The film doesn't need them and—"

"This again? Are you kidding me? I thought you were a serious actor."

"I am serious." Or she *was*. Now Mary had moved on with her life and she didn't want this to follow her. "But you lied to me," she said, in a fiery tone. "You told me this film would be PG 13, not rated R. I never agreed to be naked like that."

"Wow." Zeke snorted. "You sure have a selective memory. How can you not agree to a nude scene while you willingly take off your clothes?"

"I was coerced."

"There was a room full of people. Nobody talked you into anything you didn't want to do."

"That's not true!"

"You loved the attention. Those extras we hired to play football players were practically slobbering over you and you ate it up."

Tears blurred Mary's eyes and her racing heart rattled in her chest. "You're lying, and if you want me to keep promoting the film, you need to remove that scene."

"That's not how contracts work, bitch. If you stop promoting *Zombie Prom at the Disco*, I'll sue you."

"I... I..." Mary scrambled for a retort. But what could she say? She didn't have the resources to sue him. She *would* stick up for herself, though. She wasn't an eighteen-year-old girl with stars in her eyes anymore. She was older now, and wiser. Mary knew where to hit Zeke where it hurt. "I promised to promote the film, but I didn't promise to do a good job of it," she said. "I don't see any of your other actors' TikTok accounts getting the traction mine is gaining. If you want my best work, then you need to listen to me."

"I already got your best work. It's your naked ass—and front —wiggling on camera that we needed." Zeke hung up on her before she could respond.

What a jerk! No, *monster*. Hot tears of rage burned Mary's cheeks. She wiped them away just as someone rapped on her car window, scaring the bejesus out of her. Looking up, Mary saw Aidan, the last person she wanted to talk to right now.

Since the car was turned off and she couldn't roll down the window, she cracked open the door.

"Is the battery dead?" he asked. "Do you need a jump start? Oh... you're crying."

Mary wiped her wet cheeks with her sleeve. "I'm not crying."

"What's the matter?"

"Why should you care?"

"Look, I know things didn't end well between us, but that doesn't mean that I don't care. If you're in trouble, then maybe I can help."

Her conversation with Zeke attacked her confidence like a woodpecker hammering a tree. Maybe if she shared it with someone, it would ease her load. Making an impulse decision, Mary went for it. "I'm going to be in a movie," she said clearly.

"A porn movie? Is that why you're crying?"

"No!" she shrieked. "Why would you say something like that?"

"Because you were so desperate to become an actress. Plus, you're hot. That's one of the things I really miss about you, compared to Lara. Especially after she's had Larry." He cringed. "I've said too much."

"Ya think?" Why had she thought that confiding in Aidan was a good idea? "I'm in a horror film, that I'm quite proud of actually," she said. *Except for that one scene...*

"Wow." Aidan's eyes widened. "Horror?"

"Yes, and..." Mary scrambled for something to explain her tears. "I'm sad that the press circuit will be over Zoom, instead of in person. It would have been fun to fly around the country. But please keep this secret. I want it to be a surprise for Hannah and Gran." She narrowed her eyes at him. "I know you're great at secret-keeping. You're a real expert." She slammed the door without another word and drove off toward town.

By the time she'd reached the movie theater, she was feeling better. Mary checked her reflection in the mirror just to be sure and was pleased to see that except for a little puffiness under her eyes, it was impossible to tell that she'd been crying. She refused to let Zeke, or Aidan, and a locker room full of doomed football players, ruin her day. She was putting the finishing touches on Steven's office this morning, before he arrived later this afternoon to see the result.

Mary took out the key Steven had given her to unlock the front door, but it was already open. Loud music blasted from the speakers and as she entered the lobby, she saw Nick, his son-in-law Shane, and a few others installing cabinets in the concessions area. Nick wasn't known for a strong work ethic, so seeing his crew on a Saturday surprised her.

"Hiya, Mary," Nick called. "What do you think about the new cabinets? They finally came in."

Mary walked closer so she could see. She'd already inspected them when she'd accepted delivery yesterday morning but seeing them against the freshly painted walls was different. "The color really pops," she said, nodding her approval. "I didn't know you'd be here today."

"Today and tomorrow." Nick nodded. "On account of taking a vacation next week."

"What? Nobody told me that."

"I cleared it with Steven already, and he said it was okay."

Of course he said it was okay. Steven was too lovably nice for his own good sometimes. "When are you leaving?" Mary asked.

"Wednesday. For a week," said Nick.

"I'm coming too." Shane changed drill bits. "We're going to Sun River."

"Oregon?" Mary asked.

Nick nodded. "That's right. An RV trip with my poker buddy Herman. Anyhow, I told Steven that we'd work double this weekend to make up for it."

"Great," Mary said weakly. "Thanks for letting me know." *Finally*.

"By the way," said Nick. "There's a bunch of junk in that storage room that needs to be cleared out before we can refinish the floors. I'm not an artsy-fartsy person like you are, but some of that stuff looked interesting. You might want to take a look."

"I'll do that. Thanks." Mary nodded goodbye and headed to Steven's office.

At least the office was in good shape. Or, horrible shape since the theme was horror. All that was left to do was install the manacles, which Mary had crafted to also be hanging house-plant holders. She wasn't sure the room had enough light for philodendrons, but she was going to try it. The room was supposed to be dungeon-like, not soul-sucking too. She wanted Steven to be happy here.

Before Mary got to work, she said hello to Celine and Dion. Dion was stretched out and staring at her, while Celine was coiled under a heat lamp, fast asleep. "Hey, you two. It's nice and warm in here, isn't it?" She took off her coat and began her tasks.

Using the stud finder was easy. Drilling holes in the wall was a piece of cake. But as her decorating vision came to fruition, Mary fretted. Aidan's first thought was that she was a porn actor. What would other people think when they saw that film? Her worry was too awful to bear. She finished the room, and it looked amazing, but instead of being pleased, her anxiety was on overdrive. The sooner Steven got here, the better.

Your office is all done and looks incredible, if I say so myself, she texted him.

Can't wait to see it! he replied. *I'll be there in forty-five minutes.*

Since she had time to kill, Mary decided to deal with the storage room. Taking her phone with her, she headed to the basement.

She and Steven had sorted through some of the items over the past few weeks. Godzilla was gone, and they had donated the box of purple glass. Valuable posters were at the frame shop right now, awaiting permanent placement in the lobby. They'd tossed the popcorn tubs from the 1980s and random bags of trash. But there were still over a dozen boxes to investigate.

Mary opened the first one and found tins of powdered pink soap. Weird! Who'd ever heard of powdered soap? This box went directly into the garbage pile. The next box was so old that the cardboard was disintegrating. When Mary opened the lid, she found a case of pop. She picked up a can. "Tab," she read aloud. "Never heard of it." When she saw that the expiration date was 1982, she shoved the carton into the recycle pile. Another box had coin wrappers. The one after that had straws. But the final box she examined contained an unexpected find.

"Is this some sort of book?" Mary asked as she dug into tissue paper. No, it wasn't a book, it was an album, made from what looked to be synthetic leather. Armadillo, maybe?

Bringing the album closer to the light, Mary opened the cover and saw a letter. Plastic film covered the page, and the stickiness had turned into diagonal lines of goo across the handwriting. Holding it up to the light, Mary read the inscription.

My darling girl,

This isn't how I wanted our story to end. Pretend that I'm riding off into the sunset with music playing instead of leaving you like this. You can still have a delightful day in Sand Dollar Cove. Watch a movie. Play on the beach. Fly a kite. Visit the ice cream shop. But promise that you'll forget me...

"How sad," Mary murmured. "I wonder who wrote this letter?" Maybe the pictures would give her more information about the letter writer, or who the album belonged to. She turned the page.

The first few photos were of Rhododendron Lane, the popular make out spot in Sand Dollar Cove. Mary recognized the spot instantly, even though the rhododendrons were half their current size. There was a picnic scene, and a roast chicken, and a kite flying in the sky. After flipping the page, Mary saw a handsome man with blond hair and a horseshoe mustache holding a baby. There was also a woman with brown curly hair rocking the infant in a chair. Mary didn't know who the people were but assumed the pictures belonged to the former theater owners. Maybe the couple from Port Angeles who had purchased the business for their son? Perhaps the baby in the picture was their little boy.

But now, Mary turned another page and saw that the baby had grown up to be a girl.

Mary stared at the picture. It was almost like looking at herself in another era.

The girl-who-wasn't-Mary wore her hair in two pigtails spiraled into sausage curls. Red yarn bows adorned both sides of her head. She had on a golden-brown pinafore over a white blouse with puffy sleeves. Nothing about the outfit was remotely like anything from this century. The girl's eyebrows were different, too, and her mouth was oval instead of heart-shaped. But still, the resemblance was clear. Mary felt chills run down her spine and it wasn't because she was cold.

How strange. Who was this child?

"Maybe it's the Swedish DNA," she told herself. Scandinavians had flooded Washington State in the late 1800s and early 1900s, many of them working in logging. Now that Mary knew she was part Swedish it made sense that she'd look like the ancestors of other Swedish immigrants.

Cheryl might know more about the girl in the picture. Mary would ask her grandmother later when she went home.

Bringing the album with her, she hurried upstairs to the warmth of Steven's office, just as he arrived looking like a shorn sheep.

"Steven!" she cried, setting the book down on his desk. "What did you do to your hair?"

"Do you not like it?" He patted the cropped sides. They faded into a longer top section that swooped over to the right. "I went to that hair salon you recommended and—"

"It looks great," Mary said quickly, concerned that she'd hurt his feelings. "I love it." She did, too. Although part of her missed the man bun. "You look handsome with your hair at any length, but now I can do this." She threw her arms around his neck and brushed her fingers across the buzzed edges at his hairline. "And this," she said as she kissed the back of his neck above his collar.

"That tickles!" Steven laughed, and Mary pulled away. "Don't stop," he hugged her closer. "I didn't say stop."

Mary kissed below his ear and then Steven sneak-attacked with a kiss so hot it made her forget about everything. She couldn't remember the fight with Zeke, or the horrible things Aidan had said. She forgot her annoyance about Nick taking off in the middle of the job. Steven erased all the men who had disappointed her. He held her tight, sat her on the edge of his desk, and kissed her tenderly. Mary savored the feeling of Steven's body's warmth against her own.

"So, you *do* like my haircut, right?" Steven asked as he stared into her eyes.

"Yes." Mary nodded. "I most definitely do."

"This is how I wore it when I was a lawyer, and had to look professional."

"Oh."

"It wasn't until I settled my aunt's estate, quit my job, and told my dad off—really had it out with him—that I let it grow, just for the fun of it. Stress had ruled my life. That's what Corey told me."

"Your gladiator friend?"

"Yeah." Steven nodded. "I was miserable all the time. Working twenty-four-seven. It was an awful way to live." He sat next to her on the edge of the desk. "It wasn't only the long hours, it was also the pressure of my caseload. I believe passionately in the criminal justice system. Most of my clients were victims of poverty or drugs. They made bad choices because they had no choices to begin with. But..." He looked out at the velvet-draped windows—blood red, for extra drama. "I also represented people who did horrendous things. Sex offenders, child abusers, you name it."

"That must have been incredibly difficult."

Steven gripped the desk's edge with white knuckles. "It was. But public defenders are an essential part of the American democratic system. Every accused person deserves a lawyer, and the public defenders I worked with were some of the best. We worked our tails off to make sure our clients had adequate representation, even the ones we knew were guilty. That way, when justice prevailed and they were convicted, we'd played our role in helping justice run its course."

"I never thought about it that way."

"I'm not sure why I started talking about this." Steven rubbed his chin. "Oh yeah, my haircut."

"I love your haircut, and thanks for sharing with me how difficult it was to be a public defender."

"It's easy to fall apart when you work at the courthouse. People eat too much, drink too much, gamble too much, and take their stress home to their families. Not everyone, of course, but some people do. Like my father." Steven frowned.

Mary linked her arm through his and squeezed his hand. "I thought your father was a politician?"

"He is, but before that he was a prosecutor. Vick, that's his name. He never hit me, but boy would he shout. At me. At my mom. At the grocery store clerk... I heard every curse word before I was five years old."

"That's awful, Steven. No child should be exposed to verbal abuse like that."

"He lied, too. Half of the words that came out of his mouth were lies. My dad wanted me to believe the worst in people, especially the ones who were kind to me, like my Aunt Helena."

"How horrible."

"Yeah." Steven raked his fingers through his freshly cropped hair. "Once I changed course, all that stress went away. I had time to think, and walk, and then run. I finally had the time to think about what I wanted to do with my life, and more importantly, who I wanted to be."

"That's good. Is that how you decided to move to Washington?"

"Yeah." Steven swallowed. "Pretty much. I did a nationwide search on cineplexes for sale, and Sand Dollar Cove popped up."

"Luckily for me."

"Best decision I ever made." Steven squeezed her tight.

"Thanks for sharing it with me."

"So you like my haircut?"

"Absolutely. But I liked the man bun, too." She rested her chin on his shoulder. "I like you in every which way, except when—" Mary stopped herself, just in time. His body, his choice. But it was too late.

"Except when what?" Steven asked, the corner of his mouth twitching.

"Except when you wear Crocs," Mary admitted. "Especially with socks." Her plan had been to throw them away when he wasn't looking, but maybe confessing the truth about how she felt was better.

"I didn't know you were such a fashionista with men's footwear."

"I have strong opinions about plastic shoes."

"What about my barefoot running shoes? I'm guessing they won't meet your style criteria either."

"Are those the rubber shoes with the individual toe sockets?"

"Yes."

"Ah..." Mary wrinkled her nose. "Well..."

Steven laughed. "I'm just messing with you. I wear Nikes."

"Phew!" Mary chuckled too. "Speaking of design choices, ta-da!" She waved a hand around the room. "What do you think of your office now that it's finished?"

"I was admiring your handiwork before you got here. Mary, this room looks incredible. It's like I'm on the set of a haunted house."

"I'm glad you like it." Mary's gazed drifted over to the photo album. "Oh, wow. I almost forgot." Mary jumped off the desk to get the album and sat down on the rug next to the snakes, where it was warmer. "Check out this bizarre book I found in the basement. The photos look like they're probably fifty years old. The cover is interesting, too. It must be some sort of synthetic leather from the 1970s that hasn't aged well."

"That *is* an unusual-looking cover." Steven sat next to Mary and took the album from her. "It looks like rattlesnake."

"Rattlesnake?"

Steven nodded. "I'm not sure if it's synthetic or not, but that's what it looks like to me." He flipped through the pages.

"Look at the girl," Mary said, pointing to a photo. "Doesn't she look like me?"

"Kind of." Steven peered at the photo and then at Mary. "Maybe around the eyes, a bit."

"I wonder what happened to her? Did she grow up to become a teacher? Or a nurse?" Mary wondered out loud. "There weren't as many options for girls back then." Or did her life take a bad turn...

Turn around and face the camera, Zeke had said. The prop director sprayed her with blood. Mary felt the oozy mess slide down her nakedness. The hungry eyes of the cast and crew consumed her, savoring her humiliation.

I'm not your prom queen, she had rasped, horror sticking in her throat like a splintered chicken bone. *I'm your nightmare.* Only she was the one in the nightmare, and once that film hit the screens, her nightmare would haunt her forever.

Steven had shared his work trauma with her. Was she brave enough to share her own? She'd tried telling Aidan earlier that day, but clearly, he had been the wrong choice in every regard.

Mary took the album from Steven and set it aside. "I need to tell you something that you're not going to like and that is hard for me to say," she began.

"Are you breaking up with me?" Steven blurted.

"What? No. Why would you think that?"

"Because you're so out of my league."

"How am I out of your league? You're the one with the law degree."

"But I'm not a lawyer now. I'm a small business owner with a mildew situation."

"Okay, let's pause here." Mary expelled a deep breath. "It seems we both have some attachment issues to work out."

"So we're officially dating then?" Steven asked, with a sly grin.

"Yes."

"You're my girlfriend? My smokin' hot girlfriend?"

Mary laughed. "Yes, if you say so."

"Can I take a picture of us and send it to Corey?" Steven took out his phone.

"Later, when I've fixed my—"

"Smile!" Steven smushed his face next to hers and took a selfie.

"Steven!" She grabbed his phone to delete the photo. "Oh

wait, that picture's cute. Celine photobombing us is adorable." She passed it back. "Okay, you can send that one."

"I'll text Corey later. You were going to tell me something, and as your boyfriend, I'm giving you my full attention." Steven took both her hands in his own and held them gently.

Why was this so hard? Why was a rock in her stomach carving through her chest and up to her heart? Like it was granite, slicing her insides into pieces. Mary swallowed, not knowing where to start, so she began at the beginning.

"When I was eighteen, I starred in a movie," she said. "Called *Zombie Prom at the Disco*."

"That's incredible!" Steven exclaimed. "How cool!"

"No." She shook her head sadly. "Not cool at all." She launched into her explanation, pouring her heart out about what had happened. When she had finished, Steven's face was beet red.

"It wasn't your fault," Steven said, his eyes sparking with anger. "None of that was your fault. Zeke exploited you. You're a victim, Mary, not someone who should feel embarrassed. And you're still being victimized. How many TikTok videos has that monster had you make?"

"A few dozen. But I'm clothed in the TikTok videos." Mary looked at the snakes for a moment. "I'm not embarrassed about the TikToks."

"Good." Steven let out a sigh of relief. "But that doesn't change the fact that someone who abused your trust and good nature is still abusing you."

"I know. It really sucks. That's why I've been afraid to tell people."

"I don't want you to be afraid." Steven hugged her. "You don't need to be scared anymore. I'll help you."

"How? I don't have an agent. I did have a contract, though, but I didn't study it enough when I signed it, which is my fault and—"

"It wasn't your fault at all." Steven placed his hands lightly on her shoulders. "Are we clear on that?"

"But it *was* my fault." The tears that had flowed that morning, rolled again. Something about her was messed up. She often looked for love and approval from people she shouldn't trust. That type of foolishness might have been understandable when Mary was younger, but once she'd reached adulthood, she should have known better. Now, she *was* trying to change; she really was. That's why she'd been so careful to take things slowly with Steven. But her past choices haunted her. "When I lived in LA I was a naive idiot who was too stupid to read the contract and too weak to stand up for myself," she said.

"You weren't weak." Steven's tone was soothing. "That's victim blaming. You were eighteen and being preyed upon by strangers." He hugged her tighter. "I'm so sorry that happened to you. I'll make them axe the whole thing. We'll file an injunction and prevent it from airing."

"But I want it to air," Mary said, her voice muffled by Steven's broad shoulders. "I was proud of being in the film. I still believe it's a good picture, I just want my naked bits cut out of that locker room scene."

"Okay, we'll make them cut that one scene, then."

"Can you do that?" Mary reached for a tissue in her pocket and blew her nose. "How?"

"I have reciprocity in Washington, but California doesn't offer reciprocity. Corey practices in California, though. He can submit my pro hac vice application, which means I'll be able to practice law there for this one case. Then I'll file an injunction and temporary restraining order to prevent it from airing, so they'll need to edit you out if they want to release the rest of it."

"I'm not sure I followed any of that."

"Sorry for the legalese. It means I need to make some phone calls, but I'm going to take care of this for you. I'm sure Corey will help me, too. Let's sit down at my desk properly and you can write out the information I'll need. Names and phone numbers, stuff like that. Can you do that for me?"

Mary nodded. "Yes."

Steven stood and helped her to her feet. Mary wiped tears away with the tissue and watched as he removed a yellow legal pad from his desk.

She'd seen Steven as a movie buff, herpetologist, piano player, and lovable creative before, but now she was seeing him as a lawyer, too. He was impressive, that's what he was, and for some reason he wanted to be her boyfriend. Her heart fluttered like a tiny butterfly fighting against a cold breeze. Hope clung to her like gossamer. If anyone could make her Zeke problem go away, it was Steven. Maybe her future would still be bright after all.

EIGHTEEN

"That's Sven Nilsen," Cheryl said, pointing at the picture of the man with the horseshoe mustache. "But I don't recognize the woman or little girl." She sat in her recliner and turned the pages of the photo album one by one.

"Sven Nilsen?" Mary asked. "The name sounds familiar." It was the day after her confession to Steven about her participation in *Zombie Prom at the Disco*. Mary sat in the living room wearing her fluffy purple bathrobe, drinking coffee with Cheryl and Hannah.

"Wasn't Sven the former chef at The Summer Wind?" Hannah asked.

"That's right." Cheryl gazed at the photo.

"Did you say he was so hot he could sizzle bacon all on his own?" Mary asked, suddenly remembering.

"And I stand by that description." Cheryl licked her lips. "Sizzle, sizzle."

"Okay, I need to see this man's face," said Hannah. "Can it be my turn now?"

"Sure." Cheryl passed over the album to Hannah, who sat next to her.

"I didn't think the man was that good-looking." Mary sipped her coffee.

"It's hard to look past the mustache." Hannah crinkled her forehead. "Nobody wears them like that anymore."

"Not true," said Cheryl. "Sam Clafin had a similar mustache in *Enola Holmes*."

"I think that was more of a walrus mustache," said Hannah. "Or maybe it was a handlebar one..."

"Can we please stop talking about mustaches and focus on the fact that the pictures of the little girl look like me and that's creepy?" Mary exclaimed.

"I don't think the girl looks like you," said Cheryl. "The only thing you have in common is blonde hair."

"I don't know about that." Hannah flipped another page. "There's something in the girl's eyes that looks a little bit like Mary."

Appeased now that Hannah recognized the similarity too, Mary shared her theory. "I was thinking it could be a Swedish DNA thing."

"Maybe." Hannah turned to Cheryl. "Tell us more about Sven."

"Gosh, let me think." Cheryl settled into her chair. "I moved here in 1961 when I was nineteen years old. Sven arrived when I was thirty-four. I remember that because I had just bought my Ford Pinto station wagon. It was blue, with wood side paneling, and I got a good deal on it because my dad was still alive back then, and he was friends with the man who owned the dealership. Boy, was that a great car."

"Sven," Mary prompted. "You were telling us about Mr. Mustache."

"Oh, that's right. Sorry." Cheryl set down her coffee. "Sven worked at The Summer Wind for less than a year. Oscar Lexter, the former owner of Seaside Resort, fired Sven after he was caught hot-sheeting in Triton's Cottage."

"Hot-sheeting?" Hannah asked.

Cheryl raised her eyebrows. "Like a gigolo!"

"I still don't understand what hot-sheeting means." Mary leaned forward in her chair.

"He was having affairs in the hotel rooms," Cheryl explained. "Paid or unpaid, I don't know. I told you Sven could make bacon sizzle all by himself. That's not the only thing he could heat up. Not that I would know anything about that. I was a single mom with a seven-year-old, and that made me ancient as far as a hot stud like Sven was concerned."

"Wait a second," said Hannah. "I'm remembering something you told me a while ago. Wasn't Oscar's wife involved with Sven, too?"

"Iris?" Cheryl nodded. "That's right. She had a thing for him, but I don't think she was Sven's type either, which made it weird that I saw them flirting so much. To him, I was old, but Iris was ancient."

"Where does Sven live now?" Mary asked. "Maybe I should return this photo album to him."

"Or maybe it belongs to the woman in the pictures." Hannah tightened the belt on her bathrobe. "There's that letter on the first page, after all."

"Read it to me," said Cheryl. "I didn't have my glasses on and might have missed something."

Hannah opened to page one in the album and read out loud. "'My darling girl. This isn't how I wanted our story to end. Pretend that I'm riding off into the sunset with music playing instead of leaving you like this. You can still have a delightful day in Sand Dollar Cove. Watch a movie. Play on the beach. Fly a kite. Visit the ice cream shop. But promise that you'll forget me.'"

"Sven must have given the album to the woman with the baby," said Mary. "What a dirtbag."

"I believe the correct term is 'absentee father' these days," said Cheryl. "Although dirtbag works, too."

"But you don't recognize the woman or the little girl?" Mary asked again.

"Nope. Sorry. So many people moved to Sand Dollar Cove in the 1960s and 1970s that it was impossible to know everyone. Then the town shrank in the 1980s during the recession."

"Now we have remote workers flooding in," said Hannah. "Our small town sure is certainly changing."

"And not necessarily for the better," Cheryl added.

There was a pause in the conversation, and then Hannah changed the subject.

"So, how was your date with Steven last night?" she asked. "I noticed you got home past midnight."

"We ordered pizza and watched a movie."

"Until midnight?" Hannah frowned. "So much for taking it slow."

"I *am* taking it slow," Mary countered, annoyed with her sister's disapproval. "I know what I'm getting with Steven, a fun-loving, smart, empathetic man who cares about me."

Hannah looked at her sideways. "The next thing you know, you'll be raising rats to feed his snake—and you hate rats."

"Celine and Dion eat frozen guinea pigs and white feeder rabbits, actually."

"Celine and Dion?" Cheryl asked. "Who are they? I thought Steven's snake was named Elvis."

"Elvis is his ball python," Mary clarified. "Celine's his reticulated python and Dion is an albino Burmese."

"Wait a sec." Hannah's nose wrinkled. "He has *three* snakes? Not just one?"

"Yeah." Mary lifted her chin. "And those snakes are another reason to admire Steven. He takes incredibly good care of them, especially Celine and Dion, who aren't as young as they once were, and need the thermostat to be at exactly—" A startling shriek from upstairs interrupted Mary's sentence.

"I did it!" Jeremy shouted, as he bounded down the stairs. "I got an A on my math test! My teacher just posted the grades online."

"Congratulations," said Mary. "That's awesome. All that studying paid off."

"Yeah," said Hannah. "Congrats."

"Well done, young man," said Cheryl.

"Thanks." Jeremy beamed. "Wait until I tell Kenzie. She's a million times better than my teacher. If she didn't tutor me, I'd have failed." He took out his phone.

"What did I miss?" Brittany ran into the room from the kitchen. "Is everything okay?"

"Better than okay," said Jeremy. "I got an A on my math test. It was worth thirty percent of my grade, so this really pulls my average up."

"That's wonderful." Brittany hugged him. "I'm so proud of you."

"Yeah. This is such a huge relief," said Jeremy. "I don't know why my teacher waited until Sunday morning to post the grades, though. It's like she doesn't care about us at all."

"I'm sure that's not true," said Brittany. "You can't expect teachers to work on the weekends. Maybe she—"

"Why are you defending her?" Jeremy asked.

"I'm not defending her," Brittany said. "I was explaining that—"

"She's a horrible teacher. I already told you that, but you don't listen." Jeremy folded his arms across his chest.

"Keith's dad was her mentor teacher," said Brittany. "He said—"

"Our old math teacher?" Mary asked Hannah.

Hannah nodded.

"So you'll listen to Keith's dad's opinion of my teacher but not mine?" Jeremy glared at Brittany. "Why does that not surprise me at all?"

"I *am* listening to you," Brittany said. "Keith's dad said that—"

"I don't care what he said." Jeremy pointed at Brittany. "And I don't care what *you* say either." He stomped up the stairs.

"What did I do?" Brittany asked the room.

"It's a tough age," said Cheryl. "Hang in there."

"I hope I can." Brittany flopped next to Mary on the couch. "I'm counting the days until he graduates and gets his diploma, but then what? We can't afford for him to live in the dorms at Grays Harbor State, so he'll still be living here at home, butting heads with me."

Shoot. Mary still hadn't told Brittany about Jeremy's plans to live with his father next year in Seattle, like she'd promised. Ian wasn't exactly Brittany's favorite person, but she deserved to know that Jeremy was moving in with her ex. "What about—" she began to say, only to realize that Hannah was already talking.

"No offense to Keith, but his dad was my least favorite teacher ever," said Hannah. "I wouldn't trust that man's opinion on anything to do with education."

"Really?" Brittany asked.

"Cross my heart." Hannah made crisscross marks over her chest. "He never walked around the classroom. He never graded homework. He had a monotone voice that put everyone to sleep." She shuddered. "That man would have been fired if it weren't for tenure."

"Oh." Brittany's shoulders rounded forward. "He told me great things about Jeremy's teacher, and that students do well in her class if they try hard."

"Jeremy *did* try hard," said Mary. "Kenzie's basically retaught him the whole syllabus, as far as I can tell. Kenzie should be the one teaching the class, if you ask me." Maybe this was her opportunity to keep her promise to Jeremy. "And I think there's another solution for next year that you might want to consider."

"Really?" Brittany looked at Mary. "What?"

"Jeremy mentioned to me that he might want to go to community college for a while in Seattle, and then transfer to Grays Harbor State. He wants to train to become an EMT and then a firefighter."

"A firefighter?" Brittany's eyes opened wide. "What? This is news to me."

"Yeah, he wasn't sure how you'd react, so he asked me to tell you first." Mary stuffed her hands into the wide sleeves of her bathrobe and hugged herself. "He'd move in with Ian."

"Live with his dad? That's a horrible idea." Brittany frowned.

"He wouldn't be home at Ian's house very often," said Mary. "He'd be going to school, and working, and out with friends. It would be an excellent opportunity for him to explore the city."

"And a great opportunity for the two of you to have more space," Hannah pointed out. "You just said you wished he could move into the dorms and get some independence. This would be a nice halfway point."

"Max loved his time in the city when he attended the University of Washington," said Cheryl. "It made him appreciate coming back home to Sand Dollar Cove once he'd graduated."

Brittany squeezed her eyes shut. "I wish parenting teen boys wasn't so hard."

"Said every mother in America," Cheryl muttered.

"I think he's on the right path." Mary took the last sip of her coffee and put it down on the glass coaster. "He goes to school full time and holds down a part-time job. He was willing to be tutored so he could bring up his math grade."

"He was willing to be tutored to spend time with Kenzie, is more like it," said Brittany.

"They're not dating," said Mary. "Officially, at least. Kenzie was upset that he didn't invite her to the winter formal."

"Oh." Brittany pulled a lock of curly hair behind her ear. "I didn't know that."

"It's not your fault for not knowing," said Cheryl. "The boy doesn't tell you anything."

"He doesn't tell me anything, either," said Hannah. "Then again, I'm hardly ever here."

"Jeremy talks to me a lot," said Mary. "And I'm telling you that you've done a good job raising him. He's on the right track. I think his plan for moving to Seattle next September is a good one. Training to become an EMT is a wise idea, too, because it's so hard to become a firefighter these days. One of my old co-workers at the coffee stand told me that."

"It's all about the pension plan," said Cheryl. "If I could go back in time, I would have strutted my stuff in front of the fire-house until someone noticed me."

"Gran!" Hannah exclaimed.

"A sweet, hunky fireman willing to take a chance on a single mom," Cheryl said, looking out into the distance. "Back when my boobs were still perky, and I could stand up straight."

"Thankfully women's empowerment has advanced a lot beyond those days," said Hannah. "I don't need a man with a pension plan, I've got my own 401K to save for retirement, and Mary has a Roth IRA."

"I do?" Mary asked.

"Yeah. I helped you set one up with the insurance money from Dad."

"Oh. That's right. I knew I had investment accounts, I just forgot what they were called."

"I'm proud of you girls." Cheryl smiled. "You're living lives I could only dream of. Education. Running Seaside

Resort. Starting your own business. Enjoying life with birth control."

"Gran!" Hannah chirped, for the second time that morning.

"Always remember to take your birth control," Cheryl cautioned. "It's the best invention in the entire world."

"Speaking as the mom of a teenager, I'd have to agree," said Brittany.

"My point is that the world has changed," said Cheryl. "Sand Dollar Cove isn't what it was like fifty years ago, especially for women, and thank goodness for that. I'm glad my granddaughters live in a world with opportunities. I didn't have the choices you have when I was your age. Maybe if I had, I wouldn't have been a housekeeper for fifty years."

"There's nothing wrong with being a housekeeper," said Hannah. "You did valuable work."

"I know it," said Cheryl. "I also know that it was better than the alternative."

"What was that?" Mary asked.

"Being a single mom with no way to support my family at all," Cheryl said ominously.

"Mom could have supported us, if she had wanted to," Hannah said.

Mary agreed.

"I wasn't talking about your mom," said Cheryl. "But now that you've brought Kelly up, she didn't have many job skills to work with beyond running a video store cash register."

"Mom had our house and some savings, and she squandered all of it," said Mary. "Don't defend her."

"I'm not," said Cheryl. "Kelly did wrong by both of you. She had choices, and she chose poorly."

Mary felt that Cheryl was right; women did have more opportunities for advancement now than they had fifty years ago, and yet Mary had still walked into a situation where she was exploited. She still wished she could travel back through time and make different choices. Steven had told her it wasn't her fault for following Zeke's instructions, and that as a victim, she shouldn't blame herself. But that didn't stop her unease from bubbling up.

Maybe this was the time to finally tell her sister and grandma about Zeke and the movie? Or maybe she should wait to hear from Steven first... She'd rather tell her family the good news about landing a starring role in a film than the bad news that came with it. Hopefully she'd never have to tell them about the bad parts at all.

NINETEEN

"Good news," said Steven, as soon as Mary walked into his office on Monday morning. "I just submitted my pro hac vice application in California. My next step is to file the injunction and temporary restraining order. That'll make Zeke take you seriously."

This was really happening. Someone was finally standing up for her! Mary threw her arms around Steven. "Thank you," she said, her voice muffled by his shoulder. She closed her eyes and breathed in the scent of laundry detergent that clung to his shirt. Her future felt hopeful, like the fresh scent of spring rain. Now that Steven was fighting for her, maybe that locker room scene could be washed away like a bad stain.

"I'm so sorry this happened to you." Steven enveloped her with powerful arms. "But you're not alone anymore. I'd take on this case even if you weren't my girlfriend."

"Did you just take that as an opportunity to call me your girlfriend again?"

"Me? Never."

Their lips crushed together and Mary linked her arms

around his neck. She lifted on her tiptoes and tilted her head to the side as she savored every moment of contact. Here was a man who seemed to truly care for her. Here was a man she could trust. At long last, Mary had a partner who respected her creativity and didn't belittle her for her flaws. The intensity she felt for Steven was so strong that she knew she was making the right decision. There could only be one decision. The choice was clear. Her heart yearned for him in a way that made each heartbeat sing his name.

"Oh Steven," she murmured when their lips parted. "Life feels like it was black and white before I met you, and now everything is in color."

"I knew moving here was the right decision." He gazed into her eyes. "It was a leap of faith that paid off."

Mary grinned. "Glad it worked out for you."

"It definitely worked out." Steven was about to kiss her again when a knock at his office door interrupted them. Their bodies pressed together for one hot second before Steven sighed and stepped away to the side. "Come in," he called.

"Hey, Steven," said Nick, entering the room. "Shane and I are setting things up to refinish the floor in the basement before we leave for Oregon on Wednesday. Did you want us to do the floor in the storage room too?"

Steven looked at Mary. "Do I?"

"Yes." Mary nodded. "You do."

"That would be an affirmative then," said Steven.

"Okay, well, I'll have my crew clear those shelves out of there this afternoon, but what do you want to do with the boxes?"

Steven groaned. "I can't believe how much junk was down there."

"We're almost done sorting through it," said Mary. "There can't be that much more." She looked at Nick. "Will you have enough time to refinish the basement floor all in one day?" It would be just like Nick to do a rush job. Hannah always said he was lazy.

"Sure," Nick said in a way that didn't reassure Mary at all. "Piece of cake."

Ugh. The sooner they cleared the storage room the better, so that Nick's crew could get started on those floors. Mary thought about the task ahead. If she and Steven worked fast, the room could be ready by lunchtime.

"It would be great if you could start on the floors in the storage room today," she said. "By one p.m. That'll give you more time for the main room in the basement tomorrow." Mary looked Nick directly in the eye. "I know Steven said it was okay to take off for a week of vacation, but we both expect quality work. Just because it's the basement doesn't mean you can cut corners."

"Yes, ma'am." Nick let out a puff of laughter. "You're a bossy one, aren't you? Like your sister."

Mary folded her arms across her chest. She didn't like Nick's tone, but she took the comparison to Hannah as a compliment. "I'm not bossy, I'm the designer, and my client deserves this place to be perfect. He's paying you for high-quality workmanship and I know you can deliver." Mary smiled icily. "Right?"

"Like I said before, yes ma'am." Nick tipped an imaginary cap to her and left the room.

"Wow." Steven whistled. "I didn't know you could be such an enforcer."

"Nick needs to be kept on a short leash," said Mary. "That's what Hannah told me, and I have no reason to doubt her." She pecked Steven on the cheek. "Now let's go deal with that storage room."

With a wave to Celine and Dion, they both headed downstairs.

"This shouldn't be too bad," Steven said as he held the door open for her. "Most of the crap is already gone."

"Yeah, we've been picking away at it." Mary lifted a bag of packing peanuts. "The main thing is to move the shelves out of here."

"I was thinking we could bring them up to my office while they do the floors."

"Or we could store them in the women's restroom. It'll take two weeks for the floor to cure before we can bring them back here."

"Yeah, that's a good point. Don't move anything heavy. You're the brains of this operation, not the muscle."

Mary chuckled. "I'll try not to throw out my back carrying this Styrofoam." Mary hefted the bag over her shoulder, grabbed a smaller box of napkins, and took the items upstairs to the restroom. When she came back down, she found Steven dismantling the shelves.

"I thought it would be easier to move them in pieces," he explained.

"Good idea."

Together, they carried five slats up to the restroom. At this point, Mary tied her sweatshirt around her waist. The basement was cooler than the balmy upstairs, but she was breaking a sweat from the work.

"I'll get one of Nick's people to help me move the frame out of here," said Steven.

"I can at least help you shove it out of the room," said Mary. "Now that the slats are gone, the shelves are light."

"Well, okay. But if you hurt your back—"

"I'll be fine," she promised. Mary grabbed one side of the shelf frame and Steven grabbed the other. "On the count of three," she directed. "One, two, three!"

Working together, they slid the unit three feet to the right, which is exactly what Mary intended to happen. What she didn't intend was for part of the wall to come with the shelf!

Plaster crumbled to the ground. White dust shot into the air like a mushroom cloud. An earthy smell filled the room.

"Oh no!" Mary cried. "We ripped open the wall!"

"What in the world?" Steven exclaimed.

"I'm so sorry." Mary wiped her dusty hands on her jeans. "Moisture must have made the metal stick to the drywall, or something." She kicked her feet out, her toes covered in rubble.

"Are you okay?" Steven touched her shoulder. "You got the brunt of it."

"I'm fine." Mary waved her hand in front of her face to clear the air. "I'll probably have a coughing attack in a minute or two."

"Be careful with your eyes. It looks like a tin of baking powder exploded on your face."

"Really?" Mary untied her sweatshirt and wiped her cheeks and forehead.

When Mary pulled her sweatshirt away, she saw it was covered with a chalky residue. "I've never seen a shelving unit stick to the wall like that. It's like it was glued to the plaster." Now that she could see clearly, she peered at the wall. What in the world? "Steven!" Mary cried. "There's a door!"

"No..." He stepped forward. "Well, I'll be damned."

"Where do you think it leads?"

"I don't know." Steven took out his phone and turned on his flashlight. "Let's open it and find out."

"We'll be explorers," said Mary.

"Adventurers, like we're in an Indiana Jones sequel."

"Exactly." Mary blinked dust out of her eyes and her vision cleared. "But why is the door wrinkly?"

"Huh?" Steven angled the flashlight.

"Look." Mary brushed dirt off the door and revealed a wrinkled finish. "That's not paint or wallpaper."

"What is it? All I see is dirt."

"Let me try this." Mary used her sweatshirt like it was a rag and wiped white dust off a huge swath. "Whoa!" she cried. "I've seen that coating before. Is that... Could it be...?" The diamond pattern was eerily familiar. She turned and looked at Steven. "Is this door covered in rattlesnake skin?"

Like the photo album.

Like the book with the blonde girl in pigtails.

Was there a connection?

"No way. Rattlesnakes are this thick." Steven held out his fingers. "It would take a bazillion rattlesnakes to cover a door this size."

"But look." Mary pointed to the edges of each pattern. "That's where the snake's belly would be, right? They're stitched together somehow. Glued, maybe."

"It's not rattlesnake."

"Then what is it? It's got to be some sort of snakeskin, right? Look how long the strips are."

"I think we're getting off track." Steven turned off the flashlight.

Mary continued wiping down the door. "The resemblance to the photo album is uncanny. And you said that photo album was made of rattlesnake, so I wonder if the same craftsmen made both pieces." *Sven Nilsen, maybe,* she thought to herself. She shook out her sweatshirt and retied it around her waist. "Let's see what's behind the door."

"I'm not sure that's a good idea. What if—"

But Mary was already trying the handle. "Locked, dammit." She shook the handle hard but all it did was rattle. "I wonder if there's a key around here?" She spun on her toes.

"It's probably another storage room. Nothing to get excited about."

"If it was only a normal-looking door, sure, I'd agree with you. But a snakeskin door? That's not normal. I've never heard about someone decorating a storage closet with snakeskin." Dropping to her hands and knees, Mary crawled along the floor.

"What are you doing?" Steven asked.

"Looking for the key. It's got to be here somewhere."

"Maybe it's on the key ring the former owners left for me."

"Hopefully so, because I'm not seeing it down here."

"Let's focus on moving the shelves out of here so that Nick can work on the floors. We're running out of time to make that happen."

Mary sighed. Steven was right. She rose gingerly to her feet. "Okay, good point. Plus, maybe we'll find the key behind one of these shelves. It might have fallen through a crack or something."

"I know you're excited," Steven said, as he took the heavy side of the shelving frame. "But it's probably a broom closet."

"But why the snakeskin?"

"We don't know that it's snakeskin. It could be a weird 1970s wallpaper."

"Well, maybe," Mary conceded. "But I think it looks similar. It's like a larger-scale version of the album." They stopped pushing the shelving unit when they reached the bottom of the staircase, so that Nick's crew could carry it upstairs. When they re-entered the storage room, the door called to Mary like a mystery waiting to be solved. "Why would someone spend so much time decorating a door, only to cover it up with shelves?"

"Who knows why interior designers do what they do?" Steven winked at her. "I never argue with creative brilliance."

"Flattery will get you everywhere." Mary was about to hug him when she realized how filthy she'd become. She didn't smell that great either. She took another look at the door. "Do you think that whoever decorated that door might have been a herpetologist?"

"Maybe. But most herpers I know like to study snakes, not paste dead ones to their walls."

Was Sven a snake enthusiast? Cheryl had never mentioned that about him. Mary thought back to the photographs in the album. None of them had pictured snakes. The only thing remotely related to reptiles was the cover.

"What are the chances that you have the key to that closet upstairs in your office?" she asked.

"Slim to none," Steven admitted, as he picked slats off the next shelf. "But maybe Nick has some locksmith skills. We can find out."

"Absolutely." Mary wiped sweat off her forehead. She didn't know what she was looking forward to more: finding out what was behind that door, or going home and taking a shower.

"Are these the shelves we need to move?" Shane asked, as he came down the stairs to the basement.

"That's right," said Steven.

Shane looked Mary up and down from head to toe. "What happened to you?"

"I got a bit dirty, moving boxes." Mary was annoyed. It was none of his business what she looked like.

Shane's eyes opened wide. "No, I mean that giant scrape on your arm. It's bleeding."

"What?" Steven gasped. He looked at Mary. "Shoot, you're bleeding."

"I don't feel anything," said Mary as she looked down at her arm. A diagonal slash across her arm oozed blood.

"I've got a first aid kit in my office." Steven gently pressed his hand to her back. "Let's get that cleaned up."

"I must have scraped my arm when I was moving shelves," Mary mumbled. "It's not a big deal."

"You leave the shelf-moving to the professionals," said Shane. "I'll take it from here."

"I'm perfectly capable of helping," Mary started to say, but when she saw the worried look in Steven's eyes, she stopped arguing.

He brought her upstairs, washed her arm in the restroom sink, tortured her with antiseptic, and then applied a half dozen bandages. "When was your last tetanus shot?" Steven asked.

"I don't know. Is this a tetanus shot situation?"

"It could be." Steven's forehead wrinkled with concern. "What if you scraped your arm against a rusty bit on that old shelf? We don't know what caused the scrape."

"It's not that bad."

"It could scar! And I'd never forgive myself." He kissed her fingertips. "Your beautiful arm."

Mary giggled. "I promise I won't scar."

"But lockjaw, that's a serious matter."

"Lockjaw?"

"The old-fashioned word for tetanus. At least call your doctor and check your vaccination status."

"I think that's online now." Mary took out her phone. "I remember seeing that when I got my last Covid booster." She searched through her email and pulled up the website. It took her another couple of minutes to remember her password. But finally, she was into the system. "Huh," she said, Steven's worry beginning to infect her. "It says my last DTaP booster was when I was four."

"Four years old?" Steven exclaimed. "That's it, I'm taking you to the doctor."

Mary sighed. This was not on her agenda today. "I can handle that myself." She scrolled through the contacts on her phone until she found the number for her doctor. "You've got tons to do, including looking for that storage closet key. But thanks for the offer to take me."

"Call me as soon as you're warded against tetanus." Steven hugged her on her good side. "And ask the doctor about scar prevention. I mean it when I say I don't want anything happening to that beautiful arm of yours."

"You mean this arm?" Mary extended her hand out in front of them and angled the phone at their faces. "Grimy selfie time!" She snapped a picture of their side hug. Steven wasn't the only one who wanted to document their budding relationship.

TWENTY

The next morning, Mary's arm still stung, but Cheryl had gooped it up with so much Neosporin that she felt confident it wouldn't get infected. The doctor hadn't been worried about the scratch at all but had given Mary a tetanus booster and a stern lecture about forgetting to get her flu shot last fall. After stopping by the old coffee stand where she used to work for some java on the house, Mary arrived at the movie theater with a cappuccino for herself and a regular drip for Steven. They'd talked about meeting there at nine a.m. to make sure that Nick's crew got to work on the floors, work that was supposed to have started the day before. But when Mary pulled up to the movie theater, she didn't see Steven's minivan. Nick's truck was there though, and she viewed that as a promising sign.

Before she got out of her car, Mary sent Steven a quick text. *I'm here and I brought caffeine.* She added a heart for good measure.

You're my hero, Steven replied with three hearts in a row. *Sorry I'm late. Got a leg cramp while running.*

Ouch! Are you okay?

I walked it off. Feel fine now.

Take care. Now I'm here, I'll make sure Nick's getting going on the floors.

Great, Steven texted. *He really needs to get moving on that.*

I agree.

I'll be there as soon as I can.

Celine, Dion, and I will be waiting for you, Mary texted. She picked up the coffee and exited her car.

Walking into the warm theater was a welcome relief. The quick trip from her car had left her chilled. Steven's office was even warmer, of course, because of the pythons. She left the coffees on his desk and greeted Celine and Dion. Then she went out to the lobby where the shelving units were pushed to the side, instead of in the women's restrooms where she'd wanted them to be stored temporarily. Hannah had been right; Nick was completely unreliable. "Nick?" she called through the empty lobby. "Shane?" When nobody answered, she figured they must be downstairs, hopefully working on those floors.

Hurrying down to the basement, Mary found Nick and Shane standing around two unplugged floor refinishing machines, eating donuts.

"Hey, Mary." Nick held out the pink bakery box. "Want one? There's a maple bar left."

"Thanks, but no thanks." Mary looked around the room. "Today's the big day for the floors, huh?" she asked, trying to avoid a confrontation. What she really wanted to know was why the hell hadn't they started yet.

"Yeah." Nick helped himself to the last maple bar. "I assume you talked to Steven this morning?"

"I texted him a little bit ago," said Mary. "He'll be here any minute." That wasn't exactly true. As far as she knew he was still walking off his leg cramp, but Mary didn't want to give Nick any excuse to delay the work further. "Steven's eager to see the floors be refinished," she added.

"Yeah." Shane dusted powdered sugar off his hands. "Same. But not as eager as I was to explore that tunnel."

"Tunnel?" Mary asked, confused.

"What a surprise *that* was," said Nick. "What did you think when Steven told you about it?"

Told her about it? Steven hadn't told her anything. Why not? But Mary certainly wasn't going to reveal private details about her boyfriend's lack of communication with these two. "I was as surprised as you were," she bluffed.

"Surprised is right." Shane licked his fingers.

"We were going to start on the floors yesterday afternoon," said Nick. "But once we jimmied open that door and saw the tunnel behind it, that changed our plans."

The door.

The rattlesnake door.

It wasn't a broom closet after all!

It led to an underground tunnel?

"Of course it would change your plans," said Mary, using every acting skill she knew from her former improv classes. "I only wish I had been there to discover it with you." At least she could see it now though. Mary looked toward the storage room, itching to ditch Nick and Shane and explore that tunnel herself.

"It seems a shame that we had to seal it up," Shane said a second later. "I still don't see why we had to do that."

It was closed? Shoot! Why? Mary tried to find a delicate way of finding out. "Sealing it up," she echoed. "Why was that again?"

"Because Steven said it was unsafe," said Nick.

Shane scoffed. "Suddenly he was a building code inspector."

"The rooms looked stable to me." Nick picked up the last pastry from the box. "They were well lit, too, what with those purple skylights." He waved a donut in the air. "Skylights as circular as this jelly roll."

Purple skylights?

Like the ones they'd seen at the underground tour in Seattle?

Goosebumps raced down her arms. There had been that big box of glass coasters they'd found in the storage room...

What if they weren't coasters? What if they were tunneling supplies?

Could Sand Dollar Cove have an underground, too?

No... that was impossible. Her imagination was running away with her. Mary had lived here her whole life and never heard of an underground. Probably it was just one tunnel.

Her phone buzzed and she looked at the screen and read the text from Steven.

Just arrived. Can't wait to see you.

"Steven's here," Mary told the workmen. "Good luck with the floors today. I'm just going to check in that storage room and see if I left my..." She scrambled to think of something to say. "Hairbrush."

Hairbrush? Was that the best she could come up with? Annoyed with herself, Mary raced to the storage room. When she arrived, she gasped.

The back wall had been replastered.

The door was sealed off!

Not only that, it appeared as if the door had never existed at all.

What was Steven up to? Why hadn't he told her about this?

He'd called her last night after her doctor's appointment. They'd FaceTimed before falling asleep that evening. Mary had thought it was romantic. Then this morning she had texted him and he hadn't mentioned the tunnel either. Why was he keeping this from her? This was huge! Why hadn't Steven called her right away?

Full of questions, Mary marched upstairs to find Steven and get answers. He was in his office, crouched in front of the snake enclosures, whispering sweet nothings to his pets. Witnessing him being such a tender caretaker softened her ire a bit, but then she remembered that he'd lied to her. Well, not exactly lied, but an omission of truth of this magnitude was still a huge freaking deal, and after her experience with Aidan, Mary had a low opinion of sneaky boyfriends.

Sneaky... was that what Steven was? Mary's heart squeezed painfully in her chest. She hoped not. She really, really hoped not.

"Hi, Steven," she said, from her spot at the doorway. "Good morning."

"Good morning to you, too." He smiled and stood. "I've been looking forward to doing this since the moment I woke up." Steven crossed the room and swept her up in his arms, kissing her with a passion that made her pulse race.

It was like being caught up in a fantasy, and Mary desperately wanted the fantasy to be true. She wanted Steven to be her exuberant prince charming, even if he wasn't.

Mary pulled away. "I spoke with Nick and Shane. They're starting on the floors now." She looked directly into his eyes, waiting for him to expand on that. To tell her that the crew was supposed to begin work yesterday, only they made a major discovery that he didn't have time to tell her about.

"Good." Steven nodded. "It'll be interesting to see what the floors look like when they're done."

Mary felt the tickle of tears in her eyes, but she fought them with every ounce of strength she had. *I'm being lied to,* she thought mournfully. *Again.* Was that her lot in life? To be manipulated by untrustworthy men?

To be manipulated by untrustworthy people, she added, thinking of her mom.

She looked down at her fingernails, which she'd recently painted in a bright shade of purple. "The basement will be off-limits for two weeks. Nobody will be able to go down there once the floor is curing."

"That's right." Steven walked over to the lone window and opened the blinds.

"Did you ever find a key to that storage closet?" Mary watched him, but his back was turned, and she couldn't see his face.

"Yeah, I did," he said.

Yes! Her heart lurched like she'd just finished a roller coaster. Steven was true after all. She shouldn't have doubted him. He had only taken his time telling her, that was all.

"Oh?" Mary asked innocently.

"I found the key on the ring they'd given me after I won the auction." Steven lifted the blinds all the way up. "But all that was in that closet was a mop and a bucket." He turned around to face her. "Should we go over the plans for the mural in the lobby now? The muralist will be here in a couple of days, right?"

She should confront him. Right here, right now. That's what her brain told her to do.

But her heart told her to ignore it. Her heart told her to let the untruth be.

Act like things were okay.

Pretend so he would love her.

If she fought it, she'd have to break up with Steven, and he was the best thing that had happened to her in ages.

"I'm excited about the mural," Mary said, stalling for time.

"I'm proud of this whole project." Her eyes drifted around the room. The satin-finish black walls. The floor-to-ceiling velvet curtains creating the illusion of a window. The "Zombie Emergency Kit" on the chest freezer.

Zombies... If Mary accused Steven of lying and broke up with him, what would happen to her legal fight against Zeke? She needed Steven's expertise on that. Mary was completely out of her element.

Weak.

Helpless.

Pathetic.

Unable to protect herself.

It was like she was performing the same script, year after year, and the other actors changed roles, but Mary's was always the same. Pretending to be injured so her mother could steal. Acting like a seductress so the movie would succeed. Falling in love with the wrong person. Trusting people that were unworthy of trust. She was the damsel in distress and her heroes always turned out to be villains.

What was it Hannah had said about Mary rushing into things? Her sister had warned her about her tendency to make rash decisions. Maybe the best thing Mary could do for herself right now was give herself time to think, before she acted too hastily.

"I'd love to discuss the mural," she said, "but I have a follow-up appointment for wound care at the clinic."

Steven rushed over to her and picked up her hand. "You said it wasn't that bad and the doctor said not to worry!"

"That's right," Mary answered truthfully before continuing with her falsehood. Now she was the one who was lying, and that felt awful. "It's just that the nurse needs to check it again, to be safe." She squeezed his fingertips. "It's probably nothing, but like you said, I don't want to risk scarring."

"Absolutely not." He kissed the tip of her nose. "Not with

arms as pretty as yours."

"I think you're the one with the good-looking arms." Mary squeezed his biceps. "I'll be back when I can." Her voice cracked as she said it. Would she ever come back? Would she ever be able to trust Steven again?

She had to.

She had a job to finish, renovating this theater.

And she needed Steven's help with Zeke.

Crap, she was in a heap of trouble. Not knowing what to do about any of it, Mary said goodbye to Steven, put on her coat, and left the movie theater.

Gray clouds blanketed the sky, blocking out the sun. The temperature was a crisp forty-two degrees, and the air was heavy with unfallen raindrops. Mary could smell the rain coming and pulled up her hood. She trudged to her car, her mood sinking with every step. The rain started right when she reached the curb. Looking down at her feet, she saw the drops hit the concrete one by one, like polka dots. It was meditative, watching the rain fall like that. Soothing, almost. She snapped the chin strap underneath her hood and felt the rain pelt the impervious fabric of her raincoat.

At least I'm strong enough for rain, she thought, as she let the Pacific Northwest weather wash over her. The spring shower felt good, even though her jeans were getting wet. But she couldn't stand on the sidewalk forever. Steven might come out and see her here and ask questions. Then she'd have to talk to him again, and what would she say?

Mary looked both ways to make sure there wasn't any traffic, and then stepped off the curb and walked around her car. When she got to the driver's side she reached for the handle.

It was then, looking down, that Mary saw it.

Something she'd probably seen a hundred times, but never noticed before.

Purple glass, partially crusted over by asphalt.

TWENTY-ONE

She followed the purple glass circles like Dorothy on the Yellow Brick Road. They were hard to spot, unless you knew what you were looking for. At the end of every block was a bank of glass skylights. Mary had walked over them hundreds of times before and had never noticed them, just like she paid no attention to sewer covers or storm drains. But now that she was specifically looking for them, she found them. Many were covered by asphalt, and she could only see tiny spots of purple where the road had worn away and the amethyst glass shone through. Every time Mary saw another glimpse of purple, she felt a hitch in her breath from excitement. The path shot west, toward the ocean, and closer to Main Street. Then it took a hard right and veered into an alley behind the kite shop.

Sand Dollar Cove *did* have an underground. There wasn't just one tunnel, there were many!

Mary dodged dumpsters and parked cars. She passed a little cottage that she knew belonged to the owner of the whale watching company. Exiting the first alley, she crossed the street and entered the second. Mary kept walking, following the skylight banks until she reached a familiar sight—the large googly eyes of cartoon roller skates.

"The senior center!" she exclaimed. Rain fell so hard now that it was difficult to hear the sound of her own voice. In fact, it was so noisy she almost didn't hear her phone ring. She hurried underneath the shelter of a back porch stoop before she answered. "Hello?"

"Mary it's me, Steven. Are you okay?"

"What?"

"Your car is still parked in front of the theater. I was worried you were mugged or fell and broke your hip."

"Broke my hip?"

"It can happen to anyone. One wrong step, and bam!"

"Oh..." Now that she'd lost faith in him, she couldn't tell if he was being sinister, or sweet.

"That's what happened to my Aunt Helena."

"I'm not in my eighties, so you don't have to worry about that with me," she said decidedly. Steven *was* sweet, she decided. He was a bold-faced liar, but he still had a sensitive soul. "I've never heard of anyone being mugged in Sand Dollar Cove. But..." Her eyes drifted over to the roller skate mural. "I needed to run over and check on my gran before my doctor's appointment. She was a bit wobbly this morning." That was technically true, although Cheryl was *always* wobbly.

"Is everything okay?"

"Her back hurts. Osteoporosis is rough."

"Please let me know if there's anything I can do to help."

"I will, thanks."

"And watch out for hip fractures with her."

"Got it. I'll text you later." After she hung up, she found two more skylight banks, the last one only ten feet away from the ramp that led to the back door of the senior center. Her thoughts swimming through turbulent emotions, Mary ran up the ramp and knocked on the door.

Brittany opened it wearing an apron. "Mary? What are you doing here? You're soaking wet."

Mary didn't know where to begin. "I'm here because... Well, the thing is..."

"Shut the darn door!" Keith's voice bellowed. "You're letting the heat out."

Brittany frowned. "You better come in out of the cold."

"He shouldn't talk to you like that," Mary whispered hoarsely. "Why do you put up with it?"

"He's my boss," Brittany whispered back. "And he has a good heart."

Mary wasn't sure about that, especially when she saw Keith adjust his glasses on his nose and peer at her like an eagle spotting prey.

"What are you doing here?" Keith asked. "Brittany's in the middle of supervising lunch for the guests and doesn't have time for socializing."

"I've already checked the numbers for the diabetics," Brittany shot back.

"I'm not here to see Brittany, I'm here to see my grandma," Mary said quickly, not wanting to cause any more problems for her landlord. "I came in through the back door because it was closer, and the rain was falling so hard." She unzipped her coat and hung it on a hook.

"Oh. Okay," said Keith. "If you end up staying for lunch though, I need to charge you fifteen dollars."

"I'll be gone by then." Mary adjusted her purse. "This will be a quick visit. I just need to ask Gran some questions."

That was it. As the words came out of her mouth, she knew what she had to do. Mary would ask Cheryl what she knew about the underground tunnels. *If* she knew about them at all, that is. Cheryl had never mentioned them before, not even when Mary had come back from the underground tour in Seattle. Cheryl wasn't the only person she could ask, either. This place was full of untapped knowledge, Mary knew.

She crossed through the swinging doors into the main room of the center and felt a glowing pride when she entered the welcoming space. It looked every bit as amazing as it had at the party, minus the balloon arch. Some people relaxed on the new sofas, others played cards by the window, and an older gentleman played blues on the piano.

The piano... Mary remembered Steven's performance on the keys, and how he'd come to her rescue the night of the party when the WiFi had cut out. What an incredible performance that had been. That was the night she'd officially fallen for him. But still, she'd held off, and kept Steven at arm's length for a little while longer before they began dating so that she could be absolutely sure he was trustworthy. At least, that's what she had *tried* to do.

Mary walked through the room as Cheryl waved from a cozy spot in the corner, at a table covered by fabric. Patti sat next to her, working a sewing machine, and Don was on the other side, holding a bright red pincushion shaped like a tomato.

"Well, look who it is," said Cheryl, with a huge smile on her face. "My favorite interior designer."

"Guess what?" Patti took her foot off the presser pedal and the sewing machine became quiet. "I'm making tablecloths for our Easter breakfast."

"It won't really be on Easter." Don jerked his thumb toward the kitchen. "Keith refuses to open the doors up on Sundays."

"Plus, some of us will be busy with church that day." Patti pulled out a pin and handed it to Don, who promptly stuck it into the tomato. "I wish my granddaughter Isabella could come, but she'll be with her mom that weekend."

"We convinced Keith to dress up like the Easter bunny and pass out jelly beans to the grandkids on the Monday after," said Cheryl.

"What?" Mary sat down. "I don't want Keith to give me candy."

"Not you, silly," said Cheryl. "The little grandkids."

"My daughter's driving up from Olympia with the twins." Don looked at Patti. "I can't wait for her to meet you, dollface."

Patti blushed. "I'm looking forward to it. I'm still waiting to see if my son Ryan will drive up, too."

"How did you get Keith to agree to wear a costume?" Mary asked, temporarily forgetting her mission.

"That was your grandma's doing," said Don. "I had no idea she was that evil."

Cheryl chuckled. "If you're going to have a hunchback you might as well channel your wicked witch vibes."

"Gran, what did you do?" Mary asked.

"Didn't I tell you?" Cheryl smoothed the pink fabric in front of her. "Maybe not. You've been so busy with Mr. Snake Charmer that I hardly see you anymore."

"Sorry about that," Mary said, wanting to protest that it wasn't true, but forced to admit that it was.

"That's okay." Cheryl patted her back. "I like Steven. He seems like a keeper."

Mary's heart lurched.

"Wait until you hear what happened," said Don. "It's hilarious."

"The mayor and three city council members were here last Tuesday," Cheryl explained. "To do Keith's annual performance review. And I was miffed with him for how he's been treating Brittany."

Patti clucked her tongue and shook her head. "She should dump him, if you ask me."

"Agreed." Mary nodded her head.

"The mayor wanted to know what I thought of Keith as our director," Cheryl continued. "I couldn't say anything bad about him after he helped us with our emergency housing situation last year, so I went for a sneak attack instead. I told the mayor how delighted I was that Keith had agreed to dress up like the Easter bunny."

"You should have seen the look on Keith's face." Don tossed his head back and laughed.

"Patti was brilliant, too," said Cheryl.

"I don't know if I'd say brilliant," said Patti. "All I did was say how excited I was that this would be the start of an annual tradition. I've known Brittany since she was a little girl, and I don't like hearing her mistreated either."

"Keith tried to get out of it by saying there wouldn't be enough funding to order the costume." Don stabbed a pin into the tomato. "But one of the council members offered to pay for the whole thing herself."

"Wow. I sure do miss a lot when I'm off in la-la land," said Mary.

"You should stop by more often so you can hear the news." Cheryl shifted in her seat. "So, what brought you in this morning?"

Mary hesitated. She'd been planning to jump in and tell Cheryl that Steven had lied to her, and how she could no longer trust him, but something held her back. It wasn't loyalty to Steven, so much as lingering affection. No; affection was too light of a word. Longing was more like it. Mary longed for Steven. Part of her wished she could go back in time to the state of unknowing, and still believe in the fantasy again. That he was the man she wanted him to be. A person she could fall in love with, or perhaps already loved. So instead of telling Cheryl about Steven's betrayal, she asked about the glass skylights instead.

"Remember those glass coasters you gave me for Christmas?" Mary leaned forward. "I saw them embedded into the alley outside. There was a whole path of them, one block after another, and I think they might be skylights."

"Skylights?" Don asked. "To where?"

"To an underground," Mary explained. "Like the one in Seattle."

"I've never heard about Sand Dollar Cove having an underground before," said Cheryl. "Have you, Patti?"

"No." She shook her head. "And I've lived here since I was a teenager."

"Then why would the glass circles be there?" Mary asked.

"Decoration maybe?" Cheryl suggested.

"Or maybe the early city planners were trying to seem cool, like Seattle," Don suggested.

"Sand Dollar Cove wouldn't want to copy Seattle," said Patti. "It was a cesspool back then."

"Still is if you ask me," said Cheryl. "A bad day in Sand Dollar Cove is better than a great day in Seattle."

"You definitely don't think there's an underground?" Mary asked.

"Not that we're aware of," said Cheryl.

"That's not true," said a voice, followed by a yippy bark. Ann-with-the-poodle pulled a chair up to the table. Her dog poked his head out of her purse, like he was eager to join the conversation too.

"You've heard of an underground?" Mary asked.

"Only rumors." Ann sat down next to Don. "And it was a long time ago. I was in high school. Class of seventy-two."

"You're practically a baby," said Cheryl. "I was a single mom in seventy-two."

"What was the rumor you heard?" Mary asked, not wanting her grandma to veer them off track.

"That there was a secret high-stakes poker club that was invite only. Or rather, an illegal gambling operation." Ann removed her poodle from her purse, set the tiny pup in her lap, and continued her story. "I overheard my parents talking about it. My dad was a deacon at the Methodist church and didn't want to believe that it was true, but my mom had heard it from our housekeeper who knew a card dealer. I remember my dad saying that if that rumor was true, he would have heard about it by then. But my mom said that nobody would have told him because of his position in the church."

"How does that have anything to do with an underground?" Patti asked.

"Because," said Ann, "the gambling happened in a basement."

"Lots of places have basements," said Cheryl. "That doesn't mean there's an underground."

"It does if the basements are connected." Ann fed her poodle a treat from her pocket. "Our housekeeper said that one of the entrances was at the T Bone Bluff."

"The steak house?" Mary asked.

"Yup." Ann nodded. "Of course, this is all hearsay. I don't even know if the T Bone Bluff has a basement."

Mary scratched her head. If it did have a basement, it would also have glass skylights outside. That would be a dead give-away. And if she could enter the tunnels from the restaurant, then she might be able to access whatever Steven tried to cover up at the movie theater, without him knowing. He shouldn't be the only one with secrets! She could find out what he was up to.

Then and there, Mary decided. Nobody could stop her from uncovering the truth. She would enter the tunnels and take control of her life. Mary was through with people lying to her, she was done with being manipulated, and maybe, just maybe, she was ready to stop acting like how other people wanted her to behave.

TWENTY-TWO

"Why do you look like the villain in a Bond movie?" Jeremy asked as he slung his backpack onto the kitchen table.

Mary, who was dressed in her oldest pair of black leggings, a turtleneck, and a black wool sweater she'd found at the thrift store, double-checked her outfit. "That wasn't intentional. I threw on some old clothes that I thought would be warm. What are you doing home from school?"

"I came home for lunch because I'd forgotten to bring one and the school cafeteria is nasty." Jeremy took out a container of leftover spaghetti from the fridge and popped it, uncovered, in the microwave.

"Oh. Right." Mary filled her water bottle. She wasn't sure what gear she'd need for her adventure but figured that water was a good idea. When she'd left the senior center, she'd come home to change and gather supplies.

Besides old clothes, water, and a couple of protein bars, Mary had grabbed the photo album, too. She wanted to compare the fake leather cover to the leather on the storage room door underneath the movie theater, assuming she could open it from the inside of the tunnel, that is. But right now, she was having trouble stuffing everything into her backpack.

"You still haven't explained why you're dressed like a Bond villain," said Jeremy, as he waited for his lunch to reheat.

"Why Bond villain and not Bond girl?"

"Because you're old."

"I'm twenty-three!"

"Exactly." Jeremy chuckled. "I'm just messing with you. You could be a Bond girl if you wanted."

"If only Hollywood agents had agreed." Mary tried one more time to cram the album into her backpack and ended up scratching it with the zipper. "Crap," she muttered.

"What is that thing, anyway?"

Mary wasn't sure how much to explain, about the album or her afternoon plans. She didn't want Jeremy following her in case the tunnels were unsafe. But it couldn't hurt to tell him about the photo album.

"It's this weird book I found in the storage room of the movie theater." She pried it from her bag and showed it to him. "Gran said the man is Sven Nilsen, the former chef of The Summer Wind restaurant. But I don't know who the woman or the girl are."

Jeremy looked at the first picture right as the microwave beeped. "What's with the mustache? He looks like a walrus."

"That was the style back then, I guess."

Jeremy flipped the pages. "Whoa! This little girl looks like you."

"You see it, too? Gran didn't see the resemblance. I thought it must be my Swedish DNA."

The microwave beeped again, and Jeremy collected his food. "Look," he said as he shut the microwave door without cleaning up splattered marinara. "I was wondering if I could ask your advice about something."

"Sure." Mary sat at the kitchen table and shoved the album

off to the side so it would be safe from the spaghetti. "Ask me anything."

Jeremy sat next to her. "It's about Kenzie. I want to invite her to the spring formal."

"That's a brilliant idea! I bet she'll say yes."

"Do you think so? Or are you just saying that?"

Mary nodded vigorously. "I know so. She dropped some heavy hints at the senior center party about wishing you'd asked her to the winter formal."

"She did not."

"She did, too. Maybe you just didn't hear her."

Jeremy twirled his fork in the spaghetti. "Are you sure? She's way out of my league. I told you she got into the University of Washington, right? To the Paul Allen School for Computer Science and everything?"

"No, I didn't hear that, but congratulations to her."

Jeremy sighed. "My mom's slowly getting on board with me moving in with my dad this fall and going to community college in Seattle, but that's what I mean about Kenzie being out of my league."

"Community college is a smart idea." Mary rested her elbows on the table. "Especially if it means avoiding student loan debt."

"That's what my mom thinks, too. She doesn't want to spend a dime on me if she doesn't have to."

"That's not true," Mary said, coming to Brittany's defense. "Your mom loves you and would probably shower you with cash if she could, but money's tight. She works for a nonprofit, after all."

"Yeah, well…"

"Look," said Mary, sensing an opportunity to repair things between Jeremy and his mother. "I know it feels like your mom is nagging you all the time, but she tries to offer good advice because she loves you, and you should be grateful."

"Grateful that she's nagging me?"

"Yes!" Mary slapped her palm on the table. "Do you know what type of guidance my mom gave me? She taught me how to act like I had twisted my ankle so she could steal booze while I diverted everyone's attention."

"Did you?" Jeremy's eyes grew wide.

"Yes, and I was brilliant at it until my mom stole a bottle with an antitheft device and set off an alarm. The shopkeeper grabbed me by my neck and the gig was up."

"Sick."

"Not 'sick,'" said Mary, knowing he meant that as a compliment. "Despicable. But I did it because I was good at it and Hannah wasn't, and I wanted to make my mom happy." She was getting off track here. "I wanted my mom to be okay, and I knew she didn't appear well when she was sober." Mary clenched her right hand into a fist and cupped it with her left one. She bowed her head a moment, thinking about what she had said.

She was a natural actor. She had been all her life. But that didn't mean she liked acting. It had been a survival mechanism for getting what she wanted.

"I'm sorry that happened to you." Jeremy patted her back a few times and then cleared his throat.

Mary lifted her head and met his gaze. "All I'm saying is your mom loves you, and she's a decent person, and maybe you should give her a break now and then."

He nodded. "I'll try, but what I really need your help with is figuring out how to ask Kenzie to the dance."

"Oh, well, what have you come up with so far?"

Jeremy swallowed the bite he was chewing. "My idea was to straight out ask her: 'Kenzie, would you like to go to the dance with me?'"

"That's one way to do it."

"You hate it."

"No," Mary said. "I think the direct approach would work fine. But do you have any other ideas that have more, I don't know..." She made jazz hands. "Pizzazz?"

"That's why I need your help." Jeremy tapped his fork against the leftover's container. "I do have this one idea, but it's probably dumb."

"Let me be the judge of that."

"Okay. Hang on a sec, I'll be right back." He scooted out of his chair and left the kitchen.

Mary glanced at the clock above the oven. She should be finding the entrance to the underground right now, not caught up in teen drama. But she knew this was important. When Mary was in high school, she would have appreciated a little social coaching. Cheryl was so much older, and always at work. Hannah had lived at home while she attended Grays Harbor State, but had also worked at Seaside Resort, which meant she'd never been around. Mary knew what it was like to bumble along, figuring things out as she went, with nobody to guide her. That had led to a lot of poor decisions over the years.

"How about this?" Jeremy asked, entering the kitchen holding a white cardboard sign that said *Kenzie, will you go to the dance with me?* in thin black letters. "I figured this way I wouldn't have to say anything."

"I love it!" Mary nodded her approval. "Women love public displays of affection. It's a little hard to read from a distance, though. My suggestion would be to fill in the words, so they look more like block letters than normal writing."

"Could you help me with that? My handwriting sucks."

"Sure. We can do it tonight."

"Could it be now? I wanted to ask her after school, and I need to go in ten minutes, or I'll be late for sixth period."

"Oh. Ah... sure."

"Great. You're a lifesaver." Jeremy put the poster on the table, narrowly missing a splatter of spaghetti. Mary hopped up to get a kitchen rag to wipe that away. He opened the junk drawer and brought out a box of crayons.

"The marker ran out," he explained. "Will this work?"

"Sure. I don't see why not." Mary lifted the lid of Crayolas and selected a dark purple. "Is this color okay?"

"I guess."

"I'll draw the outlines, and you color them in with black." Mary peeled back paper from the tip. The waxy scent smelled like childhood.

Carefully, one letter at a time, Mary outlined. As the crayon pulled across the cardboard, the scent grew stronger.

The waxy scent.

The smell of Crayolas.

Somewhere, from the deep recesses of her memory, Mary remembered the coloring book Cheryl had given her when they visited Kelly at the corrections facility in Gig Harbor.

Now she was drawing letters, but back then, she colored in balloons. There was a clown holding balloons standing next to a giraffe and a seal bouncing a ball on its nose.

Mary sat with the memory, mulling it over, trying to steep it stronger so she could remember more from that time, but all she could picture was the coloring book. She didn't remember the prison. She didn't know what Kelly looked like back then, or if she'd been wearing an orange jumpsuit and been surrounded by guards. All Mary's brain offered her was circus pictures.

"This looks great," said Jeremy, as he filled in the last letter. "Thanks so much."

"No problem." Mary put her crayon back into the box.

"Now are you finally going to tell me what you're doing in that Bond girl outfit and taking my flashlight that you didn't ask to borrow?"

"That's yours? I found it in the junk drawer."

"I don't mind you borrowing it, but what's the deal? Are you going spelunking, or something?"

"Like in caves?"

Jeremy nodded. "There are some cool ones in Olympic National Park."

"Yeah, well, no. I'm not going cave exploring." Mary thought about it. She wasn't ready to tell Hannah where she was going, because then she'd have to explain about Steven lying to her, and it hurt too much to contemplate that conversation. If she told Cheryl, her grandma might think it was too dangerous, and try to talk her out of it. But from a safety perspective, it was probably wise to tell at least one person what she was up to; she just didn't want Sand Dollar Cove's underground to become an adventure course for every teenager in the neighborhood.

"I'll tell you," she began, "but you have to promise to keep it a secret, because I don't want anyone to get hurt."

"Is it dangerous?"

"Maybe..." Mary was already regretting mentioning it, but it was too late now. "Promise?"

Jeremy held up his fingers. "Scout's honor."

"I didn't know you were a Boy Scout."

"Former Cub Scout." He pointed to her backpack. "That's where the flashlight came from."

"I think there might be tunnels under downtown Sand Dollar Cove," Mary blurted. "If my suspicions are right, there's an entrance somewhere in the T Bone Bluff."

"Whoa!" Jeremy's mouth gaped open.

"Yeah. But don't tell anyone, because I'm not sure if it's safe or not."

Jeremy's phone chimed. "That's my alarm." He picked up the poster. "I want to hear all about the tunnel tonight. But be careful, okay?"

"I will," Mary promised. "Good luck asking Kenzie out."

As Mary watched him go, she thought how funny it was. Jeremy hadn't cleaned up his lunch dishes or the poster supplies, but he'd been responsible enough to set a timer on his phone so he wouldn't be late for school. Was that what being eighteen was like? If so, maybe she shouldn't be so hard on herself and the crappy decisions she'd made when she lived in Hollywood. Looking back, she realized she hadn't been stupid. She'd been a teenager and a survivor. Maybe it was time to give herself some grace.

It was also time to stick up for herself. To stop being a pushover. To stop allowing herself to be lied to over and over again. That's why exploring the tunnels was so important to her. If Mary could discover the truth about this one particular thing, then maybe she could discover the truth about everything. Maybe she could become a walking, talking human lie detector who could ferret out untrustworthy people in the future. She was ready to stop believing in people who betrayed her. It was time to become the hero instead of the victim.

TWENTY-THREE

"What are you doing here?" Kelly asked. She wore tight black pants and a black sweater. "And why are you dressed like me?"

"I'm not dressed like you on purpose." Mary clutched her backpack in front of her protectively. Running into her mother hadn't been part of her plan. But now that she was walking through the parking lot of the T Bone Bluff, it seemed inevitable. She slung the bag over her back and tightened the straps. "I'm—"

"Here to apologize for embarrassing me last week?"

"What?"

"You and your boyfriend ordered your dinner to-go, mid-meal, like you couldn't stand having me as your waitress."

"Because we *couldn't* stand it," said Mary. "It was awkward."

Kelly's face pinched, the lines around her mouth from years of smoking becoming more pronounced. "I knew moving back here was a bad idea."

"Then why didn't you stay in Aberdeen?" Mary thought about taking off, to avoid the uncomfortable conversation, but she stood her ground. "Hannah and I didn't ask you to come back."

"You certainly don't want me here, that's for sure."

Mary didn't argue.

"For your information," Kelly said, lifting her chin. "I met a handsome firefighter named Randal at that party you threw at the senior center. We've been dating for a month now and Randal thinks I'm great."

"That's..." Mary scrambled for a word to say, "nice, Mom, I hope it works out for you."

Kelly looked at her phone. "And now I'm going to be late for my shift since you ambushed me in the parking lot."

"I did no such thing! I'm out for a walk, that's all."

"In this weather? It only stopped raining an hour ago."

"Which is why I waited for the perfect time to go outside." Mary clung to her backpack straps to keep her hands from shaking. This conversation had made her jittery. "Have a great day at work," she said, before charging away.

"And you have a nice walk," Kelly shouted, in a way that sounded like an insult.

Mary watched her feet as she trudged across the parking lot. Her temper simmered like water about to boil. Why was Kelly like this? Why did her mom have to be so awful? It didn't seem possible, but sobriety had made Kelly's personality worse, not better. It was a lot easier to deal with her when she lived in Aberdeen and Mary only had to see her every couple of years, even though Aberdeen was just a short drive away.

Mary tried to put all of that behind her, though, and focus on her mission. It was one p.m. now, and time was passing quickly. She needed to find the entrance to the tunnels as soon as possible. That's why she'd been exploring the parking lot when Kelly had crossed her path.

The trouble was, the parking lot had been repaved so many times, there wasn't one glass circle to find. If there was an entrance to the underground, it might be inside the T Bone Bluff, perhaps via the basement. After that encounter with Kelly just now, Mary didn't want to have to go inside and talk her way into a tour.

Another option was to retrace her steps back to skylights she'd found on other streets and see how they led to the restaurant. That seemed like the quickest way to find the entrance.

Mary zigzagged through town, looking down at sidewalks and searching for the purple glass skylights. But she didn't find any until she got to the back entrance of the senior center and was standing underneath the roller skates again. Shoot. It was like coming to a dead-end. Mary had explored every inch of the senior center. She knew it didn't have a basement.

Closing her eyes, Mary tried to picture the streets like a grid. Using her imagination, she drew a line from the movie theater, across the alley, and to the senior center. That's where she knew for certain the purple glass could still be found. If she could stretch the line out, like she was drawing with a purple crayon, where would it go next?

The T Bone Bluff. It had to be. Trying one more time, this time with her head up, and walking by faith, Mary walked straight from the senior center to the restaurant, crossing three blocks and reaching the entrance. The imaginary line in her head went straight to the front door. With no other options, Mary walked inside, where the hostess greeted her.

"Hi," said Mary. Sand Dollar Cove was a small town, but with so many newcomers she didn't recognize the woman standing in front of her. "I was hoping to order a side salad to go."

"Sure," said the hostess. "You can do that from the bar."

"Great." Mary took a deep breath. "Is it okay if I use the restroom first?"

"Go for it. The bar's that way when you're ready to order."

"Thanks." Mary nodded and went to the restroom. Mainly

she wanted time to think of an excuse to be in the T Bone Bluff. But once she entered the women's restroom, she saw something she'd seen dozens of times before but had never paid attention to: a supply closet! Feeling excited, Mary looked over her shoulder to make sure she was the only one in the room, then she flung the closet door open.

She discovered toilet paper.

"Bummer," Mary muttered. She used the facilities, washed her hands, and headed to the bar. Ordering a salad seemed like a good idea. Maybe she could chat the bartender up while she was at it and ask if he knew if the restaurant had a basement.

It was then, on her way back through the lobby, and down the short hallway to the bar, that she saw it: the clue to everything. There, surrounded by cow pictures, was a small painting that looked like it must have been commissioned in the early 1970s, when the T Bone Bluff still had a bandstand where the parking lot was now. The painting was of the bandstand itself, and the back of the restaurant. Mary stood in front of the painting and was gobsmacked by what she saw. The artist had included the tiniest details, right down to a pathway of purple glass, decorating the sidewalk!

Mary closed her eyes again and used the information from the painting to picture where those skylights must be. Yes, they'd be in the parking lot, but they would also be at the back entrance of the restaurant. Ditching her plans to chat with the bartender, Mary hurried back through the lobby and outside, ignoring the hostess calling after her that "restrooms were for customers only."

Mary was running now. Her anticipation was so keen that she couldn't have walked slowly even if she'd tried. She didn't come to a halt until she was behind the restaurant, where it formed a seam next to the parking lot. Mary stepped off the pathway and into the landscaping strip. It was shrubs mostly, with clumps of daffodils poking up. But at the edge of the dirt, behind scraggly bushes of Oregon grape, Mary saw a trapdoor leading to a cellar. She crouched down next to it and tried to lift one of the doors, but they were padlocked together.

So close, and yet so far... Mary groaned with frustration.

She picked up the padlock and wiggled it, wondering if maybe she could use a hairpin to pry it open.

Then, her adrenaline exploded like fireworks when she realized the padlock wasn't locked.

It unclicked easily in her hands!

Mary put the lock into her pocket, took out her flashlight, lifted the trapdoor, and angled the beam of light into the dark.

There were stairs!

Mary propped the trapdoor up and stepped inside. She took one step, and then another. But when she was halfway down the staircase, the trapdoor slammed shut. Wind must have knocked it down, or gravity. Shivering, Mary clicked her flashlight to the highest setting and didn't stop until she reached the bottom and her feet touched concrete.

The cellar, if that's what it was, had nothing in it except for old metal shelves similar to the ones in the storage room of the movie theater. Not just similar, identical. The recognition made Mary smile. Surrounded by shelving units, Mary didn't see any doors, but that didn't mean one wasn't there. She angled her flashlight for a better look at each wall, and then stretched out her arm and brushed her fingertips across the wall board. Every surface felt the same except for one part that felt wrinkled.

Not wrinkled—leathery.

Using all her might, Mary pulled that shelf forward, assuming it would be heavy. Only it glided easily. Looking down, Mary saw metal tracks embedded into the concrete. The shelves swung outward, and behind their false back, Mary discovered a door.

A door covered in snakeskin.

Tiny hairs on the back of her neck stood up.

Was that python?

Mary took out her phone and snapped a picture. She needed documentation in case nobody believed her. Once she'd slipped her phone back into her bag, she opened the door and looked inside.

A wooden plank sidewalk snaked into darkness. Maybe this had at one point been a light-filled path, but with the paved parking lot up above, the tunnel was plunged into pitch-blackness.

Mary propped the door open this time, using a rock she found on the ground. She didn't want a repeat of the trapdoor surprise. Still, she felt uneasy. Entering the tunnel was like walking into a tomb.

Mary took out her phone again and texted Jeremy the picture of the python door.

Found it.

Cool, he replied.

Now that somebody knew for sure where she was, she crossed the threshold and stepped onto the wooden planks.

Mary walked deeper and deeper into the tunnel, like she was in the bowels of the earth. Shelves lined the walls of the tunnels, but instead of flush against the wall, they were perpendicular. She didn't know what they used to hold but suspected it was alcohol because she found an empty keg. Mary tried to keep a mental map of where she was in her mind, but it was difficult. She passed a door but was too creeped out to open it. Then she passed another, and another. It wasn't until she saw her first patch of purple sky that she breathed easier. Not only from the relief of seeing daylight, but from ventilation shafts filling the tunnel with fresh air.

Mary looked upward and saw dozens of glass circles above her head, glowing amethyst.

It was easier to see now.

It was easier to breathe now.

When Mary saw a door to her right, she opened it.

"It's a room," she said aloud. Hearing her voice made the situation seem less scary. "I'm going to film this so I can show Jeremy."

She held her flashlight in one hand, and her phone in the other, documenting her discovery.

"I'm standing underneath I-don't-know-where and I've found a room that has round tables in it." She stepped inside. "There are metal folding chairs, too, but most of them are rusty. Nothing is on the walls except for this faded poster." Mary zoomed in with the video. "It looks like a calendar from 1979 with a bunch of naked women at the top. Gross." Mary turned off the video for a moment. What had gone on in this room? Illegal gambling, maybe? That might have been what the tables were for. She left the room and turned her camera back on so she could film what she discovered next.

"I've left the room and am walking down the tunnel. You can see that it gets extremely dark for a bit until we reach the next block of purple light. Some of the walls have wooden support beams. From the size of the boards, it looks like old-growth cedar. That's probably why they're in such good shape. Old-growth wood lasts forever. That's what my science teacher said when we went on a field trip to the Hoh Rain Forest."

Great. Now she was rambling. But keeping up a running conversation for the camera helped calm her nerves.

"I see another doorway now. I'm going to open it." She pushed the door inward and gasped. "There's a bedframe, and a stained mattress." Icy fingers tiptoed down her spine. What had gone on in here? "There's a nightstand too, with a kerosene lantern. That would have been handy if I had matches. This flashlight is pretty weak."

The bedroom, if that's what it was, was sketchy, and Mary

didn't want to spend any more time here than she had to. Besides, she still hadn't found the rattlesnake door.

"I'm headed back to the tunnel," she told the camera. "My goal is to find out how it connects to the movie theater. I know there's an entrance in the cinema's basement, and I want to see what's on the other side of it."

Along the way she found dozens of rooms. Some were empty. Some had card tables, and some had beds.

"My flashlight's getting weaker now, so I'm turning it down to the lower setting, so it lasts longer," she narrated for the film. "Sorry if it's harder to see the video. I think I'm getting closer to the movie theater now. That last part must have been under the senior center and then—oh, wow! Look at this!"

She panned out, so that the camera could see the murals painted on the walls around her. Mountain ridges of peaks she didn't recognize, and a forest blazing on fire covered one part of the room, and a water view covered the rest. Owls peeked out of cedar trees and a family of deer grazed in a meadow by a lake.

"There's a large room!" Mary exclaimed. "With tables and chairs and what looks to be a stage. Every inch of the wall is painted with scenery."

Mary propped her phone up on one of the tables and hopped up onto the stage and waved. She looked straight at the camera, her stage presence feeling as powerful as ever.

"It seems like this was an auditorium of some sort, or maybe..." She turned around. "A casino? A pool hall? I'm not sure. But somewhere around here has got to be that doorway, I think. It could be the doorway to the theater, I don't know."

She scrambled off the stage, picked up her phone, and walked around the circumference of the room, admiring the murals. She was looking for another tunnel, but all she found was the one she'd entered from.

This room was a dead-end, and she hadn't seen one inch of snakeskin.

Could there have been a doorway she'd missed along the path? There were the ones at the front of the tunnel that she'd skipped, but Mary had thought she'd opened each one since.

Mary was about to head back through the tunnel when she heard a buzzing sound.

No, not a buzzing sound. It was more like the whir of a motor.

Racing over to the wall, Mary listened closely.

Was that Nick and Shane on the other side using the machines to refinish the floor?

Sure enough, there was a doorway that she'd missed, painted to blend in with the mural. Pulling the handle with all her might, she couldn't get it to budge, because it must have been the door that Nick and Shane had sealed shut. Pressing her ear against the doorway, she heard the flooring equipment.

Mary took out her phone and filmed what she'd found. "I'm standing on the other side of the rattlesnake entrance," she said, before panning around the room. This was what Steven had tried to hide from her. But why? What's so bad about this place that he didn't want her to discover it? The murals were beautiful. And what did it have to do with him? It made no sense that he'd hide it from her. None whatsoever.

She switched from movie to camera mode, snapped a picture, and turned on the flashlight app so she could see better. The flashlight she'd borrowed from Jeremy was dimming, as if the batteries were weak.

Tonight, after she'd cleaned up and her hair didn't smell like basement anymore, she would march to Steven's apartment and demand answers. No, wait. She would dump him first. He shouldn't have lied to her.

It hurt, thinking about ending things. It hurt more than Mary wanted to admit. Plus, there was the business about Zeke and filing the injunction. Mary wouldn't be able to handle that on her own.

Or maybe I could, she thought with a rush of newfound confidence. Now that she knew what needed to be done, she could hire a lawyer. She had that emergency account with the money from her father's life insurance. She also had the retirement account Hannah insisted that she start. Mary would rather cash out all of it and protect her reputation than do nothing. She was tired of people screwing her over.

"I'm ready to fight," Mary whispered as she clenched her fist around her phone.

They were easier words to say underneath the purple skylights. But once Mary entered pitch-blackness again, her courage wavered as unsteadily as the fading flashlight.

"Come on, flashlight," she said encouragingly. "Don't die on me now."

But the light became weaker and weaker, as the battery drained.

Mary swallowed hard and walked faster.

She was almost at the T Bone Bluff. She passed the doors she didn't explore the first time.

Almost there, she told herself. She was sure of it. *I just need to walk a hundred more feet perhaps and—*

Smack!

Mary saw stars. Everything went black except spots of lights bouncing in front of her from hitting her head. She must have walked into a wall.

Mary stumbled forward, feeling nauseous, and hit one of the shelves that lined the tunnel. She grabbed onto it, trying to steady herself, but was so wobbly on her feet that she leaned sideways, causing the shelf to pitch forward, hitting the one next to it.

The cacophony of a million roller skates stamping on the ground followed next.

The shelving units fell like dominoes, one after another, down the line of the tunnel.

Mary heard more than saw them. It was too dark to make much out.

But when the final shelf fell, she used the last little bit of light from her phone to see what had happened.

Mary screamed.

The tunnel had collapsed.

TWENTY-FOUR

Buried alive. Mary's recklessness had buried her alive.

"This is my fault," she whispered in agony. Her head throbbed, and she probably had bruises all over, but at least it didn't feel like she had broken any bones.

Not that being mobile did her any good. The movie theater side of the tunnel was a jumble of fallen shelves. The web of dislocated metal would be impossible to pass. Support beams had fallen on the other side of her, blocking her path to the T Bone Bluff.

Mary was well and truly trapped.

She pulled out her cell phone, which was now at four percent, and dialed 911. But this deep underground it was impossible to get a signal. Sand Dollar Cove had spotty cell service to begin with.

She'd been able to text Jeremy earlier, though. Maybe she could do that now.

Help, she typed. *I'm trapped in an underground tunnel. The entrance is below the T Bone Bluff.*

She sent the message to the house group chat with Jeremy,

Brittany, Hannah, and Cheryl but wasn't sure any of the texts went through, especially when they didn't answer her.

Searching for a signal must have weakened her phone's battery further.

Now it was three percent.

A few minutes later it died completely.

"Help!" Mary shouted. "Can anyone hear me?"

Shouting hurt her head, but she couldn't give up.

"Help!" she cried again. "I'm trapped down here!"

She tried to pick through the rubble until her already weak flashlight died.

She shouted until her throat was raw from screaming.

Then, when adrenaline had worn her out to exhaustion, she sat in the darkness, hugging her backpack, and slowly sipped water.

"I might need to ration it," she whispered. "Who knows how long I'll be here?"

Mary wept.

What had she done? How had she gotten here? Mary's hurting brain tried to think through the steps that had brought her to this messy end, but the only thing she could clearly picture was crayons. A circus tent and balloons. A clown riding a unicycle. What the hell was that about? Her mind was a muddy mess.

"Help!" she cried. "Get me out of here!"

Time ran away with her as she huddled in the darkness, but she continued to call out for assistance.

"Mary?" a faint voice called. "Mary, is that you?"

"Yes!" she screamed, her voice stronger now. "It's me! It's Mary!"

Where was the voice coming from? Mary couldn't tell. She strained her ears and heard a click, click, clicking sound coming from behind the jumbled shelves.

"Hello?" Mary called, afraid that she'd been imagining the

voice.

"Mary, stay put. Mama's coming for you."

Mama's coming for me? Now Mary knew she was hallucinating. Kelly had never come to her rescue, not once in her entire life. In fact, the opposite was true. Kelly was the source of Mary's childhood misery.

"I'll be right there, darling girl. Stay put. Are you okay? Mama's coming."

Mary hugged her knees and bowed her head. She must be dying. That blow to her head was worse than she'd realized. Now she was hearing voices.

"I'm almost there, sweetie. Hang on."

I'm sorry, Gran.

I'm sorry, Hannah.

I'm sorry I rushed into this without telling you.

I'm sorry I act like things are perfect when they're not.

Would she ever learn?

No, because now it was too late. Her poor choices had trapped her for good this time, and there was no way out.

"I can see you. Can you see me?"

Mary couldn't see anything. That light peeking from her left was only her imagination playing tricks on her.

"Dammit. This last bit is tricky. These shelves are like a maze. But don't you worry, darling girl, Mama's coming."

Mary closed her eyes against the darkness. She wiped her nose on her sleeve.

I'm sorry, Hannah.

I'm sorry, Gran.

"There, there." Warm arms surrounded her. "Don't cry. Mama's here."

Mary felt a warmth she could barely remember, her mother's skin pressed against her own. Her mother's hands stroking her hair. Her mother's lips whispering kisses on her cheek.

"Are you okay, Mary? Are you hurt?"

A light shined in her face, causing Mary to see red behind her closed eyes. She fluttered her eyelids open and saw Kelly staring down at her.

She wasn't hallucinating.

Her mother was right there next to her!

"Mom?" Mary asked. "What are you doing here?"

"I heard you screaming for help, and I came running."

"But how?"

"I heard the crash first, so I came down to investigate."

"So... and... what?" Mary put her hand to her head.

"Did you hit your head? Do you have a concussion?"

"I don't know. But could you call 911? My phone won't work."

"Neither will mine," said Kelly. "I dialed for help as soon as I heard you screaming. But even if a crew could get down here, they wouldn't know the secret passages and the main exits are blocked."

"Secret—"

"So here's what we're going to do. I'm going to lead you out of here before my phone dies and the flashlight app won't work. Okay? Do you think you can move? Or are you too injured?"

"I can move." Mary tried to nod and winced. "It's just my head that hurts."

"Okay. Stick with me, kiddo, and I'll get you out of here. I know these tunnels like the back of my hand."

"How?"

"Never mind how. I'll tell you all that later. Let's focus on getting you out of here, first. Here. I'll deal with the backpack, you just move one foot in front of the other and listen to the sound of my voice. Got it?"

Listen to the sound of my voice.

I love you.

I'm doing this because I love you.

"What?" Mary asked.

"I said, hold my hand. We need to climb over this first piece of metal. Lift up your right foot. No, your other right foot. That's good." Kelly guided Mary's body through the first obstacle. "Now we're going to bend sideways here to get over this next piece. Careful, it's unstable. Attagirl. You're doing great, baby."

Listen to the sound of my voice.

You're doing great, baby.

You're doing great with your grandma.

"Mom." Mary clutched her stomach. "I think I'm gonna puke."

"That's okay, baby. It wouldn't be the first time someone's barfed down here. You just let me know when, and I'll hold back your hair."

"I'm good now."

She gulped. It was a false hope. A second later, Mary vomited up everything in her stomach.

"Okay. It's okay." Kelly pulled back Mary's hair.

"Sorry about that."

"No need to apologize."

"Can I have a sip of water from my backpack to rinse out my mouth?"

"Absolutely." Kelly unzipped the bag and handed her the bottle.

They were both trapped in an uncomfortable position, bounded on each side by fallen shelves. Mary swished out her mouth, spat, and handed the bottle back to Kelly. "I'm ready," she said. "Let's keep going."

"Good girl. You're such a good girl."

You're such a good girl.

I want you to be happy.

I can't give you a good life like your grandma can.

That's why I'm signing these papers.

Mary's thoughts thickened like mud and kept sticking in uncomfortable places.

"Here we go, baby girl," said Kelly. "This part's real tricky, but I know you can do it. Put your foot here and then push yourself up." Kelly demonstrated and then looked down at her daughter. "Can you do that for me?"

"Yes. I think so."

"Then we climb over and jump down." Kelly landed on the other side but shone the light so Mary could see.

Mary boosted herself up and hopped to the ground.

"Nice and safe," said Kelly. "Good job."

Nice and safe.

I want you to be nice and safe.

I'm signing these papers because I love you.

I can't be a good mother to you. Cheryl can.

"That's true about Gran," Mary said.

"What, sweet girl?" Kelly asked. "I didn't say anything about Cheryl."

"You didn't?" Mary asked, feeling confused.

Kelly squeezed her hand. "Let's keep going. We're getting closer."

Mary was having increasing difficulty following instructions. Kelly touched her right leg when she wanted Mary's right leg to move, and tapped her left shoulder when it was time to bend to the left. That was the only way Mary was able to make it.

"We're almost there, baby girl. Mama is so proud of you!" Kelly rubbed Mary's back.

Mama is so proud of you.

It breaks my heart signing these papers, but I'm not going to fight it.

Your grandma is right.

You and your sister are sweet girls, who deserve a good life.

Cheryl will be a better mom than I ever could be.

Kelly leaned across the table and selected a red crayon from the box. She opened the coloring book to the last page, which was blank, because it was the endpaper.

Mama loves you this much, she said, drawing an enormous heart. *I love you so much that I'm doing the hardest thing in the world for me. I'm giving you to your grandma for your own good.*

"Where's the crayon?" Mary asked. "What happened to the crayon?"

"Crayon? What are you talking about? Oh shit." Kelly gasped. "There goes the flashlight."

"Mom. I'm scared." Mary clung to her hand. "Don't let go, okay?"

"I won't let go, I promise. But you're going to have to trust me. Can you do that?"

Could she? Put her faith in the most untrustworthy person in her life? Yes, she could. Because of that red heart. Because of that conversation, long ago, that Mary was only now starting to remember. Kelly had made the most trustworthy choice of all. She'd put Mary and Hannah's well-being first when she'd relinquished custody to Cheryl. She could have fought it. She could have drawn out the court battle for months. Years, even. But she didn't. She gave her daughters to Cheryl, free and clear.

That's what the coloring book was about. That's why the scent of crayons triggered difficult memories. Mary had been coloring the day she'd visited Kelly at the prison and her mom had agreed to place her and Hannah in Cheryl's care. Mary wanted to hold onto that memory before she lost it again. Her mind was addled, but this was too important to forget.

She squeezed her mother's hand. "I trust you."

Kelly squeezed back. "Okay," she said gently. "Here we go. I'm going to have to feel our way out of here. We're past the shelves now. I just need to run my hand along the wall until I find the door to the second brothel room and then—"

"Brothel?"

"Yeah. That's what this underground was for. Brothels and illegal gambling. My mom was a cocktail waitress here."

"Video store," Mary mumbled, her head hurting so much that it felt like it would split into halves.

"That was my foster mom, Amy, who owned the video store," Kelly explained. "Amy was my real mom, as far as I'm concerned. But my birth mom was named Grace, and she worked as a cocktail waitress down here after my dad ran out on us. There. I found the door!" Kelly pushed it open, and it became even darker, although that didn't seem possible. "Only bats and rodents can see down here," said Kelly. "Now we walk through this room, around the bed frame—ouch! That was the bedframe." She grabbed Mary's shoulder and steered her to safety. "Then we find the ventilation shaft, behind the secret door, and we can climb up the ladder into the dining room."

"Of Gig Harbor?" Mary's throbbing headache made her woozy.

"What? No. Why would you mention Gig Harbor?"

"The red heart. I see it now." Mary was really beginning to lose it.

"What red heart?"

"I see *you* now," said Mary.

"How can you see me? It's pitch-black in here."

"Thank you for your sacrifice," Mary murmured. Fatigue overwhelmed her. Someone had mentioned a bed. "I think I'll take a nap now."

"No, Mary! Don't fall asleep!" Kelly dragged her forward. "I'm getting you to safety. I won't let you die down here. Nobody should die down here, ever again!"

They were the last words Mary heard before she passed out cold.

TWENTY-FIVE

"Good morning, sis." Hannah pressed a cold compress to Mary's forehead. "Or should I say good afternoon? It's almost noon."

Mary's eyes fluttered open. She was in her room and the window was cracked open. She could smell the scent of the ocean breeze outside. "What day is it?" she asked groggily.

"Wednesday. You really gave us a scare."

Mary tried to remember what happened, but the images scattered. Kelly had been there. Maybe? Mary tried to sit up and felt woozy.

"Take it easy," Hannah cautioned. "Here, see if you can drink this 7Up. The ER doctor said to get some fluids into you. He said nausea is normal when you have a concussion, and based on what Mom said, you puked your guts out."

"I did?" Mary sipped the lemon-lime soda. It felt good in her parched mouth.

"Wow. You seem a bit confused still." Hannah patted Mary's arm. "You should have heard the crazy stuff you were saying last night before you fell asleep. Something about rattlesnakes, which is weird because Mom didn't say anything about snakes being underground."

Underground. The tunnels! The brothel...

"Can I have my phone?" Mary asked. "I think I took pictures. Maybe they'll jog my memory and I'll stop being so confused."

"Confusion is normal with a concussion. The doctor said that, too." Hannah handed Mary her phone. "Promise you'll give it back to me if it makes your headache worse."

Hannah fussing over her felt good; comforting, in fact. Mary waited as her phone turned on.

"I charged it for you last night," said Hannah. "It was completely dead. So was your flashlight."

"Where's Mom?" Mary asked while she waited for the phone to boot up.

"With that firefighter she's dating. Randal seemed decent. Do you remember the rescue?"

"Mom came for me," Mary said, still unable to picture it but knowing it was true.

"That's right." Hannah nodded. "By the time you got to the ladder the first responders were already on the scene, investigating the implosion. Paramedics, firefighters, police, the mayor —everyone was there. Guy and I saw the lights and sirens after we had picked up Gran and were rushing home to tell you that... Uh, never mind. Anyhow, we didn't think it had anything to do with us until Jeremy texted us that picture you sent us and said he was worried about you. He'd seen the emergency vehicles go by from his drive-thru window at McDonald's."

"I texted Jeremy a picture of the python door," Mary said, remembering.

"I called him right away, freaking out, and at first he didn't want to tell me because you'd made him promise not to say anything, but he did when he realized you might be in danger."

"I can see the pictures I took." Mary tapped on the gallery.

"There's the python door," she said, turning her phone to Hannah and pointing. "I remember that." Next came the videos.

Hannah climbed up on the bed next to Mary and watched her tour of the tunnels. "Unbelievable," Hannah muttered. "And those murals, too. I had no idea that was here in Sand Dollar Cove this whole time."

Seeing the film footage, and hearing the sound of her own voice explain everything, jogged Mary's memories further. "Mom said there was an underground brothel and casino."

That's what was on the other side of the snakeskin door.

That's what Steven tried to hide from her.

"Steven knew about it," Mary said, finally ready to share her heartbreak. "And he lied to me." She quickly explained about the movie theater entrance, and the rattlesnake door.

"Wow." Hannah gasped. "That's a lot. Why would Steven hide it from you? He must have had a good reason to, right?"

"I can't believe you're defending him!"

"I'm not. But the whole thing is strange. Steven's been out of his mind with worry. He was there at the rescue and followed us to the hospital. He would have camped out downstairs all night, except Gran told him to go home because his pacing back and forth was so noisy it kept her up."

"I'm glad she sent him home. I don't want to see him."

"You don't?" Hannah asked. "Oh, sorry. I texted him as soon as you woke up, but I can tell him to shove off when he gets here."

Mary sighed. "No, that's okay. I should tell him myself." She didn't need her sister to fight her battles for her anymore. "But could I have a cup of coffee first? I'm getting a caffeine headache on top of everything."

"The coffeepot's already on. I'll go grab you a cup. Gran says hello, by the way, and that she loves you. She was going to brave the stairs, but I held her off because it's too dangerous."

"Good call," said Mary. "The last thing we need right now is for Gran to fall and break a hip."

Hannah hugged her. "I'm so glad you're okay. You're my bestest, most favorite sister ever. I hope you know that."

"I'm your only sister. But right back at you." Mary kissed Hannah's cheek.

"I'll go get that coffee for you. Be back in a jiff."

As soon as Hannah left, Mary heard a soft knock on the door. "Come in." She propped herself on the pillows.

It was Jeremy and Kenzie. They both poked their heads inside the door. "Is it okay if we come say hello?" Jeremy asked. "We have a few minutes before we need to head back to campus for fifth period."

Mary waved them inside. "I thought sixth period was after lunch."

"That's on Tuesdays and Thursdays," Kenzie explained. "Mondays and Wednesdays are classes one, three, and five."

"Block schedule." Jeremy pulled out Mary's desk chair and was about to sit down before he must have thought better of that and offered it to Kenzie instead.

"Thanks," Kenzie said, her cheeks turning pink.

"Are you okay, Mary?" Jeremy asked. "How mad are you about me blabbing?"

"I'm not mad at you at all." Mary hugged herself. "You did the right thing, Jeremy. I'm sorry I asked you to keep a secret that was too big to hide."

"Yeah, well, at least your advice turned out good." Jeremy poked Kenzie in the shoulder. "Guess who agreed to go to the spring formal with me?"

Kenzie blushed even redder. "Took you long enough to ask me," she said with a giggle.

"Oh, man. I almost forgot." Jeremy hurried to the door. "I'll be right back." He darted down the hallway.

"So, do you have a dress picked out?" Mary asked.

"I'm not sure yet." Kenzie scooted her chair closer. "It depends on the dance's theme. The decorations committee is still deciding. Half of them want 'Parisian Moonlight' and the other half want a zombie theme, like that TikTok video that's going viral."

Mary's ears perked. "Viral zombie TikTok?"

"Yeah." Kenzie nodded. "Have you seen it?"

Mary shook her head. "I'm not sure. Describe it to me."

"You can't see the TikTokker's face because it's blurred out by ghostly makeup, but her dress is shredded like lettuce in a taco salad. She does this weird, jerky dance, and then the voice-over comes on and she says, 'You've murdered my love for you. Your cursed heart means nothing to me anymore. I—'"

"Don't dance with the dead," Mary said, at the same time Kenzie did. "I think I *have* seen that one."

Holy cow! Did she do it? Did Mary have a TikTok video finally go viral? What did this mean for the movie release, or her legal fight against Zeke? The distribution company would be more eager than ever to get *Zombie Prom at the Disco* on the big screen. Mary was thinking about this right as Jeremy burst into her room holding the photo album.

"Here it is!" He waved it in the air. "You left this in the kitchen, and I thought you might want it back."

"Thanks." Mary pointed to her dresser. "You can set it there."

"I didn't know you scrapbooked," said Kenzie.

"I don't," said Mary. "It's this—"

Jeremy's phone chimed. "That's our alarm." He held out his hand and pulled Kenzie to her feet. "Sorry, Mary, but we got to go. I hope you feel better soon."

"Yes." Kenzie waved. "Me, too."

"Thanks," said Mary. "Bye." As soon as they left, she opened TikTok. Her last video had been seen four million times! There were thousands of comments. It would take ages to read them all. She scrolled through, reading as many as she could.

Cool dress.

Is this from a movie?

Name?

What beach is that?

Title please?

Mary turned over the screen right when Hannah entered the room holding a breakfast tray. "You're not the only one in the family with barista skills," Hannah smiled proudly. "I brought you fresh coffee, with milk, and blueberry muffins that Brittany baked this morning just for you."

"Thanks so much."

Hannah put the tray on Mary's lap. "Take it slow, though, okay? Maybe I should bring you a bucket in case you puke."

"My stomach feels fine now, I'm just hungry."

"I can help you shower when you're through. Get the crud out of your hair."

Mary looked down at her pajamas. "I don't remember changing."

"I helped you with that. But all I could do was blot your face with a makeup remover wipe."

"Thanks for that." Mary drank her coffee and as the rich aroma filled her senses, she considered something Hannah had mentioned earlier. "You said you and Guy were rushing home last night to tell me something. What was it?"

Hannah sat on her hands. "Now seems like a horrible time to share. Drink your coffee, and we can talk later."

"Tell me," Mary prodded. "I can handle it." She meant what she said. She wasn't the same person that she was last spring when Aidan had broken her heart. She wasn't the same person she was at Christmas. She was stronger now, more capable. Not just capable—*fearless*. Mary had explored that tunnel on her own, after all. That was some serious hero energy.

"Well, okay, if you insist." Hannah held out her left hand and showed Mary the gold band, studded with diamonds, on her ring finger. "Guy proposed last night, and I said yes!"

"Oh Hannah!" Mary put her coffee on the nightstand. "I'm so happy for you." She held out her arms for a hug. "That's wonderful news."

"It is, isn't it?" Hannah hugged her carefully, so as to not knock over the breakfast tray.

"But then I went and ruined your big night," Mary said, feeling awful.

"Nothing was ruined." Hannah squeezed her again. "Not even that creepy underground tunnel. At first glance it looked like it had collapsed, but it turns out it was just a tangle of bookshelves or something. The army corps of engineers is coming out later to investigate. According to what Brittany heard from one of the seniors at the center."

"Let me look at the ring again." Mary clasped Hannah's hand. "It's gorgeous. Guy picked out the perfect one."

"You don't think it's too much?" Hannah tilted her hand this way and that. "The side diamonds are as big as my earrings, and those are almost too much, and—"

"If you don't like it, I'm sure Guy would take you back to the jeweler and let you pick whatever you wanted."

Hannah pulled her hand to her heart. "No, I love this one, I just worry about whether I deserve something this fancy."

"You do. You absolutely do." Mary loved shiny things, but in this case, she was happy that her sister was wearing the bling machine. If anyone deserved a happy ending, it was Hannah.

"Just promise me that the next time you see Aidan you wave it in his face and blind him with diamonds."

Hannah laughed. "Will do."

A car pulled into the driveway, the sound audible through the cracked window.

"Speak of the devil," said Mary, assuming it was from the DeLacks' driveway.

Hannah hopped up and peeked through the window blinds. "It's not Aidan, it's Steven." She looked back at Mary. "Do you want to see him, or should I send him away?"

Mary wrapped both hands around her mug for comfort. "I'll see him. But could you help me take a quick shower? I don't want to greet him smelling like barf."

TWENTY-SIX

What would she say when she saw Steven? Mary thought about it as she washed her hair.

"Are you okay in there?" Hannah said from the other side of the shower curtain. "You don't feel dizzy, do you?"

"I'm fine." Mary adjusted the nozzle and rinsed out the suds. She squirted conditioner into her palm and massaged it into her tresses.

"If you're sure you're fine, I'll go downstairs and greet him," said Hannah. "It sounds like Gran already let him in, but I better hold him off before he charges upstairs and sees you naked. Unless you want him to see you naked...?" she added.

"I don't know what I want right now," Mary admitted. "Except to not stink."

"It smells like you used a whole bottle of Suave, so I think you're covered. Holler if you need help getting dressed. Okay? I put your clothes on the sink."

"Thank you, favorite sister."

"You're welcome."

Mary heard the bathroom door close. She knew that she could stay in the shower as long as she wanted to, but she also knew that Steven was waiting to see her, and part of her wanted to see him, too. She was hungry for the confrontation. She was ready for the fight.

After she rinsed her hair, Mary turned off the water and reached for her bath towel. She quickly dried off and put on her clothes. Mary applied moisturizer and brushed her teeth but didn't bother with makeup or drying her hair. Downstairs, she heard muffled voices, and then Steven's solid steps on the stairs. This was it. He was in her room waiting for her.

The thought made her jittery with nerves and excitement. She flicked her wet hair over her shoulder and looked at her reflection in the mirror. "Friends?" she whispered. "We can never be friends. You've murdered my love for you. Your cursed heart means nothing to me anymore. I don't dance with the dead." That was how to do it. Jenaly Macintyre wouldn't put up with this garbage, and neither would Mary.

The confrontation was now. And Mary was ready for it. She was a fully-formed human being who could stick up for herself and do brave things.

Mary rolled her shoulders back and opened her bedroom door. She intended to wear a fierce expression, but as soon as she saw Steven, she smiled. She couldn't help it. Seeing his hazel eyes so full of concern, and his arms overflowing with dozens of roses, triggered the part of her heart that still cared for him deeply.

"Mary," he said, taking a few steps across the room. "Thank God you're okay." When she didn't immediately leap into his arms, he took a tiny step backward. "I'll just, ah, put these here where you can see them." Steven set the enormous vase of roses on the dresser she shared with Hannah. "How are you feeling?"

"I've been better." Mary folded her arms across her chest and leaned against the doorframe.

Steven froze. "I bet." Instead of coming closer to her, he sat on the edge of Hannah's bed, which was neatly made and several feet away. "How's your head?"

"It hurts." She took a deep breath and walked over to her bed, sitting on the rumpled covers. "My head hurts a lot, but not as much as my heart does knowing that you lied to me."

"What? I didn't lie, I—"

"Yes, you did," she said in a definitive tone. "About those tunnels. You told me that the only thing in the storage room was a broom closet, not a secret passage to an underground lair."

"It wasn't a lair, it was an entertainment establishment I didn't want you, or anyone else, to know about. That's why I had Nick seal off the door."

"But why? I don't understand it."

"I can explain." Steven pushed hair off his forehead.

"I thought you were honest."

"I *am* honest."

"Not to me, you weren't," said Mary. "You lied directly to my face."

"Well, so did you." Steven's cheeks reddened. "You told me you were going to the doctor to see about your arm, when really you went and explored the tunnels without me."

"Because I had no other choice! You didn't want me to know that they existed, and I still don't understand why."

"I was right to hide them from you. Those tunnels are dangerous. You almost died down there."

"Are you an engineer?" Mary leaned forward. "You couldn't possibly know how stable they were, and that's still no excuse for keeping the truth from me."

"I had to keep them from you, Mary. You don't understand." Steven rested his elbows on his knees and put his face in his hands. He stared at the carpet for so long that the pause in the conversation became awkward.

"Explain it to me then," Mary said, when the silence became too unbearable.

Steven lifted his head, and tears wet his cheeks. "As soon as I saw the snakeskin door, I knew what it meant."

"A-ha!" Mary pointed at him. "That's another lie. You told me it wasn't made of snakeskin."

"It was. I don't know how many rattlesnakes had to die to stitch that much skin together, but it was a lot." Steven wiped his palms across his knees.

"What does the snakeskin door mean?" Mary asked, her eyes drifting over to the photo album.

"That my Aunt Helena was involved. That she was heavily involved in criminal activity like my dad told me. Only I always thought *he* was lying. My dad was the monster, not my Aunt Helena. He was the horrible person, not her. But when I saw that door covered in snakeskin, I knew that everything Dad said about Aunt Helena and her time in Sand Dollar Cove was true."

"Wait, what? Your family had a connection to Sand Dollar Cove? That's news to me."

Steven nodded. "My great-aunt used to live here."

"Why didn't you tell me? You said that you'd just so happened to move here because the theater went up for sale."

Steven looked out the window. "That was another omission of the truth."

"A lie, you mean," Mary said, a sharp edge to her voice.

"A lie," Steven agreed as he looked back at her. "I don't even know where to start."

"At the beginning, and don't leave anything out."

Steven's shoulders slumped forward. "I knew my aunt had lived here. That was the draw for me moving to Sand Dollar Cove. Aunt Helena had always told me how wonderful the town was, and how this was a community where people looked out for one another. She talked about how beautiful the ocean was, and how you could drive your car right up onto the beach."

"If she loved it here so much, then why did she move back to Vegas?"

"Economic opportunities," Steven said. "In any case, that's what she told me. But my dad said it had to do with illegal activity, only I didn't want to believe him. I accused him of lying because he was jealous of how much I hero-worshiped my aunt. Dad told me I was a fool to trust Helena and that she had been arrested for vice."

"Vice?" Mary wasn't sure if she had heard him right. "What?"

"She was a madame," Steven said, spitting the words out one by one. "A brothel owner. A person who made money off ensnaring women into the sex worker industry. Here in Washington, she was an entirely different person than the aunt I knew in Nevada. Or maybe she was an awful person there as well, and I was too ignorant to see it."

"Helena ran a brothel in Sand Dollar Cove?"

"An underground one." Steven nodded. "That was what was behind the snakeskin door. According to my dad, a woman was murdered by a patron, and that's what drove my aunt away to Nevada. As soon as I saw the rattlesnake skin, I came face-to-face with the truth."

"You could have told me that," said Mary. "If you really cared for me, you would have been honest, instead of tricking me."

"I *do* care for you." Steven scooted off Hannah's bed and knelt in front of her. "Mary, I care about you so much. That was the other reason I didn't want you to know about the tunnels or my Aunt Helena's involvement in them."

"You still could have told me," Mary insisted. "I would have understood."

"No, you wouldn't have, because there's something else." He squeezed his eyes shut and his forehead furrowed.

"I'm listening," she said cautiously.

Steven looked at her. "It's about that photo album you found."

"You mean, that one over there?" She pointed at her desk.

"Yes." He crossed the room and picked it up. Steven stared at the leather cover reverently, as if he was holding something sacred. "I should have known the truth when I saw the cover. Part of me did, I think, but I refused to admit it. I wanted to believe it was a coincidence. I wanted to hope that it was some sort of sketchy synthetic leather from the past, but no. This is rattlesnake." He sat next to her on the bed. "Helena covered everything in snakeskin. Purses... shoes... wallets... You might have seen that belt she gave me. It's my favorite one."

Mary nodded. She remembered the day he'd worn it. The day of their lunch at The Summer Wind, and how she'd wanted to hook her finger into his belt and pull him closer, for a kiss. Part of her wanted to do that now. The weak part of her. The part of her that wasn't fierce enough to fight for her honor and demand her own worth. The part of her that wanted to act like things were okay because it was easier to pretend than admit the truth. But no: Mary could be tough. She'd walked through a cauldron of trauma, not just in the past twenty-four hours, but the past twenty-three years as well. Mary had emerged from those flames like burnished steel. She'd bend, but she'd no longer break.

"Your aunt had something to do with the album?" Mary asked, wondering what Helena's connection to Sven Nilsen might have been.

"Yes, but I'm not sure how." Steven flipped through the pages. "You were right, though. This girl does look like you. Part of me worries that it's one of your relations. A cousin. An aunt. I don't know... Someone... That person might have been one of the sex workers that worked in my aunt's brothel."

My birth mom was named Grace, and she worked as a cocktail waitress down here...

A half-remembered conversation flitted across Mary's memory, making her headache worse. She raked her fingers through her hair and massaged her temples with her thumbs.

"All those things you told me about your mom," said Steven. "About her history with drug and alcohol abuse. About her DUI. About her felony for vehicular assault."

"*You* told me about the felony," Mary countered. "I grew up ignorant of all of that."

"It's a lot to process," he said slowly.

"Wait," said Mary. Her head throbbed so much that it was hard to connect the dots. "You said cousin or aunt, but..." She yanked the album away from him and looked at the little girl's picture again. Her eyes reflected back as if Mary was looking in the mirror. "Are you saying you think this little girl is my mother?"

"I've been wondering that ever since I entered that tunnel and realized my dad was speaking the truth." Steven put his hand over his mouth and shook his head. "My aunt might have exploited your grandmother."

"That's impossible," said Mary. "My grandma Amy owned a video rental shop in Aberdeen." But even as she said it, Mary knew it wasn't true. Her memories from yesterday were still cloudy, due to the concussion, but something about that statement felt off.

Steven rested his hands on his thighs. "People carry trauma in different ways. I learned that being a public defender. Some people are resilient in the face of hardship, like dandelions growing in sidewalk cracks, and other people are like orchids and need perfect conditions to be successful. It could be that your mom grew up in such difficult circumstances that she never fully recovered."

"'My darling girl,'" Mary read, looking at the note at the front of the album. "'This isn't how I wanted our story to end.'"

She looked at Steven. "Whoever made this album loved the little girl very much."

"Unfortunately, love isn't enough when it comes to good parenting," he said darkly. "I'm sorry for my family's part in all of it."

"What do you mean, 'your family?' I thought we were just talking about your aunt."

"Her first husband was involved too, only I never met him. His name was Alfredo Lexter and he owned the T Bone Bluff. That's one of the reasons I was so eager to leave when we went there for dinner together. I thought it would be cool to see it, but it was too sad. Aunt Helena said he was a drunk who used to 'beat her to within an inch of her life.' Her words, not mine."

"How awful."

"Yeah. I knew that part of the story was true. But she never told me about the underground. My dad must not have known about it either. He told me about her exploiting sex workers, but didn't give specifics."

"I wonder if Alfredo Lexter was related to Oscar?"

"Who's Oscar?"

"The original owner of Seaside Resort," Mary explained.

"Could be. A whole crew of mobsters came out here from Vegas when Sand Dollar Cove was founded. At least that's what my dad said, and he built his reputation on putting gangsters behind bars."

Mary let out a huge sigh. "This *is* a lot for me to process," she admitted. "And I'm still not feeling very good. I need to rest, and then I need to speak with my mom."

Steven nodded. "That might be a difficult conversation. I'm sorry."

It *would* be a difficult conversation, but not as hard as what Mary was about to say next.

"I can't be your girlfriend anymore," she said matter-of-factly. "I refuse to date someone who lies to me. I can still help finish the renovations of the movie theater, but if you want to find a different designer, I'll understand."

Steven held her gaze, even though his lower lip quivered. "I don't want anyone else... to do the movie theater." He stood and stuffed his hands in his pockets. "I need to go. It's feeding day, and the guinea pigs have probably defrosted by now." He left without saying goodbye.

Mary watched him go, wishing she could call out to him, ask him to stay, and pretend like nothing bad had happened.

But she didn't. Her acting days were done.

TWENTY-SEVEN

"Ordering a golden milk latte might have been a bad idea," Mary said, looking at the cup in her hand. "Mom might not like turmeric. I have no idea."

"I thought hot chocolate was a safer bet, but you didn't ask me." Hannah held a casserole from Guy, who had insisted on contributing to the housewarming brigade and been a bit miffed that he wasn't included. But Mary was the director of this show, and she wanted it to be mother and daughters only.

"Are you ready to do this?" Mary asked as she lifted her fist to knock. "This is your last chance to back out."

"And let you face her alone?" Hannah scoffed. "No way."

"Thanks." Mary flashed her sister a grateful look. "But let me do most of the talking, okay?"

"You got it."

Mary rapped on the door. The address Kelly had provided surprised both sisters. It was a ranch-style house in a nice part of town. There wasn't a water or golf course view, but it was in walking distance to the local elementary school. Mary looked over her shoulder while she waited for Kelly to answer. A cluster of kids walked down the sidewalk as the school bus pulled away. Parents followed them, some pushing strollers.

"This is a pleasant neighborhood," Hannah observed.

"I was just thinking the same thing," said Mary. "This was the type of street I wish we had grown up on, with a mom or dad to greet us when we came home from school."

"Instead, we had each other." Hannah bumped her in the hip with her own.

"That's right." Mary lifted her chin. "We walked home to Gran's house together."

The door opened a second later and Kelly stood in the doorway wearing a pink velour tracksuit. Dark black eyeliner rimmed her eyes, and she wore a pale pink lip gloss that gave her a washed-out look. But despite the mask of makeup, Mary could see the anxiety in Kelly's eyes as she greeted her daughters. "Hi," she said shyly.

"Happy housewarming!" Hannah held out the casserole. "Here, take this. My arms are about to fall off."

Mary shot her sister an annoyed look. Hannah had promised that Mary could do the talking, but she was already jumping in, as if Mary needed help. She *didn't* need help. Mary was fully capable of leading this conversation. "Hi, Mom," she said. "Thanks for inviting us over. We really appreciate it."

"You kind of invited yourselves over, but that's okay. I wanted to see how you were doing, and I also wanted to show you Randal's house. He's on duty today, but you've really got to meet one of these days." She opened the door wider. "Come on in."

"Thanks." Mary walked through the door into the living room. Two leather couches and a giant television swallowed most of the room, but there was also a bookshelf full of tiny porcelain figurines.

"That's a lot of Dalmatians," said Mary after she walked over to see them.

"One hundred and one, to be exact." Kelly brought the casserole into the nearby kitchen and put it into the refrigerator. "Randal's not just a firefighter, he's also a Disney lover."

"Cool," said Mary. "And firefighters and Dalmatians are part of American pop culture that—oh, wow..." She paused, mid-sentence. "Is that—"

"A fire hydrant in the living room?" Hannah asked.

"It's not a real one," said Kelly as she came back into the room. "Well, it was a real one, but it doesn't work anymore. It's more of a sculpture at this point, like art."

"Yeah." Mary nodded vigorously. "A statement piece. I totally get that." She thought it was hideous, but couldn't allow herself to get sidetracked by decorating disasters. "Here," she said, handing Kelly the drink. "I brought you a golden milk latte, my favorite drink."

"I never would have guessed that." Kelly wrapped both hands around the cup. "And thank you. I love spicy things."

As soon as Mary turned her head, she saw a lamp made of a fire helmet. Good grief! *Focus,* she told herself. *Let the decor go.*

"Please, sit down," said Kelly.

"Thanks," said Mary as she sat next to her sister. "And I wanted to say thank you for the other day, back in the tunnels, when you rescued me. Saved my life, even."

"I wouldn't go so far as saying that." Kelly wrung her hands. "Randal and the other rescuers would have found you soon enough."

"Still, I don't remember much, but I remember you being there, and helping." Mary set the bag she was carrying on the ground. "I brought something to show you, that I found on the other side of the tunnels in the movie theater basement."

"Oh?" Kelly raised her eyebrows. "What?"

"This." Mary passed over the photo album "Do you recognize it?"

Kelly shook her head. "Never seen it before in my life."

Mary stood and made her way to the other couch to sit next to her mom. "Gran says there's a picture of a chef she used to know named Sven Nilsen in it, but we don't know who the other people are."

"Sven Nilsen?" Kelly gasped.

"That's right." Hannah got up and sat on the other side of Kelly. "Did you know him?"

"He's my father. Or was my father. He wasn't father-of-the-year material, that's for sure." Kelly flipped open the album.

Mary locked eyes with Hannah over their mother's head. *Sven was their grandpa?*

"'My darling girl,'" Kelly read. "'This isn't how I wanted our story to end. Pretend that I'm riding off into the sunset with music playing instead of leaving you like this. You can still have a delightful day in Sand Dollar Cove. Watch a movie. Play on the beach. Fly a kite. Visit the ice cream shop. But promise that you'll forget me...'" Kelly put her hand over her heart. "This is my birth mother's handwriting. I recognize it because she sent me a few letters later on in life when I bounced around foster care."

"I didn't know you were in foster care," Mary said quietly.

"Yeah, for most of my childhood." Kelly turned the page and looked at the picture of Sven and Grace. "There was a friendly couple when I was six that wanted to adopt me, but my mother refused to relinquish custody. I went back into the system again and those parents adopted someone else."

"So that little girl is you?" Hannah asked, as Kelly continued to flip pages.

"Yes. Only I've never seen these pictures before. I didn't know they existed."

"You said your mom was a waitress who worked in the tunnels," said Mary. "Am I remembering that right?"

Kelly nodded. "As far as I know."

"A waitress," Mary clarified. "Not someone who worked in the brothel."

"You can say prostitute, or sex worker," said Kelly. "I won't be offended. I served time with a lot of them. Most of them were booked for drug crimes, and all of them had sad stories."

"We're trying to understand, Mom," said Hannah. "But we know nothing about your past."

"That's right." Mary nodded. "Would you be willing to tell us? Even if it's hard to share?"

Kelly leaned back on the couch, her eyes still glued to the photographs. "Sure. Might as well. Not that it will change anything." She flipped back to the opening picture of Sven and Grace.

"I was born in 1971. I was four years old when we moved to Sand Dollar Cove. My mom got a job as a waitress at the T Bone Bluff, and my dad was the chef at The Summer Wind."

"Who babysat you when they were at work?" Mary asked.

Kelly shrugged. "I have no idea. I was too young to remember any of it. But what I do remember was my parents drinking and arguing. I remember one huge fight in particular, because that's when my dad left. One day he was here, and the next he was gone."

"That might have been when Oscar fired him," said Hannah. "He caught him sleeping with one of the Seaside Resort guests."

"Could be," said Kelly. "My mom still had the waitressing job at the T Bone Bluff though, so we stumbled along there for a while, just the two of us." Kelly looked at some more pictures. "You know, you asked me who took care of me, and I said I didn't remember, but I do, kind of. There was a grandma-type lady who used to watch me named Helen, who was really nice."

"Helena!" Mary exclaimed.

"No, I think it was Helen. Or Elena?" Kelly looked up at the ceiling. "I guess it could have been Helena, I don't exactly remember. Anyhow, that's how I knew about the tunnels. My mom would work waitressing shifts down there, too. I didn't understand at the time that there were also brothels, but I figured that part out later when I grew older and tried to process what I saw."

What I saw... "Did anyone hurt you?" Mary asked, terrified of knowing the answer.

"No." Kelly shook her head. "Helen kept me safe. She said if anyone touched me, she'd sink her fangs into them."

"Or her rattlesnake would," said Mary.

"What?" Kelly sat up straighter and looked at her.

"Did she have snakes?" Mary touched her arm, right where Elvis liked to coil.

"Maybe." Kelly shrugged." I don't remember." She twisted her bottom lip and flipped back to the letter. "What I do recall is one day, my mom left, too. She just wasn't there anymore. Helen took care of me for a while, saying that my mom would return, but she never did. That's when I met my first social worker and moved to Aberdeen."

"Wow," said Hannah. "Wow. Wow. Wow."

"Later, I heard that one of my mom's friends died down there." Kelly shook her head somberly. "She was strangled to death."

"That's horrible," said Mary.

"Yeah." Kelly nodded. "I don't know where my birth mom ended up, but at least she avoided that fate."

"Thank you for sharing this with us, Mom." Mary rubbed Kelly's back. "I know it couldn't have been easy."

"I didn't want to tell you girls, or Cheryl, or even your father, because I knew you'd think less of me. I wasn't even good enough for my own parents to stick around."

"That's not true," Mary said fiercely.

"Of course not, Mom." Hannah picked up Kelly's hand.

"I think your mom loved you," said Mary. "Look at this

beautiful album she made for you. Maybe she knew she couldn't do a good enough job taking care of you, and hoped that someone else would do a better one."

"Or maybe she was afraid you'd be exploited in the tunnels," said Hannah.

"Or maybe she was in danger of being exploited herself," Mary said in a quiet voice. Steven had said that Helena did horrible things. Who knew what she was capable of? "Are you sure nobody hurt you down there?"

"Positive," Kelly whispered. "That didn't happen until later, in my third foster care home."

"Oh, Mom!" Mary threw her arms around Kelly, and Hannah did too. "I'm so sorry that happened to you," Mary said, tears dotting her cheeks. "I had no idea."

"Me neither," said Hannah.

Her mother's history of abuse and neglect explained so much about her life. What was it Steven had said about trauma? That people carried it in different ways? He had been right. Kelly's life had been one traumatic experience after another. It was no wonder she had struggled.

"I wanted you girls to have a better childhood than I had been given," said Kelly, her face blotchy from crying. "I knew Cheryl could provide you with a stable life in a way I never could."

"You made the right decision," Mary said, breathing in the citrus scent of her mother's hair. "You did a good job with that choice. Gran gave us a wonderful childhood."

"She really did," said Hannah. "We didn't have much money, but we were always safe and loved."

"That's all I ever wanted for my daughters, but I knew you wouldn't have it if I were pulling you down," said Kelly.

"Well, you're not pulling us down now," said Mary, as she brushed tears off her mother's cheeks. "We are full-grown women, and maybe it's not too late to start over in a whole new way with you."

"Really?" Kelly looked from Mary to Hannah, and then back at Mary again. "Do you mean that? Even after I stole from you and tricked you into helping me steal when you were little, and all of that?"

"Yes." Mary nodded. Her heart was one hundred percent in. Her brain told her she still needed to be cautious. But most of all, her soul told her that now the truth had been revealed, the cycle could be broken. Grace had abandoned Kelly. Kelly had abandoned Mary and Hannah. But Mary refused to abandon her mother. Generations of hurt and betrayal ended today.

"My darling girl," Kelly whispered, as she hugged Mary with one arm. "My darling *girls*," she said again as she hugged Hannah too. "A second chance to be your mother would be a dream come true."

"Then let's make it happen," said Mary. "I'm willing to take a chance, if you are."

"Same with me," said Hannah. "I'm ready to move forward, too."

TWENTY-EIGHT

"Are you going to call off your dog, or what?" Zeke asked. It was Friday morning, and the phone call woke Mary up. She looked over at Hannah's bed and saw that it was unmade. Hannah, who usually stayed at Guy's apartment, had spent the night here with her sister to keep her company while she recovered from her ordeal.

"What are you talking about?" Mary asked Zeke, as she hopped out of bed and peered through the doorway down the hall. The bathroom door was closed, and the shower was running. She had at least a few minutes until Hannah returned.

"Don't play dumb," Zeke said in a nasty tone. "You hired an asshole lawyer to disrupt *my* artistic vision."

"Speaking as a fellow artist, your creative vision works much better without the outlier of an X-rated scene that humiliates me."

"We've been over this before, bitch!" Zeke yelled.

"But not with my lawyer present." Mary was surprised by how calmly she was speaking, despite her racing heart. What did Zeke mean about her setting her lawyer on him? Was

Steven continuing to represent her even though she'd dumped him? "When's the last time you spoke with my lawyer?" she asked.

"I got off the phone with him just now, and yes, I'll agree to your demands. Just promise you'll call off your dog. You've put the whole film in jeopardy with your hysterics."

"No, *you've* put the film in jeopardy with your narcissism. I'm the one getting tremendous early attention with my TikTok account. I don't see anyone else on the team with a video that's racked up over seven million views. Do you?"

"No," Zeke admitted bitterly. "And if it weren't for that, I'd take your naked ass to court."

"Keep talking to me like that, and I'll shut down distribution completely." Mary looked at the enormous bouquet of roses Steven had left on her dresser. The petals were fading now, but they kept their beauty. "Apologize for swearing at me."

"I'll talk to you however I want!"

"Apologize," Mary demanded. "Or I'm calling my lawyer back right now and asking him to go for the nuclear option."

She waited. One. Two. Three. Four. Five seconds and Zeke had said nothing. "Well," she said. "If that's the way you want it. Goodbye—"

"Wait!" Zeke exclaimed. "I'm sorry for calling you a bitch. I should have said 'ice princess.'"

"No, you shouldn't have called me any name at all. That was unprofessional of you."

"Right. Unprofessional. I'm sorry. Now, will you go post another TikTok? We need you."

"Sure. As soon as I've talked to my lawyer, and he confirms that you've agreed to cut that scene."

"I'll call him right now. I promise."

"Do that." Mary hung up. *Jerk.*

"Oh good, you're up," Hannah said as she entered the room

wearing a towel wrapped around her head. "I was hoping we could have breakfast together before I take Gran to the senior center and head into work."

"I can drop Gran off." Mary opened the closet. "I'm not an invalid."

"I realize that." Hannah massaged hand lotion into her elbows. "But nobody would blame you for wanting to take it easy for a few days."

"I'm fine." Mary put on her bathrobe. The conversation with Zeke had rattled her, but she was also proud of how it had ended. She was grateful to Steven for his help, and shocked that he hadn't abandoned her. But mainly she was proud of herself for confronting Zeke and demanding an apology. Mary took a deep breath and looked at herself in the mirror that hung above the dresser. Somehow, she'd transformed from a survivor to a fighter. When had that happened? Her eyes drifted to the flowers again. She needed to talk to Steven today. But first, she owed Hannah and Cheryl the truth about what had happened to her in Hollywood.

"As soon as you're done getting dressed, I need to tell you something," Mary told Hannah. "Something important."

"What is it?" Hannah asked, with a note of alarm.

"Let's wait until Gran is there, too," said Mary. "I only want to explain it once."

Five minutes later they sat at the kitchen table around a plate of Brittany's cranberry-walnut muffins. Brittany had been on a baking kick ever since her latest fight with Keith. She sat there too, next to Cheryl, holding a mug of coffee. Mary hadn't intended to include her landlady in this discussion, but since Brittany was also her friend, and part of her life, she was glad she was there. From the corner of her eye Mary could see sunflowers, lilies, daffodils, and roses littering every horizontal surface from the kitchen to the living room. Steven hadn't let up with the flowers. He never included a note, but everyone knew they were from him.

"So what's the big news?" Cheryl asked. "Why the grim face?"

"Yeah," said Hannah. "You're scaring me, and that's saying a lot, because you've already given me a good fright this week."

"What I'm about to say will freak you out further." Mary set her phone on the table, but didn't bring the screen to life yet. "Remember when I moved to Hollywood?"

"Of course we remember," said Cheryl. "My mobility might have declined, but the noggin works just fine, thanks very much."

"Yeah. Well... the thing is..." Mary held her breath for a second. *Here goes.* She explained it all in one breath. "I landed a starring role in an indie film, only I didn't want to tell you because there was a naked scene with the back of me—and the front—and now it's coming to theaters everywhere and I was really upset about it, but Steven has made them edit the humiliating scene out."

"What?" Hannah asked.

"Here." Mary tapped her phone and brought up the trailer. "Let me show you." She enlarged the screen and hit play.

ZOMBIE PROM AT THE DISCO flashed across the screen, and then there was Mary, dressed as Jenaly Macintyre innocently dancing at prom.

"Morning," Jeremy mumbled, strolling into the room.

"Shh!" Brittany hushed him. "We're watching Mary's movie trailer."

"What?" Jeremy rushed over to the table.

"Start it from the beginning and turn up the sound," said Cheryl. "I can't hear it."

"Okay." Mary set the video up again.

As trailers go, this one was pretty good. It built mystery,

excitement, and fear into a ninety-second clip that left viewers wondering what happened next. But Mary was so emotionally invested in the project that she wasn't sure if her judgment was accurate.

"That's sick," said Jeremy, after it ended. "It's just like that TikTok video that Kenzie loves."

"*I'm* the TikTok video," Mary admitted. "That's me, too."

"Really?" Jeremy looked impressed.

"Yeah." Mary was glad that Jeremy approved, but his opinion wasn't the one that mattered to her the most. She was still waiting for Hannah and Cheryl's reactions, and from the expressions on their faces, it seemed like they were still making up their minds.

"I should have told you earlier," she mumbled. "I'm sorry."

"I'm speechless," said Hannah. "I don't know what to say."

"I can't believe you kept this from us," said Cheryl.

Mary hung her head and picked at a torn cuticle. "I should have told you earlier. I'm sorry."

"Don't be sorry." Hannah leaped from her chair and jumped up and down. "This is amazing!" she cheered. "Mary, you did it! You really did it!" Hannah threw her arms around her sister and nearly knocked her over. "I can't wait to see you on the big screen."

"Me too," said Cheryl. "I would have been fine seeing your naked bum, too. It's not like I haven't seen it before."

"I would have been totally fine seeing it too," said Jeremy, with a smirk.

"Har, har," Mary fake-laughed.

"Jeremy," Brittany chided. "Don't be inappropriate." She smiled at Mary. "I'm thrilled for you. Honestly, thrilled. When does the movie come out?"

"May fourteenth." Mary disentangled herself from Hannah's clutches. "You can let go of me now."

"I'm never letting go." Hannah squeezed tighter. "I'm just so proud of you."

"You're smothering me."

"Oh." Hannah released her. "Sorry."

"May fourteenth, huh?" Cheryl mused. "Didn't you say the movie theater would be finished around then?"

"That's right." Mary nodded. She was wary of the mischievous look she saw in her grandma's eyes.

"I bet Steven is every bit as excited for you as we are." Cheryl sipped her coffee.

"When are you going to give him a break?" Jeremy asked. "It's getting really annoying having him ding-dong-ditch bouquets every few hours. The house smells like a funeral parlor with all the flowers."

"How do you know what a funeral parlor smells like?" Brittany asked.

"I don't," Jeremy admitted. "But that's what Kenzie said."

"Okay, well, I'm sure Mary has her reasons for rejecting him," said Brittany.

"Do you blame him for trapping you in the tunnel?" Hannah asked.

"He didn't trap me," said Mary. "Getting stuck in the tunnel was my fault. I blame Steven for lying to me. That's unforgivable."

"Is it, though?" Cheryl asked.

"You think Mary should date a liar?" Hannah asked.

"You're marrying one," said Cheryl.

"That's not fair!" Hannah exclaimed.

"We all love Guy," said Cheryl. "But he lied about his identity for months and you still forgave him."

"This is true," Hannah admitted. "But Mary has the right to make her own decisions."

"I'm through with dating liars," said Mary. "That's my decision."

"Whoa. Hang on." Jeremy helped himself to a muffin. "Is Steven not telling you about the tunnels really such a horrible lie that you'll never be able to trust him again? It's not like he got a stranger from Kansas pregnant, after all."

"That's right." Cheryl nodded. "He lied to protect your feelings and keep you safe. I can understand why he did that."

"Even though it was stupid of him not to tell you," said Jeremy. "You're tough enough to handle anything."

"I agree," said Brittany. "I'd add that sometimes the people we love do stupid things, but we need to forgive them, anyway." She looked at her son. "I'm sorry that I was so hard on you about your math grade. I should have recognized that you were struggling and needed extra help, instead of insinuating that you didn't care about your grade. I'm really proud of all the hard work you've done studying to bring your grade up and improve your report card."

Jeremy looked at his mom. "And I'm sorry I didn't tell you I borrowed your car the other night to take Kenzie out, and scratched the rear bumper."

"What?" Brittany slapped the table. "Why didn't you take your car?"

"Because it was Kenzie's and my first official date, and your car is nicer."

Cheryl chuckled. "Your car *is* nicer, Brittany. Take it as a compliment."

"Steven's not Aidan," said Hannah, pulling the conversation back to Mary. "I spent quality time with him when you were in the ER, and I've never seen a person so distraught. He cares about you a lot."

Was her family correct? Should Mary give Steven a second chance?

"Why don't you go see him this morning and talk things over?" Cheryl suggested.

"Yeah," said Jeremy. "At the very least you can tell him to cool it with the flowers before someone has an allergy attack."

"Okay," Mary agreed. "I'll talk to him."

Wow, she was getting so good at tough conversations, she almost found herself looking forward to this one.

TWENTY-NINE

What she needed was a script, a rehearsed speech she could give to Steven when she saw him. Mary thought about that while she washed her face and brushed her hair. "Lying is unacceptable," she practiced saying as she applied mascara. "But maybe we're both guilty of that. I shouldn't have lied and said I was going to the doctor about that scratch on my arm, when I wasn't." There. That wasn't so hard. Mary dabbed on lip gloss. She could follow up with something that shared how she felt. Standing straight, Mary looked at herself in the mirror, pretending like she was speaking to Steven. "I really want us to try again."

Could they, though? Or was it too late? The mere thought of Steven never being in her life again scared Mary to her core. She thought about his enthusiasm, and his zest for living that was so like her own. Or had been until Aidan had broken her heart and she'd sunk into depression. But now she was back, and it had taken a lot of hard work to get here. *Work* work, like starting her business and tackling jobs, and emotional work, like confronting her issues with Kelly and re-examining her family history. Mary was better equipped to be in a relationship than she had ever been before, and she knew that the person her heart wanted was Steven.

Steven, with his zany shirts, and wild personality.

Steven, who tenderly cared for his pet reptiles like they were the most adorable creatures on the planet.

Steven, who had battled Zeke for her, and emerged triumphant.

Steven, who had bought out the Sand Dollar Cove florist to prove his devotion.

Had Mary done anything to prove her devotion? No, she hadn't, and the thought pained her. Steven had worn his heart on his sleeve for her all along, but part of her had always held back, standoffish, afraid to risk her feelings.

That changed now.

"Gran?" Mary called, as she raced down the stairs. "Is it okay if you're a little late to the senior center today? There's something I need to do first before we leave."

"Take all the time that you need," said Cheryl from her spot on the recliner. "*Good Morning America*'s on and I'm enjoying my second cup of coffee."

"Thanks." Mary opened the junk drawer and took out the crayons. Markers would have been better, but she was in a rush. She went down the hallway to Jeremy's room, feeling guilty about invading the teen's privacy, but she needed to find his stock of poster supplies. His room stank like antiperspirant and dirty socks, but she quickly found poster boards on the ground, next to his desk. Helping herself to one, she went back to the kitchen and got to work.

Balloons. Mary drew balloons first because she always started with balloons. The scent of Crayolas brought back memories, only now she could deal with them. Her life might have been a circus, but she was the ringmaster, in full control of her destiny. Mary drew a striped tent, an elephant, a seal bouncing a ball on its nose, and her best imitation of a strong man, holding a snake. *That* made her smile, especially when she gave him a man bun. She drew a tightrope walker right above, that would have looked more like her if she had been a better illustrator. Finally, at the center of the poster, in huge block letters, Mary wrote: CAN WE START THIS CIRCUS OVER? Because that was the crux of it. Her life involved lots of wild elements, and she wanted Steven to be with her for the show.

"I'm almost ready to leave," Mary told Cheryl as she held up the poster. "I made this for Steven. What do you think?"

"I think he's lucky to have a Turner woman, that's what." Cheryl collapsed the footrest of the recliner. "If it's okay with you, let's bring some of these flowers to the center. We're running out of room and I'm afraid I'll knock a vase over."

"Great idea. Let me run up and grab my purse and I'll be right back." Mary charged up the stairs, two at a time, and burst into her room.

The window was cracked, like always, and she heard one of the DeLacks pull up into their driveway. The DeLacks with their mundane life, sniping away at each other, without an ounce of imagination. Even their squabbling was boring. Mary chuckled. How silly of her that she had ever wanted to be one of them. She couldn't picture her life now, chained to Aidan. What a disaster that would have been. Fresh air or not, it was time to close that window once and for all. But as she crossed the room to slam it shut, she heard music. Not radio music, coming from Aidan's car, but the soft sound of the guitar. And then there was singing, too, and that's when Mary smiled.

She ran to the window, threw open the blinds, and pushed the glass all the way to the side. She poked her head out, grateful that there wasn't a screen to stop her.

There, standing below her window, was Steven, strumming a guitar. He sang Elvis's famous song about fools rushing into love, and it was as if Mary heard the words for the first time. She felt every note, every syllable, and every sentiment. She couldn't help falling in love with him, either.

Mary gazed down at Steven, and she smiled. She couldn't believe he was really there, singing for her, in front of the entire neighborhood. She heard a window over at the DeLacks' house open and then slam shut. Hopefully baby Larry didn't wake up, but if he did, Steven's sweet serenade would sing the infant back to sleep.

"What are you doing?" Mary called down, after the song had finished.

"Begging you for one more chance." Steven looked up at her with both hands on his guitar. "I'm sorry I lied to you. I should have told you about the possibility of the tunnels as soon as we saw that door."

"I should have told you how upset I was when I realized you were lying to me, instead of making up a story, acting like everything was okay, and then exploring them on my own."

"Does that mean you'll forgive me?" Steven asked with a hopeful look in his eyes.

"Hang on a second." Mary turned away from the window and picked up the poster she'd made. Then she lowered it carefully over the windowsill and angled it so he could see it. "Still want to be part of my circus?" she called down to Steven.

"Yes!" He spun the guitar around so that it hung off his back from the strap and grabbed onto a lower branch of the vine leaf maple tree that grew next to the house. "I'm coming up!" he called as he wedged his right foot against the trunk.

"Careful!" Mary cried. "Why not use the stairs?"

"Because that would take too long, and it's already been seventy-three hours and eighteen minutes without you." He reached for another branch and hauled himself upward, the guitar bouncing against budding leaves.

"You're going to hurt yourself."

"It would be worth it."

"I would have opened the front door for you."

"This way, you don't have to."

Steven was close enough now that she could see the soft greens and browns in his hazel eyes. A light sheen of sweat glistened off his forehead from the exertion of climbing. The vine leaf maple had a sturdy base but grew spindly at the top, and Mary panicked when she saw the branches bend and heard a snapping sound. "Steven!" she cried.

"Almost there." He clasped onto the window frame with both arms, and Mary leaned back out of his way. One foot came over into her room, and then another. The poor guitar bashed against the side of the house with a hollow groan.

"I probably should have left the guitar in its case," Steven said, as he unslung it. He put it into the room first, but sat on the windowsill, hesitating, like he was waiting to be invited to enter.

"What are you waiting for?" Mary held her arms open wide. "It's been seventy-three hours and nineteen minutes since I saw you, and longer than that since you've kissed me."

Steven launched into the room and swooped Mary up in an enormous bear hug. He lifted her off her feet and swung her around. As she slowly slid down his body until her toes touched carpet, she smiled. Then she crushed her lips against his with an untamed fierceness, hungry enough to ravish him then and there—if her grandma hadn't been downstairs waiting for her.

"My gran," she whispered a few minutes later when they paused to catch their breath. "She's..."

"The one who told me you'd be home and to keep trying," said Steven. "I love Cheryl, she's amazing." He lifted her chin up with a gentle brush of his thumb. "But not as much as I love you. Can I say that?"

"I'll allow it. You're my boyfriend, after all." Mary plucked her phone out of her back pocket and grinned. "Say cheese," she said, as she held out her arm to click a selfie of them both.

"Let me see it," said Steven. "In case I have twigs stuck in my hair."

"I love you rumpled." Mary brushed a leaf off his fleece jacket. "Just like I love you any way."

Steven held her close, and their hearts beat as one. "The snakes are going to be so happy we're back together," he murmured. "I can't wait to tell Elvis."

EPILOGUE

It was Wednesday, May 14th, and the newly renovated Sand Dollar Cove Cinema was packed. Everyone Mary knew was in the audience that night. School friends, co-workers from the barista stand where she used to work, senior center members, and practically everyone her sister worked with at Seaside Resort—everyone had bought a ticket. They'd dressed up, too, because this was a red-carpet event. The theme was "Disco Prom," and Mary wore a one-sleeved dress made of a stretchy bronze fabric that hugged every curve. Steven had on a vintage brown tuxedo with a ruffled lapel, that was delightfully hideous in a 1970s way, especially the cummerbund. Cheryl wore a sequined pantsuit that Patti had sewn for her, and had decorated her wheelchair with ribbons. When Guy rolled her through the double doors into the lobby, she had made a stylish entrance. Kelly was there too, along with Randal, whom everyone had now met and agreed was a nice catch.

"This is everything I could have dreamed of, and more," Steven whispered in Mary's ear, as he held her hand and welcomed guests while they flowed into the lobby. "The mural turned out great."

"It really did." Mary looked up at the painting that graced the walls. *Sand Dollar Cove is Out of this World!* read the lettering. A family of green aliens, drinking soda and eating popcorn, shot out into space. The solar system boasted sand dollars and starfish where the planets were supposed to be.

"The selfie station is going great," Mary said, looking over at Godzilla. "We can expect a bunch of tags on social media later on."

"You're brilliant." He kissed the top of her head. "Your creativity is taking this business to the next level."

"You're the one with the business vision," said Mary. "This place would still be a dump if you hadn't bought it."

"Yes, but— Wait... why is *he* here?" Steven put his arm around Mary protectively and smiled in a way that showed all his teeth.

Aidan and Lara DeLack walked through the door. Aidan wore a suit and Lara had on a pretty maxi dress and chandelier earrings. Mary could tell that she'd made an effort with her appearance, and thought she looked beautiful.

"Don't be mad," said Mary. "I invited them since I've known Aidan so long, and since Lara is my neighbor. I didn't know if they'd come or not."

"If you invited them, then they are welcome guests." Steven gave her another side hug before letting go and extending his arm for a handshake as the DeLacks approached. "Aidan," he said. "It's great to see you, man. Thanks for coming."

"This is so exciting," Lara gushed. "You must be thrilled." She fluttered her fingertips in the air. "I've never been to a movie premier before, let alone known the lead actress. Wait until I tell my friends back home."

"Though of course, this is your home now, right, babe?" Aidan asked, wearing a punch-me expression.

"Uh, yeah..." Lara's smile disappeared. "This is where I live."

As Mary watched them walk over to Godzilla, she made a mental note to reach out to Lara later, and perhaps invite her over for coffee. It must be lonely for the new mom to be here. It had been nearly a year now, but Mary wasn't sure if Lara had made any friends.

"I told you we'd be late, and look what happened," Keith grumbled, two steps ahead of Brittany. He had once again ignored the dress code and wore chinos and a polo shirt.

"I've never put on blue eyeshadow before, and it was tricky," Brittany explained. She picked up her dress so she wouldn't trip, walking in platform heels. "Sorry we're late," she said as she air-kissed Mary. "I didn't know that Farrah Fawcett curls were so hard to emulate."

"You look wonderful," said Mary.

"Check out this crowd," said Steven.

Mary looked over her shoulder to see who he meant and saw Jeremy, Kenzie, and a dozen of their friends walk up, dressed in shredded prom clothing and ghoulish makeup. Throwing her hands up in the air, Mary cheered. "The zombies have arrived!"

"Are you ready to do this thing?" Steven asked.

Mary nodded. "You bet."

Steven gave the signal, and a tone sounded, followed by an announcement that it was time for everyone to find their seats. He and Mary entered the theater and found their spots near her family in the newly created section that accommodated Cheryl's wheelchair and met requirements for the Americans with Disabilities Act.

"I'm so proud of you, sis," said Hannah.

"We both are," Guy added.

"My daughter, the movie star," said Kelly.

"Thanks." Mary sat down and nodded at Steven encouragingly. "This is Steven's big moment, too. He worked hard to bring this theater back to life."

"I couldn't have done it without your help." Steven gave Mary a happy kiss. "Be back soon." Then he picked his way through the audience and stood in front of the stage. Once everyone was seated, he waved at the crowd. "Ladies and gentlemen—and zombies—welcome to the grand reopening of Sand Dollar Cove Cinema."

"Yay!" Cheryl called out, leading the audience into an eruption of cheers. Randal let out a piercing whistle.

"Not only is this our reopening, but it's also part of one of the worldwide celebrations at theaters across the country of the brand-new film *Zombie Prom at the Disco*, staring Sand Dollar Cove's own leading lady, Mary Turner!" Steven extended his arm over to Mary and the spotlight followed.

"That's my sister!" Hannah cheered.

Mary stood briefly and waved. Her pulse didn't slow to its normal rhythm until the lights were turned down, Steven was by her side, and the opening credits rolled.

The movie wasn't awful. It wasn't blockbuster material, but it wasn't bad, either. Now that the locker room scene was gone, Mary felt proud of her performance. There was something thrilling about seeing her eighteen-year-old face up on the big screen, captured for posterity. Five years ago, Mary had been naive, insecure, and gullible. She saw that now. But she could also see that she'd been bold, beautiful, and brave. Those were qualities that she carried with her to this day, and Mary was proud of the new life for herself she'd created.

When Jenaly Macintyre stared back at her and uttered the famous lines, now shared millions of times as trending audio on TikTok, every teen in the audience said them too.

"Friends?" the crowd echoed. "We can never be friends. You've murdered my love for you. Your cursed heart means nothing to me anymore."

When the final credits rolled the audience broke out into

thunderous applause that didn't stop until the house lights came up again.

"We want more Jenaly!" Kenzie cried.

"Jenaly. Jenaly. Jenaly." Jeremy led people in a chant.

"Go strut your stuff, zombie girl," Steven said with a wink. "Give the people what they want."

Mary laughed and went up front. "Okay, Sand Dollar Cove," she said as she lifted her hands. "This is how you do the TikTok dance." She gave a quick tutorial and soon had everyone dancing along with her. "Have a safe ride home, and remember," she told the crowd. "Don't dance with the dead!" Mary strutted up the aisle and people followed, like she had an entire crew of backup dancers. It was a golden moment, one that she would cherish forever, and one that would live online and gain the film more attention, because every teenager had their phone out and was filming her performance.

When she reached her family, Steven hopped up beside her, jerking his limbs along in the awkward dance she'd choreographed. Hannah and Kelly did, too. Guy and Randal waited with Cheryl since the aisles were so crowded.

"Don't dance with the dead!" the audience echoed.

Mary led the pack through the doors and out into the bright lights of the lobby. She and Steven locked arms and stood by the door, thanking theatergoers for coming. Exhausted, but glowing, Mary felt like one half of Sand Dollar Cove's "It" couple. She just hoped the noisy crowd hadn't bothered Celine and Dion, who were resting in Steven's nearby office, like always.

"I bet Zeke will call, begging you to make a sequel," said Steven, when everyone but family had left. "You're going to need an agent."

"I don't want an agent, or a career in Hollywood anymore." Mary snuggled up to him. "I want my interior design business and my life right here, in Sand Dollar Cove, with you."

"Are you sure about that?" Steven kissed her cheek. "Say

the word, and I'll move to LA with you and fly up to run this place on weekends."

"I'm sure." She rested her head on his shoulder. "I don't need to pretend to be someone else anymore, because I'm proud of being me."

"As you should be." Steven kissed the tip of her nose.

The warmth of the moment was interrupted by a string of curse words. Mary and Steven both turned to see what the commotion was about. Keith, his chinos drenched with soda, faced off against Jeremy, who stood in front of him with an empty cup.

"You're lucky that was soda and not piss, asshole. Never talk to my mom like that again."

"Jeremy, it's okay," Brittany said, her face splotchy. "I can handle it."

"*That's* how you handle it?" Keith's eyes flashed fire. "You're such a lousy mother it's no wonder your kid's a train wreck."

Mary lunged forward, her fists clenched. "How dare you!" she shouted. "Jeremy's my friend." She looked at the teen. "Don't listen to him, okay? You're awesome."

"You are, you know," Kenzie told Jeremy. "You really are."

"My son is not a train wreck," Brittany said, her voice growing stronger.

"You've put up with Keith's verbal abuse for too long," said Cheryl. "It's time to dump the bastard."

"Yeah," said Hannah. Guy and Randal were there, too. The entire Turner family stood in a tight unit.

"Keith's not a bastard," said Brittany. "He's a good man. Tonight was really stressful, and—"

"I'm sorry I lost my temper back there," Keith interrupted. "It's just that you know I have an early day tomorrow, and you promised that—"

"No, *you* look," said Mary, squaring her shoulders. "You aren't allowed to treat Jeremy like that."

"Or Brittany," Cheryl added.

"Right." Hannah nodded.

"That's it," Keith shook his head. "Drama, drama, drama. I never should have dated a middle-aged woman to begin with, because you're clearly a basket case." He gave Brittany a cold look. "I think it's time we ended things, don't you?"

"You're breaking up with me?" Brittany gasped. "But we work together."

"For now." Keith widened his stance. "And let me remind you that *you* work for *me*."

"I don't work for you," said Brittany. "I serve the seniors of Sand Dollar Cove."

"Fire her and you're looking at a labor violation lawsuit faster than you can say 'douchebag,'" said Steven. "I'm licensed to practice in Washington State and will represent Brittany for free."

That's my boyfriend, Mary thought with pride. *A hunky protector in a polyester suit.*

"I didn't say I'd fire her," Keith said quickly. "I just said..." He looked at Brittany. "That I'd like to date a woman my own age again, instead of a dried-up forty-five-year-old."

"Who has a bucket of popcorn I can throw at this jerk?" Jeremy shouted. "He needs something to go with his soda!"

"Here." Kelly handed him her bucket. "You can take mine."

Brittany threw her arms out to block Keith from Jeremy's wrath. "Go home, Keith. I don't want to see you again unless I'm being paid by the hour, and I'm surrounded by senior citizens."

"Fine by me." Keith snorted. "Have fun with your totally out-of-control son. I should have dumped you ages ago."

Popcorn would fly. Mary knew it. She looked at Jeremy as Keith walked away and saw the bucket shake. But instead of flinging kernels at Keith's backside, like Jeremy probably wanted to do, he put his arm around his mom and hugged her. Every moment of Jeremy's life was a toss-up between adulting and childhood, and right now, he was letting Keith walk away unscathed because that was the mature thing to do.

Jeremy was doing the right thing, and Mary was proud of the choice he made in that moment. But that didn't mean she had to be mature. She no longer had anything to prove to anyone.

Apparently, neither did Hannah.

Mary ripped the popcorn bucket out of Jeremy's hands just as Hannah grabbed the one Randal was holding, and together they showered Keith with a buttery explosion that would ring up the dry-cleaning bill from hell.

"Jeremy is not out of control!" Mary screeched like a banshee.

"Yeah," said Hannah. "And Brittany's a great mom who doesn't deserve your crap."

Keith shook popcorn kernels off his sticky sleeves. "You two are nuts," he said. "Your whole family's crazy." Then he did the unthinkable. He pointed at Cheryl. "I might not be able to revoke your membership, but you can forget about your food assistance discount. I know where you live. You're paying full rate, from now on."

"But I qualify for that discount!" Cheryl exclaimed. "I live on social security."

"Don't worry, Cheryl," said Guy. "I'll pay your fees."

"And I'll make sure that Keith doesn't do that to you, because it's probably illegal," said Steven.

"We'll see about that," Keith snarled, before rushing out of the building.

Mary looked at Jeremy and Brittany. "Are you two okay?"

"I think so," Brittany said, with a wobbly smile.

Jeremy shook his head and grinned. "I knew you were Bond

girl material, Mary, but your sister?" He glanced at Hannah. "That surprised me."

Mary looked at Hannah and then back at Jeremy. "My sister's a badass," she said, a huge smile on her face. "Just like me."

"Never mess with a zombie princess." Steven put his arm around Mary and looked at her with pride. "She bites."

Mary nestled into Steven's embrace and felt a deep sense of security and peace. Jeremy and Steven were right. She was stronger than she had ever been before. The wounds of the past that had haunted her for decades were no longer buried and could now heal. She had uncovered her family secrets, confronted her demons head-on, and forged a way forward. She'd stopped acting like a victim and had become the hero of her own story. The future glowed with promise.

"Wait a sec," she said, as she lifted her head off Steven's shoulder. "This evening can't be over until we do one last essential thing."

"What's that?" Hannah asked.

Mary waved her family and friends to the corner of the lobby. "We need a group photo with Godzilla."

"I love the way you think," said Steven as he squeezed her hand. "Lead the way, Jenaly Macintyre. I'd follow you anywhere."

Mary lifted up on her toes and kissed his cheek. "I don't want to be anywhere else in the world besides right here in Sand Dollar Cove with you."

A LETTER FROM JENNIFER

The world can be a stressful place, and I'm absolutely delighted that you chose to spend your limited free time relaxing with one of my books. I hope that Mary and Steven's story made you feel like you've taken a whirlwind vacation to Sand Dollar Cove, and even had a chance to meet Elvis—the snake, that is.

Sand Dollar Cove is a fictional place, but the Pacific Northwest does have several real-life underground tours. In Washington there are Bill Speidel's Underground Tour in Seattle and the Port Angeles Underground & Heritage Tour. In Oregon, there is the Pendleton Underground Tour. I've also spotted purple glass skylights on the streets of Snohomish, Washington. My teenage son was quite annoyed with me for stopping to take a picture.

Speaking of teenage sons, our next visit to Sand Dollar Cove centers on Brittany, and her new life after Jeremy goes off to college. I can't wait for you to find out how she turns her life around and discovers another chance at love. You can find out more about my Sand Dollar Cove series by signing up for my newsletter. Your email will never be shared, and you can unsubscribe at any time.

www.bookouture.com/jennifer-bardsley

I also invite you to follow me on social media. Facebook is my favorite way to connect with readers. In my VIP reader group Jennifer Bardsley's Book Sneakers (https://www.face

book.com/groups/jenniferbardsleysbooksneakers/), I give away free books every Friday.

Finally, I'd like to say a huge thank you to everyone who takes time to write a quick review on Amazon and Goodreads. Reviews make a huge difference in terms of helping my books reach new readers.

The next tour to Sand Dollar Cove is boarding now. Come take a journey with Brittany that's full of heartbreak, mystery, and joy.

www.jenniferbardsley.com

facebook.com/JenniferBardsleyAuthor

x.com/JennBardsley

instagram.com/jenniferbardsleyauthor

tiktok.com/@jenniferbardsley

ACKNOWLEDGMENTS

Thank you to my agent, Liza Fleissig, my editor, Lucy Frederick, my critique partner, Penelope Wright, my copyeditor, Jenny Page, my proofreader, Liz Hurst, and the wonderful team at Bookouture for bringing the world of Sand Dollar Cove to life. Thank you especially to my readers who have traveled with me from one little town in the Pacific Northwest to the next. I appreciate you tremendously, and hope that if you ever get the chance to visit Washington State, my books help you remember to bring layers, sturdy walking shoes, and a highly competent raincoat.

PUBLISHING TEAM

Turning a manuscript into a book requires the efforts of many people. The publishing team at Bookouture would like to acknowledge everyone who contributed to this publication.

Commercial
Lauren Morrissette
Jil Thielen
Imogen Allport

Cover design
Emma Graves

Data and analysis
Mark Alder
Mohamed Bussuri

Editorial
Lucy Frederick
Imogen Allport

Copyeditor
Jenny Page

Proofreader
Liz Hurst